For Jerry-Jew!
with very best -
for your life in
and after Fondly
David
March '97

RU$$IA

RU$$IA

··············

A NOVEL

David Evan Kaun

FITHIAN PRESS ▪ SANTA BARBARA ▪ 1995

Published by Fithian Press
A division of Daniel and Daniel, Publishers, Inc.
Post Office Box 1525
Santa Barbara, CA 93102

Design by Eric Larson
Set in Electra and Helvetica

LIBRARY OF CONGRESS CATALOGING-IN-PUBLICATION DATA
Kaun, David Evan
       Russia : a novel / David Evan Kaun.
           p.   cm.
       ISBN 1-56474-119-2 (cloth) — ISBN 1-56474-112-5 (pbk.)
       1. Capitalism — Russia — Fiction. 2. Americans — Russia — Fiction.
       I. Title
       PS3561.A8573R87   1994
       813'.54 — dc20   94-27514
                                         CIP

To the memory of my father,
Albert E. Kaun

CONTENTS

RU$$IA

PROLOGUE

■ ■ ■ ■ ■ ■ ■ ■ ■ ■ ■ ■ ■ ■ ■ ■ ■

*I*n less than an hour, Aven would accept the mandate of his people. Pride filled his every breath as he contemplated his future—first tsar of Mother Russia in over a century.

"Madness!" he thought.

As director of MOP (Ministry of Persuasion), Aven had led the Russian transformation from a stark, lifeless society of the 1980s into a land of optimism, joy, and an abiding faith in God and free enterprise. The Marxist cant learned so well in school had been turned on its head. The land of Lenin and Stalin had become the most fully developed of all the capitalist nations. A prairie fire ignited in the tinsel land of Southern California had swept the eastern shores of Amerika by the late 1980s. In less than a decade, the conflict, hostility, and periodic tension between East and West that had dominated so many lives and drained the resources of nations seemed a distant memory—a bad dream best forgotten.

For an instant, Aven's thoughts turned to Rena. Rena's image, remote and ill-defined, faded quickly. Rena was, he knew, only a footnote to all that had transpired.

Two seemingly unrelated events were to have a profound effect on Russia and on much of the rest of the world. In the aftermath of the calamitous and debilitating cultural revolution, the leaders of China had begun their inexorable march toward full capitalism. A momentary lapse came in the spring of 1989, when well-meaning though naive students, the sons and daughters of China's ruling class, took the term *democracy* too literally and too far, ultimately creating a Woodstocklike environment in the midst of Beijing. Cleaning up after the rowdy youngsters took a stern hand and caused some consternation around the world. But all was quickly forgiven. China was on the road to full partnership with the world's great economies.

Aven smiled. The dramatic rise in China's living standard had created problems for the Soviet leadership. In his position as an assistant secretary to the Minister of Persuasion, Aven had to deal with this yellow materialism, as it came to be know at MOP.

The concerns raised by a surging nationalist sentiment within the Soviet borders took some time and energy but did not divert the ministry's primary focus. Most of the staff, including Aven, felt that Gorbachev, once allied with Yeltsin, could deal with the sporadic local protests. Dealing with the reality of economic backwardness, however, was another matter.

For years, the Soviet leaders had been waging an ideological war within the nation's borders. Western capitalist mentality represented all that was corrupt and degrading in human life. Aven and his colleagues were holding their own, if not winning this struggle for the mind of the Russian citizen. Occasional set-backs were perplexing—bluejeans, followed by jazz, punk rock, and chartreuse hair. But with the conflict centered around youth-cult commodities, MOP, assisted by the KGB, was able to limit the damage. For years, the puppet nations to the West had acted as an effective shield against any massive influx of Western capitalism, ideas, or products.

China's great leap backward into capitalism presented an altogether different problem. No buffer of geography existed between the countries who had earlier been allies in a promising but short-lived struggle for world communist domination.

The tailor was putting the finishing touches on Aven's robe as Aven reflected on the irony of these concerns. The real threat to the Soviet state was not China's proximity but rather the special character of the yellow materialism. China's leap backward had resulted in an abundance of consumer goods. Food, clothing, and housing were now available in quantities far in excess of what most Russian citizens might desire for their great-grandchildren. Rumors of prosperity across the Eastern borders were rampant throughout Aven's land. Work at MOP progressed at a fever pitch. The dream of a classless society, of a humane communist state destined to spread its values (and control) across the earth, had to be kept alive.

Aven had been confident of MOP's ultimate triumph. Communism would prevail. In rare moments of candor, Aven had admitted to Rena that the success of his ministry was assured, ultimately, by the vast Soviet nuclear arsenal. A successful counter-revolution within the state was not possible without active outside intervention, and no such intervention was likely. The combined forces of the United States and Western Europe, even in the face of a passive, docile, and finally disintegrating Warsaw Pact, were no match for the Russian ICBMs, along with the new class of submarine-launched cruise missiles. China had followed Japan's lead, devoting all of her economic resources to the production of consumer products. Thus, a military threat from the East had all but vanished.

Moments remained. Aven glanced at his note cards. Ronald Reagan had also used note cards, a trait that attracted considerable cynicism among left-leaning intellectuals in Russia and Amerika. Self-satisfied elitists in both nations had misjudged this man's visionary powers. Despite much skepticism, as deep as it was broad, Star Wars had altered the course of history and of Aven's life.

Thanks in part to a chance meeting between Edward Teller and Nancy Reagan (who was with her astrologer), by 1994 all of the U.S. ICBM sites, as well as every population center of over twenty-five thousand, had been provided an invulnerable ballistic missile shield. The once great and proud Soviet nation had no choice but to surrender under terms dictated by the forty-second president of the United States, Danforth Quayle. Despite the soft winds of glasnost, along with moderation in Eastern Europe, Danforth remained as steadfast in his opposition to the Soviet system as he was supportive of Star Wars. The unfortunate and mad antics of the Iraqi dictator Hussein helped speed a sequence of events that were to thrust this young man from Indiana into the Amerikan presidency.

With the failure of Gorbachev's reforms, the party hardliners had regained control and were preparing to reintroduce the Brezhnev Doctrine. They hadn't bargained for the astrological powers of Edward Teller, Nancy Reagan, and Danforth Quayle. Armed with ultimate moral and military superiority, President Quayle demanded total surrender. Three days later, on the first of April 1995, Amerikan occupation forces arrived in Aven's homeland.

Gaylord entered the dressing area. As the two men moved down the long corridor, Aven couldn't help but wonder what earlier tsars must have felt as they assumed absolute rule over all of Mother Russia.

Part I

DAY ONE

■ ■ ■ ■ ■ ■ ■ ■ ■ ■ ■ ■ ■ ■ ■ ■

*E*verything seemed normal enough. The faint sound of the alarm soon took on menacing proportions. Aven moved quickly yet with care so as not to wake Rena. This was an arrangement they had agreed to when Rena moved in. Aven took care of the morning duties, leaving the flat orderly with fresh tea on their small stove. Rena's work as a free-lance writer allowed her to set her work hours, in sharp contrast with Aven's routine. Work at the Ministry of Persuasion began promptly at seven-thirty.

The alarm had been set for five forty-five, assuring that the morning newspaper would be waiting. It was as if Aven's mind couldn't focus without the front-page news. Whatever the story might be—troubles on the China border, Stalin's death, victory at the Olympics, or another football title for the local team—the bold headline provided the stimulation Aven required to start each day with unfaltering optimism and confidence.

Along with good looks and wit, a supreme sense of self-confidence, regardless of what was going on around him, accounted for Aven's success. As the youngest of three children, with parents possessing no influence in the party, Aven's admission to the finest university at Moscow was a surprise to family and friends alike. But not to Aven.

The banner of the paper that lay folded near the door occupied all twelve columns, with type far bolder than usual. During the moments that Aven was opening his paper, millions of his countrymen were reading the same headline. For most citizens, the words would evoke a profound sense of unease. Aven felt no such feelings.

IN THE INTEREST OF WORLD PEACE RUSSIA UNDERTAKES
MASSIVE REORGANIZATION
Amerikan Representatives Due in Moscow Today

It had been less than three weeks since President Quayle had delivered the Amerikan ultimatum. Aven knew the story well. It was all he and his colleagues could do to prepare the nation. The Soviet surrender had to be seen as little more than a thoughtful resurrection of glasnost. Despite the efforts of Gorbachev and Yeltsin, conservatives had regained power shortly after the "liberation" of Estonia, last of the Baltic states to leave the Soviet orbit. Unilateral disarmament in the name of *perestroika* seemed only a decree away. With a populous far from enthusiastic about capitalist "freedoms," hardliners in the party had little difficulty in removing Gorby, muzzling Yeltsin, and making clear to the world that Russia had no intention of abandoning its historic mission. The first task in returning to this historic struggle had required a massive rebuilding of the Soviet military forces.

The conservative leadership had failed to consider the upcoming Amerikan elections. With vague reference to his health, George Bush had decided to relinquish the presidency after one term. Many felt the real reason was his strong desire to hunt and fish. As president, Bush had done a good bit of this, but the more time he spent in his adopted states of Texas and Maine, the less fond he became of the District of Columbia. At the Republican Convention in the summer of 1992, Bush, a man born to the CIA, unleashed his final well-kept secret. In stepping down, he reminded the stunned convention of the profound wisdom in his decision four years earlier, the surprise selection for running mate. In fact, Bush had chosen quite wisely. While he himself had loved the idea of *being* president, he had no ideological agenda or any interest in one. His young running mate was the perfect complement, having a strong ideological agenda but no idea whatsoever about what it meant to *be* president. The latter proved no weakness as he obeyed like an adoring schoolboy the directions of Marilyn, who defined his every thought and action. With the comforting return of the Russian threat, the Amerikan electorate and Republican delegates eagerly turned to their conservative-hardline vice president.

Danforth Quayle was one of the few national figures who had not declared an end to the Cold War, and within days of his inauguration, he began the resurrection of Star Wars. Subsequent events occurred in a blur of diplomatic activity. When, in the late winter of 1994, the Russian generals were provided with a demonstration of the Amerikan SDI capability, they met amongst themselves briefly before agreeing to the terms of surrender.

In actuality, Aven's ministry had had an easy time in explaining the "thoughtful return to Gorby's vision." An essential ingredient in the return was cooperation with Amerikan officials. The two nations agreed, discreetly, to a variation of the surrender terms imposed upon Japan nearly half a century ago. Reorganization of every facet of Russian society would be determined by

Amerikan officials, officials who would remain deeply in the background. For the past several days, Aven and his colleagues played this theme so cleverly that many believed nothing was really going to change. Aven was too much the realist.

As he read the news and finished the last bite of toast, Aven realized that the headline was unlike any he had ever perused. And yet his spirits were as high as ever. He did the dishes and put the tea on for Rena. The springtime walk to the ministry, unimpeded by rain or snow, took close to twenty minutes. For the past three years, Aven had been in no hurry to get to work. This morning, however, he found himself eager to see how his nation—as well as his world—was to be restructured.

He moved quickly to the front door and just as quickly retraced his steps. Aven ran his left index finger over the table's glowing surface. Nothing. He couldn't help the broad smile. It was a lesson learned well from his mother years ago. There was no more fastidious a homemaker in their small community. And how many times did he hear his mother's admonition, the Russian peasant saying that had been passed from generation to generation of homemakers, "Dust, but verify." He left the flat knowing that Rena's love would remain undistracted.

Aven's route allowed precious solitude for much of his walk to the ministry. The Party leadership had years before recognized Aven's unique powers of persuasion along with his ability to focus entirely on complainants' problems and to come up with unique "solutions" to the most complex situations. Aven was put in charge of the crisis-complaint division within a few weeks after his arrival at MOP, spending his days in constant conversation with one, two, three—sometimes a roomful—of disgruntled fellow workers or citizens. Invariably, these individuals left the meeting feeling better. It made little difference as to Aven's ability to change the objective circumstances—something Aven in fact was rarely able to do. What mattered was Aven's ability to motivate and persuade, and at this Aven was a master. He did his work so well, however, that for the first time in his life, promotion had eluded him.

This morning Aven's mind was not on work. The exhilarating headline, the wondrous uncertainty, the unimaginable possibilities, took Aven to an earlier time. Before MOP, the path of his own life had been wondrous and unimaginable. He was his parents' favorite. In his early years he could do no wrong. His teachers called on him whenever they wanted to show the rest of the class what dunces they were. During the recess periods, Aven's peers forgave his unfailingly correct responses, and on those rare occasions when he wasn't selected as one of the team captains, he was always the first player chosen.

Along with wit and dominating athletic skills, Aven's physical appearance soon attracted the young ladies. Only a few centimeters taller than his peers, it was the supple power of his body that served him well in all sporting endeavors. That, and the ever present animation in his gray-green eyes. During his years at the gymnasium, Aven achieved the highest marks in all of his classes, led his school's track, swimming, and gymnastic teams to the regional championships in four successive years, and introduced countless attractive young girls to the mysteries bound up within their own bodies.

Even today, as he walked in the gentle morning solitude, Aven did not find this adoration at all peculiar. True enough, he could think of others whose success in academics or sports or with women had evoked feelings of envy and hostility. Such feelings eluded him. Before entering the university, Aven had been the subject of universal admiration, no different and no less qualified than that bestowed upon him by his mother at the moment of his birth.

Although Aven had had the highest marks recorded in the past several years on the mathematics and physics entrance exams, his heart, mind, and already well-demonstrated abilities lay elsewhere. He had used the latter to charm his way into the School of Social Studies and Rhetoric. While the intellectual demands of the program were well within his capacity, the volume of reading and writing was far more than he had ever experienced. And his new classmates were among the brightest students from the vast Soviet nation. For the first time in his life, Aven had to make choices. Some came easily.

Disengagement from competitive athletics was simple. There were none at the university. The nation's top athletes were employed full-time, with international competition their sole preoccupation. Inter-university sports competition did not exist. During his time at the university, Aven continued spending just enough time in the gym to maintain his well-toned body.

The more difficult choice came in his other extracurricular activity. From the age of eleven through age seventeen, Aven had spent many pleasurable hours with the most attractive girls in his community. Never having had to make choices among these admiring creatures, he could see any and as many of them as he might desire for as short or as long a period as was his fancy. The normal youthful battles among the sexes—hurt feelings, petty jealousies, or paranoid possessiveness—never touched Aven. There was a singular aura about him that allowed his relationships with members of the opposite sex to be conducted without ill feeling. Young women were ecstatic and grateful for any attention that he might bestow upon them, and he never consciously took advantage of this adoration. His male comrades looked on in wonder. They, too, held no ill feelings towards Aven and his "way with the girls." Without trying to understand, Aven did know there was great delight to be had in the intimate company of beautiful young girls, and in taking his pleasure, he gave full measure in return. He never felt the need, nor had he been compelled, to limit his sources of rapture. This part of Aven's world changed as he entered the university.

From his first moments in Moscow, Aven was, as always, attracted to the best-looking coeds in his classes, and he had no trouble gaining their attention. But for the first time in his life, he experienced female anger and rejection. A chill ran down his neck as he recalled Riva, the lovely country girl from his Marxist theory class. Aven had offered to help with the first chapter of *Kapital*. Very quickly the evening turned from a discussion of commodities to the most intense lovemaking. Aven remembered the adoration in Riva's eyes as he took her back to the student flat. As was his habit, with no malice intended, Aven paid little attention to her for several days after. Instead, he openly turned his attention to a number of other young women. Shortly after the evening with *Kapital*, Riva came into class, dumped a bucket of rotten herring on Aven's head, and ran from the classroom screaming hysterically, "you stinking cod," or words to that effect. Aven was quite perplexed at the time.

It was shortly before the first examination period. To conserve time, Aven had arranged for concurrent dates with Rona, the upperclass student who ran his rhetoric section, and Renalda, his history classmate who seemed to be unable to take her eyes off him. The room was well prepared—soft music on the radio and a candle-lit table with a bottle of wine and three glasses. Renalda and Rona arrived moments apart. Aven had barely enough time to tell them how good it made him feel to see them and how sensuous and seductive they looked. The two women stared at each other and then at Aven. Almost as one they raised their right arms from the elbow, while bellowing into his face an old peasant curse, "Thrust *this* up your eye," and left his room. He met Rena the next day.

Aven became aware of the sounds of children. The swings and climbing toys, new to the park, were an instant success. The number of complaints from the grandmother-nannies about keeping the young ones occupied had fallen dramatically. Aven had walked halfway to the ministry. His thoughts returned to Rena.

The previous evening's fiasco with Rona and Renalda had weighed heavily on Aven's mind as he entered his literature class. He remembered how difficult it had been for him to concentrate. This had never happened before, and he realized for the first time in his life that women could provide deep consternation as well as comfort.

"What's the matter? I've never seen you confused in class, and you haven't smiled the entire hour."

With his head still in turmoil he didn't realize these words were directed to him.

"Oh, Rena, sorry. I didn't know you were talking to me."

"That's what I was saying. Aven, I've been watching you. You're not yourself. Any dolt could have answered the professor's question. And you have such a sour look on your face."

Aven had been aware of Rena since the start of the year. Despite her unpretentious clothing, he had recognized the body of a well-trained dancer. There was an elfin glint in her otherwise somber brown eyes. Rena was by no means unattractive; she simply had not caught Aven's fancy. Perhaps it was because of her obvious intellect. From the start, Rena pushed the professor to justify his assertions about whatever literature the class was discussing. It was clear to Aven, if not the professor, that Rena's probing was never meant to show up the class or the professor. Rena was interested in ideas and the logic of argument. She was the closest to a true scholar Aven had ever encountered. And Aven may well have been intimidated by her—unconsciously, of course. For whatever reason, until that morning, Aven had not found Rena sexually appealing.

"I'd really rather not talk about it. I'm fine, it's just that...."

"You're not fine. I don't mean to be pushy, but if you'd like a cup of tea this afternoon, perhaps I can help. You know, Aven, I'm pretty good at getting to the bottom of things."

Rena said this with a smile, and for a brief moment, something inside Aven stirred. Aven realized that beneath that rich academic veneer there was a rather attractive female after all.

"Thanks, Rena. My last class ends at four this afternoon. Let's have tea then."

Since that afternoon, nearly a decade ago, Aven had not made love with any other woman. This was not the scenario he had had in mind when they brought the pot of tea to their table in the cafe a few blocks from school. He did not yet know Rena. As she spoke to him, as she listened to his puzzlement over the peculiar antics of Riva, Rona, and Renalda, as she spun her web of analysis that was simultaneously sensitive, thoughtful, critical, and humorous, and as her eyes began to glow with an obvious fondness for Aven, he found himself smitten—lost—awash with feelings of desire that were unlike any he had known before.

"So, what I'm trying to say to you, Aven, is that university women are different. The days of subservience are over. We are not rejecting men, only holding them to a new standard. The same that they have expected of us throughout history."

"Rena, the tea is cold. Let's go to my place."

"Aven, you are the brightest man I have ever met, and by far the most handsome and sexiest. But for some strange reason you've never had to use the brain God gave you in your amorous endeavors. I'd like nothing better than to go to your flat. I expect that there is much I could show you. But, Aven, not this afternoon...and not any afternoon, until you come to understand one word. We have been talking for over two hours, and I'm sorry to say, I don't think you know what it is yet."

"Gender gap? Androgyny? Missionary position?...Self-actualization? Oh, Rena, you've said so much. How can it possibly be expressed in a single word?"

It was some time before she answered.

"Commitment. Aven, what we want is what we have always given to our men—complete, unconditional, and unending devotion. Your father was the only man in your mother's life. So too with my mother, and our mothers' mothers, as far back in time as you care to go. Oh yes, things have changed for some of us. We have been accepted, if somewhat grudgingly, into the universities and into—or at least near—the halls of authority and power. We are permitted to have our own careers and professions, so long as we tend to the house and our husbands and children as well. I want to be a writer. And I will be. And I also want a family, with children, and a husband to love and to be loved by. But I won't accept the conditions imposed on my mother and all the women of her generation and before. No longer will the man be exempt from the marriage vows. Aven, your behavior towards Riva and the others is precisely what we will no longer tolerate."

"But, Rena, you know...."

"Sorry, Aven, but we will settle for nothing less than commitment."

For the first time that afternoon Rena's voice took on a stern and demanding tone.

"Okay...okay. What you've said makes a lot of sense. And it might be nice to have just one girl for a change. But do you think it's too late to go back to my room for a while?"

"Aven, my charming bright Aven, yes it's too late to go back to your room this evening. And I expect it will be a goodly while before the time is right."

"What do I have to do? I've already said I...."

"It's not simply saying the marriage vows. Every male despot does that easily enough. For me to give myself to you—and that's what I'd be doing if I went to your room—I want to know that I am the only woman in your life. I know myself, and it won't work any other way."

Aven was near tears of anger and frustration. Rena had become incomprehensibly attractive. Never before had he failed in gratifying similar though far less compelling desires. With some effort he controlled the sound of his voice.

"What must I do?"

"You will know easily enough, Aven. If I am the only woman in your life, you will no longer get fish from Riva or fists from any of her female friends. You will not give them cause to treat you so. We can study together. I'd love to have lunch with you often, and tea as well."

For weeks Aven maintained an excruciatingly platonic yet totally faithful relationship with Rena. They saw each other often—walks to and from class and the library, lunch, tea, an occasional lecture or afternoon chamber concert, and visits to several of the museums. Aven quickly discovered Rena's passion for classical music and art. Through all of this they were never truly alone. From the first, it was clear that Rena would dictate the terms of their relationship. Aven quietly acquiesced. His internal tumult was another matter.

During this time, Rena talked often of her own life. She was an only child and, like Aven, much adored by both parents. Sara and Albert had met while studying at the university. Sara had been active in the dissident movement of the time. Both were persecuted for their liberal views. Despite his inability to make more than a humble income, Albert had refused to let Sara work. Out of the deep love she felt for him, Rena's mother agreed. She took care of the house and her husband, and soon Rena as well.

Neither expressed any regret over their situation. They were happy in their love for each other and for Rena, happy in their thirst for knowledge, in their interest and understanding of the world around them, and happy in the unshakable belief that a better world was not far off. If they were too old to see much of this new earth, surely Rena was not. Despite her attractiveness, Rena was not active socially. Rena's closest friends were her parents. Rena spent her hours reading and developing her musical and artistic skills. She soon became an accomplished dancer. She loved painting, but her knowledge of classical music far exceeded her talent with a brush. By the time she was twelve, Rena had already decided on a career as a writer. Her optimism, intelligence, and determination, along with a mild thaw in the internal political affairs of the nation, allowed her entrance to Moscow University. Rena brought to her studies and life at the university the very same dedication to truth and knowledge possessed by her parents.

"Next Friday."

"Next Friday what?"

They were finishing the pot of tea.

"I'd like to go the symphony, and then perhaps you could show me your room."

Aven laughed to himself as he remembered. The cup of tea he had been holding assumed a cossacklike life of its own. Fortunately, they were in a rather remote corner of the cafe. He had also felt a moist warmth in the seat of his pants. Aven had long since forgotten the program at the concert hall. But the evening's music had just begun. He vaguely remembered Rena commenting about the Purcell, something about the first movement lacking in vitality. His mind was elsewhere, racing ahead to what the rest of the evening might bring. At least he wouldn't have to worry about Rena finding traces of other women. He had almost forgotten what it was like to be with anyone else.

"It's on the second floor."

Aven had not fully recovered from Rena's long-awaited pronouncement. He steadied himself while placing the key in the lock. It took some time.

"Come on in. I'm sorry the place is such a mess."

The words rushed from his mouth involuntarily.

"Please sit down. I only have orange spice tea. I agree, the Piston was flaccid in its shaping…I mean the Purcell." Aven gasped to himself. How could he confuse the two, especially knowing how much Rena objected to even this gentle twentieth-century composer?

Fortunately, Rena had moved to the other end of the room and was looking with interest at Aven's one oil painting.

"Aven, you don't really like this, do you?"

They were talking past each other. Aven was nervously spinning the radio dial when Rena came up behind him. She gently turned the knob all the way to the left.

"Not tonight, my pet. We won't need others to make music for us."

Rena wrote and conducted the entire program. The extended overture provided a hint of the evening's major themes. Neither of them spoke, nor could they had they tried. After the first few measures, Aven was able to follow Rena's pulsating rubato style through the climax of the piece.

"Rena, I…I can't find the words to…."

"Hush, Aven my love. You'll need all of your strength. The symphony has four movements."

And what a magnificent work it turned out to be. From the quiet opening through the development, the first movement evoked the passion and pathos of Tchaikovsky and Brahms combined. They continued without pause into the lento-appassionato, their glistening bodies moving in perfect octaves. The rapid scherzo opened with the most exquisite tonguing that either of them had ever known. The trio, by contrast, was fairly traditional, with slower waltzlike motions allowing them energy to return to the opening delicacies. The fourth movement was the longest, and the most breathtaking. From the first aggressive attack, the two moved through repeated climaxes, yielding in tempo for the briefest time, only to resume their bacchanalian excess. Not long after, sleep seemed so welcome, and necessary.

It couldn't have been more than a minute or two when Rena put her hand on his shoulder.

"Aven, not yet. We still have the encore."

Rena was gone when Aven woke the next morning. For the remaining time at the university she had rented a room in a private boarding home. Aven kept his second-floor concert hall where their love making continued as it had begun. Their monogamous existence caused him no obvious distress. The comfort of his relationship with Rena allowed him to concentrate on academic matters as needed. They graduated together, Aven fourth and Rena first in their respective programs. Rena began work as a free-lance writer. Though a gifted essayist, for some time she had only modest success in placing her work. She also insisted on keeping her room, a short distance from his flat. These were the only two subjects over which they quarreled. Aven gave up counting the number of times he had pleaded with her to move in. She was just as stubborn about her writing.

"I know you value truth, and I know you think writing to suit the dictates of the circulation manager is the worst form of prostitution."

"You're damn right. Most poor souls have no choice. They sell their services to the highest bidder. But you—I've told you why I write as I do. From the time I first wrote, my mother told me that I had a gift from God and that not to express my thoughts and ideas as I felt them would be a sin. That is how she and my father both conducted their lives. Aven, I can do no less."

"But your mother said nothing about moving in with me. I'm sorry I didn't know her. Perhaps if we had met she would have kept you from this stubbornness. And you talk of sin, keeping two places with housing conditions as they are."

Rena's voice softened.

"Aven, it will not always be like this. I promise. But until my writing is better received, I must keep the room. Please don't ask me to live off your earnings."

The present intruded on his thoughts. The upper floors of the ministry were in sight. Aven realized that he had been walking in an aimless fashion.

"Curious," he thought. "the past seems to be deflecting me from my destination."

But as always, Rena had been true to her word. The first jubilant days of glasnost had seen the opening that would eventually permit Rena's biting commentary an audience. With the acquisition of this independence, Rena gave up her room. Given the intimacy of their relationship, Rena's move was only a formality. But Aven could honestly say to himself that he had attained all that he wished out of life. He ignored the frustration with the ministry much of the

time. Advancement was something he had been accustomed to all of his life—
but the enchantment Rena brought to his existence was more than ample balm.
Most of the time.

Aven entered through the large glass doors, which reflected outward, a sym-
bol of the building's function within the state. Success was measured by the degree to which MOP was invisible to the citizens it served. Much of the time the
ministry earned high marks. Nevertheless, the continual decline in the nation's
economic well-being was enough to keep Aven and his modest staff fully occupied. Besides directing his section, Aven took on for himself most of the serious
individual and small group complaints. However insoluble the concerns might
be, Aven rarely failed to persuade his "patients" that their lot could be much
worse. It was his extraordinary ability to divorce himself from the concerns and
apprehensions of others that made him so effective.

"Good morning."

Upon greeting the lift operator, Aven's thoughts turned to his work.

"Morning, sir. Gonna be a real interesting day."

Aven hardly heard as he tried to recall what was in his appointment book.

"Oh, yes, Otise, interesting indeed!"

Only one entry had been made in the book for Monday. The notice came
late Friday afternoon. The newly appointed Amerikan shadow Director of the
Ministry was arriving at eight o'clock, in exactly half an hour. Aven closed his
eyes for a moment. He remembered—her name was Doctor Paula T. Barnum.

"Fifth floor, sir."

"Well, Otise, have a good day."

"The same for you, sir."

The six members of his staff were at their desks. With substantial obstacles
bedeviling his country, the mood in the office had been subdued for some time.
A cloak of apprehension greeted him. For the briefest moment, Aven was taken
aback. But just as quickly, his optimism returned. He tried to lighten the mood.

"Good morning, comrades. I trust you all had a refreshing weekend."

The laconic response told him he had failed.

"Oh now, cheer up. It's just another day, another half-kopec."

Aven didn't wait for a response. He entered his modest office and opened
the file that had been placed on his desk. It contained one page.

ATTENTION

To: ALL MEMBERS OF THE MINISTRY OF PERSUASION
FROM: I. M. PAVLOV, DIRECTOR

On Monday, 1 April, 1995, at PROMPTLY 8:00 AM, you will

be expected to be in place in the central B.S. Room. At that time Dr. Paula T. Barnum from the UNITED STATES OF AMERIKA will begin the orientation program.

Dr. Barnum is a distinguished administrator. She began her studies at the University of California, Los Angeles, transferring to Vassar, where she received her B.A. (Human Growth and Development), and completed her D.B.A. (Advertising) at Harvard University. For the past two years she has been the C.E.O. at her nation's most successful private ministry of persuasion, Ribald, Snow, Joubh, and Smith.

Whatever your feelings might be about recent events, Dr. Barnum deserves our undivided attention and cooperation. DEVIATIONS WILL NOT BE TOLERATED.

HAVE A GOOD DAY

"Of course this will be a good day," Aven thought. "It would have been easier to think of working under the supervision of a man, but who knows, a woman's touch might be just the thing to smooth our occupation status."

Aven wouldn't need to leave the office immediately, since he could walk to the Boris Stemtide Room located one floor below.

The assembly hall was large enough for the ministry's two hundred workers, seated in ten gently arced rows, a design that lent a degree of intimacy not found elsewhere in the building. Aven joined the section heads seated on the podium. The two empty seats were obviously to be occupied by old Igor and the Amerikan.

"I wonder if it's Miss or Mrs.," he said under his breath and abruptly corrected himself. "All professional women from Amerika are Mzzz. these days."

At eight o'clock, Igor Pavlov walked onto the dais and approached the microphone.

"Comrades, Dr. Barnum needed a few more minutes in the powder room. She will be with us shortly, and she begs your indulgence," adding in a stage whisper, "as if we have any alternative."

As he finished, the door at the rear of the hall opened. Aven was among the first to see her. Those facing the podium realized she had entered only as she passed each successive row. Conversation grew softer, reaching a stunned silence as she stepped onto the stage. In his most erotic fantasies, Aven had never imagined such beauty. He felt himself losing all sense of time and place—falling helter-skelter through a silent barren realm. Into this void came a high-pitched though muted squeal. Mzzz. Barnum had begun to speak.

Aven had not fully recovered from the initial assault and could not recall all of what she said. Paula T. Barnum's voice, whiny, just a bit too high-pitched, and without any timbre, also took his mind away from her words.

"...to be here. It was a really long flight, but...miss this moment for anything. Before I go any further...to say hello to all of you from the folks back on the mainland, ah, I mean the States."

Aven began to adjust to the sound, and at the same time Mzzz. Barnum's visual image came back into focus.

"We're all on the same boat now, and it's with a feeling of comradeship that I come to you today. Some may resent the fact that you had so little to say in selecting the ship's captain. Some of you may begrudge the fact that I am a woman."

Paula extended a demure smile, brushed the back of her hand across the left side of her forehead, and tried to whisper, "Of course, I'm just as sure that some of you don't mind at all."

The brittle sound returned.

"But whatever your own private thoughts, I trust that uppermost in your minds is the task that lies ahead. It gives me chills just to think about it. Owwwweeee."

Paula put her clenched hands to her side, knuckles thrust forward and knees together, as a shiver seemed to extend through her entire body. Regaining her composure, she continued.

"In extensive briefings in my country, I've learned that the staff of the Ministry of Persuasion contains some of the most talented and creative minds in all of your nation. That is why your ministry has been selected as the lead...."

Aven's mind wandered away from her words.

"Was all of Amerika like this?" he wondered.

He had heard the song on several occasions.

"How did it go? Amerika the beautiful...for ample waves...purple mounds...fertile plains..."

Seated behind and a good bit to the left of Paula T. Barnum, Aven saw much of her in profile. Her face, as if chiseled by Michelangelo, was framed in straight blonde hair, each short strand aligned to perfection. The subtle coloring of her eyes and lips blended naturally with her tan skin.

"My God, what I wouldn't give to climb those mountains...to explore her plain."

Aven shuddered.

"I haven't had such ideas about another woman...."

A familiar shrillness returned.

"...that is why I'm confident that together we can do the job. In my country we have perfected the methods of public control. The three necessary ingredients required of government if it hopes to accomplish anything worthwhile are *appearance, appearance,* and *appearance.* With my background in public relations and your expertise in persuasion, we can't lose. Together we shall lead this nation—and allow me the privilege of saying OUR nation—out of its malaise and into the warmth and promise shared by all of the world's free-market economies."

"If it weren't for Rena, I'd be happy enough with a little warmth and promise from her."

Aven realized, with some unease, that for the first time in their relationship, Rena appeared as an obstacle. He didn't permit the embryonic guilt to bloom.

"...why it is essential that we act boldly. We have precisely one week to create this nation anew. Seven days. But we can do better. I fully expect that next Sunday will be a day of rest. It's now time for lunch. At one o'clock I'd like to suggest that you return to your desks. My staff has provided a copy of the new three-year plan for each of you. The plan is rather substantial, and you will need time to familiarize yourselves with it. Meanwhile, I will be consulting with Director Pavlov regarding his replacement. His retirement ceremony, along with the naming of his successor, will take place in the morning. Once again, trust me—everything is going to work out just fine. See ya!"

This last news was as startling as the speaker's entrance had been. Aven and the other division heads looked at each other in collective wonderment. None had known of Igor's retirement. Aven couldn't help overhearing Mzzz. Barnum's comment to Old Igor as he moved to the microphone to close the meeting.

"If you don't mind, I'll stand. I just had this skirt pressed."

"Comrades, it's time for lunch."

Igor's voice shook.

The entire MOP staff remained seated while Igor led the guest from the hall. Aven looked at Paula as she left the stage. He couldn't be certain, but it seemed that she held his gaze for a moment longer than her movement past him required.

Lunch was eaten in silence. Aven sat at the division leaders' table, where he had a particularly nice view of the park through which he had walked and reminisced earlier in the day. His thoughts were of the future.

"Whom would she choose?"

Having been without advancement for so long, Aven had almost forgotten the excitement such prospects could bring. He failed to respond to the subdued greetings as he returned to the office. On his desk was an oversized loose-leaf notebook whose title seemed modest in comparison: Three-Year Plan. Aven sat down and pulled the volume closer, thinking he should at least take a look at it. The first page was nearly blank.

> We meant to change a nation,
> and instead we changed a world.

> —RONALD REAGAN
> *Farewell Address to the Nation*
> *January 11, 1989*

While never admitting it to Rena, Aven had thought highly of the old Amerikan president. He admired Reagan's unfailing optimism, his easy charm, his world-class communication skills, and, perhaps most of all, the female adoration bestowed on the former Hollywood favorite. Aven wondered whether he and the Amerikan shared common ancestors. This was not the case, of course, but he did not find the fantasy disturbing. His interest in the three-year plan was immediately heightened. The table of contents followed:

"One hundred pages."

Aven was struck by the emphasis. He remembered his college days and the exuberance he and his classmates had felt when reading Karl Marx.

"The economy is fundamental, all else is superstructure," or words to that effect.

While beginning to feel quite comfortable with such kinlike surroundings, Aven felt something else as well. It was hard to identify—a faint sense of apprehension perhaps, but far too obscure to trouble him.

"I might as well begin at the beginning," he thought as he turned the page.

INTRODUCTION TO YOUR NEW
ECONOMIC POLICY

It is with the greatest of pleasure that we welcome the Russian citizens to the family of freedom-loving nations. I know
all too well of the disagreements that have divided our
peoples for much of this decade. But we can rather easily let
bygones be bygones. American citizens have already done so,
and they ask only that you follow our recommendations in
the spirit in which they are intended.

Not so long ago, in the late 1970s, our nation was faced with
much the same malaise you have experienced recently. We
had lost our way. But we had not lost our ability to find the
kind of inspirational leadership that every great nation needs
in time of crisis. The words and actions of Ronald Reagan
gave us the spiritual and creative guidance we so desperately
required. Mr. Reagan was truly our savior, and his words
[with only the slightest modification] offered in his first Economic Report are no less apt today than they were when published on February 10, 1982. The plan we offer to your people
can have no more appropriate introduction....

Perplexed at the religious overtones, Aven moved a few pages forward. The
introduction had been written by President Quayle. The Russian press had long
been critical of the current Amerikan president, with much made of his evan-
gelical style. As Aven recalled, the president's opponents in the election of 1992
had tried to use the fact that he was a born-again Christian. This desperate
gamble served to push Quayle's margin of victory to sixty percentage points.
The Democratic candidate, whose name had vanished from Aven's consciousness long ago, had received less than fifteen percent of the total vote. The young
president's historic victory had been marred only by the low voter turnout, as
only twenty-two percent of the Amerikan electorate voted that day. This latter
fact, along with the disdain felt for the youthful Amerikan, had lulled the Russian military into a false sense of omnipotence. Aven turned to Reagan's Economic Report.

In the year [ahead], the first decisive steps [will be] taken toward a fundamental reorientation of the role of the [central]
government in [your] economy—a reorientation that will

mean more jobs, more opportunity, and more freedom for all
[Russians]. This long overdue redirection [perestroika] is designed to foster the energy, creativity, and ambition of the
[Russian] people so that they can create better lives for themselves, their families, and the communities in which they
live. Equally important, this [perestroika] puts your nation on
the path of...rapid economic growth.

[Your new] economic program is based on the fundamental
precept that government must respect, protect, and enhance
the freedom and integrity of the INDIVIDUAL. Economic
policy must seek to create a climate that encourages the development of private institutions conducive to INDIVIDUAL
responsibility and initiative. People should be encouraged to
go about their daily lives with the right and the responsibility
for determining their own activities, status, and achievements.

Aven's heart was pounding. These thoughts often entered his own consciousness. Rena never shared his views on the primacy of the individual.

"Perhaps if I had been able to express these ideas with the simple elo-
quence of the old Amerikan president. But with the new peace terms, Rena's arguments on behalf of community are moot anyway."

Aven continued reading, although an exaggerated elation inhibited his concentration.

...describes the policies which have to be adopted to reverse
the debilitating trends of the past, and which will lead
to...sustained growth in the years [ahead]...Finally, this
[plan] explains the impact these policies will have on the economic well-being of all [Russians] in the years to come.

For several decades, an ever larger role for the [central]
government...has sapped the economic vitality of [your]
nation....Over the past decade[s] the government has spun a
vast web of regulations that intrude into almost every aspect
of every [Russian's] working day. This regulatory web ad-
versely affects the productivity of [your] nation's businesses,
farms, and educational institutions....

> ...ever greater intrusion by the [central] government...has played a major part in a fundamental deterioration in the performance of [your] economy....This deterioration in [your] economic performance has been accompanied by inadequate employment opportunities for [your] growing work force.
>
> Reversing the trends of the past is not an easy task. I never thought or stated it would be. The damage that has been inflicted on [your] economy was done by imprudent and inappropriate policies over a period of many years, [but with all we have learned in my own nation, along with the talented cadre of supervisors led by Doctor Barnum, I feel confident in saying you can] undo it all in a few short months.

Aven was having a difficult time containing the sense of vitality these words provided.

"The old president writes with an elegant simplicity. No wonder the Amerikans speak with such respect and awe of the Reagan Revolution, almost as a religious crusade."

Aven closed the book, marked his place, and walked to the window. He reflected on what his role in this new world would be.

"I'll no doubt have a better idea tomorrow, after the new director is selected."

Returning to his desk, Aven found a pen, opened the book, and began to underline as he read.

> ...first and foremost objective...to improve the economy by reducing the role of the [central] government...
>
> ...a substantial reform of [central government] regulation...
>
> ...a reduced role for the [central] government means an enhanced role for [provincial and] local governments
>
> We should leave to private initiative all the functions that INDIVIDUALS can perform
>
> To spur [private] business investment and productivity growth,...new tax laws [will be required]...

"Pure genius!"

Again Aven paused to break the tension. It was all so simple.
"How had our leaders been so blind? And for so long?"
Aven put the pen away and continued reading.

> The poor performance of the [Russian] economy over the
> past decade[s] has had its impact on [your] position in the
> world economy. Concern about the [ruble has been] evi-
> denced by a prolonged period of decline in its value on for-
> eign exchange markets.

"How true," Aven thought.

Old Gorbachev had established the convertibility of the ruble in the early
days of his well-meaning efforts. And the ruble's plummeting on the foreign exchange markets certainly contributed to Gorbachev's downfall. Aven had come
to the last page of the introduction.

> The policies of the past have failed. They failed because they
> did not provide the environment in which [Russian] energy,
> entrepreneurship, and talent can best be put to work. Instead
> of being a successful promoter of economic growth and IN-
> DIVIDUAL initiative and freedom, government became the
> enemy of growth and the intruder on INDIVIDUAL initia-
> tive and freedom. [The three-year] program...seeks to create
> a new environment in which the strengths of [Russia] can be
> put to work for the benefit of all. That environment will be a
> [Russia] in which honest work is no longer discouraged...a
> country that looks forward to the future not with uncertainty
> but with the confidence that infused [your] forefathers.

> In closing, I hope you will permit me a personal comment.
> The message above was written by me as I took on the leader-
> ship of my own country in 1981. During the eight short years I
> was in office, I had the great pleasure of coming to know
> some of your leaders and, more importantly, of coming to
> know you. Upon leaving office I said to the American people
> in my farewell message something that I would like to say to
> you now: Once, during the heady days of the Moscow Sum-
> mit, Nancy and I decided to break off from the entourage one
> afternoon to visit the shops on Arbat Street—[as you well
> know] that's a little street just off Moscow's main shopping

area. Even though our visit was a surprise, every Russian there immediately recognized us and called our names and reached for our hands. We were just about swept away by the warmth—you could almost feel the possibilities in all that joy. Today we no longer need to talk about "possibilities." The warmth and joy that I now feel are positively overwhelming. I know you will soon come to feel the same way. We are all God's children. We in America have been living under His blessing for some time, and He is about to shed His grace on thee.

RONALD REAGAN
President, USA, Retired
Consultant

Aven didn't finish the few pages remaining in the preface. He couldn't. He had had no idea when reading the morning headline what the day would bring, nor could anything have prepared him for what had already transpired. He had been deeply shaken by the magnificence of Mzzz. Barnum's physical beauty, and now the lyric poetry of the old Amerikan president overloaded his senses. He sat quietly, his shirt damp with perspiration, allowing the multitude of feelings to wash over him. None were very precise, but he knew he felt good. A vast expanse of natural beauty coupled with eloquent common sense that was Amerika had been brought to his country in the form of Mzzz. Barnum and the three-year plan.

"Five twenty-two! That's impossible. But I can read the rest of the material in the morning, when my mind clears."

Aven and Rena usually had a glass of wine before dinner, a pleasant ritual Aven wanted to continue.

"If I leave now, I'll be able to take the outer path through the park."

This route was twice his normal walk, but the added fresh air seemed as attractive as it was necessary. Aven had to walk to the first floor, since Otise, along with all of the ministry staff, had already left. The late afternoon air, mild and gentle, provided a stark contrast with the atmosphere created over the course of the day. Aven walked toward the park.

"What will I say to her?"

Along with the stimulus provided by the impending reorganization and the role he might be playing, Aven was faced with a unique problem.

"There's no way I can tell Rena anything of my reaction to the Amerikan. But what do I say? She'll want to know every last detail."

The few people he passed along the edge of the park were more animated in their conversation than usual.

"Everyone is anxious about what changes the Amerikans have in store for us."

Aven smiled to himself.

"I wonder what their mood would be if they had seen Mzzz. Barnum? The women would really have something to be nervous about…and the men? I'm not even sure how *I* feel."

The quandary confronting Aven was new. In his relationships with women before Rena, he had never had to explain his behavior. Women were happy with any time that he might spend with them. There were those three women at the university, but Rena's appearance had all but erased them from his memory. Since Rena came into his life, there were no other women to explain away. Until this morning.

"I better think of something."

Rena opened the door. They kissed briefly but not without warmth. Immediately upon entering the front room, Aven was engulfed in a sense of panic. Rena's expression conveyed an attitude of anger and disbelief.

"Does she know? How could she? My God.…"

Her soft voice broke the self-inflicted interrogation.

"Aven, what is the matter? You look like you're in a trance. Come on now, we've kissed like that many times."

"No, Rena, it's not me. I was just concerned. You look upset…and angry."

"I'm sorry, darling. I've been in a foul mood since early this morning."

Aven felt his stomach leap toward his throat.

"It's the damn essay. There's so much to say about the deteriorating work of our young composers and artists. Every time I start to write I become paralyzed with anger."

Aven's stomach slid back into place.

"This effort to mimic technology is beyond belief. What's happening to our souls? Computers may be necessary in the design of missiles and everything else that is useless around us, but why must the last remnant of our heritage fall victim as well?"

Aven had witnessed this scene many times and knew that her tears would soon be flowing. He reached for his handkerchief.

"But, Aven, enough of me. My problems will keep. Let's have our wine and talk of something interesting. Your day must have been fascinating. What happened? Did the Amerikans come? Are they any brighter than they appear to be? Is there any chance at all for our country? What did you do all day? Come, dinner isn't near ready. We have lots of time. I want to know everything."

Aven's stomach resumed its upward drift.

The front room was small. A few simple furnishings gave it a quiet dignity. Rena and Aven's combined income had allowed the purchase of two works of Rena's favorite young Russian artist—one of the few who had not joined the modern abstract/analytic movement that was so upsetting to her. In one corner of the room Rena had located a small antique coffee table flanked by the two comfortable leather chairs that had arrived some sixteen months after she had placed the order. While Aven's position allowed them the privilege of purchasing such furniture, Aven had no say over production and delivery delays. Rena had not complained. She was so delighted to have them.

Rena poured wine for both of them.

"Aven, please, do come and sit down."

"Actually, Rena, there isn't a whole lot to tell. I spent most of the afternoon reading material the Amerikans provided for us. In the morning we met the new Amerikan administrator, someone named...uh, P. T. Barnum, I think. Anyway, all pretty boring stuff. Oh yes, I almost forgot, they'll be naming a new Russian director for the ministry. Old Igor got the sack. Came without warning, but he was starting to lose touch. An awful lot of pressure lately. Probably just as well. That's really all. I suppose things will pick up in the next few days....Hey, Rena, I've got a great idea. How 'bout putting the stew on simmer? Let's go to the club for dinner. We both need to get out. You've had an awful day, and I've had hardly any day at all."

Through this entire evasive monologue, Aven kept his gaze on the wine glass, turning it by the stem, gently moving the red liquid from side to side, and taking a sip now and then. He looked up at Rena. Since he entered the flat, his stomach had been in constant motion. This time it was his heart. It sank.

"Aven, if you don't mind I'd just as soon not go out tonight. If you want to go to the club, that's fine with me."

"Rena, come on, you're just upset with the essay."

"No, I don't think it's the essay. As a matter of fact, I couldn't wait for you to get home tonight so that I could put the damn thing out of my mind."

She hesitated, as if uncertain of what to say next.

"Maybe I was expecting to hear some good news about the Amerikans."

"Well, I didn't say they were bad."

"I know you didn't, but you didn't really say anything. Oh, Aven, maybe you're right. Perhaps the essay is what's nagging at me. Maybe you will know more in a day or so."

Rena tried to lighten the mood she had created.

"Oh well, they do say that Rome wasn't built in a day, don't they?"

Her heart wasn't in it.

"Rena, look. I'm positive there will be more news. It's just that today was all a jumble. It's hard for me to make sense out of what happened. Don't be so blue. It's not like you. You make me feel as if I've done something to hurt you, or disappoint you, and I haven't...have I?"

Rena relented.

"Darling, I need ten minutes to freshen up. Call the club and tell them to chill their best bottle of wine."

Aven's heart and stomach were finally calm. It was another organ that moved involuntarily.

The club chef was among the best in Moscow. The wine was wonderful, and they drank more than usual. They were the last to leave. Aven was intoxicated with the wine and the waltzes played by the pianist. By the time Aven had paid for the cab, Rena had moved into their private concert hall and was beginning to undress.

"That was a nice evening, Aven. Thanks."

"Rena, I'm glad. You know how I hate to see you upset. I'd never do anything to make you unhappy."

"I know that, Aven."

Aven undressed quickly, considering the excesses of the evening. Rena was on her side, knees pulled up, and head resting on both hands. Aven slid under the covers, pressing his body against hers. He caressed Rena's exposed shoulder with his right hand. Arousal was instantaneous.

"Aven, dear, not tonight...."

DAY TWO

■ ■ ■ ■ ■ ■ ■ ■ ■ ■ ■ ■ ■ ■ ■ ■

His head throbbed slightly from the previous night and the empty space beside him turned the mild ache into a spasm of despair.

"*She's gone!*"

At that moment the room filled with the smells of tea and eggs and onion.

"Aven, I'm sorry. I couldn't sleep. That cursed essay, it came back to me in the middle of the night. But I did make some progress, and I decided to take a break and fix your eggs. You never have time to prepare them yourself. Tell me I didn't disrupt your sleep?"

"Oh no, ah, no, not a bit."

Several seconds passed before he spoke again.

"Rena, you're such a love. What have I done to deserve you? From the day we met you've been the only woman in my life. No matter what the crazy Amerikans dream up for us, nothing can ever change that."

"I know that."

Rena put the breakfast tray over Aven's lap, bent down to kiss his forehead, and left the room, only to return with the morning news.

"Enjoy your breakfast, my love."

"Where are you going now? Why do you keep coming in and out?"

"Eat your food and read your paper," she said firmly. "I need to get back to the essay. We can talk this evening. I'm sure something will happen at the ministry today, and, Aven...I love you."

Aven had been living with Rena long enough to recognize the familiar and the uncommon in her behavior. He imagined that if he was deathly ill, she might attend to him, but short of that, her words told him to find other amusements. But he could not recall the last time she had prepared his eggs. The vagaries of Rena's behavior faded from his mind as he turned to the news.

AMERIKAN ADVISORS ARRIVE, LED BY P.T. BARNUM
Ministry of Persuasion to Be Focal Point of
Reorganization Effort

The story itself was not informative. It did mention old Igor's "long-planned" retirement but said nothing about his replacement. Aven had difficulty thinking of anything else. Rena might just as well have brought him stale toast. Aven finished his food, showered, dressed, and left the flat with only a perfunctory good-bye. He walked quickly.

"Daaamn it, the dishes!"

He continued walking through the park with undisturbed concentration. Aven knew in his heart of hearts that his chances were nonexistent.

"If the ministries of military and economic affairs had had even a fraction of our skill, old Igor might well have been on his way to Amerika this very moment," he thought. "But that is precisely why I have no chance. I'm better, but I'm the youngest, with the least experience, and I've been stuck in the crisis-complaint section for too long."

Aven's confidence ebbed.

"Good morning, Otise, and how's the family?"

"Morning to you, sir. Thanks for asking. Everything's fine now. You know, we weren't prepared for triplets. And Roma and I had hoped she could get back to work after the baby. But with three, it was tough for a time. Roma's a wonderful woman, and really thrifty. The kids were just six months old last week. Be a while yet before they are walking...."

"Well, that's wonderful, Otise. Have a good day."

He made a game effort to appear himself as he greeted his staff. The three-year plan was on his desk where he had left it. Aven checked his appointment calendar. There was nothing until lunch. And there it was:

> 12:30 P.M.: Retirement ceremony in Main Dining Hall
> *to be followed by*
> NAMING OF NEW (VICE) DIRECTOR
> ~~NAMING OF NEW (VICE) DIRECTOR~~
> ~~NAMING OF NEW (VICE) DIRECTOR~~

The words reverberated on the page.

"This is craziness. My life's been good, I like my work, and am good at it. And I have Rena. There's no reason to indulge myself in this morbid self-pity."

Aven realized the ministry staff would be actively involved in reorganization and that he would remain a key participant. His mood brightened some as he reached for the book on his desk. After finishing the preface, he turned to the first page.

> The plan for your economy which is provided here is really quite simple. It is based on the seminal works of three great thinkers: ADAM SMITH—FRIEDRICH A. HAYEK—MILTON FRIEDMAN. No condensation of the writing of these men can do justice to the full majesty of their work, and the American government will provide each ministry library with copies of their publications. A set of recommended readings is given on page 81 below, and it will behoove all of you to do this reading in the weeks ahead (ESPECIALLY THOSE SEEKING ADVANCEMENT IN YOUR NEW GOVERNMENT).

To Aven's surprise, there were only three entries.

RECOMMENDED READING

Adam Smith	*The Wealth of Nations**
Friedrich A. Hayek	*Road to Serfdom*
Milton Friedman	*Capitalism and Freedom*

*NOTE WELL!!! UNDER NO CIRCUMSTANCES SHOULD THE READER CONFUSE THIS VOLUME WITH ANOTHER ENTITLED

The Theory of Moral Sentiments

THIS WAS A WORK DONE WHEN PROFESSOR SMITH WAS VERY YOUNG, AND HE HAS FULLY RE-CANTED ALL OF THE FOOLISH IDEAS EXPRESSED THEREIN. THE BOOK HAS BEEN OUT OF PRINT FOR SEVERAL DECADES, BUT ISOLATED COPIES MAY STILL EXIST. IT IS BEST THAT THEY BE SHREDDED WHEN FOUND.

"Shredding? An Amerikan oddity, I suppose."
Aven rang for his secretary.
"Mila, please run down to the library and check out these three books."

"These are unfamiliar. Aven, are you sure they're in our library?"

"It won't be long before we become intimate with these authors—the Tolstoys and the Gorkys of our time. If we haven't received them yet, be sure that the library notifies us the moment they come in."

"I'll go right now. Is there anything else?"

Aven had resumed reading as he mumbled.

"No thanks, not at the mom...."

On the middle of the second page he came to the subheading: BASIC PRINCIPLES.

> For some time now thoughtful people in many nations have seen the relationship between Adam Smith and Capitalism much like that between Jesus Christ and Christianity. Indeed, Adam Smith is the father of Capitalism, and *The Wealth of Nations,* our Bible. His followers are numerous, but none have been more vital in providing a modern-day translation than his sons, Professors Hayek and Friedman. In the next brief section we rely heavily on Professor Hayek's work in defining the contemporary intellectual and spiritual basis of the economic plan. Professor Friedman's work then provides the operational guidelines for the day-to-day organization and functioning of the modern 21st-century capitalist state. With a clear understanding of this material, there is no reason why the Russian people cannot have a society every bit as splendid as America's, perhaps more so.

> The *Wealth of Nations,* written well over 200 years ago, remains a book of today and forever. The central and timeless theme can be found in the following nine canons:

Aven had to move away from his desk. He was tempted to ask Mila to go out for a bottle of vodka. The one he kept in the lower drawer had been drained during the most recent crisis conference. He looked at the clock.

"I can't have a drink at this hour," he groused, "and I should be sober for the noontime festivities, I suppose."

He did feel somewhat discombobulated. Despite the religious fervor in the introductory paragraphs, the beauty of Ronald Reagan's phrasing had won him over. The language today, however, was beginning to take its toll.

"Is this a plan for economic reorganization or personal redemption? Is Mzzz. Barnum going to be a director or a deacon?"

It was without any enthusiasm that he returned to his desk and the nine "commandments," as he thought of them.

I. It is not from the benevolence of the butcher, the brewer, or the baker that we expect our dinner, but from their regard to THEIR OWN INTEREST. We address ourselves, not to their humanity but to THEIR SELF-LOVE.

II. The property which every man has in his own labour, as it is the ORIGINAL FOUNDATION OF ALL OTHER PROPERTY, so it is SACRED and INVIOLABLE.

III. Man neither intends to promote the public interest, nor knows how much he is promoting it...he is led by an INVISIBLE HAND to promote an end which was no part of his intention.

IV. The natural effort of every individual is to better his own condition, when suffered to exert itself with FREEDOM and security, is ALL POWERFUL...

V. CONSUMPTION is the SOLE END of all production...

VI. The uniform, constant, and uninterrupted effort of every man to better his condition...is frequently powerful enough to maintain the natural progress of things IN SPITE OF both the EXTRAVAGANCE of government and of the greatest ERRORS OF ADMINISTRATION.

VII. It is the highest impertinence and presumption...in kings and ministers to pretend to watch over the economy of private people....They are themselves always, and without exception, the GREATEST SPENDTHRIFTS in society.

VIII. What is PRUDENCE in the conduct of every private family can scarce be folly in that of a great kingdom.

IX. According to the system of natural liberty, the sovereign has ONLY THREE DUTIES to attend to; three duties of great importance...[1] PROTECTING SOCIETY from the violence and invasion of OTHER INDEPENDENT SOCIE-TIES...[2] PROTECTION, so far as possible, for EVERY MEMBER of society from the injustice or oppression of EVERY OTHER MEMBER...[3] the duty of erecting and maintaining certain public institutions, which...can never be in the interest of any individual, or small group of individuals...to erect and maintain.

It took Aven the better part of an hour to finish the page. He paused frequently in mid-sentence, reread passages, or simply sat with a vacant look on his face.

"Oh...my...God."

Aven covered his eyes with the palm of his right hand, leaned back in his chair, with his head continuing backward after the chair had reached its maximum tilt, as the words came in a halting crescendo from the depths of his soul.

"Self interest! Private property! Invisible hand!....The power of *freedom!....Limit the tyrannical and profligate government!....CONSUMPTION!"*

All of the most fundamental values that had dwelt deep in his bowels, longing for but denied expression by the dictates of society and his own ambition, had been released by the massive purgative powers of Smith's nine commandments. Aven had been BORN AGAIN. He whispered to himself, "Hallelujah, I've been saved, and the nation as well."

Aven had almost completed the major body of the document when Mila's entrance distracted him.

"Sorry to disturb you, but Director Pavlov is on the phone. He said he hoped you would be able to see him before the ceremony in the dining hall. Poor man, he seemed quite apologetic. What shall I tell him?"

"Poor old Igor. He wasn't prepared for the dismissal. None of us were."

Aven turned to the clock on his desk.

"There's not a lot of time before lunch. Tell him I'm on my way."

Aven closed the book, straightened his tie, put on his jacket, and walked towards the elevator.

"Two please, Otise."

"That's a popular floor this morning, sir. Seems everyone's been speaking to the director. Kind of hard for him, I suppose. With all this talk of change, makes me a little nervous myself. Here you are, sir."

"Thanks, Otise. And don't you worry. I'm sure everything is going to be fine."

The director's office was at the far end of the hall. Aven noticed one of the maintenance staff working at the door, removing Igor's name.

"Hello, Jenna. I think Director Pavlov is expecting me."

"I'll tell him you're here, Aven. He's really in a bad way. I hope you can cheer him up."

"Oh, I'm sure I can....I like your blouse."

"Thanks, Aven."

Aven was not prepared for what he saw.

"He's aged a dozen years since yesterday morning."

Aven's mind spun futilely for the right words.

"Sit down, Aven, I've just been speaking with Doctor Barnum. So much has happened in the past twenty-four hours. It's all come too quickly. So suddenly....I...."

"Igor, I'm terribly sorry about the directorship, seems awfully unfair."

"Aven, that's not what I wanted...."

"No, don't belittle yourself. You've done a fine job with the ministry, and all of us greatly admire...."

"No, no, Aven, just let me...."

"Igor, it's good to talk about your feelings. After all, I am your friend. All of us are. The Amerikan decision to replace you makes no sense. I'll bet it was a mistake."

"I'm afraid not."

"Well then, if not, it was surely unwise. Perhaps they have other plans for you. That's it, I'm sure. You've done too much good work, and the Amerikans are not foolish. They must have something in mind, right here at the ministry."

"I hope you're right, Aven. I've spent the past thirty-seven years at the ministry. It's all I know, and the thought of leaving is inconceivable. What would I do? Where would...?"

"You're worrying for nothing. Igor, believe me, the Amerikans will find a place for you, I'm sure."

"Aven, I've never had reason to question your judgment. Thank you. I feel much better, as if this enormous burden of the past day never existed. A place, that's what I need, desperately. But Aven, you've almost succeeded in making me forget why I wanted to talk."

"Oh, I thought that when I came in you needed, ah, Jenna had mentioned...."

"Aven, the reason I asked you to come in was because of my conversation with Doctor Barnum."

"What's old Igor talking about if it isn't his job?"

And in the same instant that he asked himself this question, the answer seemed obvious.

"His job!"

Aven did all he could to remain nonchalant.

"She did make quite an impression yesterday. What do you think, Igor, what's it going to be like working *under* her?"

Aven gave Igor a mischievous wink as he spoke these last words.

"Aven, I think we need to be serious for a moment. She and I have been talking about my replacement. She wanted to know about each of the section heads."

"I hope you were able to say good things about me."

"That's the odd part of the conversation. We discussed each section head in order of seniority. When we got to you there was very little for me to say."

"That son-of-a-bitch. He brought me here to tell me that!"

Igor must have sensed the change of mood.

"No, Aven, I don't think you understand. I can't say for certain. Doctor Barnum tried to be noncommittal, but I think she's decided on you."

"On me for *what*?"

Aven was more confused than mollified by the direction of the conversation.

"Igor, you just said that Mzzz. Barnum showed very little interest in knowing anything about me. You also know that I am the youngest of the section heads, with the least...."

"Aven, I'm terribly sorry. A few moments ago you did so much to lift my spirits. And I seem to have returned the favor by raising your dander. It *is* a puzzle, I admit. When we spoke earlier today it really did seem that the Amerikan had no desire to learn anything about you."

"That's precisely what you said a moment ago. I'm sorry too, Igor, but you're speaking nonsense to me."

The director waited for Aven's obvious fury to subside. He resumed in quiet tones.

"Aven, if you recall, I did say that I couldn't be fully confident. She kept her own counsel. There was a moment yesterday, just as she stepped down from the stage after greeting all of us and announcing my dismissal...."

Igor paused again, as if these last words had diverted his train of thought. Aven could feel his own anger being displaced by genuine befuddlement. The director regained his thoughts.

"In thinking back, I realize that we hadn't taken two steps towards the exit when she asked me for the name of the 'young man sitting at the far right of the group on stage.' Her question took me by surprise, and I looked to see who she was talking about. Aven, she was asking about you."

"And that's your evidence?"

"Aven, look, it's near time for the ceremony. I told you it was just a feeling. Perhaps I shouldn't have said anything to you...."

Aven's emotions had calmed considerably, and he realized that old Igor was trying to be helpful.

"Igor, let's forget it. I know you have my interest at heart...as you always have."

Aven stood and walked around the desk. As the director rose from his seat, Aven hugged him with genuine warmth.

"Igor, I honestly believe that things are going to work out well for both of us. Do keep your chin up, and I will do the same."

"My dear Aven. No one ever leaves your presence in a foul mood. Go now, I'll see you at lunch."

"Bye, Aven. I bought it at the Imperium, only last week. I'm sure they have Rena's size. If you want, I'd be happy to buy one for you on my way home."

"Old Igor's even got Jenna talking nonsense," Aven thought.

"Jenna, I'm sorry, my mind was elsewhere. What...ah, what are you referring to?"

"Oh, you men are all alike, so forgetful. Aven, the blouse. You commented on it when you came in."

"Jenna, sorry. It is beautiful on you, and thanks for offering. But you know Rena, she really has peculiar taste in clothes. If it isn't something her mother would have worn, Rena wants no part of it. I've given up long ago trying to buy anything that she hasn't seen first."

"I understand, Aven. If you change your mind, let me know...bye."

Shortly after leaving the director's office, Aven entered the dining hall, stopping briefly in the men's room that had been set aside for Igor and the section heads, and found his place at the end of the head table. As usual, the section heads said little to each other, but today an air of mutual suspicion also hung over the group. Aven was aware of these feelings but did not contribute to them. His normal optimism had been strengthened by the morning rebirth.

Punctually as always, Igor entered the dining hall with Mzzz. Barnum, whom he escorted to the table.

"Oh, Igor, if you don't mind, I'll stand until after the ceremony...."

Aven couldn't help but overhear, as the two were only a few feet away.

"Oh, yes, your skirt. Fine, my remarks will be brief."

The director moved slowly to the portable podium, grasped both sides of the lectern, paused as he looked about the dining hall, and took a deep breath.

"Comrades, I welcome you for the last time as your director. My affiliation with each of you these many years provides me with the greatest sense of accomplishment and satisfaction. I shall cherish your colleagueship forever. And now, as is necessary in every facet of life, we face new challenges. You will, under new and younger leadership, meet those challenges with the same spirit that has served our beloved nation so well."

Aven noticed that Mzzz. Barnum had begun to display some signs of restlessness.

"In concluding, let me say that while I depart the directorship, I hope that there will remain a place for me among you."

The entire assembly rose as the applause echoed well beyond the walls of the hall.

"Thank you…thank you. And now it is my privilege to introduce once again, Doctor Barnum."

The applause was restrained, and Aven could feel himself redden slightly. He took his seat along with everyone else.

"Good afternoon…*comrades*…"

Aven had forgotten the sound of her voice.

"…and after being amongst you and your people for more than a day now, I feel quite stoked using the term. I'm sure you've had an opportunity to read through the planning document our government has provided, a wonderfully concise blueprint for the betterment of your people. And don't ya think that Adam Smith is the jamminest dude?"

Aven, who had always been at the top of his classes in English, wondered to himself.

"I thought our Amerikan idiom and slang classes were fully comprehensive, but stoked?…jamminest dude?"

"…and my staff and I are just as anxious to begin as you are. Before we depart on this journey, we need to say a word about the past and recognize the very dedicated leadership of those who have helped pave the way. As you are fully aware, I'm sure, we have such a person with us today. Your director, Igor Pavlov, has dedicated his life to the work and workers of the ministry for the better part of four decades. I mean, that's intense. Words can't begin to express our gratitude."

Mzzz. Barnum stepped to the side of the podium, beaming directly at the director, and began clapping the tips of her fingers. Once again, the walls of the dining hall were unable to contain the applause that spread from table to table. Aven glanced around. There was not a dry eye in the room.

"Thank you…thank you…thank you. Igor thanks you as well. But we have not yet had our full say. In my country there is a time-honored tradition for movements like this one."

As she spoke, a member of her staff handed her a small package.

"Igor, my government has asked me to present this small token of our respect and appreciation."

Paula held up a shining gold wristwatch.

"I'm sure Igor won't mind if I read the inscription—'to Igor with admiration, from all of us in the U.S.A., made in Ja—'...whoops...."

A tinge of red crossed her cheeks.

"There is one more thing we need to say to Igor."

Turning again towards the director, she continued.

"Igor, don't think that because you are stepping down from the directorship there won't always be a place for you at the ministry...."

Aven's ears and eyes lit up, as did Igor's. Igor was looking directly at Aven. The smile on his face was one of pure bliss. Aven felt good as well.

"Yes, Igor, a very special place for you. I have made arrangements for your portrait to be hung in the lobby, directly facing the main entrance. No one shall again walk into the ministry without knowing of your presence."

The room was silent. Aven's eyes focused directly on the glistening plate in front of him. His body seemed paralyzed.

"And now it's time to move forward. I have two brief announcements before lunch. The work for the remainder of the week, creating our new world, will require the utmost effort from each of you. It will be best to begin in the morning well rested. I'm sure you will welcome this afternoon's holiday. The second item concerns your new director."

It was as if Igor had never existed. Aven's thoughts took a radical turn.

"Why not?" he asked himself. "I am by far the ablest."

Aven remained as he was, not moving a muscle. Or so an outside observer might have thought.

"...and while my staff and I were not in the least bit surprised to discover many qualified to take on such responsibility, we have found one to be uniquely suited to the momentous task ahead. He is a young man of remarkable ability, totally awesome in every facet we investigated, a man who has successfully handled every problem and person thrown before him. In a word, he's...intense...."

Paula's theatrical pause seemed an eternity to Aven.

"Comrades, I am really pleased to introduce your new director. Let's all welcome to the helm Aven _____"

Again the dining hall was still. Not a word, not a sound. And then it broke. The members of the ministry, first a few, then, within a matter of minutes, the entire staff, were standing, applauding, whistling, and shouting their approval. During this frenzied ovation, nothing came into focus for Aven. His senior colleagues remained somewhat sedate and were among the last to rise. At that moment, however, nothing could have troubled him. The world was perfect. A now familiar sound broke this idyllic spell.

Mzzz. Barnum had leaned over with her hand on his shoulder and tried to whisper.

"Congratulations, you great big Adonis. If you don't mind, I think we should get started this afternoon, just the two of us."

Aven felt a slight increase in pressure on his shoulder before she moved to her seat next to Igor. During the next half hour, Aven ate as best he could, while accepting congratulations from everyone as they left to take advantage of the un- expected holiday. He was the last person in the hall. As he put his napkin onto his plate, he was overcome with a sensation of panic.

"Where is the Amerikan's office?"

The sensation was short-lived.

"Get a hold of yourself."

Aven realized the Amerikan could be in only one place—old Igor's office.

"*Former* office," he thought to himself. "It's my office now."

He wondered if the workman had managed to put his name on the door.

"I suppose I can wait until morning, if I have to."

He would. There was a blank space on the door where Igor's name had been.

"I'm back here, Aven."

Aven was going to have to learn to avoid any hint of shock when the Amerikan began to speak.

"This is not going to be easy," he thought, "but to be director, I will make myself do anything."

He walked into the office with an air of confidence.

"Hello again. I assume you had no trouble finding *your new office.*"

Mzzz. Barnum was standing by the window overlooking the street below.

"Aven, I suggested the ministry staff take the afternoon off, but actually there is a great deal of work we need to do before morning. And I think we best get started."

"Oh. Ah, of course. I do want to tell you how much I appreciate the confi- dence you and your government have put in me, and to say...."

"Later, if you don't mind. At the moment we need to settle some pressing issues. Why don't you sit down at the desk. I'd prefer to stand."

With the first smile of the meeting, she added, "After all, it is *your* desk."

All business again, the Amerikan took a file from her attaché case.

"Aven, after today we have five days in which to create our new world. Ac- tually four, because I intend for us to finish before Sunday. We can do it, pro- viding the ministry is *properly* organized."

Aven had not been prepared for the alacrity with which the Amerikan worked.

"Perhaps this is what is meant by Yankee get-up-and-go," he thought.

The Amerikan paused for a moment as she set the file before him. Aven took advantage of the opportunity to speak.

"That's fine, Mzzz. Barnum. Whatever you want accomplished, I'm sure we can do. But I don't think I understand what you mean. With respect, the ministry has been the most effective agency in our country for some time now."

"But not good enough. Your staff includes some of the best minds in Russia. Believe me, I've had them investigated thoroughly. But the same cannot be said for the equipment. I don't mean to be condescending, but face it, Aven, your country has been in the Dark Ages when it comes to computers and every other form of transistorized equipment."

"That's not true. Our missiles...."

"I wasn't really referring to your military capabilities. But even there...well, never mind. The point is that there is much more that can be done to enhance productive capacity. You and I, in fact everyone at the ministry, will be able to lead the way ever so much more effectively with the proper equipment and organization."

"Please, please forgive me. This is happening so quickly. I don't really mean to argue, and I am fully aware that you have final authority in all matters pertaining to the three-year plan. Indeed, let's get started."

"Fine. Actually, it's all rather straightforward. We simply need to agree on the staffing situation for tomorrow."

Aven could feel the look of bewilderment on his face.

"Perhaps I *am* moving too quickly. Let me explain. This afternoon an American cadre of technicians will be refitting the ministry with all of the necessary equipment. In the morning, the staff will find state-of-the-art equipment throughout the ministry."

For the first time during the conversation, Aven felt somewhat at ease.

"I think I understand. And it makes a great deal of sense as well. I must say, your Amerikan technicians certainly are swift."

"They have to be, or they wouldn't be working. But that does raise one additional point."

"What's that?"

"It concerns the ministry workforce."

"I don't quite understand. I thought we agreed our workers were among the best in the nation. I can't think of who else...."

"We do agree. But with the new supercomputers and other automated equipment, we won't need everyone. Some workers will have to be laid off."

"Laid off? Laid off what? I think I'm confused again."

"Fired, canned. History!"

Aven understood the word *fired* and didn't pay much attention to the rest of what the Amerikan was saying.

"Who? How many? When? What will happen to…?"

"Calm down now, Aven. In a prosperous economy, no hard-working person need fear for a job."

"All right, I think I understand most of what I read in the three-year plan, but who? And when?"

"Here, I've prepared the revised organization chart. The original staff has been reduced by fifty workers. Most everyone staying on has been assigned to their previous divisions. Of course, with your reassignment, some changes had to be made among the section heads."

Aven, still rather shaken, looked at the file Paula had given to him. The new assignments were pretty much what he would have done himself.

"On the next page are the names of those whose services will no longer be required. We retained all of the section heads of course. Otherwise, we've cut pretty much across the board, clerical and analysis. Much of the maintenance equipment will also be automated, and it will be nice to be rid that slow-moving elevator."

Aven turned the page. It was all he could do to keep the luncheon herring and beets down. He recognized each name.

"Jenna. Mila. Otise. Why…why?"

"Jenna worked for Igor, and he's no longer here. We combined your section with Victor's, and he preferred to keep Rhonda. And as I've just told you, the elevator will be automated."

Aven hadn't heard a woman speak to him like this since his first year in school.

"But Mila has worked with me since I've been at the ministry. There could be no more loyal employee."

"I believe that, Aven, but I just don't feel she'll be adequate for you, now that you are director."

"Who will be? There is no one else at the ministry that I would trust as much."

"We have selected an assistant for you. He should be here in the morning."

"*He*? And there must be some work for Otise. He and his wife just had triplets, and…"

Aven stopped midsentence. There was something about the Amerikan's expression. A hardness had come into her eyes. And into her voice as well.

"Perhaps we've made a mistake. Based on your record, you appeared ideally suited for the directorship, and I have always considered myself an excellent judge of character and ability. Possibly this time…."

"Let's not discuss it further."

Aven regained his composure.

"It has been the Russian way of doing business that has done so much harm to our citizens. Your system, our new system, will bring untold advantages to all my people. Mzzz. Barnum, the reorganization plan seems perfect. Ah, I do have just one more question. How long will Otise and the others remain at the ministry?"

"The termination notices have already been delivered and will be waiting when they arrive home. They will, of course, be paid for the entire day. And by the way, Aven, I do wish you'd call me Paula."

Aven returned her smile.

"That's fine with me, ah, Paula. What's next?"

"I think we should do something about this office."

"I don't understand."

"Come, here to the coffee table. It's more comfortable."

Aven walked across the room, with the Amerikan a few steps behind.

"Sit anywhere. Can I get you some port? Igor departed in such a rush, and he left the liquor cabinet well stocked."

"Ah, why yes, Mzzz....Paula, port sounds...."

Paula set two glasses on the table as he spoke, filling each with the deep amber liquid. She paused for a moment, as if unsure of what to do next.

"Oh, what the hell," she said, and sat carefully in the stuffed chair next to Aven.

Aven sipped the port while trying to think of something to say.

"What about the office? What do you have in mind?"

Paula had also lifted her glass. It was empty by the time she put it down.

"Men are all the same. Aven, the furniture, the vinyl flooring, and, can you believe, *roll-up* window shades? I mean, really...this place is grossola. It's zuke city."

Aven guessed that she was not taken with the room and realized he was going to have to get an updated Amerikan dictionary.

Paula got up, holding the arm of her chair briefly as if to gain her balance, and walked to his desk. She removed a glossy brochure from her attaché case.

"Take a look at this. I think you will see what I have in mind."

The sleek cover had an abstract pattern in several pastel shades of gray and pink. Running in a northeasterly direction were the bold letters:

GDANSK DESIGN FOR THE MODERN OFFICE

Aven turned the cover.

"This is no ordinary desk," he realized.

The desk was unlike any he had seen before, made of the richest woods, with a curved top possessing the graceful lines of an ocean schooner. He felt the excitement within him, turning the pages quickly.

"Pretty gnarly stuff, isn't it?"

"There she goes again. Perhaps she is referring to the type of wood."

Paula was smiling as Aven responded.

"This furniture is beautiful. I don't think I have ever seen a desk like this. It's Danish, isn't…?"

"No silly, it's Polish."

"*POLISH!*"

Aven looked back at the cover and realized what his eyes had missed.

"Come on, Paula, is this some kind of joke?"

"There's nothing funny about the Polish phenomenon. If you recall, they were the first of the Warsaw Pact to adopt our system and have prospered ever since. In those first halcyon days of Polish reform, private investors from all over the world sought advantage in the new opportunities. Several Danish venture capitalists provided the funding for Gdansk Design. They've been flourishing ever since."

"I understand. The furniture is lovely, and it appears to be very sturdy."

"Of course it is, Aven. Everything from Gdansk is solid."

They spent some time searching through the brochure. Agreement on the desk came quickly, but there were the lamps, the chairs, a small conference table, and a liquor cabinet. The smaller the object, the more difficulty they had. Paula always prevailed, but Aven found little difficulty in giving in.

"Well, that should about do it. I know you're going to love everything we've chosen. Let's see, what is it, an hour or two time difference? I think we can call in the order right now. Would you like do the honors?"

"We can just call in the order? Just like that? And how long will it take?"

"That's been my only complaint with the Poles. They're still slow with their deliveries. Everything we want is a special order. I don't imagine they can promise delivery sooner than the day after tomorrow."

For years the major part of Aven's work involved keeping his citizens content in the face of Western capitalist prosperity. Paula's words told him how successful the ministry had actually been. Aven walked over to the phone on his desk.

"What's the number?"

"You have to dial eight hundred first."

Aven placed the order and returned to the table with the bottle of port.

"Can I pour some for you?"

Paula nodded her approval with a smile.

"And, Paula, I suppose we need to do something about the carpets and drapes, too."

"Oh, Aven, I hope you don't mind too terribly much. I took care of that yesterday. The installers will be here later this afternoon. Come on now, don't look so glum. You'll see, what I ordered for your office is totally rad."

"Okay, but I was enjoying choosing the furniture."

Aven took a substantial swallow of the wine before changing the subject.

"If there's no other pressing business just now…?"

"There isn't."

"…well fine. There is something that's been bothering me. I hope you don't take offense."

Paula was also well into the second glass of wine.

"Aven, dear, we're going to be spending a lot of time together. We need to be straight with each other. Let's have it, both barrels."

Aven finished the wine in his glass.

"I don't quite know how to say this, but every now and then I have a hard time understanding you. I was always a top student of English, but you use some words—*rad, dude, zuke*. I can't figure…?"

Paula giggled as she poured the remainder of the wine.

"There's nothing wrong with your English. It's me. Occasionally, not too often I hope, but especially when I get excited, I revert to my college slang. You know I went to UCLA for a couple of years, very impressionable years. We had our own special language."

She stopped abruptly and brought her attaché case back to the table.

"Here," she said, handing him a well-worn document. "Spend an hour or two with this in the next few days, and you won't miss a word."

Paula leaned forward and touched Aven's knee gently.

"You know, you are a studmuffin.…"

Aven at least understood the look in her eye.

"Which reminds me, has the film *Field of Dreams* ever come to your country?"

The look on his face told her no.

"Well, how about *Bull Durham* or *Wyatt Earp*?"

"No, never heard of them. In the last few years very few foreign films have been shown here. Why do you ask?"

"No particular reason, really. There was an actor you remind me of, Kevin Cosno, or something. I forget his last name."

The conversation had run its course. The ticking of the clock on the wall behind them caught their attention.

"Where did the afternoon go? It's well past five, and I still have files to review. Aven, I know that, ah, what's her name? Rena? Yes, Rena will be waiting for you. Let me get a car for you."

"Thanks, Paula, but you needn't bother."

"No bother, Aven, and besides, the new director shouldn't have to walk to and from work."

Aven saw her point, and he accepted in silence. Paula picked up the phone.

"Hello, this is Doctor Barnum. Yes, and I'd like to have a car in front for the new director.…When will it be fixed? Well, send my Beamer instead."

She hung up.

"The car will be downstairs by the time you get there. See you in the morning, seven-thirty, right?"

She left the room, almost before Aven could get out of his chair.

Aven took Igor's copy of the three-year plan along with him. A modest-size red sedan was waiting.

"Excuse me, but what kind of car is this? Is it Amerikan?"

"No sir, it's Doctor Barnum's private automobile. I believe it's German. Where to, sir?"

As usual, the streets were nearly empty. It took only a few minutes for the driver to find the flat.

"Too bad about Otise and the others," Aven thought, "but otherwise, eggs and onions, the directorship, new furniture. Not a bad day. So far! I wonder how Rena will take the news?"

He didn't have to wait long to find out.

"Aven, love, I'm happy for you, and very proud of you as well," Rena whispered as she continued to hold and kiss him. "Come, come in. I didn't get anywhere on the essay today. My thoughts have been with you and the evening ahead."

Aven was not prepared for this torrent of physical and verbal ardor. He followed Rena into the front room. The wine glasses were in place. New on the table was a candle, its flame filling the room with a seductive glow and aroma. Aven remained silent as Rena poured their wine.

"Drink my darling, and tell me in your own words. We've got all night."

The warmth of her expression had won him over that day outside of class many years ago. But this evening she seemed unable to contain herself. Love appeared to gush from every pore.

Aven's passion was overpowering, but he knew Rena too well. There would indeed be lovemaking this night, all in good time, after dinner and after his news. He put the notebook on the floor beside his chair and reached for his glass.

"Yes, it actually happened, Rena. But how did you know? Of course, one of my colleagues called you after lunch."

"No one called, Aven."

"But then how did you…?"

"Do you think there was ever any doubt in my mind? It's been our deepest failing. The talent of so many young Russian citizens has been allowed to go unused. Seniority has meant everything, and with it a withering of our nation's productive capacity. Aven, whatever the faults of the Amerikans—and there are many indeed—they do seem to reward talent and ability. Your colleagues at the ministry are able workers, but it's plain for all to see how you stand above every one of them."

Rena continued with renewed eagerness.

"Now tell me how it happened. When did you learn? How did you feel? Tell me everything. Dinner is ready. I'll need only a minute to warm the soup…."

"I would be lying if I said I didn't have some expectations about the directorship, but so long without advancement, I tried not to let my hopes go too high."

Aven paused to put the glass down.

"That may explain why I had so little to say last evening. But today was wonderful. After all, how could it have been otherwise, starting with your eggs and onions…."

Aven reached across the table and put both of his hands high up on Rena's thighs.

"Aven! What happened after breakfast?"

He sat back, sighing softly.

"The luncheon for old Igor wasn't until twelve-thirty. There was the announcement about the new director at that time as well. I spent most of the morning finishing the Amerikan plan. Oh yes, I brought a copy home for you."

Aven reached down for the notebook.

"You must read it. Especially the opening section on economic reorganization. It *is* a brilliant document."

Rena took the book and returned it to floor.

"I will," she said, "but not tonight, my darling."

Aven felt no desire to protest.

"I took a walk before lunch. The morning's reading had been very stimulating, and I needed the calming effect of the park. Before the meal was served, the Amerikan offered a few nice words about Igor's retirement, and then she made the announcement. It all happened so quickly, and…."

"She?"

"Oh, didn't I tell you? The Amerikans sent a woman to head the occupation, aah, reorganization effort."

"It's an occupation, Aven. You know you don't have to use the ministry words here. I expect the Amerikan leader will be competent, *especially* a woman. Go on. What did Igor have to say? How did you react? What happened after lunch?"

Aven wanted to say more about Mzzz. Barnum, but decided not to.

"Well, I think Igor was pretty happy with the retirement ceremony. He received a lovely watch, and his portrait will hang in the entrance. Probably take some time for him to adjust to a life of leisure, but he'll do fine. As for me, I really don't remember how I felt, stunned, in a dream...."

"And when you woke, after lunch? I assume the new director had much to take care of?"

"Not really. Actually I spent most of the afternoon talking to the Amerikan...."

"Does she have a name?"

"Mzzz. Barnum. P. T. Barnum, I think it is. Well, she, Mzzz. Barnum, and I talked about reorganizing the office. I moved into Igor's office."

"I guess you'd have to settle on the makeup of your staff before getting down to work. Mila will still be your secretary. She must be thrilled."

"Actually, the Amerikans are going to provide me with an assistant. We meet in the morning."

"But what about Mila? She's so good, and she knows you almost as well as I do. I think they're making a dreadful mistake. Who's the lucky person to get her?"

"I, aaah, I'm not sure yet. She's probably going to be...reassigned."

Aven took several deep breaths. It was not his custom to deceive Rena, and he found the experience awkward.

"But it wasn't so much rearranging the staff...."

"Well then, what was it?"

"New furniture."

"Aaaaaavennn! Please be serious."

"I am being serious. The Amerikan wanted to start with the furniture, and you said it yourself, they're the ones giving the orders. The office was unimpressive, and I think the change will be important to our work. We'll see soon enough. Implementation of the Amerikan plan will begin in earnest tomorrow, and according to Pa— Mzzz. Barnum, everything should be in place by the end of Saturday. Whatever you think about the Amerikans, they do move quickly."

Aven spoke with his old conviction and confidence, two of the traits that Rena most admired in him.

"I think I've grilled you enough today. I love you. Stay still. Dinner will be ready in a minute."

Aven continued drinking his wine.

"She's a great woman. Even when we don't see eye to eye on things, she can love me without compromising her ideals...."

The pleasant daydream was interrupted by the sound of music and Rena's voice.

"Dinner's ready. Wash up and let's eat."

Rena had put out her favorite tablecloth. It had belonged to her parents, a soft rose-colored linen that enhanced the sensuality of Rena's exquisite creations.

"What's that?"

"Oh, you silly, we've had this many times, it's...."

"No, no, Rena, I mean the music."

"Ah, yes, the music. We don't listen to this very often. It seemed appropriate for tonight."

"Are you going to tell me what it is?"

"Bach."

"Oh."

Aven's knowledge of music had come entirely from Rena, and outside of their bed, he had never been an enthusiastic student.

"The soup looks delicious."

Dinner took the better part of two hours. Her soup, a salad that had obviously been prepared by an artist, the special garnishes added to last night's stew, his favorite custard, all of this floated on a brook of merlot that they had saved for just such an occasion.

"Rena, I don't think I've ever been happier. Why is this all happening to me? The directorship? Real possibilities for our nation? You? Is this only a dream?"

They returned to the front room. Rena had removed the wine glasses and replaced them with their opal liquor vessels. It was difficult to differentiate the sweet Benedictine, their words, and the music. All seemed to meld together.

"Dearest, you have a very full day ahead. The dishes will keep. I think we need to get to bed."

Rena must have noticed a flicker of disappointment scurry across Aven's face.

"No, Aven, I don't mean to *sleep*. At least not for a while. I think you will like the program I've chosen. It's Bach."

"Oh."

But this time his interest was rising.

"Any particular composition? The man was rather prolific, wasn't he?"

"We were listening to it this evening, the second suite for cello."

Aven was pleasantly surprised when he entered their concert hall. Despite the coolness of the room, Rena was lying naked on the bed, knees bent and her gorgeously athletic legs widespread. Her head was raised slightly from the pillow, and her breasts and arms were beckoning to him.

"After all, love, the man who is about to lead the Ministry of Persuasion ought to be master in his own bed...for tonight."

Aven's technique was near perfect. He drew his long supple bow, slowly at first, with uniform pressure from the frog to its tip and back repeatedly. Every fiber in Rena's body was soon vibrating in a mournful tone, and the soundpost quivered inside her arched body. It was not long before the mournful sounds turned to a harmonious wail. The tension in Aven's bow ebbed, and none too soon. Rena's delayed but contented breathing told Aven that she was asleep. After a few minutes he nudged her lovingly.

"Aven, I can't. Lets go to sleep."

"But, Rena, Bach wrote *three* suites for cello. We have two to go."

"*Six*, Aven, and...."

Aven too was sleeping only moments later.

DAY THREE
■■■■■■■■■■■■■■■■

*A*ven stretched his hand towards the alarm. Rena opened her eyes and brushed her hair aside.

"Good morning."

"Good morning."

As if deaf, they embraced while the clock protested loudly.

"That was a nice evening. I love you."

"I love you, Rena. Oh shit," he exclaimed, finally acknowledging the intruder. "We must have overslept. It's after six."

A grin appeared as he realized his mistake.

"I'm being picked up this morning, and tomorrow, and the next day."

He leaned over to kiss Rena.

"Go back to sleep, a car will be coming for me at seven-fifteen. I've got plenty of time."

He went out for the news.

SURPRISE APPOINTMENT AS NEW DIRECTOR OF MOP
Igor M. Pavlov Given Place of Honor Upon Retirement

"Wrong on both counts," he thought to himself, but as he read on, the story had a sobering effect. Still, he knew the importance of the headline.

"The first words our citizens read every morning of their lives, and all they really remember."

Aven completed the rest of the morning's ritual, including the dusting, with time to spare. The red car was waiting.

"Rena, I'm sorry to disturb you."

She smiled and reached for him.

"No, the driver's waiting, but I wanted to have a new picture for my office, that wonderful shot of you by the lake. Do you remember where it is?"

"I'm not wonderful, it's the lake, our lake. It's in the center drawer of my desk. I love you, Aven."

Rena pulled the covers back over her body with a contented sigh.

"I found it. Bye. See you this evening."

Aven opened the rear door of the car. He arrived at the ministry in less than five minutes.

"Good mor…" was all he managed.

Otise was no longer there. Not far away was an oversized portrait of Igor, unsmiling. It looked as if the photograph had been taken immediately after the luncheon yesterday. The interior of the elevator had been done over. Aven pressed the shiny button. The doors closed to unfamiliar music. The light rose from number to number. When "5" was lit, the elevator and music stopped and the doors opened.

PING.

Laughing to himself, he pressed the number "2," pleased that no one had been along to see his mistake.

PING.

Aven walked from the elevator. His name was on the door, and he paused briefly to admire the artist's work. Paula was sitting at the old desk, talking on the phone.

"That will be fine. Tell him we're on the second floor."

"Good morning, Paula.…You're right, the carpeting and blinds look great. I hope the furniture arrives soon."

Paula got up from the desk. Her blonde hair provided a stark contrast with the deep green silk dress. In the whirlwind of yesterday's events Aven had forgotten her staggering beauty.

"Good moooooornin, Aven. I sure hope you were able to kick back last night, cause the two of us have a killer day ahead."

Aven tried to recall what he had done with the slang dictionary.

"I'm in the top drawer, I mean I'm fine, can't wait to get going."

Paula was standing close to him. The scent of her perfume distracted him. He walked past her and placed Rena's photograph, unwrapped, on his desk.

Paula seemed to sense his discomfort.

"You can relax a bit, Aven. After lunch we begin the section briefings with the ministry staff. Your executive assistant will be here soon, and the two of you will want to get acquainted before the staff meeting."

Aven tried to concentrate on what she was saying. It was not easy.

"His name is Gaylord Creamer. We worked together at RSJ and S. They don't come any better."

As Paula spoke, there was some commotion in the outer office. It was a male voice, which grew louder as the door opened. Paula ran to greet the stranger, hugging him with earnest affection. Aven could not fathom the sight before him. The man Paula was embracing was well built, of average height and weight. He was dressed in a suit of lavender leather, with scarlet shirt and tie. His short curly hair was black with stripes of red, white, and blue running from the center of his forehead across the top of his head. His face was also black. As he approached, Aven felt a desperate need to hold onto his eyes, lest they fly from his head and strike the stranger.

"Holy mother of Saint Christopher, this guy's as queer as a three-kopec bill!"

"Aven, I'd like you to meet Gaylord Creamer. The two of you will be seeing a great deal of each other in the days ahead, and I know it's going to be a splendid partnership."

As Paula left the office, the stranger extended his hand to Aven.

"How ya doin, Jack."

Seeing no alternative, Aven took the stranger's hand.

"Fine," he mumbled.

The stranger seemed unfazed by Aven's tepid greeting as he offered to go out for tea. Aven sat at the coffee table, where he and Paula were the day before in such contrasting circumstance. He had always maintained a degree of respect for the Amerikans. Until a few minutes ago he had also admired their spontaneity. He had become accustomed to Paula, and besides, she had some significant redeeming features. But the stranger—Aven looked up. He was back.

"Here we are now."

His reaction altered as the stranger continued speaking. Aven hardly had time to recover from the visual shock when he began to feel amazingly relaxed. As the stranger continued talking, his outrageous clothing, the patterns in his hair, his skin color, all faded from Aven's consciousness. An altogether different image arose, of a man speaking to him as a friend, openly, without hidden motive—a man he could rely on implicitly, whatever the future might bring. This was a new experience, and he was reveling in it.

"...but tell me, how does a man like yourself, born of nobility, wind up working in a New York advertising firm?"

"Aven, why do you say 'born of nobility.' My mother pushed drugs on the streets of the Big Apple. I never met my father."

"Your name is *Lord* Creamer, isn't it?"

Aven could see the rows of glistening white teeth expand before his eyes. He understood, and returned the smile, with only slight embarrassment.

"I'm sorry, *Gay*lord. Then tell me something else."

"Shoot."

"Your gold tie pin, it's a, a six-sided star. Why do you wear it? You're not...?"

"Jewish? Actually, I am."

"But you don't look...."

"Aven, I'd never say this in front of Paula, but *looks* can be deceiving. I've been Jewish all my life."

"But you said you never met your father, and your mother pushed drugs...."

"That's right. One thing I know for sure. My father *had* to be black. My mother was raised in an orthodox Hasidic household. She rebelled, took up a life on the streets."

"But Creamer's not a Jewish name, is it?"

"My mother's name was spelled with a K. I changed it."

Gaylord winked as he added, "Seemed to fit my personality better."

Both men were quiet. A silence not at all awkward for two friends. Aven resumed the conversation.

"Tell me about Paula."

"That will take a while. She's quite a story, but I suppose we can begin. I met her at the agency. She moved into the CEO job about four years ago and asked to have me as her executive assistant. We hit it off right away. The company tripled its accounts within a year of her appointment. I think she felt she could trust me. We got on like troopers from the start."

Aven found himself completely absorbed in Gaylord's story. It was obvious that Gaylord was a man of considerable talent and loyalty. Aven felt fortunate to have found such a friend.

"Paula said little about her early years. I know that she had a tough time when she started college. She went to the University of California. Not Berkeley. Los Angeles was the place for her. The Southern California politics warmed her heart, and the sun took care of the rest of her.

"But UCLA was a disaster. She was invited to one or two sorority rush parties, but that was about it, not a single bid. It's hard for her to talk about that time, but I know that she's still bitter. You can tell when she's had a few drinks. She decided to transfer to a place where no one partied. That's why she went to Vassar, she says. If you ask me, I think that her voice didn't attract that much attention either. The move was a good one. After graduating cum laude she continued on at Harvard. I think that her drive to succeed was stimulated by the rejection at UCLA."

"What about men? With looks like hers, you'd think...?"

"That's a puzzling thing about Paula. Sure, she's always had men sniffing around, but nothing that went anywhere. Hard to tell why. Probably the right guy hasn't made an appearance."

"Really?"

"That's right. But there is a man in her life. He died a long time ago. Funny, come to think of it, it was this week, April sixth or seventh, over a hundred years ago."

Gaylord had been looking off to the side as he spoke. He turned back to Aven.

"Her great grandfather, Phineas Taylor Barnum. It's clear that he's had a tremendous effect on her. I'll tell you more about him at lunch. Paula should be back any minute."

Gaylord was obviously quite familiar with Paula's behavior, as the brittle sounds in the outer office indicated.

"Well, you two look like bosom buddies already. Isn't Gaylord a dream? Sorry to break this up, but the economic advisers are ready to meet with us. And after lunch, it's reorganization, *big time.*"

Paula paused as she noticed the bag on Aven's desk. She opened it.

"What a lovely picture. This must be Rena. Aven, she's beautiful. Don't you agree?" as she handed the picture to Gaylord.

"More like a young Holly Hunter if you ask me."

Aven was confused and embarrassed. He said nothing. Gaylord put the photograph of Rena on the table. Still in a mild fog, Aven followed along as Gaylord and Paula left his office and walked to the elevator.

PING.

The music began immediately. Paula tried to hum along but gave up quickly.

"I spent some of the happiest times on the beach at Waikiki…a raging place.…"

PING.

"Look, before we go in, I should tell the both of you, the university has sent us their very best young minds. These people will be working directly with the ministry section heads all week. They're economists, and they rarely smile. But don't take it personally, it's the nature of their work. Totally dismal."

They had arrived at the door to Aven's old office. Nothing looked the same. The inner partitions had been removed, and the walls had been repainted white, with heavy borders at the floor and ceiling painted a crisp shade of blue. Numerous graphs and charts had been hung with some care, like paintings in a gallery. A lighter blue carpeting lent a warmth to the considerable expanse. Aven liked what he saw. His eyes focused on the contents of the room.

"Ah, GDANSK design…I wonder if…?"

Several handsome desks were arranged in a U shape, with the base of the U located at the far end from the door where they were standing. There were twelve desks in all, four in each section. A personal computer occupied a small portion of each desk, and a circular table four or five meters in diameter stood, grandly, within the three segments of desks. Several chairs were located around the table, each situated on a centered leg that permitted a full circle swivel. The chairs themselves were of a deep maroon fabric, a color similar to the note pads and pencils located on the table.

"Well, Aven, this is it, the most up-to-date design in functional office space. It's a combo conference-research room that allows for multi-use and maximum efficiency in management. A radical twenty-four, seven kind of place, doncha think?"

Aven replied as if he understood.

"I'm quite impressed."

At that moment he noticed that the twelve desks were occupied by individuals, each wearing a white jacket with blue collar, blending well with the walls behind them. His gaze moved slowly around the room. In one sense what he saw was not unusual—four women, three of whom appeared to be Caucasian and the fourth of some Latin extraction, and of the men only two were not white. Despite these variations, there was a sameness about them that Aven found odd. Then it came to him. He, Paula, and Gaylord had been in the newly and lively appointed room for several minutes and had been engaged in an animated conversation. Yet these men and women—with heads buried in their computers, faces without expression, and bodies without movement save for the tips of their fingers—acted as if they were invisible. He had never seen a more somber group of workers.

"Aven, these are the analysts from the university, mostly from the University of Chicago, all disciples of Professors Hayek and Friedman."

With those words, Paula took Aven by the arm and escorted him to the first group of disciples working to their right. The one woman and three men turned from their terminal screens in unison. Their expressions gave no hint of what they might be thinking, though they willingly extended their hands as Paula introduced Aven.

"Aven, Professors Lowe Taksis and Freeman Treyd are experts on domestic and international questions, while Nat Law and Leslie Fair will be of assistance on all questions regarding governmental action. By the way, Professor Fair replaced the one misfit from Harvard who had managed a seat at the table some years ago, a Hungarian named Ekon Plannink."

Aven thought he detected the beginnings of a smirk on Professor Fair's face, but it didn't mature.

Under Paula's lead, the trio swept across the room, as she resumed the introductions.

"Your business and labor leaders will find much wisdom here, Aven. Professors Constance Costa, Margot Price, and Demond Supplé, who, by the way, comes to us from the University of Paris, are experts in business management, sales, and production. Professor Minnie Wages knows all that is necessary about labor policy."

Aven was about to ask a question, but it was not to be.

"We've saved the best for last," as Paula moved in dramatic fashion to the remaining desks at the base of the U. Aven noted the absence of women, although there seemed to be some ethnic diversity among the four men.

"Aven, it's an honor to present Professors Max Utility...Al O'Kate, who comes to us from Dublin...Theo Ree, who did his undergraduate work in Seoul, and last, but hardly least, the man closest to my heart, Professor Sonny Fourkaste."

At this point, Gaylord, who had remained in the background through the entire set of introductions, moved towards Professor Fourkaste. Two wide grins appeared as Gaylord and the professor greeted each other. Also unusual was the way they extended their hands high and crashed their palms together several times. Only then did the two shake hands, in a manner that Aven had not witnessed before.

"How'ya doin, brother?"

"I'm fine, Jack...waas happenen?"

Their grins were infectious, and Aven began to smile for the first time since entering the room. Paula broke in again.

"Okay, gentlemen, let's let the professors get back to work. We'll be with them again this afternoon. Right now I think it's time for lunch."

As they left, Gaylord called back over his shoulder, "Hey you cats, don't work too hard."

"Gaylord, I do wish you wouldn't be so flippant. They are awfully serious, I grant you, but they have serious work to do...but I mean, we're talking nerd city in there."

It was Gaylord who tried to get things back on track.

"Come on you two, I'm starving."

In the interest of health, they decided to walk down to the dining hall, Aven leading the way for a change.

Paula took Aven's arm.

"This is for the staff, we're next door."

It was then that Aven noticed the new large double door a few meters down the hall. On its two upper glass panels were the words:

PRI   VATE
EXEC   UTIVE
DINING   ROOM

The room was painted in a rich brown similar to the tones of the luxuriant carpet. Oil paintings, landscapes that Aven could not recognize, adorned the walls. The one long dining table had approximately twenty richly upholstered chairs spaced around it. Sounds of elevator music quietly filled the room.

As they sat down, a young man whom Aven recognized came to the table.

"The lunch today is cold potato soup, roast duck with asparagus, and chocolate mousse. The wine is a 1957 Minskevasser. Can I get you anything else?"

"That sounds divine. I'd like soup, but these gentlemen will have the full lunch."

The young man left the table.

"My staff will be with the ministry sections. I've asked Professor Law to meet with the legal section in my office. This is one of the more complex aspects of the reorganization, and I think you should sit in. Oh, here's the wine."

The conversation was without focus. Paula left without touching her soup.

Aven took a sip of wine.

"Not to change the subject, but where did you get that ring? It's enormous. I don't think I've ever seen anything like it."

Gaylord glanced at his left hand.

"Oh, it's a beauty, isn't it? An old buddy of mine from San Francisco, long time ago now, 'bout 1990 I think, a cool dude, Joe Montana was his name, gave it to me. Said he had more than he knew what to do with, which reminds me, let me tell you a little more about old Phineas."

As Aven's brow began to furrow, Gaylord resumed.

"P.T. Barnum, you remember, Paula's great grandfather."

The grooves on Aven's forehead faded.

"Quite a guy. He, more than any man I can think of, captured the essence of America."

Aven put down his fork and leaned forward with an expression of genuine interest.

"Funny how much he was *mis*understood, and still is, by some."

"Go on."

"You can sum up his life in a few words; he *gave* Americans what they wanted...."

"Gaylord, you're not trying to pull my leg are you? That doesn't sound particularly profound."

"At the same time, Aven my friend, he *made* Americans want what he gave them. But he paid the price for his efforts. A lot of people saw him as a pretty low-down character. I remember reading that ol' Phineas would 'ultimately take his stand in the social rank, among the *swindlers, blackguards, pickpockets*, and *thimble-riggers* of his day.' Others saw him as a '*great genius*, and a man of *superlative imagination, indomitable pluck*, and *artistic temperament*.' No doubt he had a lot more enemies than friends, but for a time his own biography was second in sales to the Bible."

Gaylord paused to scrape the last bits of mousse from the tall dessert glass. Aven was transfixed by Gaylord's tale and did not move a muscle as Gaylord continued.

"He was a pretty straight shooter. Often said that his prime aim was to make money and that the public kind of liked to be fooled some of the time. His detractors frequently used his words against him. They claimed that he believed a sucker was born every day and that his motto was 'Fear God and cheat your neighbor.' Both versions are true. I guess, it's just a matter of perspective."

"Gaylord, keep going. What sorts of things did he do? How did he make his money?"

"Phineas had the ability to *create demand* where no one else would ever think to look."

Both men looked at their watches.

"Too bad, the legal briefing begins in fifteen minutes, and I know Paula wants us to be there from the start. Let me give you a couple of examples before we go. He persuaded people to come and see some really weird things. Found an old slave, a black woman, who he advertised as George Washington's nurse. Folks believed Phineas when he claimed she was a hundred and sixty-one years old. They came from all over to see his mermaid. He called her his 'Fejee Mermaid' and claimed she was half human, top half was part of a mummified monkey that he had attached to a dried fish. They couldn't pay him fast enough to get a peek. In fact, he was pretty much a freak specialist—midgets, giants, Siamese twins. He made the public pay through the nose and had them believing they were having a good time. They probably were, actually."

"A super salesman for sure, but he had to be a man of his times. Hard to believe that anyone could pull off that sort of thing these days."

"Aven, you're not the only one to think that way. Wait until you see our Paula at work."

Both men turned toward the large entry doors, but Gaylord was the only one to speak.

"Hi there, P.T. We were just talking about you."

"Well, I hope it wasn't anything awful," she squeaked.

"Not at all, Paula. Gaylord's been telling me about your great grandfather...."

"Ooooooooeeeee, he was stellar, wasn't he? But we do have to get going. The briefing will begin as soon as we get upstairs."

Several of Aven's colleagues were seated quietly at the conference table. The twelve economists were wearing freshly pressed white and blue jackets. All but one were staring intently into their computer monitors, fingers flying. The terminal in front of Professor Law was not visible. Paula broke the silence.

"Good afternoon, ladies and gentlemen. Let me say at the outset that not only is the legal environment crucial to the functioning of your new society, but the principles are so elegantly simple as to be confusing at first. I thought it important that your director, Aven _____, join in this initial briefing and that we have access to all of the economic specialists if need be. Perhaps the best place to begin is with Professor Law."

Professor Nat Law had not uttered more than a word when a remarkable thing occurred, quickly and quietly. The seats at the conference table swiveled towards the left where the professor was speaking, and each chair was elevated sufficiently so that the participants had a clear view of him. This meant, of course, that those seated closest to Professor Law spun only in a horizontal plane, while those seated at the other side of the table also moved in the vertical plane, elevated enough so as to see over the person between them and the economist.

Professor Law noted their expressions and stopped midword.

"Perhaps I should explain," he said as he glanced towards Professor Al O'Kate seated to his left. "This is really Professor O'Kate's bailiwick, but I'm sure he won't mind. I must say, I was somewhat surprised myself the first time I worked in a modern combo-conference-research room. The technology is designed to maximize lines of sight and communication while minimizing movement, thereby achieving maximum efficiency. The system is fairly simple, once you think about it, not unlike an amusement park ride. I'm sure you'll all become accustomed to it in no time. And now let me get back to what brings us together. That is, the basic organizing principle of our legal system. Would any of you care to guess what it might be?"

The professor's comments about the spinning and levitation had put everyone at ease, and two or three of the legal staff members tried to speak at once. It was clear to each that their answers were similar, and all but one deferred. The senior lawyer continued.

"The legal system can have only one basis. It is founded on principles of justice and fairness, of course."

"That is not an unreasonable answer, nor is it unexpected. But it is incorrect. Forgive me for saying so, but there's not a student at the University of Chicago who wouldn't understand this by the end of *his* fresh*man* year."

Professor Faire looked up but said nothing. Professor Fourkaste, Gaylord's good friend, turned from his terminal and began to speak. Once again the seats around the conference table swiveled and changed altitude. The members of the ministry looked as if they were beginning to enjoy themselves.

"And if they haven't learned it by then, they probably transfer to Amherst or Santa Cruz, or...."

The conference chairs returned to their previous position.

"Thank you, Sonny. Perhaps if we touch on a few examples, these ideas will come into better focus. The cases of drug testing and occupational safety are instructive. In order for your economy to flourish, industrialists must be given a free hand to pursue profit where they might. An important case in point is the pharmaceutical sector, a growth sector in every modern economy. A common failing here is over-regulation, with the result that many drugs come onto the market far later than commercially feasible."

A colleague to Aven's left raised his hand.

"Excuse me, Professor Law, do you mind taking questions?"

"Absolutely not."

"Thank you. Well then, isn't it very important to test the drugs before they're put on the market? Can't you do a great deal of harm—side effects, birth defects, and even death—without proper testing?"

"That's exactly the kind of question a focus on economic efficiency highlights. Of course, there is potential harm with the premature introduction of a new drug."

The professor paused with a look of satisfaction on his face.

"But what is the cost to society of all those whose pain or illness might have been alleviated were it not for the delays due to the testing. If you recall, there was a dramatic case in point in our country some years ago. What was it called? LAIDS, or something like that?"

"AIDS, *A-I-D-S*...," came the correction from Sonny, and the conference seats swiveled and levitated before he had finished.

Professor Law resumed the Socratic lecture, and Aven and his colleagues moved almost before their seats did.

"Thank you, Professor Fourkaste. And consider the question of occupational safety. Government could come close to *guaranteeing* the health and safety of our workers, a lofty goal indeed. But you would hamstring industry in the process. And of what use would good health be if one didn't have material possessions to enjoy as well?"

Aven wasn't sure he understood the argument.

"The managers of your factories can be trusted to look out for their workers and to promote economic efficiency at the same time. Notice how lower paid workers in your factories and shops seem to care little about such issues. They're rarely the ones to grouse about safety conditions. It's the skilled workers who demand a level of protection considerably higher. Now all of this will occur *without* safety laws imposed by the government. Low-wage workers know that if they are injured, missing a day's work is not very costly, and the reverse is true for the skilled. Management loses more when a highly productive worker is injured. Is it clear, in this area, that the *proper* law is *minimal* law?"

For a time no one spoke, as if trying to digest what the professor had been saying. The staffer who had asked the previous question finally responded.

"Professor Law, your two examples are certainly persuasive, but aren't there some members of the society who might need protection—the poor, children, the elderly, the...?"

"Good question. And a question to which our legal principles respond. Take the issue of housing for the poor. In your country, much of the housing is old, rundown, and in some cases downright unsafe. With the new economic plan in place, this situation should be vastly improved within a year or two. But in the meantime, what should be done? Perhaps I should ask, what shouldn't be done?"

The professor again paused, waiting for a response.

"It won't be long before these answers come by instinct. If you *force* the building owner to improve his property, no matter how rundown it might be, the landlord will be forced to raise the rent. This, of course, will reduce the availability of housing for the poor. Obviously, if they had wanted better housing, they would have bid for it, and rents would have gone up in response to the *desires* of the tenants *without the imposition of housing codes*. By *forcing* people to live in better quality housing than they would have chosen freely, you only succeed in *forcing people out of housing*."

Once again, a broad smile of satisfaction spread across the professor's face.

"But wait a minute."

The youngest member of the ministry legal staff was on his feet.

"Why don't you just put in controls on the rent that can be charged."

Two loud gasps came from the other side of the room. The conference table chairs and their occupants swiveled nearly a hundred and eighty degrees to face Professors Margot Price and Demond Supplé. They both had turned away from their terminals. The Frenchman spoke.

"Zee *horrendous inefficiencies* of all price controls will be discussed in detail with zee ministry's industry staff in zee morning. Rent controls, minimum wages, retail price maintenance, farm price supports, all will be exposed at zat session. Perhaps zee legal staff should be invited?"

"I don't think that will be necessary, Professor Supplé."

Those at the conference table were once again facing Professor Law.

"If everyone will simply read the works referred to in the three-year plan, all such questions about the wisdom of free markets will be answered. For now, let's return to the legal issues. I think you might be interested in hearing about these efficiency principles as they apply to children and the family."

The professor talked on for some time to the undivided attention given by Aven and his staff.

"If I'm not mistaken, we still have some time remaining. What else might you like to have me discuss?"

"You haven't said anything about the criminal system. And in particular, what your principles might tell us about punishment."

The question came from one of the staff members who hadn't spoken yet.

"Ah yes, I'm glad you asked. First off, let me say that wherever possible, punishment should be by fine, not imprisonment. There are many reasons for this principle. A person who is fined can continue to work productively, contributing to the national wealth. Put him in prison and you have the cost of the prison, its construction, operation and maintenance, the loss of his income, and very likely the deterioration of his skills while in prison. Furthermore, if the individual does suffer loss of income while in prison, the likelihood of his reengaging in crime upon release is *increased*. Granted, a prison term would prevent a repeat of the crime *during* incarceration, but the longer the term, the *more likely* it is that such offenders will return to crime upon release. In every white-collar crime I can think of, a system of fines is far superior to prison."

Aven wanted to ask about the individual who couldn't pay the fine, but the professor continued.

"In those cases where the individual cannot afford to pay the fine, it would be appropriate for the government to provide for loans, but then, only if the private banking system was inadequate. Of course, jail is the only alternative for the indigent."

The young staff member who had raised the question about rent control spoke out again.

"That's all well and good, but what about violent crimes? How much would you fine a murderer, or would that depend on the kind of weapon he used?"

Professor Law seemed to ignore the sardonic tone.

"Another good question. There is a set of crimes, and murder is certainly one, that society should do all in its power to prevent. But such a simple edict is not very helpful. After all, we could provide nearly foolproof protection by arresting and imprisoning everyone. And I'm sure you can think of other schemes that would be just as foolproof, and just as foolish. The issue comes down to costs and benefits. Perhaps the point can best be illustrated in the case of capital punishment. Nothing would be more foolproof in stopping murder, at least its repeat, than capital punishment. But we use this sanction sparingly. Does anyone know why this is so?"

Several of Aven's staff members spoke as one.

"It's barbaric, uncivilized...."

"Then why do we use it at all? No, gentlemen, civility has nothing to do with capital punishment. Economic efficiency does. In the first place, capital punishment is one of those few sanctions from which there is no recovery. Not wanting to do away with the productive members of society, we tend to go to great lengths to avoid a mistake. Hence, the cost of imposing this particular penalty is extremely high, and in many cases may not equal the benefits to be derived. It may be no more costly, but may provide even more deterrent, to use these resources in locking away three murderers for twenty years rather than executing one. Also, if the penalty for murder is death, an individual who murders once may have far less incentive to stop than if the length of prison term is related to the number of such heinous crimes."

Aven could see that Gaylord was becoming somewhat agitated. Apparently this did not escape Professor's Law notice either.

"Based on the statistics of capital punishment, there are those who suggest that it is applied unfairly, that it really has nothing to do with deterrence, but rather with class hatred. Even if the statistics are correct, an economic approach to the law would indicate that such an outcome may not be at all perverse. I refer to what we call 'information-cost' theory. If we know that members of a particular race are more likely to commit a crime, society need devote fewer resources towards the determination of innocence or guilt of such persons. Mind you, this is not to suggest that all members of the race in question should be apprehended, or even executed without just cause. My only point is that the determination of guilt or innocence is costly in and of itself, and as in all matters, we must weigh the benefits against the costs."

Aven looked back towards Gaylord and then across the room towards Professor Fourkaste. Gaylord was not smiling. The professor was without expression, staring into his terminal. Aven decided to break the tension.

"Professor Law, I think we take your point that capital punishment is still with us. But surely you would agree that it occurs with much less frequency than during premodern times. In the Dark Ages, capital punishment, often of the most brutal sort, was the norm. Doesn't that indicate that we are at least *becoming* somewhat more civilized but perhaps have a ways to go?"

Aven felt good about his question, and he could tell that his colleagues did as well. It was an example of his ability to smooth surfaces, to allow everyone to feel comfortable about himself. He felt as if he were once again head of the crisis-complaint section at MOP.

"That is quite an artful conjecture, Director _____, but with all due respect, it too is incorrect."

Aven could feel his brow furrow along with a trace of anger.

"Let me explain. Medieval times were rather different. Among other things, most people living then believed in an afterlife."

Aven could tell that the professor was enjoying himself.

"I can imagine that you are perplexed. It's economics once again. In a society that believes in life *after* death, capital punishment is not irreversible. In an odd way, if the afterlife is thought of as something desirable, execution might seem to be no deterrent at all."

The professor was positively beaming at this point, and Aven saw that the mirth was spreading, ever so slightly, among the other eleven economists.

Once again the aggressive young staffer rose to speak. It was clear that he was not sharing in the levity.

"Are you telling us that there is no place in our legal system, *your* legal system for morality, for honesty, truthfulness, trust? What kind of world would you have us live in?"

The professor spoke instantly, not allowing what might well have been a most embarrassing silence.

"What kind of world indeed? We do not say our world is without morals, without honesty, trust. But,..." and the grin reappeared, "that's precisely our point. The world is moral because morality, honesty, all of the virtues you might care to mention, are themselves...."

Aven knew exactly what was coming and smiled broadly himself.

"...enormously efficient. In our wisdom we have come to live with each other in ways that allow us to do our business in the least costly manner. No government had to tell us to be honest. Man knew it the moment he had to buy and sell in the marketplace. And that is the single greatest lesson we have learned from our father, Adam Smith, and his sons, Professors Friedman and Hayek. I know you will understand as soon as you have had time to digest their writings."

He looked at his watch.

"Perhaps this is a good ending note."

"One last question please."

Aven thought to himself that he was going to have to talk with the young man soon.

"Professor, on several occasions throughout your talk this afternoon you mentioned the fact that the law, and the basic organization of the economy itself, was designed for the benefit of the *nation*, or the *society*, and not for any particular *individual*."

"Yes, I think that is correct."

"Well then, what you are saying doesn't sound any different to me than what our Marxist professors have been saying for decades."

Aven felt a stirring among all of the economists.

"Professor Law, it sounds to me like you're as much a COMMUNIST as all of them."

It was as if a hand grenade had been thrown into the room. All of the economists were out of their seats, shouting and gesticulating wildly. Aven, Paula, Gaylord, and the legal staff seated around the conference table found themselves whirling to and fro, rising and falling helplessly and chaotically. This frenzied scene continued for the better part of a minute before a piercing voice rose above the tumultuous din. It was Paula's.

"STOP IT...STOP IT...ALL OF YOU....STOP IT."

The room was still. The economists had returned to their terminals, and Aven and the others at the conference table were seated at floor level, although facing in random directions. Aven looked at Paula, who was near tears.

"Please, I've just spent two hours with my hair stylist, and now look at me."

Aven managed to say a few words to the legal staff members as they filed out of the combo room. He walked back to the table where Paula was combing her hair and Gaylord was sitting contentedly.

"Well, that was some session. Simple and powerful. I know there is a great deal yet for me to digest...."

"Aven, with your mind, it won't be anytime before you've mastered all of it. That's why you were chosen to head MOP in the first place, your mind and that *way* handsome face ya got."

Paula put her hand on Aven's as she spoke.

Gaylord looked from Paula to Aven. Aven avoided his glance.

"Thanks, Paula, I honestly hope I can live up to your expectations."

"You will."

"Okay folks, how 'bout calling it a day. It's nearly six, and I know Aven wants to get home. What are you doing for dinner, Paula?"

"I didn't, ah, nothing, Gaylord. Let's have Chinese. We can drop Aven off on the way."

Aven paid little attention to the conversation during the ride to his flat. He was anxious to get home, to talk to Rena, to tell her what he had just learned.

"Well, here we are. It was a good day Aven. See you in the morning. And be sure to catch plenty of Zs."

"Yeah, and hang loose, Aven."

"Thanks. Bye, Paula. I will, Gaylord. See you both tomorrow."

Aven turned to the door of his flat. The door opened. Aven and Rena kissed warmly.

"You won't believe…I can't wait to tell…the professor…."

Rena put an end to the gibbering with another kiss.

"Slooow down, love. Have you forgotten what we both learned in school about complete sentences? You're home late, but there's time for a glass of wine before we have to leave. We can get some food at Pero's before the concert."

Only then did he remember what day it was. For as long as he had known Rena they had gone to the chamber concerts at the conservatory. Most of them were held on Wednesday evenings. The Moscow Conservatory was home for the nation's best young talent, and Aven had to admit the concerts were not all that bad. Recently, in fact, there had been an occasional concert he enjoyed more than Rena had. To Rena's dismay, these concerts had a modern cast that she found offensive.

"I'd almost forgotten, and there's so much to talk about. But it will keep. A glass of wine sounds wonderful…my head's still spinning a bit from all that went on at the ministry."

Aven followed Rena into the front room.

"Thanks."

The wine did have a calming effect.

"If you don't mind, I won't bother to change. There's not a lot of time, and besides, people don't dress up as much as they used to. How was the day?"

"You look fine, Aven, and that jacket is my favorite. My part of the day was marvelous. The ideas wouldn't stop flowing. I think it's finished, and I like it. Not the fact that technology is so imperialistic, but the essay is good. I think those loons at the magazine will want to publish it."

"That's great, Rena. And I don't know why you call them loons. They publish just about everything you submit. Tell me, what part of the day wasn't yours?"

"Not everything my love. Not when it gets to the core of corruption in our system. The part of the day I spent talking with Hester. I'll tell you about it on the way to Pero's."

Rena spent little time in the bathroom. Another of the many things about her that Aven appreciated. How often had he heard his colleagues bemoan the time they spent waiting for the women in their lives in similar circumstances. Aven and Rena walked lightly out of the flat, arm in arm.

"Aven, I know Mellors is a colleague of yours…."

"More than a colleague, actually."

"Fine, a friend and a colleague, but, I'm sorry, he's a first-class cad as well."

"Come on, Rena, you're going to tell me that he and Hester had another fight. So what else is new? Every time he sleeps with a new woman, Hester gets all uptight, and then he brings her candy, and they're back in their nest cooing the night away."

"Hester called me today. Mellors left her."

"He wha...?"

"That's right. Mellors, world-class numbskull, walked out. Hester worries that he won't come back. He packed and left a note saying not to bother trying to see him again. She thinks he's moved in with one of his prostitute friends. I went to her place for lunch. She couldn't eat a thing, just sobbed most of the time."

"But they've been together, fighting, for as long as we've known each other, longer. It was always Hester threatening to move. There must be a mistake."

"Aven, after leaving, I called Mellors at the ministry. It's true. He's left her."

"But why? I thought Hester had become adjusted to his escapades. I had lunch with Mellors a few weeks ago. He told me then that he was going to cut down on the whoring, worried about some new kind of disease they think they've found in Iceland."

"You're not going to understand, but here's what he said. He didn't come home night before last, and in fact hadn't been home for two or three days."

"What's that got to do with his moving out?"

"Let me tell you. He came back to their flat yesterday morning around ten o'clock. Hester wasn't there, and he became furious as he waited."

Aven vaguely recalled not seeing Mellors, but so much else had been going on that it really hadn't registered.

"Hester came home around noon. After a heated argument she told him where she had been."

"At an alcohol prevention conference?"

"Don't try to be funny, Aven. Hester had felt so lonely she'd spent the night with an old friend of hers from the university."

"Now who's trying to be funny? Why on earth would Mellors get upset about Hester visiting an old girlfriend?"

"That old girlfriend's name is *Ivan*. And the two of them were lovers before Hester met Mellors."

"Well...."

"Well what?"

"Well, *that's* an entirely different story."

"Aven, love, I've only told you *one* story."

"No, that's not what I mean, Rena."

They had arrived at Pero's.

"Let's get seated and I'll explain."

Aven and Rena liked coming to Pero's. Since the restaurant had only six tables, they didn't feel far from the warmth of their own dining room. The food was always good, and the place was across the street from the Conservatory.

"Evening, Rena and Aven. I didn't see you last week. Hope nothing was the matter. The dinner's extra good tonight, one of Pero's grandmother's recipes. Would you like wine with dinner?"

"Good evening, Servo. We've just been very busy, but thanks for asking. The dinner sounds fine. Perhaps a half carafe...is that okay?"

Rena smiled her assent.

"By the way, does Pero stock Minskevasser? A white zinfandel I think."

"Never heard of it, but I'll ask Pero."

"The usual will be fine. Thanks."

Servo departed, and Aven returned to the more serious conversation.

"Look, Rena, now that you've told me the whole story, Mellors' behavior is easy to understand, and not all that...." He was going to say "not all that caddish," but thought better of it.

"Maybe for you, but not for me."

"The fact that Mellors whores around is nothing I would defend, but Hester's behavior is really unacceptable."

Aven noticed Rena looking at him somewhat more intently.

"Rena, think of the family as a unit, and that's what Hester and Mellors are all about—a unit having a number of purposes in society, not the least of which is producing and rearing children."

"I can do that, and by the way...."

"No, let's stick with this subject. Producing and rearing children. Society couldn't survive otherwise."

"Aven, we are talking about Mellors walking out on Hester, aren't we?"

"I'm sorry to interrupt. Pero thinks that Minskevasser is an Amerikan wine, from California most likely. I wouldn't be surprised if we stock it soon. Enjoy your dinner."

"Thanks. I'm sure we will...."

"Mmmmm, this does look good. Where was I?"

"I'm not at all sure, my love."

"Oh yes, the primary function of the family unit. Well, don't you see? Mellors' whoring in no way interferes with producing and rearing children. For better or for worse, the Lord made us that way."

"What way?"

"Mellors' ability to have children with Hester and to be a loving father isn't influenced by how many other women he sleeps with. Even if he were to impregnate some of them, the family remains unaffected. On the other hand, one mistake by Hester and the ability of the family unit is put into serious jeopardy. If she becomes pregnant by Ivan, it would be unreasonable to expect Mellors to care for the child as if it were his. Even more to the point, Hester's capacity to bear children is limited. One transgression on her part is far more serious than a dozen affairs Mellors might have with other women."

Rena had not taken a bite of her food for some time. She put down her fork and spoke in a most gentle manner.

"Aven, you're joking?"

"No, no. No, I'm just thinking about things as an economist might, in terms of efficiency and maximizing *social* well-being."

"And, love, I suppose you think that if Hester were to get pregnant by Ivan she couldn't have an abortion?"

"As a matter of fact, yes. Now you're starting to think like an economist."

Servo's approach reminded them that the concert would soon begin.

"I guess we better stop now. Didn't you like the fish."

"I did, Aven, honestly. Guess I wasn't all that hungry."

"I did, too. It was great. Let's go. We can talk about Hester's hypothetical abortion after the concert."

"I'd like that," she replied softly.

Rena said little on the way from Pero's. Aven's thoughts revolved around economics and the concept of efficiency. They were in their seats in good time.

"Well, Aven, I did have enough sense to check on the program. A Haydn quartet in the first half and Beethoven after the intermission, early, thank goodness. I'm not sure I can handle another new idea at the moment."

Neither composer did much for Aven, but he was content for Rena's sake. They sat for a time without speaking.

"I love this hall. I always have. It's really perfect for chamber music."

Aven acknowledged Rena's comment as he looked around the familiar surroundings. The orchestra section was not large, seating perhaps as many as three hundred. The ten rows of seats curved deeply around the stage, putting the performers almost in the round. The stage itself appeared quite expansive this evening, with four music stands and chairs, seemingly forgotten, standing in the center. Aven and Rena were seated in the balcony, which extended almost vertically for six rows at the back of the hall. In their university days, they were happy to have aisle seats in the last row of the orchestra. This evening the director of MOP and his lady had been ushered to their permanently reserved seats, center, first-row balcony. Rena had mixed emotions when learning of this new privilege. The seats were the best in the theater acoustically, but they were at the same time visible to everyone in the audience, even those in the back rows of the orchestra.

Aven's thoughts were interrupted by the restrained applause accompanying the four musicians' entry onstage. The familiar chords brought the applause to an end. Aven always enjoyed guessing which of the string players would be the last to stop sawing away, producing the sounds of a cat in heat as the pegs were twisted back and forth. This evening it was the cellist. The young musicians played with skill and a maturity that repeatedly surprised Aven. Aven and Rena had heard more seasoned groups in the larger Moscow Concert Hall, but the quality of the students' musicianship left little to be desired. The couple remained in their seats during intermission, as neither of them enjoyed the smoke-filled lobby. Aven couldn't detect much difference between the Beethoven and the Haydn.

Aven and Rena held hands as they walked home. Rena was quiet, humming to herself most of the way. Aven was pleased that he could recognize some of the themes from earlier in the evening and was otherwise content with his own thoughts.

"Aven, darling, it is late, but I'd really like to hear about Hester's hypothetical abortion. I'll make some tea."

Aven kissed Rena's cheek before Rena could escape to the kitchen.

"Of course. We can talk for as long as you like."

Aven hung his jacket in the closet, put on a comfortable sweater, and sat in the front room, waiting for the teapot to announce its wish to be attended to. He realized how awake he felt despite the late hour in a day that had been over-full some time ago. Rena poured the tea.

"Thanks, Rena…remind me where I was."

"I had asked you what Hester might do if she becomes pregnant by Ivan. I'm sure she isn't, but…."

"The reality isn't all that important. It's the theory that's seductive…no pun intended."

"Aaaven, come on now…."

"Okay, I'll be serious. Let's assume that Hester's pregnancy is what might be called an unintended by-product of sexual activity. Neither party to the act wants the child. A fairly strong case might be made for abortion under such circumstances, since neither parent is likely to have much of an incentive to care for the child, and the child himself…."

"*Him*-self?"

"Sorry, the child itself might not acquire the necessary skills to provide for him, itself, later in life. But—and this is the key to the analysis—the individual parents—Hester and Ivan in this case—are not all that relevant in making the decision."

"Who else could *possibly* be?"

"Society."

Aven paused much like Professor Law had done earlier in the day.

"There are many individuals who would pay dearly to be in Hester and Ivan's shoes and who can't have children of their own."

"But they can adopt. What do they have to do with Hester's fetus?"

Rena's voice had retained the same soft gentle intensity of earlier in the evening.

"There's a serious shortage of infants available for adoption. As I said, there are many people today who would happily pay for a child if it were available."

"Come on, Aven. What if Hester doesn't want to put her child up for adoption? You're not suggesting that she be *forced* to do so, are you?"

"Rena, try to listen. Hester doesn't *want* to put her child up for adoption for one reason only."

"Sure, you don't need a Ph.D. in economics to understand that. She *just doesn't want to.*"

"You may not need the degree, but it doesn't hurt. The reason Hester doesn't want to put her child up for adoption is simple. The *price is too low.*"

Rena put her cup on the table and her hand over her mouth.

"I wonder what was in Pero's grandmother's recipe. Maybe I'd understand you better if I had eaten more of the fish. We've gone from the sins of Hester's single act of unfaithfulness in contrast to the noble Mellors' decade of infidelity to a ban on Hester's control of her own body, to…baby selling. Aven, you're an adorable man, and that's why I love you so much."

There were other times when Rena had not taken him seriously, treating him rather like a lovable child. Aven had no difficulty in restraining the trace of annoyance that Rena's comments evoked.

"Hear me out, Rena, and then we can laugh together. There is certainly a cost to Hester's giving birth to what you would call an unwanted child. As long as child selling is *prohibited* by the *arbitrary power* of the government, Hester and others in similar circumstances will see the benefits of abortion far exceeding the cost of the pregnancy and the risks of birth. If the government allowed a free market in babies, Hester might well receive adequate compensation for her efforts and make some couple, who would otherwise remain childless, very happy. Hester is no worse off, and others are better off. It's the essence of economic efficiency."

"It's the essence of ox dung if you ask me. But love, I do understand. These are the new Amerikan ideas that have been brought over with the occupation.

Their newness alone is stimulating to you, and besides, you have to work with these people. The arguments you've been making this evening are the same as those in the notebook you gave to me the other day."

Aven's spirits lifted.

"Oh, you've read it?"

"Only the first few pages. If you ask me, that Adam Smith is every bit the simpleton that Karl Marx is…was, and the disciples of Smith sound no less dangerous than those of Marx. But love, it's late. I know we will continue to discuss these ideas. And whatever you or I might believe now, time has its own way of settling disputes. I've kept us both up until two o'clock. You have your new world to complete, and I promised Hester I'd meet her for breakfast. I think we need to get to bed."

Rena patted Aven's head as she got up.

"The cups will keep."

Rena went off to the bedroom and then briefly to the bathroom to brush her teeth. Aven did the same. They kissed and fell asleep in each other's arms.

THFRISATURDAY
■■■■■■■■■■■■■■■■

*D*uring the following three days, only a few meetings stood out in Aven's mind. Saturday was pleasant, and the daily news headlines were informative:

GREAT EXCITEMENT AT MOP
Minds Spinning, Hopes Rising

YOUNG DIRECTOR LAUDS AMERIKAN IDEAS
Happy in New Office

MOP COMPLETES REORGANIZATION IN 6 DAYS
Day of Rest Ahead

Aven's time with Rena was much like Wednesday evening, which had extended far into the morning. These discussions were serious, often tense, but Aven knew that Rena would soon come to see the virtues of free-market economics. He made his first personnel decision, and the dinner Saturday night also was memorable. Rena suggested it as he was leaving for MOP Thursday morning.

"Aven, there's an outlandish vehicle parked out front. Do you have any idea *what* it is?"

Aven liked what he saw. No longer red, and no longer squat, the object parked at the curb was a glistening gray in color. It took the space of three of Paula's Beamers, perhaps ten meters in length.

"It's the Amerikan driver; must be my car. See you this evening. The breakfast was great."

"Wait, Aven, just a minute."

Aven walked back to the kitchen.

"I realized after last night's conversation, I haven't met the Amerikans you've been working with, and I'd like to. Might even make an interesting story....But seriously, do you think we could get together sometime soon? Perhaps for dinner?"

"I, ah, I don't see why not. I'll check with Mzzz. Barnum and Gaylord. What's a good night for you."

"Saturday would be best."

Aven kissed her as he departed.

"I'm sure Saturday will be fine. Bye."

Aven hesitated as he reached the car. The driver sensed Aven's uncertainty.

"Just stand back, sir."

The door farthest to the rear swung open. Aven stepped into a coach suitable for royalty. He sat in a wide, richly upholstered black leather seat. Another seat of similar dimension and luxury was located behind him. He soon became aware of the accouterments before him. Off to the right was a small stainless steel sink with several bottles of whiskey standing to the far right. These were fastened securely to the sideboard. Directly in front was a modest size television console, and to the left were three sleek telephones.

"Is this all for me?"

As he spoke, he noticed a glass plate separating him from the front compartment. The driver's voice came from a speaker located above and to the rear of the first set of seats.

"Yes, sir."

"My goodness, I wonder when I'll have the time to use this splendid equipment."

"Soon I expect, sir."

They drove the remaining few minutes in silence.

"Here we are."

"Thanks."

Aven, accustomed to Otise's absence, had become an expert at operating the elevator. Number "2" came alive, as did the ukuleles.

PANG

After a momentary pause, Aven walked to his office. He entered to the smiling faces of Paula and Gaylord, who spoke in unison.

"Gooooooood moooorning, Aven," and Paula continued, "it's totally awesome, isn't it? I just know you're going to do smashing work here. Oh, that's the executive couch. We forgot about it Monday. I called in a rush delivery to Gdansk."

"It's okay, Aven. No executive worth his salt can get by without one. I'm sure you'll be glad to have it soon enough."

"It does look inviting, Gaylord. And how are the both of you?"

"We're fine. Gaylord and I ate out last night, and my tummy bothered me some. Probably too much MSG. Professor Lowe...."

"Oh, sorry to interrupt, but while it's on my mind, Rena was hoping to meet you, both of you. How's dinner on Saturday?"

"That's a totally gnarly idea."

"Yeah, Aven, that's cool. Paula and I would love to meet Rena."

"Great. We can settle the details later. What about today?"

"Let's see now. Our advisers will be working individually with the MOP sections through the rest of the week. You probably don't want to spend much time with the industry operations group. Pretty dull stuff as far as I'm concerned. But I've always found the sessions by Professors Taksis and Fair stimulating...."

"Paula, Aven should stop in on Professor O'Kate's meeting."

"You're absolutely right, Gaylord. He's speaking on education and training this morning. I think we should attend. Why don't you decide how to spend the afternoon. Perhaps you can get down to the gym for a swim. I have an appointment with my stylist, and then I'm going to try to do some shopping...."

PING   PLING

They entered the combo room. Three seats at the conference table were waiting for them. So too were the members of the MOP education section. Professor Al O'Kate was the only economist seated in the U engulfing the conference table. When the professor began to speak, Aven's seat adjusted only slightly. The professor was far less dynamic than Nat Law had been the previous day. Aven did manage to remain erect in his seat behind the desk. So too did all of those seated around the conference table, but it was clear to Aven that doing so was almost as difficult as understanding some of what the professor was saying. For the most part, this was simply because the professor mumbled. What Aven could hear seemed clear enough.

"In general, the allocation of resources will be determined by an 'invisible' hand. But because of the rapidity of the growth process, it will be useful to anticipate some specialized needs that are likely to arise in the near future—doctors, especially surgeons, sports officials, referees, umpires...."

At this point Aven looked to Paula questioningly. Paula gave him a reassuring smile.

"...and therefore the most pressing concern at the moment is the dearth of universities where such skills can be acquired. You will have to triple the number of major universities within the first three months of the three-year plan."

Professor O'Kate had tried to add emphasis to his last few words. With the exception of Paula and Gaylord—who seemed to take the professor's comments with equanimity—the others around the conference table were roused to a considerable state of agitation. One staffer at the rear of the table finally found the words to express his consternation.

"But Professor O'Kate, that's *impossible!*"

"And why do you think so?"

"Can your government be serious? A tripling of our universities would require nine additional campuses in the city of Moscow alone. Funding such an enormous system of higher education is out of the question. Do you have any idea what the costs would be?"

For the first time during the dull session the professor's face showed signs of life.

"Perhaps, especially since this is the section on education, some of you might recall that wonderful quote from Oscar Wilde. Let's see now, how did it go? 'Economists know the cost of everything,' or something….Indeed, I am fully aware of the costs involved in building and operating first-class universities. We wrestled with the issue for some time. As it turns out, the solution was always there, it just took the right kind of leader to see it."

A degree of restlessness was evident around the conference table.

"Let me be clear. What each university requires is a well-developed athletic program, one that will provide high excitement to the general public."

Professor O'Kate paused, much like Professor Law had earlier when making a profound point.

"Gate receipts have made all of our major universities self-supporting."

As the professor continued his explanation of the financing, he soon had his audience nodding in agreement. Aven looked to Paula and Gaylord with a smile of understanding on his face.

"Thank you, Professor O'Kate. That was truly inspiring."

"My pleasure, Paula. You know I admire the funding methods of our universities. The one thing I hated about Chicago was its outmoded sports policy. Things have certainly gotten better lately. Last year we beat Notre Dame, and if we can just get that kid from East L.A., we've got a real shot at number one. Oh, sorry, Director _____, number one in football, that is. We've always been on top in economics."

"Professor, would you like to join us for lunch?"

"Is it, ah, free?"

"All but the tip."

"Thanks anyway, Paula. I think I'd better skip lunch. Lots of work to do."

"Oh damn, that reminds me, Gaylord. I've got things to do as well. I'll check in with you and Aven later in the afternoon."

"Feel like some lunch?"

"I guess so, Gaylord. Boy, that was some potent session this morning. I'm amazed at how simple things can be if only you have the right perspective."

"You're right, Aven, perspective is the name of the game. Let's go."

The elevator was unoccupied.

PONG

"That's it."

"That's what, Aven?"

"Nothing really. I was just wondering. Is there something wrong with the elevator?"

"Not that I know of. Why do you ask?"

"Don't really know. Come on. I'm hungry."

The table was nearly empty. Three section leaders, chatting over coffee, were engaged in a fairly heated discussion—in reality, less of a discussion than a monologue.

"Can you believe this dung they're trying to pass off as theory. And don't tell me their victory over us proves otherwise. These Amerikans are just as stupid as Stalin's henchmen were and every bit as dangerous."

The other two men said little.

"Mark my words, in four days you won't see any new world at all. It's just going to be more of the same oppressive excrement in a different wrapper...."

The speaker's two companions started to leave as he was speaking.

"Do you know who that is?"

"Who, the idealistic rabble rouser with all of the questions yesterday? He's not so bad, Aven. Just young."

"Gaylord, I beg to differ. I think I know Russians better than you."

"He's a dreamer, and most likely he'll wake up as he grows up. We have the same thing in America."

"Perhaps, but what if you're wrong? How can you be sure he'll grow up? And how soon?"

"Aven, I can give you advice, not guarantees."

Aven did not reply, and Gaylord redirected the conversation.

"We have some time before the next session. Actually, it's just the last hour that will be of interest. Otherwise, pretty grim stuff. Feel like taking a walk?"

"Go ahead, Gaylord. I think I'd like some time by myself."

Aven walked quickly to his office. He dialed the number for the legal section.

"Hello...Yes, this is Aven...A little mad you say?...Well, not really, but things have been quite hectic, haven't they?...No, I was calling about a member of your staff. The young fellow who asked all of those questions of Professor Law....Yes, that's the one, quite impolite and aggressive....Oh, I see. I'd like to think that's the case, but we have three days left, and very little time for growing up....What should you do? Fire him, and don't worry, I'll have a replacement for you in the morning."

Aven dialed the personnel department. For the next hour he sat content-edly, reading from *The Road to Serfdom*. It wasn't until close to four o'clock that he recalled the meeting. He put the book down and trotted out of the office.

BING

Entering the combo room in midsession was definitely a new experience. Professor Lowe Taksis stood as he talked. In near constant motion, he paced from desk to desk. Those seated at the conference table moved like a corps de ballet, changing both vertical and horizontal position as the speaker moved at random about the U. Aven realized it would be impossible to gain his seat while the professor spoke.

Professor Taksis acknowledged Aven's presence.

"Director _____, I'm so glad you could get here. Please do come in and sit down."

With that, the professor rested his hands on the nearest desk and waited for Aven to join those at the conference table. The professor resumed his perambu-lating lecture, a fact not lost on Aven's stomach.

"We have long known that the key to prosperity and wealth lay in minimal government. Our father, Professor Smith, established this principle in his great work. The taxes necessary to carry on the proper functions of government must, by clear implication, be *minimal* as well.

A MOP staffer seated behind Aven interrupted.

"Excuse me, Professor. I did read ahead in *The Wealth of Nations*."

Aven could see the obvious sense of satisfaction in Professor Taksis' eyes.

"Didn't Professor Smith also speak of the need for taxes to be *equitable*?"

The professor's expression hardened.

"As a matter of fact, yes, he did say something about ability to pay, in one of those rare passages where scholars have had difficulty in divining the master's precise meaning. We have found it wise to focus elsewhere."

"Oh, I see. That makes sense."

Professor Taksis continued talking and walking.

"Embodied in the great work of Professor Smith, but hidden away for nearly two centuries, was an idea that helped lead a revolution. We have long known it as supply-side theory."

He took a deep breath.

"If the government *lowers* the tax rate, that is, takes a *smaller* and *smaller share* out of each worker's paycheck, then—now listen carefully—the total rev-enue that the government takes in actually increases. Yes, *increases!*"

Aven could hear the muffled gasps around him. And he had to admit to himself the professor had really uncorked a surprise.

"Many in my country pooh-poohed this idea when it was first revealed. Why, our recent great golfing president, George Bush, didn't understand it at first. If the government takes less from a worker's paycheck, the worker will have a greater incentive to work more, produce more, and earn more. It is from these higher earnings that a *smaller* tax bite will yield a *greater revenue. Q! E! D!*"

And with that final climax, the professor sat in his own seat at the far left of the room, appearing to be in a state of near exhaustion.

A quiet murmur filled the room. Members of the MOP staff looked to each other, nodding in agreement with the most recent revelation from the Amerikans. Two or three minutes passed in this manner. One of those seated at the conference table rose and began speaking in a hesitant whisper.

"I'm sorry, I can't hear you. Please speak up."

"I'll try, sir. It's just that I am confused."

"Not about anything *I* have said?"

"No, not at all. It's what I overheard at lunch."

The professor along with everyone else in the room looked at the speaker as though he had landed from another planet.

"I was having lunch with some of the section heads from Labor."

"Yes, and did you enjoy your lunch?"

"Actually, I don't remember, but the Labor group had been meeting with Professor Minnie Wages."

"I see. She's quite a dish, isn't she?"

"No, sir, it wasn't about her. It was about what she said. Seems as if she was adamant."

"About what?"

"About the need to keep wages *low.*"

"Of course, that goes without saying. Are you sure you don't remember what it was that you ate? Perhaps we should call in the lab technicians."

The professor was clearly amused.

"That's what I don't understand. She said you needed to keep wages *low* so that workers would feel compelled to work and produce in order to eat and feed their families...."

"Yes...and...?"

"And I thought you just said that when the workers were able to earn *more*, they would work harder and produce more."

The murmuring, snide comments, and chuckles ended. You could hear the MOP members' minds grinding away. Paula was filing her nails. Gaylord was smiling. The professor was not.

"Perhaps it might be useful to call in Professor Ree. I think he could help us with this seeming paradox."

It was Gaylord, speaking with his normal grin.

"Mr. Creamer, yes, I think that would indeed be helpful. Do you know where he might be?"

"I'll get him."

Gaylord returned moments later with the Korean professor, Theo Ree. Professor Taksis greeted his colleague and explained the apparent contradiction.

"We would be grateful indeed if you would clarify this matter for us."

Aven's seat swiveled to the right as Professor Ree replied.

"It is not complicated."

The professor folded his arms across his chest, a faint smile on his face.

"I'm sure it isn't, and that's why we asked you to join us. Perhaps you can elaborate."

"It is not complicated."

The professor's position and expression had not changed.

It was clear to Aven that Professor Taksis was confused.

"I'm sorry, Professor Ree, perhaps I didn't make myself clear."

Once again he tried to explain the apparent contradiction.

"Have I left something out?"

"It is not complicated."

Professor Ree got up from his desk, bowed, and left the room.

The eerie quiet returned. Paula ended it.

"Well, I'm sure that if each of us takes a peek at Professor Smith's great book tonight it will all be terribly simple. And it is past five."

Aven and Gaylord walked out together.

"You know, those Asians sure are inscrutable. See you tomorrow."

"Good night, Aven. And it's not the Asians, it's Theo Ree."

Rena was waiting at the door.

"Aven, what's wrong? Is there trouble at work?"

"No trouble, Rena. My mind must have been wandering, that's all."

The embrace and kiss continued as they walked into the flat. Aven entered the front room with a contented sigh, anticipating the taste of wine along with Rena's company. He was to have only the latter.

"Darling, the evening's so lovely and warm for April. Let's go to the park. It's been ages since we've eaten at the stand. Come on, the air will be good for both of us."

Rena rarely ceased to amaze him. She had an unfailing sense of timing, suggesting the unexpected but perfect diversion whenever he was at all troubled. They were soon on their way.

"How's Hester? Have you talked with her today?"

"Yes, on the phone. She's better I guess. Mellors didn't call. But Ivan was coming to see her in the afternoon. He seems to be having troubles of his own at work."

They soon were within the park grounds and slowed their pace. Something was in bloom. Rena always described in detail the various trees and flowers, and Aven just as quickly forgot what she had told him.

"It's a wonderful aroma, don't you think?"

"Mmmmm...yes."

They continued walking, Rena pulling him along without apparent destination.

"Aven, I managed to do some reading today. I stopped in at Kodee's yesterday on the way from Hester's. They had a very old copy of Hayek, and one of Smith's as well. They're going to call me when they get the Friedman book. Seems there was a big rush on it. So your Rena spent much of the day curled up with Mr. Hayek. I hope you are not too terribly jealous."

Rena came to an abrupt stop, pulled Aven to her, and kissed him lightly on the lips.

"Rena, why should I be jealous? You didn't let him seduce you, did you?"

"Not exactly."

"*In*exactly?"

"More like *half*exactly. Actually the man had something quite valuable to say. I assume you've already read the book?"

"Not, ah, exactly."

"All right, Aven, we're even. Let's sit down. The part I like about Hayek is that he writes from his gut. There's real feeling and experience behind much of what he has to say. He lived through the horrors of Europe in the 1930s, saw in Hitler and Stalin all of the evils of a totalitarian dictator—and he was right in good measure. His arguments against centralized planning were also on the mark. The idea that the interests of a vast and complex nation could be crystallized into meaningful directives from a handful of bureaucrats in the Kremlin was nonsense. Hayek understood, and we've been paying for this lunacy for over two generations."

Aven was wondering if his ears weren't deceiving him. Here was Rena, speaking with such passion about the son of Adam Smith, father of free-market economics. He said nothing.

"I think his ideas on the rule of law contained a great deal of wisdom as well. The notion that laws should be long-standing, not subject to the whims of a fickle public or legislature; that the nation's constitution and statutes should not grant special privilege to one class over another or place restrictions on one class, for that matter; that the majority mustn't *always* have its way, especially when basic rights of the minority are at stake. You know, Aven, he dedicated his book to the 'Socialists of All Parties.' Deep down, I think he was quite a decent human being."

"So then what do you mean by '*half*exactly'? There's not a single one of those Amerikan economists, some duller than death, that could do a better job of explaining Hayek than you have. What part of him *don't* you like?"

"Too much, I'm afraid, but let's get some food. It's going to get colder soon. We can do the other *half* at home."

They walked from the bench towards the central plaza area. There were a few others in the park. The usual assortment of young lovers and older men and women who watched with approving nostalgia. It was still cool enough to keep the young children and their parents home after dinner, but it would not be too many days before the park would be alive with a full sampling of the city's population. Rena and Aven smiled as they passed others. Acquaintance or stranger, it made little difference. The gentle surroundings of the park made friends of them all. They approached the only food stand that was open at this early date.

Some years ago, pizza had come to their country. It was an instant success. Luigi's had taken over as the first food stand to open in the park two or three years earlier.

"I don't mind Luigi's, but I liked it better when we could get sardines and black bread. Aven, what would you like?"

"Anything's fine, Rena. I'll have a beer also."

"Good evening."

"Gooduh evening to you senora. Wadda canna do for you?"

Part of Luigi's success had been the fact that he imported much of the pizza ingredients from his native land. He had also brought his large family along.

"We'd like two small pizzas with olives, and two beers. Oh, and add anchovies to mine, please."

Aven and Rena sat at the round table nearby, talking intermittently about nothing of great importance until the pizza arrived.

"Mmmmm, that *was* good...so is this place, and so are you, Aven. I only hope our new world will be as well."

"It will, Rena. Better than Luigi's pizza, even with the anchovies. Let's take the long way back."

Aven and Rena walked in the opposite direction of the flat for some time before turning onto the path at the outer edge of the park. The numbers of people they passed diminished, but not the friendliness of the greetings. The couple continued walking and nuzzling for the better part of an hour before reaching the flat.

"Well, Aven, are you awake enough to hear more about the Amerikan professor?"

"Sure, Rena, if you feel like staying up. Why don't you let me fix the tea tonight?"

They soon settled comfortably by the coffee table.

"I'm flattered that you find me more interesting than the Amerikan economists you've been listening to."

Aven leaned across the table.

"No offense, but you shouldn't take that as too great a compliment."

Rena smiled as she gently removed his hands from her thighs.

"Veeery funny, love. Would you like to be serious now? Professor Hayek is wrong on three counts."

"Oh, only three? I'm beginning to feel better already."

"AvEN!"

The look in her eyes told him that he should, as Gaylord might say, cool it.

"In the first place, Hayek's view of human nature is disturbing. He sees us all as grubby, self-seeking creatures, and the world he favors will only encourage such behavior. He wants society organized so as to minimize the harm humans do when acting at their worst. We shouldn't even think of fostering what is good and decent in people. On this basis alone, it's hard to believe that anyone can take him or his ideas seriously...and yet, we seem to more and more."

Rena's voice had turned melancholic.

"But, Rena, earlier tonight you acknowledged that Hayek had lived through and witnessed man, humans, acting at their worst. He's just being realistic. That's the wonderful thing about free markets. Each man, human, acting selfishly...."

Rena interrupted, and the intensity in her voice warned Aven not to continue.

"You can leave it at *man* in this case, and he's not being realistic. He's being narrow, cautious, constipated, and dangerous. That's the awful part. If you design a world around the worst in people, they will likely meet your expectations. But Aven, for God's sake, don't you think we can do better?"

"Your parents and grandparents thought so before Stalin."

"Fair enough, love, but does that mean we give up trying? I can't, and I hope you won't."

Aven did not reply. They both sipped their tea. A lighter look came over Rena as she resumed speaking.

"Now I agree if you say that a better world will take more than a few days to build. It may even take a few generations, in which case, love, you and I will have to see it next time around. Do you want to know what else is the matter with Hayek?"

Aven looked at his watch.

"Rena, it's close to midnight. We've got the whole night ahead of us."

Rena returned his smile.

"Well, the ninny doesn't know when to let go of a good idea. He's absolutely right about *central* planning. It won't work, nor has it ever. But Hayek rejects *all* planning, regardless of the scope—planning for the development of our city, the beautiful lake areas, or even major research projects and other large economic ventures. Oh, he says, if there is a high degree of *mutual* interest, planning *might* be permitted, but I'm sure his disciples find it easier to reject the idea of any planning whatsoever. What idiocy."

Nothing came to Aven by way of response. He respected Rena. He loved her. But her language was bordering on sacrilege. His voice was grim as he spoke.

"Rena, was there a third area that bothered you?"

"Are you sure you want me to go on? You know, Aven, this head on my shoulders has a brain, with memory cells. We could go to bed now."

"No, go ahead."

"The last point is similar to what I've been saying already."

Aven wondered if he shouldn't have chosen bed.

"Once again, Professor Hayek doesn't know when to let go of a principle. Take the setting of wages, for example. We have only two choices: people are paid according to what they are *worth* to society or according to what they might *merit*. Hayek is quite clear in the difference between the two: a person's worth is determined by—and these are his words—'*the impersonal forces of the market.*' A person's merit is some subjective concept that has to be determined, I suppose, through the political process, like minimum wages, or the idea that men and women should get equal pay for doing *comparable* work."

"I don't quite understand. If the work is comparable, won't the pay be also?"

"Not comparable in terms of market pay. That's what your economist friends would call a tautology. Comparable, say, in terms of education, responsibility, that sort of thing."

"But under those circumstances, a smoothly functioning market would lead to equal pay."

Aven spoke with a sense of confidence, almost as if the teacher's mantle had passed from Rena to himself.

Rena grabbed it right back.

"Perhaps in the textbook world of your economists, but not in the world around us. You know very well that we discriminate all the time—women, men from the provinces, Jews—these people are not allowed to enter the few well-paid occupations available. In a world where some are precluded from opportunities by their race or sex or whatever, laws requiring comparable pay are the only way people will be rewarded for what they are worth *and* what they merit."

"In a world with well-functioning markets, discrimination cannot exist. Those firms refusing to hire the *best* workers—women, Jews, Latvians—would have poorer workers or higher labor costs. Under any circumstance, they would have lower profits and would soon go out of business...unless, of course, they decided to forgo their discriminatory ways."

The grin on Aven's face seemed to extend beyond his ears.

"That's really quite a fascinating argument."

Rena's soft, low, and firm voice of last night had returned.

"And just precisely which planet is it that has those—what do you call them—*smoothly functioning markets*? Venus? Pluto perhaps? Perhaps Uranus? Aven...Aaaaavennn."

Aven realized that he had started to doze, eyes open and all.

"Oh, Rena...really, I was listening to every word, but it *is* late."

The last thing he remembered of the evening was Rena's warm body against his and a light kiss on the side of his neck.

Rena began the morning conversation.

"Aven, about last night, I'm afraid I went on too long."

"Don't be silly. You had me on the edge of my seat right up to, when was it? Two or two-thirty? In fact, I was rather upset when you suggested we call it a night. But you seemed tired, and I decided not to protest."

"That was sweet of you. And if I hadn't been so tired, you would have received full measure of my appreciation. I promise to make it up to you. But, there's something else he said."

"Who?"

"Hayek! Aven, my sweet, someday, just once you're going to surprise me and follow a simple conversation in the morning. All I wanted to say was that he...."

"Who?"

"Now I seem to have forgotten. Let's, as your economist friends are so fond of saying, *assume* it was Hayek. He did have some interesting psychological insights regarding political leadership. In chapter ten, I think. As soon as you have a chance to read it, we should talk."

"I'll read the book soon. After all, you did have the advantage last night."

Aven kissed Rena, took his tea cup into the kitchen, and was on his way.

"Bye, Rena."

"Wait. What about the dinner?"

"Oh, yes, it's on for Saturday. And I think we should choose the place. See you later. Rena, I love you."

"Good morning."

"Good morning, sir."

During the drive to MOP, Aven realized that the Amerikan economists would be leaving soon, all but Gaylord's friend, Professor Fourkaste. Saturday morning would bring a number of lower level advisers—political scientists and sociologists.

"Damn crazy fucker."

Aven's thoughts were interrupted by his driver, who was cursing and leaning on the limo horn at the same time.

"Forgive me, sir. It's just that these people act as if they've never been behind the wheel of a car. They're driving too fast for their own good."

"They do seem to be going rather fast, given the traffic this morning."

Aven entered the building after a longer than usual drive and waited for the elevator.

"Odd," he thought. "It's usually standing ready for me at this time of the morning."

Before long he stepped into the familiar confines of the elevator.

PING...PANG

Gaylord and Paula were waiting. They went over the day's meetings. Despite Paula's earlier comments, Aven was disappointed to learn that the session on industry with Professors Costa, Price, and Supplé conflicted with Professor Fair's. Rumor had it that their agenda included hostile and leveraged takeovers as well as horizontal and vertical mergers. Gaylord had confirmed these rumors, and more. The French professor was a renowned expert on the technical aspects of stock market behavior, and his talk dealt extensively with such intriguing concepts as double bottoms, low violations, ascending peaks, and the subtleties of pulling out immediately before climax.

As she left, Paula indicated her intention to come to the late morning session with them. She was particularly interested in the professor's clothing. Gaylord explained that women were not required to wear the standard uniform when giving the presentation. This major concession—the Shafley Code—had been granted to Amerikan women some years before.

"Fine, I'll meet the two of you in the combo room at ten. I can use the time to reread parts of Dr. Friedman."

Aven stood before the Gdansk bookcase. Most of the shelves were filled with reports, manuals, and other government publications. On only one shelf could a person appreciate the fine quality of wood, a white ash, with its sweeping and irregular grain. Rena's picture was on the left. Centered on the right were three books, each bound in rich leather. The titles and authors' names were embossed in a glossy black. Smith's tome, by far the thickest of the three and bound in a milky white leather, stood majestically between the much slimmer Hayek and Friedman. The fawning offspring were bound in red and blue, respectively. Aven removed Hayek.

"I'm going to have to read this soon," he thought to himself as he turned to the table of contents. There were the chapters on planning, collectivism, the rule of law, and totalitarianism, all familiar from Rena's schizophrenic monologue of the previous evening. Chapter nine, "Security and Freedom," was followed by "The End of the Truth," numbered eleven. Chapter ten was missing. Aven made a mental note to ask Gaylord about this as he replaced Hayek and opened Friedman's slim volume.

Hayek's name was mentioned prominently in the preface. In the first full chapter, demonstrating the need for economic freedom where political freedom is desired, Friedman again paid homage to *The Road to Serfdom*. Aven was impressed with Friedman's argument justifying the accumulation of great riches amongst a few. Without such inequity, the monies needed to promote any political cause would have to be raised from the contributions of many individuals, and the process of persuading such large numbers would itself be costly, time consuming, and, in the end, unsuccessful. A single wealthy individual could more easily be persuaded to provide the necessary financial backing. One did not have to worry about financial and political power being concentrated in the hands of a few, since a diversity of viewpoints was likely to prevail even among the wealthy.

Aven's own experience confirmed the force of governmental control over the news. That was what MOP had been about. Friedman argued that free political expression—an essential component in the quest for political freedom—could come only with free-private-capitalist ownership of the media. Government control, to whatever degree, would give those in power far too much say in the political process. Few politicians could resist utilizing such an advantage. Friedman's views on the role of government, placed in a contemporary context, did not differ from those set forth by Adam Smith two centuries earlier. Aven was fascinated with the argument against government provision of the nation's major parks and resort areas. He looked up to see Gaylord's glistening white teeth at the door.

"Hey, Aven, how 'bout a breath of air before the session? You've been reading that stuff all morning. First thing ya' know, you're gonna believe it. You must be finding it a trifle dismal."

"Quite the contrary. I've never been more stimulated in my life. Your ideas and economic principles have to work for us...."

"Aven, they're not my ideas. I just work here."

As they continued their relaxed walk, Aven began to question Gaylord.

"Tell me something, Gaylord. The new editions of *The Road to Serfdom*, the ones at the ministry, was there an errata sheet that came with them?"

"Ya' found a *mistake*? That's hard to believe. I thought those guys were never wrong."

From moments after they had first met, Aven had developed a real liking for Gaylord. And yet there were times—the present being one—when Gaylord's effort at humor was less than fully appreciated. Like Rena, Gaylord showed a certain irreverence towards Adam and his sons. Aven was willing to admit that the twelve disciples, by contrast, did deserve the impiety cast their way.

"No, Gaylord, I don't mean a mistake in the text. The mistake appears to be in the numbering of the chapters, both in the table of contents and on the initial page of each new chapter."

"What can ya' expect from economists? They really get turned on to *random* numbers."

"The numbers are not random, they're in perfect sequence."

"Oh...I see what you're talkin' about."

"I don't think you do, Gaylord, nor are you really trying to."

"Sorry, Aven. Shoot."

"Ten is missing."

"Ten who?"

Aven could not muffle the laugh.

"You're a good man. I have a feeling there's going to be a lot of laughs ahead."

"You're a good man too, Aven...it's time to get on back."

It took only a few minutes to walk back to the ministry. The two traded observations on the women they passed along the way. It was clear that while the best of friends, their taste differed considerably.

TING

"Gaylord, there's something strange about that elevator."

"The tenth floor is missing?"

Professor Leslie Fair was seated at her desk. A few other economists were in the room, fully involved with their monitors. Paula was already seated, and she gave Aven a fond hello as he and Gaylord sat down. Professor Fair stood, apparently intending to speak from a stationary position behind her desk. She was wearing a simple blue dress with a delicate floral pattern in pastel shades of rose and pink. Aven wondered if this is what Paula had anticipated.

Paula leaned towards Gaylord.

"Poor Miss Bonnie Brillo, she's got no globes."

Gaylord whispered in Aven's ear.

"Paula thinks the professor is very neatly dressed but flat as a pancake."

Aven glanced up to the economist. She was staring at him, with what appeared to be a look of impatience. He mouthed the words, "I'm sorry," and Professor Fair, with a slight upward jerk of her head, began to speak.

"Good morning, class. The session today concerns the most fundamental issue in your reorganization, namely, the *p-r-o-p-e-r r-o-l-e* of *g-o-v-e-r-n-m-e-n-t* in your economy. The French best captured the idea in their phrase...."

Leslie Fair paused, surveying the conference table, as if to be sure that everyone was paying attention.

"HANDS OFF...HANDS OFF...HANDS OFF."

She seemed to grow taller and slimmer with each repetition.

"Two words that will be a beacon for each of you as you navigate the waters ahead. Follow their beam, and your ship of state will have a bon voyage."

Aven sensed that the professor was rather pleased with her foray into elegant metaphor. He realized that she was lecturing directly from the book that he had held in his hands earlier in the day.

"...and thus, the proper role for the monetary authority...in our country we call it the Fed—perhaps Rube might be appropriate for your nation...."

Gaylord chuckled.

"Hey, man, she's got a sense of humor."

"Gentlemen! I do understand that economics is not everyone's favorite subject, but I would appreciate your attention."

Aven continued to study the fingernails on his left hand.

"As I was saying, since humans are inherently fallible, the money supply should be set on what we like to call 'automatic pilot.'"

Professor Fair continued her explanation, but Aven found it difficult to remain attentive. Matters did not improve as the professor turned to international trade. Aven did notice that Leslie kept looking over to Professor Treyd's unoccupied desk while she spoke. Now and then a word or phrase would register.

"...gold standard...balance of payments...capital flight..."

Aven began to wonder whether these economists thought of anything besides travel.

"...free floating exchange rates are the way to go...remove all tariffs and nontariff restrictions...free trade is the only route."

Aven stifled a comment he wanted to relay to Gaylord. As the professor turned to the topic of fiscal policy, she spoke as one might when discussing leprosy, and when uttering the name Keynes, she spat out the word as if she had bitten into a banana slug.

After what seemed an eternity, Professor Fair turned to some specific policy issues, and Aven's interest was restored. Free choice in education made good sense, though it was not as revolutionary as the privatization of the nation's parks. This issue, however, did not provide the cerebral and gut-level fireworks of what was to follow. Professor Fair had begun a commentary on the outrages of what she referred to as occupational licensure.

"…a retrogression to the medieval guild system…restriction on the free-dom of individuals…a widespread evil…the strongest case, medicine, *is no case at all.*"

At this point, Professor Fair paused.

"Director _____, it's noon, time to break for lunch. I'd be happy to sus-pend my remarks until two this afternoon, or continue on for a bit. I could finish this section within an hour or so."

Paula continued filing her nails as she spoke.

"Professor Fair, the import of your comments on medical practice will give us much more to chew on than lunch, and we can notify the dining hall that some of us will be late. I'm sure we'd prefer that you continue."

"Speak for yourself."

"Hush, Gaylord. Why don't you let the chef know we'll be a little bit late?"

Professor Fair continued. The monotonic quality of her voice did not de-tract from the beauty of her message. Aven was not even aware of Gaylord's re-turn, nor was he cognizant of the fact that it was nearing two o'clock when the professor concluded. Other than a faint trace of perspiration on her dress at the armpits, Professor Leslie Fair seemed as fresh and as tidy as when she had be-gun speaking nearly three hours earlier.

PING

They left the elevator on their way to a belated lunch.

"If you want to know the truth, I thought she looked better in the white and blue blazer."

"I thought she looked better sittin' 'stead of standin'."

"Looks aside, her ideas were stunning…and I think they'll fit our new na-tion like a glove."

Gaylord gave Aven a friendly pat on the shoulder.

"That's not bad, I just hope they're not too threadbare."

"I wish you men would stop talking economics long enough for us to get something to eat. I'm totally famished."

The waiter greeted them.

"Good afternoon. I'm sorry, but we're out of oysters. A group from the Supplé-Costa-Price session ate us out of the entire month's allotment. I wonder what must have gone on upstairs. They certainly were in a lively mood."

Somehow Aven managed to enjoy his lunch without the oysters, but not without a pang of regret. The stimulation from the session he attended, along with that provided by fantasies of what might have occurred in the session he missed, lingered through the rest of the afternoon. He did enjoy the swim and sauna with Gaylord but paid little attention to the new recreational facilities.

"That was great, Gaylord. We should try to get down there more often."

They walked to the first level.

"See you tomorrow…and don't forget, we're all having dinner."

"I wouldn't miss it, Aven."

Rena awaited Aven's arrival. For whatever reason, she did not resume the earnest encounter of the two preceding evenings.

"All work and no play makes Janeck a dull boy, and besides, Aven, you probably haven't done all the reading yet."

"Not quite, but I'm getting there, Rena. And tomorrow night we'll have you outnumbered anyway. So perhaps it's you that might welcome the interlude."

Aven wondered to himself how many other couples were lucky enough to enjoy the pleasure of such lively and intelligent banter. A give-and-take that never turned hostile.

"I'm open to any suggestions."

They went to a nearby theater and saw an Amerikan film that Rena had been lobbying for for some time. During the walk home, the events of the past few days began to sink in.

"Do you have any idea how much we've accomplished these past five days, and there's still tomorrow, *and* the dinner with Gaylord and Pa…, Mzzz. Barnum."

"I wouldn't miss it, Aven."

"That's funny."

"What's funny? Surely not the film?"

"What film?"

"Aaaaven."

Rena kicked him in the shin, gently.

"No, what you said. 'I wouldn't miss it, Aven.' Those were exactly Gaylord's words when we left the ministry."

"Sounds like we shouldn't miss it. But, love, you are right about what we seem to have accomplished. For what end remains to be seen."

Aven had opened his mouth to reply, but was too slow.

"Oops, sorry, love. That subject is off limits tonight. It slipped out. I'm at your mercy. Select my punishment."

"Another Bach cello suite?"

"Just one. I think the sixth will soothe your lust for justice."

The warmth of Bach's sixth lingered through the morning ritual. Rena remained in bed as Aven finished his tea and the dusting.

"Don't forget to dress for dinner. Bye."

"Bye, Aven."

"Good morning."

"Good morning sir…damn stupid crazy fucker…"

PI—NG

"The last day. No doubt today's sessions are important, but to tell you the truth, I can't wait for Monday to arrive."

"My, my," said Paula, "you are in a rush. Don't forget about the dinner tonight."

"Yeah, I wouldn't miss it, Aven."

"I wouldn't either, Gaylord."

"…and you *dare not* overlook *Sunday*."

"Sunday? Paula, there's nothing planned for Sunday? I thought…?"

"Planned? No Aven, it's our day of rest, and rejuvenation. Everyone needs a little, ah, spiritual revival. I always get mine on Sunday."

"That's right, Aven. Nothing planned for Sunday, just what we Americans like to call R 'n' R."

"Rock and roll?"

"Well, not exactly, but…."

Gaylord interrupted Paula, who seemed to be slightly annoyed.

"Not at all, Aven. It's an old Army term for rest and recreation."

"I can hardly wait for tomorrow myself…oweeeeeeeee."

Paula appeared to have lost the flow of the conversation and looked wistfully toward the ceiling.

"Paula, if you don't mind telling Aven and me about today."

"Oh yes, about today. Well, I thought the best way to utilize our time and resources is to put all of the ministry staff upstairs in the combo room with Professor Fourkaste…."

"But I thought…"

"Hear me out, Gaylord. I said the *staff*, not Aven."

Paula turned directly towards Aven.

"Nothing will serve to enthuse your people more, Aven, than a day with Sonny Fourkaste. They have been asked to digest a great many ideas, and it's likely they've accumulated an equal number of uncertainties, all quite counterproductive. Six hours with the professor will eliminate these. Even though the reorganization is foolproof, experience has taught us that the first few days of any dramatic change can have its problems. It will be of great help for the MOP staff to start off on the right foot. And as for you, Aven, I have arranged for the advisers who arrived yesterday to meet us right here."

"Just the three of us?"

"Yes, Aven, in this cozy office. There's a good bit of material to cover—the political structure, the family, the church. The advisers—two social scientists and a minister—are from the University of Chicago, and of course their ideas are strongly influenced by the economists. Isn't that right, Gaylord?"

"It is, Paula. In fact, economists pretty much run the universities these days."

"Like Lenin's imperialists."

"Right on, Aven, and from the way they fly around from country to country, first-class of course, with their fancy attaché cases, lap-top computers, and holier-than-thou smirks on their pasty faces, I think they enjoy being on top."

"Well, gentlemen, that's only as it should be. Look at what their ideas have done for us in America."

Gaylord, with arms outstretched, bent at the waist. "Aaaameeennnn, brothers and sisters."

"Gaylord!"

"Sorry, Paula. Oops, looks as if the colonized have arrived."

The door swung open. Three men walked in, each with an uncertain gait. In contrast to the economists, the men were wearing distinctive plaid jackets, which provided a bold contrast with the rest of their outfits. The three wore solid color turtleneck knit shirts—red, white, and blue, respectively—under their jackets. Their pants matched the shirts. Unlike the economists, who had bloodless faces, these men had ruddy complexions, especially their noses. None were wearing glasses, and beyond the bright coloring of their clothing and faces, there were no other distinguishing features.

"Good morning, gentlemen. I hope you had a good flight. Allow me to introduce Director _____ and his assistant, Mr. Creamer. Aven and Gaylord, this is Professor Mack O'Valey, our specialist on political organization, Professor Gene Puhl, a demographer whose specialty is the family, and the humble Reverend Mr. Neil Doone."

Handshakes were exchanged as Paula turned back to the visitors.

"Now, you have to tell the director, and perhaps, given the coziness of our setting, I can say Aven...."

"Fine with me, Paula."

"...what you discuss with Aven is really of no immediate interest to others in the ministry staff. I believe we should begin with the political structure. Professor O'Valey, the table is yours, and, ah, Gaylord, if you don't mind *too* terribly, would you please call up for some tea."

"Thank you very much, Paula."

The professor's voice was pleasantly engaging, and Aven knew he was going to find the session worthwhile.

"By the way, our flight was fine, except for the seats. They're terribly cramped for an intercontinental flight."

"Mack, you should know by now, the economists are the only ones permitted first-class travel. Been that way for some time."

"Too long, if you ask me. We've all been converted to their creed. Why not a little *equality*, too?"

"Hey, Mack, ya know, that word's not in their spell checker."

"Hush, Gaylord. Professor, we do have a lot to do, if you don't mind."

"Forgive me, Paula. I'll get right to the heart of the matter. Even with limitations, government is the most powerful *coercive* force in any society, powerful because it is so coercive, and essential precisely because it is coercive. The tasks that *society deems essential* and cannot be organized through the market or accomplished through voluntary actions of its citizens must, by definition, be given to government. With such powers granted to a few elected leaders, it behooves us to understand their *motivation*."

"Excuse me, Professor, Mack, isn't that obvious? People seek positions of leadership so that they can advance their nation's interests, the well-being of its pop...."

Aven noticed a familiar professorial smirk and simultaneously realized his mistake.

"Oh, of course...."

"Precisely. Leaders are no different from any other men. They *maximize* their *utility*. The butcher does it in the shop. The elected leader does it in the halls of government...."

"And the prostitute does it in...."

"Shuushh!"

"You *could* say that, Gaylord. And we need to know what actually provides the leaders with their utility. Obviously, income, power, and prestige are important, but without the *position* of leadership itself, utility will be zero. Thus, the clever insight provided by economists—those who colonized our discipline—defined utility as nothing more than being in office. Now, to be in office you need votes, the most votes. Thus, politicians maximize their utility by maximizing the votes they receive. If this point is clear, we can continue."

"Amen."

"Thank you, Reverend. Let us proceed. In a modern industrial society, we can assume first that most citizens are not born with the necessary knowledge to guide their voting decisions and second that the acquisition of such knowledge is not costless. From these simple assumptions, a number of fascinating insights can be drawn. The leaders won't always know what the public wants, and the people won't know what their leaders are or have been doing. Thus, both citizens and politicians are likely to be ill-informed about many public issues."

"Professor, I'm not following you. Are you suggesting that our leaders function in the dark?"

"No way, Aven, they just seem to be...."

"Quiet!"

"A reasonable question, Aven, to which I'm happy to say the answer is no. There are several mechanisms that allow our leaders to work, not in the bright light of day, but quite effectively nonetheless. For one, voters or their spokesmen do debate the issues in the public arena, and the leaders and would-be leaders must do so also. A modest amount of information can be transmitted in this manner, what might be called persuasion. Party ideology provides the second...."

"Amen."

"Excuse me, Professor. Your first point is quite clear, but I thought you said earlier that leaders were like the butcher...."

"And the whore."

"Shusssh!"

"...motivated by self-interest alone. What has ideology got to do with...?"

"Nothing, and a great deal as well. You are quite right, Aven, party leaders do not *have* ideologies, but they do *use* ideology as an effective way of advertising their product, namely their party and its platform. With ideological labels, voters easily learn how the leaders stand on the many issues, and the leaders can select the label that is most attractive to the voters. For example, the leaders who thought that a large part of the electorate was xenophobic by nature might advertise themselves as the War Party...."

"Or the Anti-Hopies."

"Excuse me, Professor. Gaylord, this is no longer funny. Please?"

"It's fine, Paula. A little levity in these matters never hurt, and I must admit, Gaylord does have a wry sense of humor...."

Gaylord was beaming, Paula was frowning, and Aven was liking the professor more and more.

"...now, as I was saying, the leader selects the party ideology much like a brand name."

Paula was now beaming, too.

"Of course, with free elections, the leaders cannot stray too far from their advertised ideology or party label, but neither will they be overly constrained by their party logo."

The professor paused as he reached for his cup of tea.

Gaylord spoke in restrained tones.

"Paula, perhaps we could take a short break. I'll have the tea warmed and order some lunch."

"Amen."

"That's a gnarly idea. Gentlemen, if you don't mind, I'm going to powder my nose."

As Paula left, Aven turned to Gaylord.

"Why do you suppose Paula's annoyed with you?"

"Beats me, Aven. Probably nothing. I'll be right back."

The three Amerikans chatted amiably with Aven. They were impressed with all of the Gdansk furnishings, though the executive couch evoked the greatest interest.

"I never did develop the habit of an afternoon nap."

"Oh, you really should," said Professor Puhl, "even if it's only for twenty minutes. Does wonders for the soul."

"Amen."

It occurred to Aven that these were the first words from the demographer while the preacher appeared to know only one word. Paula, Gaylord, and a fresh pot of tea arrived in rapid succession, and the group returned to the conference table.

"Information, yes, information. Mmmmm, this tea is hot. Where information is expensive, it is unlikely that many voters will find it worth acquiring...."

"Excuse me, Professor. I know you've only begun, but while the information may be costly, the issues themselves are, in your own terms, of great significance. In such a case, it seems to me that a rational citizen voter would weigh the costs against the benefits and in many cases find the cost of the information well worthwhile."

"Hey, Aven, you're all right, baby."

"Hush."

"You *are* all right, Aven, and you're going to be even better. However, the decision to acquire the information is not based on how important the issue is but rather on what impact the citizen voter can have on the issue, having acquired the costly information. In a world where millions of people cast votes, it is apparent that one vote is meaningless, nil, zero...."

"Zip. Squat!"

"Shh!"

"...the wonderful paradox is that the more people who cast ballots, the less valuable is a single vote, and from the voter's perspective, the less influential is his vote. To use Gaylord's terminology, a thoughtful citizen will realize his vote isn't worth squat. Thus, under such circumstances, what is the *rational* citizen voter to do?"

"Not acquire the information...and not vote?"

"Come now, Aven. Don't be hesitant. That's precisely what we should expect. It's what economists and all liberated political scientists call rational ignorance."

"Amen."

"A few citizens may learn about some of the issues for the fun of it, and a few will learn where the issue is of overwhelming importance. Labor leaders will learn a good bit about pending labor legislation; doctors about medical insurance laws; newspaper publishers and reporters about free speech legislation. It's only *rational* for them to do so. And because of their interest and their willingness to devote significant sums to lobbying for these single issues, they have the dominant say in the political outcome. For the average person, very little is to be gained from an active and inquiring involvement in the political process."

"I think I understand. But you have described a population whose rational actions provide the leader with no information about their preferences and how they might want to be governed. What is the leader to do without such information?"

"Use it!"

"Use what?"

"The information."

"What infor...?"

"The information that the rationally ignorant electorate *does not care*. In fact, this makes the job of governance a good bit easier than it might have been."

For some time, Aven had been in awe of the impending economic reorganization. Now the same excitement was being brought to the political process. He followed the professor's words with consummate delight and understanding. During lunch, the conversation turned informal, and Aven did raise a few questions about the desirability of a two-party system. Professor O'Valey persuaded him before they had finished their soup.

After lunch they turned to the other visitors. Professor Puhl discussed such perennial social concerns as polygamy, selective mating, divorce and the marriage market, the demand for children, allocation of time within the household, and the rationality of altruistic behavior towards one's offspring. The essence of his remarks was, however, that the family performs two essential functions in any society: reproducing the workforce and passing on the norms and mores of the society so necessary as a social lubricant. Aven was reminded of Hayek's concerns. If ever the family were to break down, society would be faced with the cruel choice of anarchy or a government-imposed code of conduct. He thought to himself, "In the former we live as animals; in the latter, as slaves."

Professor Puhl completed his remarks. The preacher had little to add beyond punctuating Puhl's conclusion with another "Amen." When asked whether he had any comments of his own, the Reverend Mr. Doone got up from his chair, walked to the shelf that supported Rena's picture and the three leatherbound books, kneeled, clasped his hands, bowed his head, and intoned, "Let us pray."

It was four-forty when the six individuals returned to their feet and exchanged good-byes.

"Have a nice flight, gentlemen."

"Gaaaaylord? Would you for once stop being such an asswipe."

"Come on, Paula, you know Gaylord. He doesn't have a nasty bone in his body, just a small streak of irreverence, and besides, you have to stop fighting. We're all going out for dinner. Rena and I have been looking forward to it."

Gaylord smiled.

"Yeah, I wouldn't miss it."

They took Aven's limo from the ministry. Aven got out at the flat, while Paula and Gaylord continued on.

"See you in an hour."

"Bye."

The door remained closed as Aven approached it. He read the attached note: "Be back in plenty of time, Love, Rena." Aven had not been in the flat for more than a few minutes when the phone rang. It was Gaylord.

"Paula asked me to call. She's going to need more time with her hair. We should be there close to seven. See you then."

SATURDAYNITEDINNER

■ ■ ■ ■ ■ ■ ■ ■ ■ ■ ■ ■ ■ ■ ■ ■

*A*lone."

The peculiarity of the situation struck him immediately.

"I hope she isn't too...."

"Hi. Sorry I'm late. I wanted to pick up some flowers."

"Hi, yourself. There's no rush. Gaylord and Mzzz. Barnum...."

"Love, you *are* among friends. You can call the lady by her first name, if she has one. By the way, shouldn't we call Pero's?"

"It's Paula. Actually, Rena, I forgot to mention, Mzzz., ah, Paula suggested that we go to one of the new places opening up on Monday. They're putting on a special dinner for us *tonight*. How can we go wrong, four rather important people, after all? What are you planning to wear?"

"My diamond tiara, of course."

Aven started to speak, but Rena was too quick for him. She kissed him on her way to the bathroom. He finished the wine in both their glasses.

"Aven, I think they're here."

Aven opened the door. Gaylord and Paula were both dressed in black—Gaylord in a black leather suit with red shirt and tie, and Paula in a linen dress adorned with a gold necklace.

"Come in. Rena will be out in a minute."

"Oweeeeeee, what a quaint little apartment...."

"Here she is. Paula, Gaylord, I'd like you to meet Rena, the reason I come to work with a smile on my face every morning."

"It's a pleasure to meet you."

"Hello, Rena, and I bet you're the reason Aven has a smile on his face when he *leaves* work every evening."

Aven could tell by her voice that Rena took a liking to Gaylord. He was less certain about her feelings towards Paula. As they were all leaving, Paula asked

Rena about the perfume she was wearing. Rena pointed to the bouquet of flowers she had brought home earlier. The two couples arranged themselves in the limo, with Rena joining Gaylord in the rear seat.

"Where are we going? And better yet, when are we going to get there? I'm so hungry I could eat a pig."

"We're go...."

"It's a good thing, Aven. That's exactly what you're gonna get."

"Gaylord, I wish you wouldn't interrupt all the time. We're going to a smashing place, Rita's Roadside Rib Rack. I think it's within a kilometer or so."

The group had long since left the inhabited sections of the city. The sound of the motor provided the only evidence of movement. As the limo came out of an extended curve in the highway, the darkness vanished. In its place stood Rita's Roadside Rib Rack. At first, the sign was all that was visible. Ten meters in height, it extended the length of a soccer field. Each letter contained hundreds of small light bulbs whose combined candle power lit up the sky in every direction. The expansive parking area was empty. The driver parked the car a few feet from the doors at the center of the building. The car was instantly surrounded by four young men dressed as infant quadruplets at a costume party. The quartet opened the limo doors while singing in ascending thirds, first one, then each in turn:

"Welcome."

"Welcome."

"Welcome."

"Welcome," finally joining in perfect four-part harmony:

"To Ri—taaaaaa's."

The party was escorted into Rita's and greeted by an older man dressed in formal attire.

"Good evening, Ms. Barnum, I presume?"

"Yes, that's us, and you must be Ronnie. Do tell Rita that these young men are adorable."

"Thank you, Ms. Barnum. If you'd follow me."

The main dining area, a single oversized room, was softly lit, with plants scattered throughout.

"Oh my, this is lovely."

"Yes, but...."

Rena's words echoed Aven's sentiments. The hangarlike room was indeed pleasantly lit and decorated, but there was only one solitary table with four chairs located in the room's center.

"Oh, this is a special dinner just for us. The permanent furnishings will be installed for Monday's grand opening."

The elderly gentleman who greeted them turned them over to a second man of similar age and attire.

"Good evening. My name is Roger."

They followed Roger to their table, which was round and attractively set. Roger scurried from Paula to Rena, helping both women into their seats.

"Randy will be your waiter for this evening. He'll be with you in a moment."

"Oh, this is going to be tooooo exciting. Like a world premiere in Hollywood."

"Good evening. I'm Randy, and I'll be your waiter tonight. As you might have noticed, there is no menu...."

Aven and the others suddenly became very interested in what Randy was about to say.

"...but not to worry. Rita's ribs are out of this world. And all you can eat. We'll be serving salad first, and then the ribs will come as quickly as you can eat them. Ruth and Rosy will be your water girls for the evening, Ralph and Rastus will be your rib runners, and I'll be standing in the wings just in case. Would you like to look at our wine and beer lists?"

"If you don't mind a suggestion, there ain't no way wine and ribs mix. I think we oughta get a large pitcher of beer...."

"Sounds good, Gaylord."

They weren't far into their salads before the conversation turned to speculation about the rib chef's credentials.

"I guess they have to go to school, as with any other profession. Paula, do you know anything about the chef here at Rita's? I'm sure he went to some sort of culinary school. I bet he has quite a fancy degree."

"To be totally honest with you, Rena, I really don't know. Seems to me that we don't require degrees of our chefs, do we, Gaylord?"

"Maybe a pigskin or two."

"Gaylord, I think you mean sheepskin, but of course you don't require a *degree*. How could you forget Professor Fair's remarks on occupational licensure. Degrees are merely an artificial barrier designed to limit entry into the profession. All the degrees in the world wouldn't amount to a hill of...."

"Which reminds me, we should ask Randy for a side order of baked beans. Here he comes now."

"How's everything? May I have your salad plates removed?"

"Wonderful, and Randy, I think Gaylord does have a question."

"Yeah, Randy, does Rita's chef work with a pigskin or a sheepskin?"

"I beg your pardon, sir?"

"It's okay, Randy, a private joke. But we would like beans with our ribs."

"Certainly, the ribs and beans will be up shortly."

Randy began the long walk back to the kitchen.

"Could we get back to the question of degrees?"

"Sure, Rena. What do you want to know?"

"Well, if I understood correctly, you were arguing that professional chefs didn't need a degree. Did you mean that such persons don't need any formal training either?"

"Rena, I don't want to debate the definition of 'formal' training. A chef needs to acquire the appropriate skills, and there are numerous ways of doing so. However, a degree from some high and mighty culinary school is little more than a means for limiting the number of chefs. A few fat and greedy chefs get together, decide what credentials are necessary, and see to it that Rita hires only those with so-called qualifications. Presto, in one fell swoop you've protected your job and kept your salary higher than it would be with freedom of entry into the profession."

"I grant you, having the degree isn't the only way to learn how to cut up ribs, but it does guarantee that the holder can do it. And it enables Rita to find a chef when she needs one, doesn't it?"

"Alas, Rena, a degree does not guarantee the holder can carve a rib, at least not in the most modern and effective way. Nor does the diploma make it easier for the Ritas of the world; it makes it *harder*, especially when the chefs decide who can teach at the culinary academies and which academies can grant the degree."

"I see the point, but then how would Rita know? Where would she learn about the prospective chef's abilities?"

"That's easy. Through the only test worth its salt—the market test."

"Oh, I get it, the wonderful wacky world of the economist to the rescue once again. And what if Rita hires a chef that doesn't know *his* porker's rib from a sow's ear? How'd you like to be gnawing away on a floppy ear right about now?"

"Hey, far out, Rena."

"Be quiet, Gaylord. Let Aven answer."

"No, that's okay, Paula. Rena's right. Chefs can botch an operation, but how many such meals do you think our malpracticing chef could serve before Rita would give *her* the boot?"

"Oh, that's fine, and in the meantime we've had one lousy meal. Hardly sounds like paradise to me."

"No, it's not. It's the real world. There's no such thing as perfect information, but the market is a wonderful institution for gathering information in an efficient manner."

"Sorry, Aven, I can't buy it. It would be more efficient if we established standards and had chefs demonstrate their abilities before entering Rita's kitchen and poisoning us."

"In paradise your scheme's a real winner. Not here though."

Paula and Gaylord watched wide-eyed as the two did battle. It was Rena's turn to serve, or was it a volley?

"Yes, here though. Our chefs establish boards to certify and maintain standards. That makes more sense to me than eating a pig's ear, even if it is rare."

"Rena, your faith in humanity is wonderful, and I love you for it, but it's often misplaced. If you've noticed, the chef's professional society, what's it called...?"

"C-H-E-F, cooks, hashers, epicures, and frauds?"

"Gaylord!"

"...maybe it should be if it isn't. The supposed monitors are the chefs themselves. Don't you see? They're only interested in protecting their jobs, and their incomes...."

"And skins."

"Gay...."

"That too, Gaylord. Rena, the examining board protects the chefs from the market, but it's the market that protects consumers from the fraudulent and incompetent chefs. In our world, there is no better way. When was the last time a group of university professors recommended dismissal of a colleague for incompetence, and the same is true for lawyers—every profession, as a matter of fact. We'd be a lot better off if we just eliminated all such licensing boards and let the market expose the incompetents."

Aven picked up his glass of beer and took a long deliberate swallow. Rena refused to concede.

"Do you really believe your own rhetoric? What about doctors?"

And in her best upper-class accent, she continued.

"Oh, terribly sorry madam, I cut in the wrong place. Pity. Neither you nor I am likely to *survive* the market test. Aven, you do get carried away at times."

It was Rena's turn to take a long sip of beer. Aven continued munching away on the plate of ribs. As he kept eating, Rena kept sipping. Aven had finished three ribs before taking a clean napkin. Randy had brought several for each diner. When Aven was finished with the napkin, he picked up his beer glass once again. Now they were both staring at each other over the top of their glass.

Aven drained his glass first and broke the uneasy silence.

"Rena, do you really think there's a difference between a doctor and Rita's rib chef?"

Rena put her glass down and started chewing on her plate of ribs, but with less zeal than Aven had exhibited moments earlier. Soon all four were involved with their ribs and their thoughts. They were keeping Ralph and Rastus busy.

"Mmmmm, these ribs are special."

"Mmmmmm, I'll say so."

"Mmmmm, me too."

"Mmmmm, yes, special…pass the beer please."

The preceding discussion had altered the mood, which Aven and Gaylord broke at the same time.

"Did I…"

"How many…"

"Sorry, Gaylord…go ah…"

"No, go ahead, Aven. Really, I'm having a great time eatin' Rita's ribs. And thank the Lord that the market mechanism worked this time."

That did it. The mood lightened, and Aven took hold of the moment.

"Paula, tell me something."

Paula warbled slightly as she replied.

"You name it, big boy."

"When we sat down this evening, there was a note reserving the table."

"Yes?"

It wasn't clear who had uttered this brief question.

"It said Ms. Paula T. Barnum. M, S, Mzzz. with an S. Paula, that's not the way you Amerikans spell Mzzz.?"

Paula seemed confused. Rena wasn't.

"Aven, Ms. has always been spelled that way."

"Well, that's silly. I don't understand it. All this time I thought it was Mzzz., you know m, z, z, z."

"Oh, like a bee, zzzzzz, zzzzzz, zzzzz."

"Rena, believe it or not, I am trying to be serious. Say 's,' each of you."

"Esss."

"Esss."

"Esssssssssss…"

"Don't you see?"

"See what?"

"M-s, M-s should be pronounced MESS. But we don't say Mess Barnum, we say Mzzz Barnum."

"Aven's got a great point. If you ask me, profound. And by the way, ladies, why did you start using Mess or Mizzz or whatever it should be? What was wrong with good old Miss and Mrs.? Men get along nicely with just one title, Mr. How come you need three?"

"Actually, Gaylord, we need three precisely because you have only one. Men have been able to live in a world *without* the need to identify their marital status. But women have been forced to identify themselves. Mrs. means someone else's property; Miss has been a sign, like 'available' or 'unoccupied.' Why have we felt the need to put ourselves on the auction block? Ms. puts us on an equal footing with men. At least in title."

A trace of a frown appeared as she looked at Aven.

"And what, may I ask, is so funny about this effort at equality? I know you'd prefer your women barefoot and pregnant, but there are a few liberated men around."

"Hey now, I'm as liberated as the next man. And I'm all for equality of title. You've just gone at it in the wrong way."

"Tell us the right way, love."

"Simple. *Our* way."

"Of course."

"No, not of course. I doubt that you understand. This Ms., Miss, Mrs. business is way too complicated. Instead of women trying to be like men, it would be far simpler for men to follow your lead."

"Aven, tell me you're feeling all right."

"I haven't felt better. What we need is some rationality. If married men were differentiated from single men, as most women are now, we'd have equality *and* rationality."

"Dear me, I'm not sure we could handle all of those blessings at the same time. But tell us, what titles would you use?"

"Easy! Mister for the single male...."

"And for the married man?"

"Master, of course. What else?"

Aven's smile bordered on the obscene, and Gaylord's was similar.

"Oweeeeeee, Aven, you blow me away...you're adorable."

Paula had no sooner finished this brief paean than Aven felt a sharp pain in his left shin. He looked across the table to Rena. Her eyes were dark, and her lips mouthed the words, "NO YOU'RE NOT!"

DESSERT

■■■■■■■■■■■■■■■■

*P*aula's squeals and Aven's pain eased. Gaylord's chuckles and Rena's smoldering, both somewhat less intense, lingered. Aven did all he could to avoid Rena's glare. Gaylord changed the subject.

"Hey, guys, if we keep eating away at Aven's ego, he's gonna be impossible to work with come Monday. Looks to me like we've done enough damage to Rita's ribs as well. They were super, Paula. Why don't we check out the desserts? I could sure go for some apple pie à la mode...."

"Gaylord, you can't be serious. That sort of cheese went out of style with rumble seats and Dick Tracy. We're in the twenty-first century now."

"You're probably right, Paula, but there's no harm in asking...."

"Well, I suppose not, if you don't mind Ralph thinking we're all a bunch of clueless dorkmunders. But I don't feel like an eggo, and I don't intend to act like an eggo!"

"Sounds as if you might be ready for dessert."

It was Randy, who must have heard Paula from his station in the far corner of the room.

"Why yes, Randy, we are. By the way, you wouldn't happen to have apple pie à la mode, would you?"

"Apple pie à la, ah, what? Can't say that we do, sir. Let me show you what we do have."

As Randy left the table, he signaled to Ruth and Rosy, who, along with Ralph and Rastus, cleared the table. Despite the distance to the kitchen, the residue disappeared rapidly. The manner in which the four young people worked infected Aven and the others.

Rena reached across the table to touch Aven's hand.

"Aven, I *am* having a grand time. Hope your shin doesn't hurt too much."

"Okay, you lovebirds. Too much of that and you'll lose your appetite for dessert, which appears to be on the way."

Gaylord was right. It wasn't long before the diners recognized Randy and his four helpers approaching the table from afar. The servers carried a large tray on which rested an assortment of odd-shaped objects. In no time, they arrived at the table.

"Our selection is terribly limited, and I do hope you will forgive Rita. The dessert chefs from Amerika, France, and Israel were able to prepare a small assortment for this evening. Soon seventeen other nations will be represented in our kitchen and on this tray. Here we have a portion of the Alice B. Toklas collection. The first adorable dish is what we call Cecil Beaton's Iced Apples. It's...."

"I'll take two."

"Gaylord, hush. Let's hear what Randy has to say about the other scrumptious-looking goodies."

"...and these are Lady Fingers, filled with Alice's infamous Bavarian cream perfect love, what the English like to call Sponge Fingers."

"And two of those."

"...we also have Vermont's Blueberry Hill frozen fruit loaf."

Randy paused, as if expecting Gaylord to order, but Gaylord had joined Rena and Aven in the giggles. Even Paula had her hand to her mouth. Somewhat resignedly, Randy pushed on through the Jewish Gugelhupf and Hamantaschen. He then moved to the far end of the tray, where the French pastries sat off to themselves.

"We have our Bananas Baronnet, Mousse au Chocolat à l'Orange, Gateau au Chocolat, and only one glacé, mocha."

Randy and his helpers stood patiently while the diners discussed their selections.

Rena went first. "I'd like the chocolate cake, please."

Aven asked for the same.

"Oweeeee, I'd like one of those adorable tarts, what did you call them, Gasoontight?

"Oh, madam, you mean the Gugelhupf. Very good choice."

"And I think I'll have two of Cecil's iced apples after all."

"Very well, and coffee or tea...? Two of each. Good choice."

It wasn't long before Randy returned with their orders. Gaylord appeared in awe of Cecil's apples, which were huge. So, too, were the other desserts. They were also quite delicious, as anyone watching could have told from the enthusiastic way that Aven and his friends attacked the sweets.

"Oweeee, this is heavenly, but the selection's rather meager, doncha think?"

"I don't know, Paula. Seemed to me there was a nice assortment. We all found something to our liking without difficulty. Usually there are so many good things, I have trouble picking only one. This was easier."

"Well, I think that you're both right, ladies."

It was Aven at his mollifying best.

"I agree with Rena that we did find something to our liking. On the other hand, from an esthetic point of view, the tray was rather barren. A few more items might have added to our perception of choice, and as Randy said, that's a problem well on its way to a solution."

"Rena's right. I was more than satisfied with...."

"Hush, Gaylord, you'd be satisfied with Cecil's apples as a steady diet. But most of us demand variety, the spice of life. As far as I'm concerned, you can't get too much of a good thing."

Paula's earlier signs of unsteadiness remained.

"When she puts it that way, Rena, I think Paula makes a good point. How many times have you argued with me about the great diversity of our own nation. One of the real blessings of the new economic system will be its facility to satisfy these many different wants."

"Aven, we *are* having such a good time, perhaps...."

"Oh no, Rena, I think there's nothing more fun than a good seeryush intellectual discussion, oweeeee. I'm not suggesting that we do an M-C-squared number or anything, but a little dig-a-nafied talk among friends, what could be groovier?"

"Two more apples."

"Hush!"

"Very well, Paula. And since we are among friends, I assume that you and Gaylord will allow me to say something about your country...."

"Rena...."

"Aven, let me finish. In Amerika, they have more choice than anyone knows what to do with. How many breakfast cereals do you really need? How many brands of toothpaste and mouthwash? And how much time and energy go into the silly efforts to persuade consumers of subtle differences where there are none?"

"Uuuuuaaaaaaaaaaaaaaaaaa!"

It was a gasp that emanated deep from within her soul. Paula took a moment to regain her composure.

"Rena, there's a new desire born every day, and the spirit of American business is to capture each and every one. Where would we be today if the founders of General Motors followed Henry Ford's foolishness?"

"Fair enough, Paula. There is a difference between no choice at all and the recognition of human diversity. That was Ford's problem, though at times, I bet even some of your own countrymen and women yearn for a Model T world. The problem is that Amerikans are offered a multitude of options in areas of life that are trivial, and in those aspects of human existence that matter, the choices are trivial. If they exist at all."

"Uuuuuaaaaaaaaa."

Paula's mouth remained open, without movement.

"As always, love, you use words very nicely, but what do they mean? Where are important consumer affairs treated trivially?"

"Not just as consumers, Aven. As humans, citizens, as members of society. Look at Amerika. We are led to believe there is diversity in their *two* political parties."

"We do have elections, and the Democrats and Republicans engage in some pretty hefty knock-down drag-out fights every four years."

"Yes, and you know there's not a dime's worth of difference between the two. If you ask me, George Wallace was being overly generous with his money."

"Well, he was just a poor ol' country farmboy from Alabama, but I think I see what you are getting at, Rena."

"I don't see how you could, Gaylord, unless you weren't paying attention to Professor O'Valey."

"I was paying attention...except for the time I spent hunting for food and tea."

Gaylord grinned at Paula, who swayed in her chair quietly.

"Well, love, I wasn't there for the lecture or for the tea. Perhaps you could tell me and refresh Gaylord's memory at the same time."

"If you don't mind, Paula?"

The glare Paula had fixed on Gaylord dissolved as she turned to Aven. With both of the women at the table happy to discuss economic rationality, Aven set sail.

"In the first place, Rena, it is quite likely that a large portion of the public, perhaps a majority, will be ignorant of political issues."

"I'm with you so far, Aven."

"But not for the reasons you might expect."

"Of course. The political leaders lie to the public; they distort the issues and corrupt the process. How could anyone not be ignorant under such circumstances?"

"Not in a political system with free elections. Such conduct would not be tolerated for very long. But even in Amerika, with open and honest elections, much of the public is ignorant...."

"Oh, I see, they're all deaf and dumb."

"Nope. Sorry Rena, they're all what economists call rationally ignorant."

Aven spoke with force and conviction. And as she had been doing through-out these monologues, Rena listened with a look of interest, blended with what seemed a tinge of understanding.

"Well, that is very interesting, but I don't see what rational ignorance has to do with two parties that look more like Siamese twins."

"Good question…in part. One could organize the political system in sev-eral ways. The question is how best to achieve an effective and stable govern-ment, one that meets the needs of the public as efficiently as possible. We can rule out a one-party system. Such a system renders choice meaningless, unless the party knows exactly what the public wants.…"

"Or is good for them."

"Yes, Gaylord, and we have sufficient evidence on the outcomes in such societies. No, I think we can all agree that there must be *at least* two political parties. This will insure that the elected leaders, whose position depends on *win-ning* fairly run elections, respond to those participating. We could have *more* than two parties…but how many is.…"

"No, don't go on. Let me guess the next word. Is it *efficient?*"

"Close, Rena, but I think economists like to use *optimal* in this situation. Interestingly enough, the answer turns out to be two, precisely the number of parties in Amerika, and the same number that will exist for us."

"Aven, do you really believe that if Randy had given us a choice between Lady Fingers and Sponge Fingers, the four of us would have been satisfied? I doubt it."

"I wouldn't have been, though I can't speak for Gaylord. But your example only proves the point. Each of us can enjoy whatever dessert we might wish without in the least reducing anyone else's choice.…"

"How 'bout Cecil's?"

"Hush."

"I speak of a society where cannibalism is banned, Gaylord. Now, in the political process, there can be only one dessert, if you wish, eaten at any given time. All of the people must live with the single party in office. You could orga-nize the process to include several parties, as they do in Italy, France, Sweden, or Israel before the PLO abolished all parties. However, in every one of these countries, a *coalition* government is usually formed after each election. Rarely, if ever, does a single party capture a majority of the vote."

"And what, my love, is so awful about coalition, or compromise?"

"Nothing, I suppose. Like mixing Cecil's apples with some Gugelhupf and a pinch of mocha glacé. People would rarely get what they want, despite fre-quent efforts at forming a satisfactory government. And if they really wanted such a blend, there would be one party formed to provide it."

"Just like the old Gay-Jewish-Black Alliance in the States. Used to be called the Rainbow Coalition. But rainbows fade during storms."

"Oh my, is it raining?"

"No, Paula, Gaylord was just making a point. So by a process of elimination, we are back to two parties."

"No sale, Aven. How about a *right-wing* party and a *left-wing* party? The politicians would be off in the atmosphere while the *body* politic would be left thrashing on the ground, wingless, leaderless. Seems to me we'd be better off with a little compromise. Better that than the public being left in the lurch. Or should I say perch?"

"Aven, baby, your Rena is some chick."

"A lovebird and more. You're right, Gaylord. And you are too, Rena, almost. When I said two parties, I didn't mean any two parties. In your world of extremes, with one party in office, a substantial part of the electorate would be extremely dissatisfied, what economists like to call a *disequilibrium* situation, or what we know better as a recipe for revolution. What's required are two parties seeking the most votes, looking to the political spectrum where most of the voters are, the center. Rarely will you have a society where voters lie in the extremes, and rarely would such a society endure."

It was clear that Aven was nearing the end of his argument. He had the extended pause down to near perfection, and the look on his face displayed triumph without arrogance.

"With a body politic so well centered, it is perfectly proper for each of the two centrist parties to accommodate any fringe elements on the extremes."

"That's the good U.S. of A., Aven, with the right-wing Republicans and left-wing Democrats flapping away to their hearts' content."

"And, Gaylord, doing little harm to the body politic or the social fabric of the nation. It's an efficient and effective system and...."

"Ah, now I think I understand, and forgive me for being so dense. Your system, or the Amerikan system that we will soon inherit, enables those *few* interested citizens with uncommon views to attend the party of their choice, so long as they don't bother anyone. Meanwhile, the great majority get to choose between two identical parties. It would take me forever to cast my vote with sooooooo much diversity."

"Rena, you're exaggerating. I didn't say the two parties were *identical*. They do have to agree on the core values of the society, but they still maintain their differences."

"Aven, how much difference, really?"

"A dime's worth."

"Hush."

Gaylord's voice apparently had stirred Paula, who seemed asleep, to momentary consciousness.

"See, didn't I tell you that seer-y-ush dishcussions can be loads of fun...?"

"Yes, Paula, and remarkably informative as well...."

Rena was looking at Aven as she spoke. Aven's reply was preempted by Randy, who had returned to the table, inquiring about a liqueur.

Paula was asleep again. Rena decided for the others.

"Thanks very much, Randy, but I think we should save it for another time. We really have had a delightful evening. Everything's been wonderful."

"Thank *you*, madam. We've been honored to have you as our first patrons, and of course, the meal is on Rita."

Rena started to resist, but Aven put his hand gently on her arm.

"I do hope we will see you again soon. Can we help with the lady here?"

"No thanks, Randy, I've handled this situation many times...it's no problem."

Gaylord picked Paula up in his arms. Aven and Rena followed. Ronnie had Paula's stole waiting. No sooner had the door closed behind them than the limo appeared from out of the darkness. Just as quickly, the costumed young men scurried around the vehicle, singing as they opened the doors.

"Good-bye."

"So long."

"Farewell."

"Come back," and joining together, once again in splendid harmony:

"*Sooo-uuooo-uuooooon.*"

Gaylord gently dropped Paula in the rear seat and sat beside her. Rena shoved Aven, less gently but with affection, into the forward seat and snuggled up beside him. The three of them were giggling as they waved good-bye to the youthful quartet.

"Oh, man, that was some dinner. I'm glad I didn't miss it."

"Me too, Gaylord."

"It was fun. Even the intellectual *dishcushen.*"

With these words, Rena grabbed onto Aven's arm, put her head on his shoulder, and was silent the remainder of the trip home. So, too, were Aven and Gaylord.

"Good night. It was great meeting you, Rena, and don't worry about Paula. I'm sure she'll be fine in the morning. See you Monday, Aven, when the fun really begins."

"Good night, Gaylord. It was wonderful meeting you."

"Nite, Gaylord."

They walked into the flat with a less than certain step, exhausted. Rena was in bed first, with Aven seconds behind.

"Good night love…I love you." It wasn't clear who had spoken these words first.

SUNDAY

■■■■■■■■■■■■■■■

*T*he images were vague. He was aware of himself, prone. His body, enveloped in a soothing warmth, was rocking back and forth in an uneven but gentle cadence. There was no sound or light. The feeling was rich and secure. The environment slowly intruded on his luxury. A light, dim at first, soon was obvious. So, too, did the stillness recede. Sound and light added to the lushness of his world. The sun caressed him, and he heard the sound of young children at play. Even in his dream he could see her smile.

He was floating on an inner tube abandoned on the shore of the lake. He and Rena had gone there often in the early years of their relationship. Although no more than twenty kilometers from the main resort area north of Moscow, few of the city inhabitants found their way there. Rena said it was because people were too lazy to travel the few extra kilometers. And most people felt the need to be among crowds, as if to confirm the wisdom of their choice. Let them. Rena and Aven had their lake, with never more than three or four other couples and a family or two with happy children occupying the glistening sandy shore.

The small lake was located in the midst of a lovely forested area. An occasional modest cabin added a touch of civilization to the scene. Aven continued to float on the undulating surface. The moist, heavy air that visited the lake area in midsummer pressed on his body. A cloud came between him and the sun, but the sun's warmth did not diminish. Like no other cloud he had ever seen, its contours and varying shades pulsated slowly and then stopped. The cloud took shape. It was Rena. Her radiant smile hardly broke as she spoke.

"Good morning, love. I hope I didn't wake you."

Rena was sitting astride him, and he was deep inside of her. The sun at the lake had entered their bedroom, the happy children's voices turned to the sounds of Mozart, the lapping waters transformed into the cool air on his feet protruding beyond the blankets, the pressure of warm moist air was Rena herself, and the inner tube had vanished as their bodies rose and fell together, much in the spirit of the music and morning sun that filled the room.

They continued, losing track of time and place, nor could either of them possibly have cared. Finally Aven was overcome by forces beyond his control. His body and soul had become too much of one with her. A part of him demanded release.

"I love you, Rena."

"I love you, too, Aven."

Rena came at the same time, though more quietly. They lay in each other's arms. Aven wasn't sure whether he would ever move again. He soon heard the sounds of water running over Rena's body, and then he heard water blithely bubbling away in the teapot. Not long after, Rena returned, wearing only her worn though cozy robe. She took both pillows to prop him up in bed, setting the tray of tea, warm rolls, and butter before him. Rena sat at the side of the bed in the rocker her parents had given her, holding an old book whose binding was in need of considerable repair.

"Rena, what can I say."

"Nothing, just enjoy yourself. You've worked hard all week. After all, even the Lord rested on the seventh day."

"But the Lord didn't have you."

"Well, love, unless the Lord was a little kinky, *she* probably wouldn't have been too interested."

They sat quietly, enjoying the tea and rolls. A happy stillness entered the room. Rena was leafing through the tattered book.

"What's that?"

"Oh, nothing special. Something I found the other day."

It was some time before Rena spoke again.

"Aven, you know, we've never been to church."

"Rena, I thought you'd never ask. Do you want to…you're not pregnant, are you? Is that…?"

"No, silly, what I was thinking about was an old-fashioned sermon. My parents took me a few times when they thought I would learn something from the sermon."

"But why now, after this morning, and…"

"This book, I guess. It's quite fascinating. The work of an old Scottish preacher, and as good a sermon as any that I can remember my parents dragging me to. Let me read to you…come on love, not the whole book, just a few passages here and there."

"Amen."

"Aven, dear, that comes later. Be still and listen. This man wasn't hung up on any particular religion, nor any particular God. In fact, the way I read him, he saw God residing in each of us, in the form of our conscience:

> It is reason, principle, conscience, the inhabitant of the breast, the *man within*, that is the great judge and arbiter of our conduct…it is not the love of our neighbor, it is not the love of mankind, which upon many occasions prompts us to the practice of divine virtue. It is a stronger love, a more powerful affection. The love of what is honorable and noble, of the grandeur, and dignity, and superiority of *our own characters…*

"Aven, isn't that beautiful? There's such strength and feeling in his words, and you know he means everything he writes."

Aven leaned toward the side, barely able to touch Rena's arm with the tips of his fingers.

"Aven! On Sunday, in the middle of a sermon. Do let's stick to the matter at hand."

> …to feel much for others, and little for ourselves, that to restrain our selfish, and to indulge our benevolent affections, constitutes the perfection of human nature; and can alone produce among mankind that harmony of sentiments and passions in which constitutes their whole grace and propriety.

"He must have felt the term *benevolence* best captured the essence of virtue, it's used everywhere."

> We have always…the strongest disposition to sympathize with the benevolent affections…generosity, humanity, kindness, compassion, mutual friendship and esteem…

"Rena, whoever he is, he does sound like a decent man. And it's hard to argue with his ideas. Why, at this very moment, my deepest desires extend to those around me, with nary a thought for my own skin. Perhaps you've been equally stimulated by the old preacher's message."

"Aven, let me read what he has to say about excess."

She turned pages back and forth.

"Here it is."

...we frequently see the respectful attentions of the world more strongly directed towards the rich and the great, than toward the wise and virtuous...and to attain this *envied* position...

"I think he's being facetious here."

...to attain this envied position, the candidates for fortune too frequently abandon the paths of virtue; for unhappily, the road which leads to the one and that which leads to the other, lie sometime in the opposite direction...

...through the whole of his life he pursues the idea of a certain artificial and elegant repose which he may never arrive at, for which he sacrifices a real tranquillity that is at all times in his power...then...

"Aven, listen to the potency of his words."

...then, *in the last dregs of life,* his body wasted with toil disease...he begins at last to find that *wealth* is a *mere trinket of frivolous utility...*

Rena rose from her chair, put the book on the table, and nestled beside him.

"Aven, the preacher is wonderful, but so are you. Besides, a little excess can't hurt—supposed to be good for the heart."

Their lovemaking was without flaw. They came together, again with Aven the more vocal of the two, and were soon sleeping in idyllic fatigue. Aven woke first. As he tried to disentangle himself from Rena, she also woke.

"Oh my, Aven, it's almost one. And don't tell me about time flying and fun, or whatever that expression was that Paula used last night."

"I won't, Rena, if you promise to let me get some rest today. You know, this is the director you've been attacking so unmercifully."

As Aven spoke, Rena was out of bed and, after a quick trip to the bathroom, returned to the rocker. She was paging through the book once more.

"Aven..."

Aven didn't have the will to resist. He had enjoyed the morning sermon and would have happily admitted that the preacher's words did have a certain grace.

"Aven, your comment about being director reminded me of some other things our friend had to say, not unlike that chapter in Hayek…here we are. He often linked wealth and power in the same category. Spoke of what he called the 'hypnotic admiration for greatness' being the 'great and universal cause of corruption of our moral sentiments.'"

"Rena, that's not fair. I don't have a 'hypnotic admiration' for anything…except you."

"I know, Aven, but listen:

> …the great source of misery and disorders of human life seems to arise from *overrating* the difference between one permanent situation and another…*ambition* overrates the difference between a private and a public station; *vainglory*, that between obscurity and extensive reputation….The person under the influence of any of these extravagant passions is not only miserable in his actual situation, but is often disposed to disturb the peace of society in order to arrive at the niche he so foolishly admires.

"Oh, Aven. I love you. I love you more than I dreamed possible. I don't want anything to come between us, ever.…"

"Rena, I promise.…"

Before he could say more, Rena was beside him. It was two o'clock when they awoke. Rena's smile indicated that she would attack no more this day.

"Stay in bed awhile, love. I need to wash my hair."

Aven picked up the old preacher's gospel. He opened the book past the title page and then felt compelled to turn back. Somewhat faded, and in an old English script in keeping with the words Rena had become fond of, he read, but was reluctant to believe his eyes:

THE THEORY OF MORAL SENTIMENTS
Adam Smith
Professor of Moral Philosophy
University of Glasgow
England
1759

Rena was drying her hair as she entered the room. She kissed Aven on the lips and her soft voice echoed at the outer edges of the fog he had entered.

"I found it the day I went looking for Hayek and the others, on the shelf

next to *The Wealth of Nations.* I couldn't resist. It was so old and seemingly ne-
glected. And, Aven, you have to admit, you enjoyed what he had to say."

The haze had partially cleared.

"But, Rena, Smith wrote this when he was young and disavowed everything
shortly after its publication."

"He *was* young, but wise as well. And you're wrong. I checked. He didn't
abandon his views at all. In fact, he continued to revise the work long after he
published his other book."

Aven did not feel up to a full-scale literary debate. He had been profoundly
affected by everything he read in the "other book," and nothing he heard this
morning had altered his faith. What Rena had read might do well for a Sunday
sermon, but the new world, their new world, began in earnest on Monday.

"Rena, why then do you think the Amerikans suggested shredding any old
copies that might be found?"

Rena looked at him for a long time before she spoke.

"Aven, you can often tell a great deal about a nation by the books they
refuse to read, more perhaps than by what they permit...."

At that moment the phone rang. Rena reached for it.

"Oh, hello...yes, it was, and we had a wonderful time...that's good...."

Rena set the receiver on the table.

"Aven, it's for you. It's Paula."

STUDDAY
■ ■ ■ ■ ■ ■ ■ ■ ■ ■ ■ ■ ■ ■ ■ ■

*H*i, Paula....Yes, we're fine....No, we haven't been doing much, just some R and R, you know, reading and...Today?...This afternoon?...I see, well, I suppose...."

He replaced the receiver and sat in the rocker.

"Aven, there isn't anything wrong? Nothing's happened to Gaylord?"

"Gaylord's fine, but Paula wants me to come to the ministry this afternoon. I'm sorry. It was the last thing in the world I expected. On Sunday yet. She said there were a few last-minute details that needed tending to, and I didn't have the heart to say no."

Aven got up and walked to Rena. He held her close.

"I shouldn't be more than an hour or two. We can go to Pero's for dinner, and then..."

"It'll be okay, love. I'll call Hester and see how she's doing. Maybe she'd like to go out for a while. You go ahead."

Rena left the house before Aven's limo arrived. As Aven waited, he thought of all that had occurred in the past few hours. Rena's love for him, her admiration for the young Adam Smith, his love for both Rena and the older and wiser Smith. Perhaps there was a reconciling of the two—at another time. The limo had arrived.

"Good afternoon."

"Good afternoon, sir....Son-of-a-bitch."

The traffic did seem heavy for Sunday. Aven walked into the ministry and glanced up at old Igor as he waited. "I wonder how he's doing."

The elevator had not arrived, and Aven, tired of waiting, walked to his office on the next floor.

The expression on Paula's face was unusual. She was standing next to Aven's desk looking at some papers.

"Hello, Aven. I'll put the phone on automatic…we won't want to be disturbed, will we?"

Paula was smiling at Aven, and her words seemed innocent enough, but there was a singular tension in the air.

"Well…?"

Aven remained still.

"Aven, don't you think it's time to ball, be laying some pipe? You know what I mean, silly, boff, boink, boost, bump. Aven baby, we need to do the do, do the bone dance, do the nasty, yeah, do the wild thing."

Aven had never seen or heard anything like it. Paula was standing before him, hands clasped and raised over her head, her entire body swaying, the words coming in rapid succession and her voice getting higher and higher.

"Avennnnnn, we gotta gash, get busy, get down, get sloppy, we gotta get some trim, grease…oooooh baby, I need a hormone fix, I'm so totally fuckstrated I got cobwebs. Aaaaaveeeen, hound me, jab me, juice me, knock boots with me, mash me, nail me, we gotta have penetration, I wanna pile, let's play hide the salami, plug me, poke me, ride my hobby horse. Come on Aaaavvvveeeeenn, score, make me scream, square my circle, stick me, thump me, work on me, womp me…."

Paula continued swaying, though less frantically, and looked beseechingly into Aven's glazed eyes.

"Paula…I'm sorry, but I don't know what you want."

All movement stopped. Paula's arms remained motionless above her head, mouth agape, as she stared at Aven for what seemed an eternity.

"You d-o-n-'-t k-n-o-w w-h-a-t I w-a-n-t? Aven, I want to FUCK, F-U-C-K, FUCK. Even you Russian boys must know how to do that."

Her arms descended. She undid the buttons at the back of her sheath dress, letting it fall to the floor.

A bolt of lightning struck, slamming squarely into Aven's head. From the first moment he had thoroughly admired her physical attributes. She was an Amerikan beauty. But without the distraction of clothing she was much more. One might try to combine the loveliness of Aphrodite and the finest ladies of her court and still not approach the purity of Paula's feminine beauty—shoulders, neck, breasts, perfectly curved hips, flat stomach, golden tufted hair, thighs, calves, ankles, even her feet and toes, every part of her bathed in a glow of perfection. Paula's expression altered. A smile replaced the petulant scowl. And then Aven became aware of something else. What began as a mild sensation suddenly sprung into full-blown agony. Aven looked from Paula to its source.

Even in his worst nightmares—or fantasies—he couldn't have imagined such a sight. As a young student, he and his schoolmates enjoyed teasing their peers who couldn't prevent an erection while reciting in front of the class. Aven had had such moments. So had every young male student. The girls would titter away noncommittally during these involuntary performances. But what Aven now saw and felt was of a different magnitude. He couldn't tell its actual size, but he knew if he didn't do something the pain would become unbearable. His penis was pressing forcibly against his pants, making their removal difficult. Paula came to help. The two of them struggled mightily, as the pressure of his inflated member prolonged their efforts. After much tugging and pulling, success was finally theirs.

"Oh, Aven, you great big beauhunk. Just look at you, and your burrito. My, my, that's some tubesteak of love...."

Aven was not listening to Paula. He was too concerned with his penis. It stood out from his body, resembling a good-sized Polish sausage. It was waving wildly in an arc of some ten to fifteen degrees, well beyond his control. He became aware of Paula once again. She had taken him by the arm, and the two of them were headed to the far corner of his office.

When they reached the couch, Paula brought the parade to a halt. She told Aven to stay still. He did, while his penis went its own way, round and round, up and down.

"Here we are now."

Paula held a large red-white-and-blue object to her mouth. As she began blowing, Aven recognized what he guessed to be an oversized condom. "Aven darling, I'll just put this life jacket on you and we'll be ready to lay some pipe."

Aven was in no position to do other than Paula's bidding. Paula lay down on the couch, putting a small cushion under her buttocks. Her arms were extended and her legs spread. Both arms and feet were flat on the couch.

"I'm your donor for the afternoon, Aven, so get busy...Aven, I want you to fuck me."

Without emotion, Aven mounted Paula, inserted his tumescence, and began, as Paula had requested, to "lay his pipe." He wanted nothing more than for this nightmare to end and pumped away without word or feeling. In the meantime, Paula's entire body was still, save for her vocal chords.

"oooooooooooooowwwwwwwwwwwweeeeeeeeee...yes, yes, yes...oh...oh... oh...oh ohohohoh...yes...yes...yes yesyesyes...ohohoohgod!...ohmygod, ohmygod..."

Aven wondered if she had expired.

"No...no...no, no, no,...yes, yes, yes, yes...oweeeeeeeee...more, more, more...stop, stop, stop...don't stop, don't stop, don't stop...ooooooohhh, aaaaahhhhh, eeeeeeeeehhhhh, yiyiyiyiyiyiyiyiyi..."

Aven began to pray, involuntarily and without real hope, that the ordeal would soon end. Then his penis throbbed twice and shrank contentedly. Aven thought he heard it sigh. He withdrew from Paula and lay on his side.

"Oweeee, you're more than a studly guy. It's six-fifteen. We've been at it for over three hours, and look, you've spooched all over the new couch. It's okay, we can have it cleaned in the morning. Oh, dear, that reminds me. We both have lots to do. I guess we should be going."

These words struck him much like the earlier thunderbolt.

"Going! How am I going to explain the delay to Rena? And the way I look? How did I let this happen?"

Aven's heart sank with each question that dashed, unanswered, through his head. He rose with difficulty. The answering machine light on his desk was blinking. Aven turned on the recording:

> Aven, love. I'm terribly sorry. I found Hester in woeful condition. She wasn't fit to walk, eat, or look after herself in the least. I went back to the flat and got a few things. I'm going to stay with her for a day or two. I hope you don't mind too terribly. And you did say that the director needed his rest for Monday. I love you, Aven. I left food. It should be enough until Tuesday. See you then. I'll call tomorrow night.

"*Saved.* I won't be late after all...no rush...no excuses...no explanations...."

Paula had come up behind Aven. She put her hand on Aven's shoulder.

"Aven, tomorrow we begin the really important work. This afternoon was something we both wanted, and needed. Our relationship will return to what it has been this entire week, colleagues, good friends...and you *were* terrific."

Paula extended her hand with less than her usual degree of self-confidence. Her smile was also tentative.

The relief provided by the recorded message from Rena had circulated throughout Aven's system. Aven felt good, eager for the new world to begin, eager to assume the lead as director at MOP. Their hands met, and his charming grin washed away the doubt in her countenance.

"Paula, no regrets."

Part II

Revolution

■ ■ ■ ■ ■ ■ ■ ■ ■ ■ ■ ■ ■ ■ ■ ■ ■

*I*n their wisdom, the Amerikan occupation forces decided to delay the elections until the three-year plan had been put in place. Experiences in Eastern Europe during the 1990s illustrated the difficulty of making hard economic choices *after* the populace had been granted a taste of democracy. Economic decay had spread deeply and widely throughout Russia, and the system capitulated more slowly than had been hoped. Thus it was that the first full and free democratic elections were delayed for an additional five years. But even the most fossilized of economies did indeed yield to Adam Smith's new world, demonstrating once and for all the cornucopia of blessings available under pure capitalism.

The daily headlines adequately conveyed what was happening. An essential task at MOP was the preparation of these banners for the nation's press. Aven had long since realized that the headline was what every citizen read—and was what was remembered, if anything, of the full story. In the early years, if Aven did not personally write the material, his staff had to obtain his approval before the daily MOP headline was faxed across the nation. It came as no surprise to Aven that the radical changes installed by the Amerikans and patterned so closely after the Reagan Revolution in Amerika would produce similar results. If there were differences, they were because Aven and his colleagues benefited from the Amerikan experience. Paula offered her own insights as well. The form of capitalism thus established in Russia was a degree or two purer than the Amerikan version had been.

The near instantaneous installation of a free-market economy had caused difficulties for many in adjusting to prices, wages, work requirements, production decisions, profit calculations, and a host of other factors that had been previously determined, however poorly, by governmental decree. With Sonny Fourkaste's help, Aven was fully satisfied with the way MOP had handled this initial phase. After that, of course, it became progressively more pleasurable to describe the ebullient course of the revolution.

The dramatic changes in the economy had an equally dramatic impact on each of the three hundred million Russian citizens, perhaps for none more than Aven. From the moment he entered the ministry following that momentous Sunday of R & R, his association with Paula was altered dramatically and abruptly. His friendship with Gaylord was to change more slowly throughout the entire period, as was his relationship with Rena. He was to become extremely close to Gaylord. Despite his sincere and thoughtful efforts, however, the same could not be said with respect to Rena.

THE BEGINNING YEARS
■■■■■■■■■■■■■■■■■

April 1995–96...FIRST DECISIVE STEPS IN PLACE **** LONG RUN PROGRAM TO DECISIVELY REVERSE PAST TRENDS **** COMMITMENT TO REDUCE GOVERNMENT SPENDING AND TAXES **** SUBSTANTIAL REDUCTION IN GOVERNMENT REGULATION **** POOR ECONOMIC PERFORMANCE OF THE PAST HAMPERS RUSSIAN WORLD POSITION **** INFLATIONARY PRESSURE DUE TO PAST RAPID GROWTH OF MONEY SUPPLY **** MOP VIEWS ECONOMIC DISLOCATION WITH CONCERN **** DISSATISFACTION AMONG GOVERNMENT WORKERS **** 15,000 MOSCOW TRANSIT WORKERS STRIKE **** MOP DIRECTOR FIRES TRANSIT WORKERS (Aven undertook this act at the insistence of Paula, who guaranteed that it would have a sobering and salutary effect on the nation's workforce. Subsequent events were to prove the wisdom of this decision.)

April 1996–97...INFLATION AND INTEREST RATES REDUCED DRAMATICALLY **** FOCUS ON LONG-TERM GOALS IN FACE OF PRESENT RECESSION **** PRESENT HIGH UNEMPLOYMENT CONSEQUENCE OF PAST FOLLY **** WORKER SKILLS TO BE UPGRADED **** ECONOMIC RECOVERY TO BEGIN SOON **** NEW TAX POLICIES: BUSINESS INVESTMENT TO INCREASE IN YEARS AHEAD **** DRAMATIC STEPS TO REDUCE GOVERNMENT SPENDING AND DEFICIT **** WORKER RETIREMENT AND HEALTH BENEFITS TO BE PROTECTED **** GOVERNMENT REGULATION TO BE REDUCED, WITH FOCUS ON NATURAL GAS, TRANSPORTATION, COMMUNICATIONS, AND FINANCIAL MARKETS (As the headlines and the Amerikans had promised, the economic boon was at hand.)

HIGHEReducation
■■■■■■■■■■■■■■■■

*H*e woke to a bleak feeling within himself and a half empty bed.

"Rena…Hester…Adam Smith…Paula."

Aven remained in a fog as the names mingled with the sound of the alarm. And then he was wide awake.

"Monday!"

As Aven bounded from bed, he recalled Rena's phone message. That the rest of Sunday remained hidden somewhere in the deeper recesses of his memory was not troubling.

"Monday…it was only a week ago.…"

Aven understood that the significant change in his status should both temper and amplify his confidence. But in finding his God he in no way lost his boldness. To the contrary. Over the next eight years, nothing of significance was to occur to alter these feelings. He left the flat clean and orderly, just as he would have had Rena been sleeping in. His limo was waiting at the usual time.

"Good morning."

"Good morning, sir."

Aven paid little attention to the driver's cursing. As they approached MOP, Aven observed a number of trucks with men standing alongside, seemingly engaged in important conversation.

"That's an unusual gathering. Do you have any idea what they might be up to?"

"Not really, sir, but I did hear talk of widening the main road to the ministry. And none too soon if you ask me."

"Oh.…"

Aven noticed that the trucks were parked quite close to the park.

PING PING PING POOONG

It occurred to him that Beethoven's Fifth Symphony had always been one of Rena's favorites, but its opening theme really was rather dull. Aven's thoughts turned to the day ahead.

PINGPINGPING PAAANG

Gaylord was seated at his own desk in the outer office, reading the morning news.

"Good morning, Gaylord. I trust you had a pleasant Sunday. What, ah, how do we start? Sorry, but you do realize that I'm new at this job. By the way, where's Paula?"

Gaylord folded the newspaper, got up from his desk, and gave Aven a comradely handshake.

"Mooornin, Aven. Yesterday was fine. We spent some time with the economists before leaving them at the airport. They're not as dull as they seem, at least not when they've had a free beer or two. Sonny and I took in a movie in the evening...yeah, it was a nice day. How 'bout yours?"

"Mine?...Oh, yesterday. I had a nice day, too, but I don't want to talk about yesterday. My mind is on today. We are in charge of this new world, after all, and today...."

"That's fine, Aven, and you *are* right. We do need to get started. Paula called just before you arrived. She won't be in for a day or two. She's working with the retailers and services on the major openings around the city. But Professor Fourkaste—Sonny—will be in momentarily. He's going to be very helpful for a while. Creating this 'new world' will be formidable at the outset, and we'll have our work cut out for us. But don't worry...."

"Hey, who's worrying? Not me, I assure you. The word's not in my, what did you call it the other day?"

"Spell checker?"

"Yeah, that's it. No kidding, I really am not worried. Excited, euphoric, exhilarated, all of that and more. And if we have our work cut out, we ought to get to it. I hope Sonny Fourkaste isn't too much longer."

As the two men walked into Aven's larger office, Gaylord spoke of his longtime friend. They had met at CCNY at an alumni gathering some years back. Sonny—the name Gaylord urged Aven to use—had been giving a lecture for the returning grads about economic prediction being as much an art as it is a science. Gaylord had arrived after the talk began and for a time was confused by Sonny's frequent reference to Rosa Scenario, who he thought was a Portuguese colleague of Sonny's. When he learned that Rosa was no lady and that the art of prediction had much in common with his own work at RSJ&S, Gaylord had made a point of meeting Sonny after the talk. The two had been fast friends ever since.

"I'm surprised he isn't here by now."

"Perhaps he was delayed. There was a lot of traffic this morning, and a small convention of trucks and cement mixers were gathered near the park area."

"That must be part of the road expansion....Oh, here he is now."

Gaylord glided toward Sonny, who had made an appearance at the door to Aven's office.

"Ho, Gay-babe, I trust you got to sleep easily enough after the flick. Man, that Russian chick was something else."

"Yo, Sonny-bo, like the innocent child that I am. And her ne'er-do-well lover wasn't too bad either. But enough of this. We gotta get Aven off on the right foot."

The two men, obviously the closest of friends, turned and walked toward Aven's desk.

"Sonny, I'm sure you remember Aven. I know you spoke at some of the sessions in the combo room."

"Just once, Gay-babe, to straighten out that pompous ass, Nat Law, on a simple medical term. Hello, Aven. Gaylord speaks highly of you. I'm here to assist where I can, and at the risk of sounding overly confident, I think you'll find me most helpful."

"Sonny-bo, with all the experience you've had expediting the American revolution, how can you miss. Man, I don't know what any of our presidents would have done without you. Sit down. I'll get us tea."

As Gaylord left, Aven and Sonny walked to the coffee table and sat down.

"Well, Sonny, this is all quite new and exhilarating. It was a pleasure to meet so many of your colleagues last week. I learned a lot from them and from the assigned texts as well. Guess I don't have to tell you what an inspiration Adam Smith has been, and his sons Milton and Friedrich as well."

"I know how you feel, Aven. To be in on the start of a revolution, and at the helm, has to be breathtaking. Actually, it's been a while since I was in grad school, but I do remember getting a kick out of old Adam. Of course, Friedman and Hayek were contemporaries of many of my own professors."

"Oh, you've met them?"

"I sat in on some of Friedman's workshops. Charming guy, so long as you've got the right answers—his. But personalities aside, there's no getting around the fact we've created the world in their image, and a great world it's going to be. It's just a matter of belief...ah, here's Gay-babe with the tea."

The three men sat with their tea for an extended period of time. Aven learned that the initial adjustment process for the Russian economy was going to require his and Sonny's best efforts. The reasons were not complicated, as Sonny was explaining.

"The key components that have been put in place today include the removal of all price controls. In addition, all government subsidies are being drastically reduced, and the ruble has been revalued downward as well. Henceforth, it shall be freely convertible with all other foreign currencies."

"I understand all of that, Sonny. It's required if we are to establish a free-enterprise, market-oriented economy. But how can such sensible policies cause us difficulty, even in, as you economists like to say, the short run?"

"Well, Aven, the difficulties will be felt by many of your citizens. Mind you, these concerns are only for the—and you have used the term correctly—for the short run. The establishment of free markets and the elimination of subsidies for food, fuel, and housing will lead to significant price increases, which in turn will lead workers to seek considerable increases in wages."

"I'm not sure I see the problem, although I do recall some discussion about wages last week. It was somewhat confusing then, too."

"I think what you are referring to was last week's session with Lowe Taksis. Just between the three of us, Aven, I would take much of what he had to say with a grain of salt."

"Yeah, that's right on, Sonny-bo. Rumor has it that the professor's theories about lowering taxes and raising government revenue came to him in the midst of a monster hangover. Seems good old Lowe had been drinking all afternoon in a D.C. cocktail lounge. After the fifth martini, he fell flat on his face on the table, teeth first. Now the professor had quite a set of choppers. The indentation they made on the table made an even bigger impression on his mental state, and he was soon chomping on tables all over Washington in an effort to sell his ideas on tax bites. He found his man in Ronald Reagan. The rest is history."

"You've got it, Gay-babe, and if you noticed the other day, the professor has this space between his front teeth. The impression left on the cocktail table's been dubbed the Gapper Curve. At any rate, Aven, the advice given to your staff members by Minnie Wages is what we have to go with. The increased costs of food and other consumer goods will not sit well with your workers, and they will be demanding wage increases to maintain their living standards. Unfortunately, such wage increases would be highly inflationary and cannot be permitted. Things would have been easier had not some of your citizens amassed large savings, what you've been calling 'monetary overhang.' With so little being produced until now, the freeing of bank accounts means we have a real job to do on inflation as it is. Add in the devaluation of the ruble, and you see why any further inflationary pressure must be resisted, including union-inspired demands for wage increases."

"Sounds to me as if we are going to have some unhappy workers out there, though not much different from what MOP has had to deal with before."

"Perhaps, Aven, but that's not the end of the story. In the freeing of your markets, a number of firms will experience a sizable fall-off in demand. In some cases, this will necessitate the closure of the business and in others, a drastic cutback in production. Unfortunately, your workers have come to see their jobs as a right, independent of how much or little effort they expend. The situation will be temporary, but difficult nonetheless."

"I see what you mean, Sonny. We'll have to use our most subtle techniques in calming the situation."

"Don't be so naive, Aven."

"What do you mean, Gaylord?"

"Subtle."

There was nothing in Gaylord's expression to suggest to Aven that he was joking in some obscure way. Aven looked to Sonny for help. Sonny obliged.

"What Gay-babe means, Aven, is that there is nothing subtle about free-market capitalism. The best means of dealing with the workforce is to be blunt, direct. Too much subtlety is often mistaken for weakness, and that's the last thing we can admit to the workers."

"Or to ourselves."

"Perhaps, Gay-babe, but your observation strikes me as being overly subtle. In other words, Aven, if the workers do exhibit signs of unrest and dissatisfaction in the early going—and I expect they will, since employees are pretty much the same from country to country—we'll have to take action that is forceful and easily understood. Fortunately, the problems engendered by the business closing and employment cutbacks represent a two-edged sword. On the one hand, the affected workers—those who lose their jobs or are laid off for a time—are likely to be quite militant, particularly in light of the price increases. However, the unemployment itself provides a rather hefty degree of labor discipline. For the remaining workers—the ones fortunate enough to keep their jobs—the sight of their brothers and sisters standing in the unemployment lines will have a wonderfully calming effect."

"Sounds like the problem will take care of itself."

"Almost. In the first place, our job will be to place the blame for the present awkwardness—the unemployment and the pressure for higher prices—squarely where it belongs."

"Take the blame ourselves?"

"Hey, Aven baby, you gotta learn it's just like the old days. You folks at MOP *take* credit and *give* blame."

"Gaylord's absolutely on the mark. Any difficulties that we experience in the near future...."

"You can cut the 'near,' Sonny-bo."

"Fair enough. We won't worry too much about the future. Our concern is with the next few months. I expect, Aven, that the unemployment will act as a calming force on the workers, but not on all of them. We'll have to wait and see, but should the need arise, visible labor discontent will have to be nipped in the bud. Otherwise, our job is to deflect the worker hostility and at the same time persuade workers that their future is looking brighter even as they stand in line for their relief checks. Before you know it, they'll be as cooperative and docile as can be."

"That's what we mean by good capitalist workers."

"Why not? As we unleash the great productive forces bound up for too long in our nation's workers and entrepreneurs, surely there will be no cause for other than cooperative and manageable workers. They'll all be sharing in the rich abundance of a capitalist economy operating at full throttle."

"Most, Aven, but some workers are apt to miss the boat. You know, get stuck in traffic as the plane is taxiing on the runway."

"In more prosaic terms, Aven, the economic boom that's sure to come will leave a few individuals...."

"In its wake."

"Hush, Gaylord."

Aven was surprised at his involuntary emulation of Paula. Gaylord appeared to be also.

Sonny continued.

"Some of the unemployed will join in the prosperity after a period of retraining. It might even be necessary for modest government help in this effort. But when all is said and done, a worker learns much more when he is paying for the education or training. However, a few individuals will not be salvageable."

"Yeah, Aven. Those we throw overboard."

It was Sonny's turn to do Paula.

"Hush, Gaylord. They are indeed thrown overboard, but if you remember your Hayek, you know that those tossed aside will land firmly in the government-provided safety net."

"You two gents ever see the modern-day safety nets? They're dropped pretty near the ocean floor. Ought to provide a lot of protection from the great white sharks swimming around in the sea. Which reminds me, don't you think it's time we got a bite to eat? Sonny, Aven, what do you say? Some lunch would be good, and besides, it'd get me off the hook."

The duo of pairwise friendships had blended into a single threesome as Aven and his Amerikan friends left for lunch. The table in the executive dining hall was nearly full, and the conversation from one end to the other was quite animated. Aven sat amongst members of MOP whom he hadn't spoken to since he had replaced old Igor. They clearly shared his enthusiasm. Aven delighted in the knowledge that many of the issues that Sonny had been discussing a short time earlier—the freeing of prices, the floating of the ruble, industry relocation, and the like—were familiar to the staff whose sections would be dealing directly with each of these special areas. Aven finished his lunch (and the day) with no less fervor than he had brought to MOP. If anything, his confidence in the economic plan, in MOP, in Sonny and Gaylord, and in himself had been enhanced by the day's conversation. Before leaving, Aven took the large leather-bound volume from the shelf.

"Reading the old professor is not the same as holding Rena, but he does provide comfort in his own mysterious way," he thought to himself.

Aven spent a good portion of the evening holding Adam, reading from time to time, otherwise simply enjoying the thoughts that wended their way through his head. Rena called shortly after he finished the dinner she had so lovingly set aside for him.

"Hi....It's good to hear your voice, too....Oh, is she?...That's too bad. But I really do think she's carrying on a bit much about Mellors....Come on, Rena, there's no need for us to fight....OK....I'm sorry. Rena, I love you....I know, and don't worry about Hester, or anything else for that matter. Our new world is just beginning. You'll see. You're just depressed because of Hester. Trust me....Fine, if you think it's necessary, I can manage until Wednesday. But not a moment longer....I love you, too....Good night."

Aven returned to Adam Smith. He was still holding the book when he fell asleep.

For the next several weeks, Aven's time at MOP was spent in much the same way as that first stimulating day. There were indeed signs of the troubles Sonny had warned of, and Aven and his staff worked effectively at maintaining the nation's morale. With Sonny's assistance, Aven wrote most of the news headlines in those early days of the revolution.

In addition to dealing with the modest difficulties the nation was experiencing, Aven had to deal with domestic problems of his own. The initial signs of tension were fairly modest. They arose for the first time when he arrived home from MOP on Wednesday, the day Rena returned from her mission to Hester.

Aven was unsure whether Rena would be home. When he had called earlier in the day, Rena had indicated that she would be home in the evening. She was not, however, certain of the time. As Aven searched his pocket for the keys, the door opened. He felt a rush of happiness, took his hand from his pocket, and the two embraced. After an instant, Rena gently released herself from Aven's grasp.

"Hello, Aven. It's good to be home, and it's good to see you. You look wonderful, as if without a care in the world."

"I've almost forgotten what it's like to hold a beautiful woman. Can't say that our world is without its share of problems at the moment, but I do feel wonderful. Oh, Rena, it's all going to work. We're meeting every challenge at MOP. Sonny and Gaylord and I have established a great relationship, but I wish I could do something to take that glum look from your face."

He again took her in his arms, this time directing his lips to hers. Rena complied, not without warmth, but with less fervor than he might have anticipated, given their time apart.

"I am sorry. You do deserve a better welcome."

"It's all right, your time with Hester must not have been a picnic, but you will get over it, and so will Hester. All she needs is a new man. She'll forget Mellors soon enough."

They entered the flat as this conversation was continuing and within a short time were sipping wine.

"Come on now, Rena, you just said that Hester had been seeing Ivan again. Her spirits can't be all that low, and I don't see why yours should be either."

"Love, it's not Hester, at least not entirely. She's seeing Ivan in the same way she sees me. We're doing what we can to help her get over Mellors. But it's not easy. You know how long they've been together, and they were in love, despite Mellors' overactive hormones. People who have loved and cared for each other for more than ten years don't just part, find a replacement, and go on with their lives as if they were merely changing sides on the volleyball court. How do you think I'd feel if we were to part? How would you feel?"

"Rena, nothing will ever come between us, you know that."

"Yes, I know that, and I also know that the world has a funny way of spinning. We can't always stay where we want."

Rena stopped speaking, and no appropriate words came to Aven. The two of them sat quietly for several minutes. Rena finally resumed the conversation, in a slightly more upbeat fashion.

"Aven, this is stupid. I'm not going to make myself feel better by lowering your spirits. Why don't we get some food, and some air, and some...."

She was unable to finish. Aven had risen from his chair and had picked her up, was holding her under her arms, and promptly waltzed her out of the room. Rena began to giggle and to protest in her best artificial manner.

"Aaaaaven, put me down this very minute...Aaaaaaaven."

He did her bidding, punctuating the request with a light but loving kiss. After fleeting visits to the bathroom, they were out of the flat.

It was a short time before they entered the park. Walking hand in hand, they said little. Rena hummed. Aven had difficulty telling Mozart from Haydn. He soon noticed the trucks from earlier in the day. Rena apparently did also.

"Aven, what are all those trucks doing over there?"

"I wondered the same thing this morning. Seems as if all of the roads in the city are to be widened. Gaylord thought that the improvement project was likely to start with the main road through Moscow, in part because it's the major access to MOP. In a way, I suppose it's a lot like the entire revolution. There's apt to be a small degree of inconvenience for some, but it will be short-lived, and better for all of society in no time at all."

Rena said nothing, and the two continued walking in the cool but pleasant April evening. There were a fair number of people in the park despite the early season. Aven was vaguely aware of the fact that most of those they passed were men, alone, and few if any seemed willing to exchange greetings.

"Odd," he thought to himself.

Aven tried to whistle along with whatever it was that Rena was humming. As he began she stopped. Aven soon stopped and they were both silent as they moved along. The upbeat feeling that was in Rena's step had ebbed.

"Aven…I'm not sure just what it is, but I don't feel right."

Aven had peculiarly mixed emotions upon hearing these words. While offering no reply, his spirits burst into flames with the possibility of Rena's being pregnant, but the glow was gone quickly as he realized Rena's practice of birth control was impeccable.

"An illness?"

The notion of being without Rena was something he could not comprehend, nor had he ever allowed himself to do so.

"Rena, what's…?"

"Aven, a while ago you used the term *inconvenience*. There's something terribly wrong, out of joint, with everything that has occurred these past three days. If I told you that Hester had lost an eye, or if I had lost the use of my legs…or if that wonderfully handsome face of yours had been disfigured by a terrible accident, wouldn't it seem odd if these events were seen as 'inconveniences'?"

Aven offered no reply.

"And if those trucks are here to help widen the road so more cars can move more people to who knows where, faster and faster, or even slower and slower, and if in the process we have to put up with a bit of dust and noise for a while, well, I suppose the dust and noise are not like losing one's vision…or good looks, but…."

"Rena, forgive me for interrupting. I know you're upset, and you've been so for too long. If you weren't such a liberated lady, and so headstrong, and if I didn't respect you as much as I love you, I'd forbid your seeing Hester for a time. Your visits with her have affected you more deeply than you think. And it's affected the *rationality* of your argument...that's an indication of how serious your trauma must be...."

He paused, realizing that for one of the few times in their entire relationship, he was actually scolding her, but she needed it.

"How on earth can you compare the loss of your legs, or Hester's eyes, one *or* two, or...and I can hardly utter the words...."

He smiled as he spoke, trying to ease the lecture.

"...my good looks, with some dust and noise? The latter are inconvenient, but they are not permanent. Don't you see how irrational you're being?"

"Aven, don't you understand that when the dust and noise, *mere* inconveniences, I grant, are gone, *permanent* changes will have occurred?"

"Of course, the road will be wider."

"Oh, Aven, you dummy, the road *will* be wider at the expense of the park, a part of which will be gone, perhaps forever."

Aven admitted to himself that he hadn't thought through the argument as well as Rena had, but he refused to concede.

"Rena, are you trying to liken Hester's eyes to the park? And your legs, and my good looks, these are all the essence of each of us being a complete person. Without them, we might still function in the world, but we would have lost a part of our humanity."

"And, my love, when the city loses a part of its park, does it, too, not lose some of its humanity?"

Rena was to have the last word on this subject, for she immediately changed the topic.

"The trucks and the loss of the park space are not the only thing. Food prices have risen dramatically, and rumor has it that there is to be a freeze on wages. How will people eat? The same rumors suggest that thousands of men and women will be losing their jobs shortly. And this mad rush to acquire Korean television sets available on every street corner, and a lot of other silly products. These men we've been passing in the park this evening, they all have such a lonely and solitary aura about them....Oh, Aven. There's something wrong, I just know it. Something terribly wrong."

Through much of this time Rena's monologue had attracted only slight notice from the people around them, a fact that pleased Aven. When it seemed as if she had drained herself of her every concern about the past three days, Aven, in a calm and thoughtful way, did all he could to explain the necessity for some of the things that were of legitimate concern to Rena. He did not try to whitewash the real issues that he, Sonny, Gaylord, and MOP were dealing with. He did explain their transitory nature. As to the "silly" commodities, Aven made no effort to deal with what he thought to be Rena being Rena. This conversation had used up the better part of the evening, and their stomachs must have rebelled at the same time.

"I'm starv...."

"So am I."

They decided on pizza, since it was both delicious and close by. A few patrons were eating at the tables near Luigi's, but to Aven's delight, no one was waiting at the counter. They placed their order. Rena asked for a double serving of anchovies. Aven had not noticed the subdued manner in which Luigi went about his business. Rena had. As they picked up their order, Rena asked Luigi if any of the family was ill.

"No, senora, evra'wonns a'good."

"I'm glad to hear that, Luigi. You didn't quite seem yourself tonight. I hope everything's OK."

"Actually, it's a'not so good."

"What's the trouble? Business should be picking up soon."

"That'sa wattsa wrong. We were told a'yesterday."

"Told what, Luigi?...Aven, do you know what he's talking about?"

"No I don't, Rena. Luigi, what were you told yesterday? And by whom?"

"An American lady, a'lovely senora, she said we'a no gonna be able to stay. Is gonna be a new pizza place. This our last'a week...in business...."

Luigi had gotten himself to the point of tears and could not continue. Rena seemed almost as upset as Luigi.

"Luigi, there must be some mistake. Your pizza's wonderful. I'll check first thing in the morning at MOP. Come on, Rena, the pizza's getting cold."

"Aven, if you don't mind, I'm not hungry. Let's take the food home. I think I need to get to bed."

Not much more was said on the walk home. Aven reheated Luigi's pizza and ate it with gusto and admiration.

"Luigi must have misunderstood," he thought to himself. "It's hard to imagine better pizza."

Rena had gotten into bed soon after they arrived at the flat. She was sleeping when Aven snuggled in beside her, though she managed a faint murmur as he held her.

The next morning Aven asked Gaylord about Luigi's. He knew nothing. Apparently Paula wanted firsthand control over all changes in the retail economy, including food and clothing as well as consumer durables. Paula was working in the field, helping to "brainwash the bumblefuck barnies," as she was inclined to define her efforts. She returned late Friday afternoon. It was then that Aven was able to discover the source of Luigi's lamentation.

Paula, Gaylord, and Aven were sitting in Paula's combo room. Sonny had left early. Other members of MOP were all quite busy, as they had been from the start of the week, and the entire building had about it a feeling of energy and movement. The three were in a relaxed mood. The many mini-muddles— M and M's, as everyone at MOP soon came to call the initial difficulties—had provided a fair amount of stimulation for Aven throughout the week. He had conquered each of them.

"Paula, I'm glad you were able to stop by."

The three exchanged pleasantries in addition to going over some of the more interesting issues that had come up during the week.

Paula was particularly excited about the progress she had made with the new lines of women's apparel.

"Ever since that goddess Raisa hit this city, the women have been eager for the latest fashion, and now they're gonna get it. The dork-head men are still clueless, but we'll get them, too, Aven."

The conversation turned for a moment, as Aven noted the first signs of labor unrest amongst some of the government workers.

"I really don't think we should have too much concern here. Russian workers are used to taking their lead from the top, and they should also be familiar with the cost of disobedience."

Gaylord added, "At least those old enough to remember Stalin."

Paula added, "Oh, Gaylord, we'd never be so wicked."

Aven changed the subject, and the mood.

"Paula, do you know anything about the food concession in the main park down the street? Rena and I were there a couple of nights ago, at Luigi's. Really great pizza. We should go there sometime. Anyway, the owner, Luigi, he came here a few years ago with his wife and two daughters. Last night Luigi said something about a new pizza place. Do you have any idea what he's talking about? Sure doesn't make sense to me."

"Nor me, Aven."

"Hush, Gaylord. Being in the field, I almost forgot how nice it was to be able to have a conversation without your constant editorial interjection. Now just what did this, what was his name, Linguini...?"

"Luigi."

"Oh yes, thank you, Gaylord. You *can* be quite helpful at times, and I do hope you know that I appreciate you despite your numerous handicaps. What was the name? Luigi, yes, why I think he's right, Aven."

"Right about what, Paula?"

"Right about the new pizza place. We're opening a series of express-food restaurants in every major Russian city—Mexican, Chinese, and Italian as well.

Each chain will be unique, but all will be patterned on the older American fast-food stand. You know the one—they've been selling adorable little hamburgers here for some time now. I think the Italian outlets are going to be called McDonatelli's."

Despite Paula's enthusiasm, Aven began to feel a slight bit of indigestion.

"We're naming the Chinese outlets MingDonalds, and the Mexican...let me see...?"

"Donald Molay?"

"That's close, Gaylord, but I just don't recall...."

"But, Paula, I grant you the name is quite clever, and our citizens have come to understand, and even enjoy, your hamburgers. But why would you, we, want to replace a wonderful old family business like Luigi's? Don't you think we ought to reconsider?"

A coldness came into her voice that added to its brittle nature.

"Aven, there is nothing to reconsider. Luingini's is being replaced for just the reasons you like it. A *family* business that does a *good* job is not what your country needs. What you need are businesses that are *profitable* and that do a *fast* job. Luciano's provides neither."

Having reminded Aven of who was calling the shots, Paula tried to soften her voice.

"And besides, you're going to love McDonatelli's. They'll have over three thousand different pizza combinations and be able to serve them piping hot in less than thirty seconds. All through the wonders of our latest freeze-dried microwave technology. Each place will have a virtually unlimited capacity and thus provide stimulating employment for many more workers than all of the bambinos in Lamborghini's clan."

From the look on Paula's face, it was obvious that the issue was closed. Under any circumstance, Aven had no desire to argue.

Several weeks passed in relative calmness. The day-to-day activity went smoothly enough, as did Aven's relationship with Rena. Aven managed to avoid walking in the park during this period, and while Rena continued to express concern with the very things Aven was helping to establish, they both realized their respective need for autonomy. They did not agree on much of what was happening, but they did understand the new nation, their nation, was still very much in its infancy, still in the process of development with nothing set in concrete, nor was anything sufficiently well defined to allow their differences to eat away at their love. The first glimmering that such was possible came over the transit workers' strike.

In response to the rejection of their wage demands, the Moscow transit workers had met in angry session for several days. At the end of long and heated argument, which was not well covered in the news, the leaders called for a strike. This, despite the government edict that such strikes were against the public interest, against the law, and disruptive of the new economic plan. The workers voted better than fifteen to one in favor of the strike and were out on the picket lines the next morning.

The strike had not been unanticipated. That same morning, Aven, Paula, Gaylord, and Sonny were meeting with the labor section at MOP. The discussion went on for less than an hour. They talked of reconsidering the wage policy, allowing a cooling-off period, closing some of the less essential businesses to ease the traffic problems, but could find no satisfactory response. Until Paula spoke. From the start of the meeting, she had sat quietly at the conference table, never facing whoever it was who was speaking but paying attention nonetheless.

"Fire the assholes."

All eyes turned to Paula as the words came whistling from her gut. It was clear to everyone in the room that she was quite angry yet fully under control.

"Fire the lot of them. We'll inform their supervisors that a crash training course will be instituted in the morning, and the buses will be running on a normal schedule in time for the Monday commute. Those fools should have known better than to strike at the start of a weekend, and...."

"Paula, perhaps we should rename the training course...."

"Hush...ah, I see what you mean Gaylord. Perhaps we should...."

The discussion went on awhile longer. Aven was quickly persuaded as to the wisdom of Paula's edict. The transit problems of the city would be minimized, and the added degree of labor discipline could only help with the transition to rapid noninflationary economic growth that was at the heart of all of their efforts. As the last details of the announcements and other plans were put into place, Aven couldn't help but marvel at the simple brilliance of the Amerikan methods. There were no losers.

"But what about the workers and their families?"

Aven hadn't expected Rena to be overjoyed with the firings, nor, however, had he anticipated the anger she was directing toward him. He had come home in his usual ebullient state. The kiss and the wine had kept him there. It would have been impossible not to mention what he, upon Paula's advice, had done. It was to be major news as of the next morning, and likely for several succeeding weeks. Nor did he feel at all apologetic as he told Rena of the day's events.

"Have you lost your senses? You don't just fire fifteen thousand workers. And what about their wives and husbands, and children? A simple MOP order has put tens of thousands of people in serious economic peril."

Rena went at him for a long time. She finally stopped. Her anger waned, or at least seemed to.

Aven responded in as steady a manner as he could. It wasn't easy, for some of Rena's hostility had bordered on the personal. But explain he did.

"The transit workers had voted for a strike with the full knowledge that it could be a lengthy one *and* that it was illegal. They surely must have reserves in their strike fund to provide for the workers and their families for an extended time. Besides, with a growing and dynamic Russian economy near the horizon, these workers will have little difficulty returning to work in the not too distant future."

Aven decided not to tell her the workers would be permanently barred from returning to transit work.

As the days and weeks progressed, Aven and Rena continued their lovemaking, often as passionate as ever, and never perfunctory. At times it was more subdued, and Rena's cries seemed tinged with a poignancy that was new to Aven. There were, however, many more nights when neither felt the desire. The evening the transit workers were fired was such a night.

The first year was nearing its end. With the exception of Rena's moods, Aven couldn't have felt better about the way things had progressed. The difficulties with Rena seldom intruded into the conversation at MOP. At work or at home, the optimistic facade that had carried him so far in the world remained. Nevertheless, Aven did allow himself the luxury of self-grievance on rare occasions. It was a late February afternoon, after a particularly successful day. MOP surveys had indicated that despite substantial unemployment and the high cost of food and housing, Russian citizens were encouraged about the future. The satisfaction level at MOP was higher than ever. Aven and the two Amerikans had taken a lengthy swim and were sitting contentedly in the sauna, relaxing, perspiring, chatting, and joking as if the world were their oyster.

"I wonder what Rena will say about the surveys. Perhaps when she sees how differently others see our revolution...?"

"Aven, what are you talking about? Rena strikes me as a most perceptive and sexy young lady...."

"Sonny-bo, Rena is a sexy dish all right, and damned smart. But she seems to have made a career out of muckraking. You know the type, forever looking below the surface...not always a good idea if you have a sensitive stomach. But, Aven, you two have been together for years, happily it seems to me."

"We have been happy, Gaylord, and in all these years I've never thought of or wanted another...."

Aven paused, as if slightly puzzled.

"Maybe you've both been working too hard. When was the last time you went out on the town? You know it's been almost a year since Rita's. Maybe...?"

"I'm not sure that would help right now. But you are right, Rena's been working seven days a week. The more work she does, the more depressed she seems to be."

Sonny interrupted with fervor.

"Hey, you two, I've got just the ticket. Aven, where was it you said you and Rena met?"

"At Moscow University. Rena and I graduated the same year, in fact."

"That's what I thought. Well, you know that MU has held the number one ranking for most of the season, and the final game with their natural rival, MIST, is scheduled for two weeks from tonight. How 'bout the four of us going? You and Rena'll have a great time, and maybe it'll help her forget some of the muck that she's been raking."

"Sonny, what in the hell are you talking about?"

"MIST and MU, you know, they've been natural rivals for close to a year, ever since MIST was established."

"Maybe I've been too busy with the daily headlines, but what's MIST? What rivalry? As Paula might say, I'm totally clueless."

"Yeah, why don't you clue in the both of us, Sonny-bo."

"Where have you two been? MIST, that's the new medical school, Moscow Institute for Surgical Technique, and they've been bitter rivals for months. If MU wins, they're a shoo-in for the national championship."

"In anything in particular?"

"Sorry, I thought you'd both know that much. In basketball."

"Whoa! I think Sonny-bo's got a great idea. A game for the national championship, your old alma mater. Why hell, I'd love to go myself."

"Maybe it would be a nice break, and I think Rena would enjoy your company. Especially Sonny, who seems to be the only one who knows much about basketball."

"I know everything about the game, Aven. My younger brother plays for the Knicks. I'll pick up the tickets this evening."

Aven returned home that evening in an up-beat frame of mind. Rena's mood did not match his, but this was not unusual. Wine, conversation, and a meal that Rena had prepared all preceded Aven's suggestion about the MU-MIST match. Rena resisted.

"Aven, don't you think we both have better things to do than to go to a game...."

She broke off mid-sentence, as if realizing how negative she was being.

"It's not just any game, it's MU. Don't you remember Moscow University, where we met? Where we fell in love? Don't you care?"

He could tell by the softer look on her face that he had prevailed. She cheerfully agreed they should join Gaylord and Sonny, and she joined Aven that night in bed with even greater enthusiasm.

For the next two weeks it was as if the economic revolution would take care of itself, and to a degree it did. All any of them could think about was the game, the Big Game, as Aven dubbed it. Interest in the MU-MIST match extended well beyond the walls of MOP. The entire city had caught the fever, and as the event neared, the economic progress of the nation seemed to be of less and less concern. With such anticipation, the actual playing date approached with excessive deliberation. But arrive it did. That night, the limo remained at the flat until Aven and Rena were ready. They departed at six-thirty, planning to pick up Gaylord and then Sonny on the way to the game. Sonny joined the other three, all seated together in the forward part of the limo.

"Does anyone know where we're going?"

"I think so. The new basketball pavilion was built a few blocks from Moscow University, in that area of run-down apartments. Good place. That neighborhood was really an eyesore."

"But what's happened to the people who were living there? Or is that another one of the problems for the free market to take care of?"

"Rena, I don't know, but you can be confident no one...."

"Hey, stop it you two." It was Gaylord who burst into the conversation.

"How 'bout for tonight we just have a good time. Neither of you will solve the housing problem in this limo."

Sonny joined in.

"I agree with Gaylord. Tonight we all oughta keep our eye on the ball."

"All right, my apologies, gentlemen. Do any of you know about the new pavilion?"

Rena did her best to be one of the boys.

Gaylord had taken an active interest in the entire enterprise since Sonny had raised the idea two weeks earlier.

"Rena, it's a super facility, used for basketball and soccer mainly, and modeled after some of my country's finest arenas. It occupies eight square blocks...."

"All of those apartments...."

"Hush, Rena."

She did, and smiled as well.

"Let Gaylord continue."

He did.

"Cost over five hundred million rubles."

"At the present exchange rate, that's nearly a quarter of a billion smackaroos," added Sonny.

"But wait till you see the place. It seats a hundred thousand for soccer, fewer for basketball, since the seats in the fourteenth tier are just too far away. Domed, with constant temperature and humidity. Quite a feat when you realize how big the place is. And of course the finest press and TV facilities imaginable."

Throughout this monologue, the limo progressed amid a solid stream of traffic. The entrance to the parking area was just ahead, and some distance beyond stood a massive and brooding structure. It looked to Aven like a stack of gray pancakes atop a thick, flat platter.

Rena's reaction was restrained.

"My, that is rather large, isn't it?"

"We're talking big."

"Not big, Sonny-bo, biggest."

They traveled some distance within the parking area, all the while approaching the leviathan. Finally, the limo pulled into an enclosed area quite close to the building. Aven noticed other limos parked nearby, along with several cars of similar shape and style to Paula's Beamer. Most were a glistening white in color, intermingled amongst a few bright reds and blacks. The limo stopped. The driver was standing silently at the door as Aven exited.

"Driver, this must be a reserved parking area. Do you know for whom?"

"The players, sir. I'll be here at the end of the game."

They entered the arena. The cavern before them was brightly lit. It seemed to rock with the sounds of youthful voices competing for attention with an army of trumpets, trombones, saxophones, and drums. The music, cheering, and lights were overwhelming. Aven, Rena, Sonny, and Gaylord all reached for their ears, while their eyes did their best to squint away the sudden brilliant intrusion. They stood huddled together on the ramp leading into the oversized cavity as if to provide each other with the moral support to proceed.

"Come on, gentlemen, don't be shy. A little noise never hurt anyone. Who knows where we sit?"

Aven's heart jumped. He hadn't seen Rena in such a good mood for months. Perhaps Sonny, who held the tickets, was right after all. Their seats were located with other MOP dignitaries, three rows behind the MU bench. They agreed that Gaylord and Sonny should sit between Rena and Aven, since the two Amerikans were much more familiar with the game and could provide the needed commentary.

The floor itself was empty save for two baskets standing about four meters high and mounted on clear rectangular backboards. The boundary lines were painted a glossy black, and the solid area near each basket and the floor area beyond the boundaries were painted a royal blue, which Aven recognized as the

Moscow University color. The floor itself appeared to be made up of meter-width wood squares in a parquet pattern.

Several levels of seats extended into the atmosphere well above the floor. Most all of the people Aven could see from where he sat were wearing shirts or sweaters of royal blue, and most of these people held paper streamerlike objects of the same color. Aven located the musicians at the far end of the lower seating behind one of the baskets. It was all so spectacular, and the four of them were content to sit with their mouths closed, allowing full sway to their ears and eyes.

After a time it appeared to Aven that every seat had been taken. And then, in an instant, the noise to which they had become accustomed increased in intensity to a level quite beyond description. The players were entering the court area from opposite ends of the arena. The MU players were clad in royal blue; the MIST team in a surgical gray. Close on the heels of both groups of players—twelve on each team—came several older men wearing formal evening dress. One of the men behind the MU players was dressed in a white tuxedo, with a royal blue cummerbund. The others wore royal blue suits with white trim. All but one of the senior MIST cadre were dressed entirely in off-white. One among them wore white set off with a scarlet bowtie.

"Those men are enormous. And most seem to be Asians. Gaylord, Sonny, do you have any idea who they might be?"

Aven added, "And who are those older men trailing behind? They look like they're going to a presidential inauguration ball, not a basketball game."

Gaylord and Sonny took turns answering the couple's questions.

"Most of the players are Tibetan. They all stand over two and a half meters and weigh in at about a hundred kilograms. We're talking big."

"Biggest."

"Tibetans?"

"Sort of obvious when you think about it. Don't forget, they've been under the thumb of the Chinese for decades. Really an exploited class, not allowed to do much besides sports. With their size and ability, well, these days it's hard to be a serious contender without them. If you notice, there are only two or three Russians on each team, and it's unlikely that more than one of them will get to play tonight."

"And those older gentlemen, the two men dressed in white are the chancellors of MU and MIST."

Aven was sure he had misheard Sonny on this last point. So too, apparently, did Rena, who shouted back to Sonny.

"I'm having a hard time hearing, the men in white must be the *coaches*, I thought you said *chancellors*."

"You heard Sonny right. The basketball program is what the university is all about, and without a winning team, there'd be little if any TV royalties or other commercial revenues. That's what it takes to run a modern university, what with the high-tech research labs and all. The gentlemen trailing along behind the two chancellors are the deans of the various science schools—engineering, medical—and, of course, MIST, being a medical school, those fellows must represent the various surgical specialties."

Rena was looking more and more intently at Gaylord as he spoke, as if questioning his sanity—or hers. Aven also found Gaylord's comments somewhat unexpected, but he could see the logic of what he was hearing. Rena apparently decided not to pursue the matter and changed the subject. She asked about the fact that everyone in the hall seemed to be wearing royal blue.

"Aren't there any fans here rooting for MIST?"

"Actually, Rena, MIST hasn't taken in any students yet. They're still in the building phase. The school opens next September, but it's important to get the basketball team in place to raise the needed funds. Medical schools don't come cheap these days."

As he spoke, all of the lights in the arena dimmed. Gaylord dropped the subject of finance.

"They're going to introduce the players."

The players from MIST were introduced first. A single spotlight followed each player onto the center of the floor as the eighty thousand fans, not including Aven and his friends, booed and jeered so loudly that the players' names went unheard. Quiet descended as the MU players prepared for their introductions.

The public address announcer obviously enjoyed his work.

"From Gartok in the western reaches of Tibet, two and a half meters, and playing pooower forward, Riiiiiiiiiick Pedma."

The silence ended, and the arena erupted into wild cheering, aided by a militant fanfare from the pep band, as Rick Pedma trotted onto the center court. The process was repeated four more times:

"Maaaaaaaaaaaagic Jamba…"

"Sleepy Kaaaaaaaaaarma…"

"Isaiah Guuuuuuuuuuuuuuunka…"

The wildest of cheers came with the introduction of "Kareeeeeeeeeeeeeeeeeeeeem Yuuuuuuuuuuungdrung…"

The five players hugged each other and returned to the bench area as the chancellor of MU was introduced to a far more subdued response. The band broke into a spirited number, and almost everyone in the hall was standing, clapping, and waving what Sonny called "pom-poms" in time with the music. Aven noticed that Rena was standing and moving slightly with the music.

The game was not without interest. The players on both sides were quite skilled. Despite their size, they moved with grace up and down the court. It was easy to tell when MU was doing well, and just as easy to tell when a MIST player scored a basket.

Aven and Rena found much to inquire about as the play unfolded: "Won't they hurt each other the way they keep banging about?—When they dive for the ball and land on top of each other, why doesn't the referee stop that sort of thing?—Isn't it unfair, all of the noise when the MIST players try to make foul shots?—Why is the chancellor getting so angry, and what is he throwing at the referee?"

"The players are in wonderful condition. They get the best physical training the nation can afford, and when injured, they receive the best of medical care.—The referee tries to interfere as little as possible. He doesn't want to get one of those fellows angry at him. A player who roughs up a referee gets a modest fine, paid for by the university alumni association, but the referee bears the pain himself.—The noise is what's called the home-court advantage. This is nothing, some fans have been known to shoot darts at the opposing players when they try for foul shots.—The chancellor has good reason to get angry. One call by the referee could cost the game, the university millions of rubles in receipts, and the chancellor his job. I understand a lot of them are being sent back to Siberia these days. And I think he threw his Knight stick."

By halftime, which took nearly two hours, the scoreboard indicated MU 112, MIST 110. As Sonny explained, a good bit of time was devoted to TV commercials, which, of course, made the entire enterprise worthwhile. The home team was ahead, and spirits in the cavern were high. The intermission itself was going to be an hour, enough time to allow the spectators time to visit one of the eighty-nine permanent concession stands as well as the hundred and ninety-six public restrooms. They had learned the precise number from the program.

"Great game, guys. Hey, Sonny-bo, one of your predictions was right on the mark for a change."

"That's not all that funny, Gay-babe, and I thought we agreed earlier to forego the shoptalk. But it has been a good game. That center from MIST, man, where do you think they found a guy like that? It was clear he didn't speak a word of Russian. Sure hate to have him as my doctor."

"Oh, Sonny, you should talk to Aven about that. And by the way, aren't you supposed to be an expert on free-market economics also?"

Sonny seemed to get Rena's point but didn't pursue the matter.

"Anyone care for something to eat or drink?"

They settled on beer and peanuts. Aven accompanied Sonny to the concession stand while Rena and Gaylord went in search of one of the many restrooms. It didn't take long to get the food. As Aven was served, he thought he recognized the person working behind the concession stand a few feet away. It looked like Otise. He hadn't seen him in nearly a year, and the man seemed depressed as well as distracted. Aven made no effort to get his attention. They were back in their seats as Gaylord arrived. Rena was much longer in returning. She also seemed to be annoyed about something.

"What's the matter, Rena? What could be better than a close-scoring game?"

"It's the restroom score that I don't care for—Men *eighty-eight*, Women *eighty-eight*. A tie! That's about the only thing men are willing to share fifty-fifty."

"But, darling, I thought you were big on equality?"

"Aven, I do believe that Paula might best express what I'm thinking right now."

The others saw Rena's point, and all four spectators were soon cheering along with everyone else as the MU and MIST players and their academic leaders returned to the floor.

The second half of the game remained close. The MU chancellor was a great deal more agitated than his MIST counterpart. He had been yelling at the referee on almost every play that went against MU, and the veins in his neck and forehead were becoming larger and redder as the game progressed.

Gaylord had an explanation.

"Aven, MU's got a great deal more riding on the game. If they win tonight, they retain their number one ranking and get millions more in next year's TV contracts. And it gives the chancellor the rubles to pay his players a hefty bonus as well. It makes recruiting—no cinch these days—all the easier. Do you have any idea what travel expenses in Tibet are like? On the other hand, MIST really isn't going anywhere yet. They'll do well enough with their basketball program, but they're gonna have to rely on the commercial contracts and product endorsements of their surgeons. Of course, with modern medicine, there's a real gold mine in such contacts."

Aven found Gaylord's answer helpful. Rena was also paying attention. At that moment a collective gasp spread through the arena. Busy in conversation, Rena, Aven, and Gaylord did not understand what had happened.

Sonny had been following the game.

"The MIST center, Dalai JammaLama, just made an impossible shot with three MU players pulling and yanking at him. The referee ignored all of the roughness. Put MIST ahead with only three seconds in the game. But MU still has a chance. After the time-out, they get the ball at half court behind by only one point. A basket wins it for MU."

During the time-out, all of the players were gathered around their respective chancellors. The deans were running to and fro bringing clean paper and sharp pencils. The university leaders were scribbling furiously, first on one sheet of paper and then on another. Aven was pleased, knowing that a number of TV commercials were being aired as these strategy sessions were played out. The horn sounded, indicating the start of play. Both teams lined up. This time the MIST captain called time-out.

"They wanted to check on each other's strategy. Now they can counteract the other's play," explained Sonny.

Another five minutes passed.

"More commercials," thought Aven as the horn sounded.

The teams lined up once again. Now it was the MU team's turn to call a time-out.

"Aven, what's going on here?" asked Rena.

"Strategy. Might as well relax. Each team gets eleven time-outs."

"Beer anyone?"

"Good idea, Sonny-bo."

When the horn blew for the last time, all eyes focused on Isaiah Gunka, the MU player with the ball. He was standing out of bounds. The referee blew his whistle and began counting the five seconds within which the ball had to be put in play. The noise in the cavern was deafening, and the referee had to get quite close to Isaiah. Aven could hear the referee's count. "One—two—" The referee hadn't reached three when Isaiah ran directly onto the court, ball in hand. He pushed aside the first MIST player in his path, ran over two more, and leaped high into the air, the ball held in one hand behind his back. He was about three or four meters from the basket when he began his ascent, and he stayed airborne seemingly forever. It couldn't have been that long, for just as the buzzer sounded to end the game, Isaiah spun with his back to the basket and stuffed the ball through the hoop. There was a momentary quiet. Then the eighty thousand fans, who had been standing for some time now, began screaming as if they had been resting their vocal cords for weeks in anticipation of this one moment. The MU players and academic staff were at center court, dancing and falling all over each other, while the MIST players and staff had the referee surrounded. Soon the referee walked over to the table at courtside and spoke to the public address announcer. This was taking place a few rows from where Aven and the others were seated. It was clear that the referee and the announcer were in heated debate. Finally, the referee grabbed the microphone and began to ask for quiet. This was not immediately forthcoming. In fact, the cheers were beginning to turn to boos. After considerable pleading, the spectators became still.

"Ladies and gentlemen, the last basket is disallowed. There were several blue-team violations on the play. Time has expired, and the final score stands as it is now posted."

The large four-sided electronic billboard hung above the court. Close to a hundred and sixty thousand eyes looked as one. The only sounds came from the twelve MIST players and their five academics. The impact of the referee's decisions couldn't have been clearer.

MU 233, MIST 234

The MIST players' cheering was drowned in a sea of boos that cascaded over and around the cavernous arena, as if never to end. But soon the many thousands of eyes found a new and common focal point. It was the chancellor of MU, who had discarded cummerbund, bowtie, red studs, and jacket. His shirt, wringing wet with perspiration, barely covered his torso. The chief referee, who had managed to maintain his clothing intact, looked very ill at ease. And for good reason. The chancellor from MU was holding the referee by the neck and shaking him violently. He continued for several minutes before dropping the referee in a heap on the floor. The chancellor's voice filled the arena:

> YOU NO GOOD CRAZY SON OF A PIG-EATING CAMEL...DO YOU HAVE ANY IDEA WHAT YOU'VE DONE? DO YOU KNOW JUST HOW BLIND-ASSED THAT CALL OF YOURS WAS? YOU'VE COST DEAR OLD MOSCOW UNIVERSITY ITS NEW LASER LAB, A LAW LIBRARY, THE ENTIRE UNDERGRADUATE PROGRAM IN SOCIOLOGY. STUDENTS WILL FEEL THE BRUNT OF YOUR SIGHTLESS STUPIDITY FOR GENERATIONS TO COME.

He stopped speaking, but his breathing came more and more quickly. Finally, he reached down to grab the sniveling referee and, along with one of the MU players who had not had an opportunity to enter the game, swung the poor man by his legs round and round, faster and faster, finally flinging him straight up toward the center of the domed ceiling high above the court. Every eye in the place followed the referee's flight, a journey that took several seconds. The force of the hammer-throwlike propulsion sent the referee all the way to the top. The referee hit the dome with sufficient force to remain wedged deeply into the acoustical tiles that only partially dampened the sound of the collision. As his feet dangled helplessly above the floor, the lusty cheers that had rocked the place earlier returned. The pep band, too, had found its second wind. If MU hadn't won, at least the score had been evened. As Aven watched the flight of the referee he thought he noticed several other sets of feet dangling from the domed top, but he said nothing.

Nor was much said on the return home. As they were going to sleep, Aven made one last effort at comforting her. "Come on, Rena…it was only a game."

THE BEGINNING
OF THE MIDDLE
■■■■■■■■■■■■■■■■

*A*pril 1997–98…VITALITY OF RUSSIAN ECONOMY, PROSPERITY OF RUSSIAN PEOPLE DIMINISHED BY PAST POLICIES AS RECENT RECORD DEMONSTRATES **** SUBSTANTIAL PROGRESS SEEN **** TAXES REDUCED **** BURDEN OF REGULATION EASED: FULL EFFECT YET TO BE SEEN **** GOVERNMENT SPENDING REDUCED **** SOUND MONETARY POLICY IN PLACE **** FAMILY INCOME UP **** EMPLOYMENT UP: ECONOMY TO ADD MILLIONS OF JOBS **** JOB TRAINING SIGNED INTO LAW **** YOUTH UNEMPLOYMENT TO BE ATTACKED: ENTRY-LEVEL WAGES LOWERED **** PRICE STABILITY ACHIEVED **** RISE IN VALUE OF RUBLE **** RUSSIAN CITIZENS ABLE TO PURCHASE MORE FROM ABROAD **** STRONG RUBLE EXPLAINS RUSSIAN EXPORT DECLINE **** RISE IN TRADE DEFICIT OF LITTLE CONCERN: SOLUTION SEEN THROUGH FREE TRADE **** GOVERNMENT REGULATION FURTHER REDUCED: FREE MARKETS TO BE ESTABLISHED IN AIR TRANSPORTATION **** GOVERNMENT DEFICIT TO BE REDUCED (True to Paula's prediction, Aven noted an enormous change in attitudes of the Russian worker. The peremptory firing of the transit workers coupled with the rapid rise in unemployment during the first several months of the revolution had instilled a new disposition among these millions of men and women. No longer did they consider their job as a right granted by the state, theirs to keep for life regardless of how they performed. A job in the new society of free markets and capitalism was now seen as a privilege, to be earned through hard work and, even more importantly, respect for the word, will, and whim of the employer. With a hard-working and obedient workforce, mindful of the very real possibility of unemployment or worse, there was no limit to what the entrepreneurial genius might accomplish, as the years ahead were to demonstrate.)

April 1998-99...EMPLOYMENT RISING **** BUSINESS OPPORTUNI-TIES EXPANDING **** INFLATION UNDER CONTROL **** BUSINESS INVESTMENT HIGHER THAN ANY TIME SINCE THE GREAT WAR **** PRODUCTIVITY GROWTH FAR SURPASSES EARLIER YEARS **** WIDESPREAD AND GROWING ANXIETY OF THE PAST ALL BUT FORGOTTEN****GOVERNMENT DEFICIT TO BE REDUCED **** EMPLOYMENT CONTINUES ITS RISE **** UNEMPLOYMENT REMAINS HIGHER THAN DESIRED **** POVERTY LEVELS NEED TO BE REDUCED **** FOREIGN TRADE DEFICIT NEEDS TO BE REDUCED **** AGRICULTURAL SECTOR HARMED BY PAST GOVERNMENT POLICIES AS WELL AS THE STRONG RUBLE **** GOVERNMENT POLICIES TO PROVIDE SOCIAL SAFETY NET **** REGULATIONS IN PLACE TO REDUCE GOVERNMENT DEFICIT **** TAXES TO BE RE-DUCED FURTHER **** REGULATORY REFORM IN BANKING AND NATURAL GAS TO BE HASTENED

HURRA HURRA HURRA
■ ■ ■ ■ ■ ■ ■ ■ ■ ■ ■ ■ ■ ■ ■ ■ ■

*A*ven was relieved to find Rena asleep the morning after the Big Game. The heated controversy at the game's end had altered her mood severely. He knew that women were sensitive to the least hint of violence, even when such aggression was justified. Last night was a case in point.

The game had run too late for the morning news. Aven wondered how MOP should deal with the temporary depression sure to result from the MU loss. He knew, however, that the citizens of Moscow would soon have other distractions. Not all of the economic problems had been fully resolved, nor all of the blessings attained, and besides, the baseball season was only a few weeks off. It was true, of course, that the Russians had not fully embraced the Amerikan pastime, but Aven was assured that even in Amerika, baseball had taken decades to catch on. Sonny had predicted that the sport would captivate Russia much more quickly. None of this, however, would ease the immediate pain of MU's loss, and it thus came as no surprise to Aven, upon arriving at MOP, to find the events of the previous evening commanding the attention of everyone in the building.

PING PING PIIIIING ping PING

Aven stepped from the elevator wondering whether a night at the opera might lift Rena's spirits.

"I think *Aida* is coming soon, and Rena likes Verdi."

He walked into the outer office to find Sonny, Gaylord, and several other members of the MOP staff gathered around the television screen behind Gaylord's desk, watching with considerable interest.

"Sorry to interrupt, fellows, but don't we have some work to do in putting the best spin on last night?"

The men who had been peering at the large screen turned for an instant toward Aven and then resumed their vigil. Gaylord responded to Aven's question.

"Morning, Aven. What's happening right now will have a lot to do with how much spin we need. The nation's Ruling Organization of Basketball, ROB, is reviewing the game. Seems as if some of Moscow U's most influential alumni have been flooding the phone lines in protest over the MU loss. They're just about to announce their decision."

Gaylord turned to look at the screen, as did Aven.

An elderly gentleman, whom the announcer identified as the faculty representative to ROB, an MU professor of French, Dr. Charle Atan, spoke:

> The committee has been carefully reviewing zee reruns of last night's disputed play. As you are all aware by now, zee play in question took less than three seconds. Thus, despite zee fact that we have had the benefit of shots from zee forty-three cameras located in zee hall, zee committee has been unable to find, a...how do you say, conclusive evidence...

At this point, the shoulders of all the viewers sank in apparent disappointment.

> ...upon which to overturn zee MU basket...

Their shoulders straightened. Aven and his colleagues jumped with joy as the import of the ROB decision sunk in. Sonny and Gaylord smiled. The two of them, along with Aven, spent a happy morning casting about for the next day's headline. It was Gaylord who penned the winning selection:

MU-MIST MATCH MISCARRIAGE MODULATED
MU Chancellor Reaches Leadership Zenith
Hard-Headed Referee Refuses to Retreat

They did have some difficulty in getting back to the economy that afternoon, but no one at MOP felt much pressure to do so. Celebration of the MU mending soon waned, however, and Aven returned to the day-to-day work at MOP with his usual vigor. The nation was adjusting to moderate unemployment, and there were the first signs of a significant improvement in the economy. A number of programs designed to retrain workers whose skills had been made redundant by the market-led reordering of production were in place.

Days blended into weeks, and weeks into months, as the new world entered and was well along in its second year, crawling, standing on wobbly legs, but soon to take those first full steps from which there is no turning back. The reductions promised in government regulation were still to be achieved, but there was no question that the economy was moving in the right direction. Rena's moodiness remained as counterpoint to these otherwise laudatory developments. Aven had long ago accepted her self-proclaimed role as social critic. To date she had found no reason to rebuke his MOP work.

Aven was sitting with Rena after dinner one evening, several months following the exciting MU victory, talking amicably. Rena had been doing some preliminary research on Russian women, a topic that Aven thought harmless enough. He noticed the time and asked if she was interested in watching the evening news. Some months ago she had acquiesced in his desire to purchase a new color TV. They had had a black-and-white set for years without complaint, since there was little they found worth watching. The situation had begun to improve under Gorby, but not sufficiently to require discarding the old set. With the widespread availability of Korean electronic products, it seemed silly not to join the masses, and they did within a year of Aven's appointment as director.

"Aven, why on earth do you want to do that? It's all happy talk about prosperity around the corner, and when we're not getting that pap, they fill the screen with the horrors of the day, the latest family stabbing or...."

"It's not pap, and much of it comes directly from MOP. There's also a lot more on the news than the 'horrors of the day,' as you so elegantly put it. You get some of that, but with the ninety-three channels, surely we can find plenty of thoughtful analysis."

"That's the worst part."

"Thoughtful analysis?"

"No, dummy, the ninety-three channels. There's no such thing."

Aven didn't understand what she was talking about.

"But we have a ninety-three month warranty, one for each channel...if the set isn't working...."

The love that Rena felt for Aven had not lessened. It was simply the fact that so much of what was happening distracted her from these feelings. This at least is how Aven understood their relationship. Rena got up from her chair and walked to Aven, armed with her most seductive expression. She leaned over, holding his head, and kissed him softly but without hurry.

"Aven, always the same sweet innocent Aven. There is nothing wrong with the new set or with any of the ninety-three channels. We get every one, crisp, clear, and in glowing KoreoKolor. But, love, we might just as well be back in Stalin's stone age. One channel is quite enough, thank you."

She kissed him again and walked to the set.

"Let me show you what I mean."

The bright picture appeared instantly, but Aven saw only a blur. Rena was turning the dial from channel to channel before his eyes could focus.

<tck> <tck> <tck> <tck> <tck> <tck> <tck> <tck> <tck> <tck> <tck>

"Very funny...I see what you mean. If you turn the dial fast enough, all the channels look alike, just the way it must have been in Stalin's day, without the KoreoKolor."

"Love, it really doesn't matter how fast I turn the dial...."

Rena stopped turning the dial at channel 4, the Russian National Broadcast Company, RNBC. The network anchor, an attractive woman in her early forties with flowing blond hair and impeccably made-up eyes, was just beginning the economic roundup:

> The latest figures for the second quarter bring *<tck>* more good news (the channel 5-RCBS announcer was an attractive woman in her early forties with flowing black hair and impec- cably made-up almond-shaped eyes) to the Russian *<tck>* people. Leading indicators (the channel 7-RABC announcer was an attractive woman in her early forties with flowing blond hair and impeccably made-up eyes) point to an un- precedented period of *<tck>* economic expansion in the (the channel 30-RCNN announcer was an attractive woman in her late forties with flowing blond hair and impeccably made- up eyes) major industrial sectors. Steel *<tck>* production is up over (the channel 27-RTBS announcer was an attractive woman in her late twenties with flowing blond hair and im- peccably made-up eyes) forty percent from the previous quar- ter. Durable *<tck>* orders have remained strong for the sec- ond *<tck>* quarter....

"I think I see your point, Rena, but it's not all that persuasive. The eco- nomic news certainly should be the same, regardless of its source. As you know, every major news channel starts its broadcast with the MOP report, and there's variety in the anchorwomen. Not bad-looking ladies, you'll have to admit."

"I don't have to admit anything of the sort. No one has any idea what those poor robots really look like underneath the wigs and all of whatever it is they plaster on their faces. I doubt if even their mothers would recognize them. And you're also mistaken about the uniqueness of the economic news alone. By now they've moved on to the features..."

And Rena turned up the volume and continued her irritating trek across the dial.

"Pretty interesting, isn't it, Aven, the way these megamillion-ruble media moguls operate. And I bet they had several of their top reporters working their heads off to prevent being scooped."

Rena's smile had a distinct schoolmarmish look as she continued.

"...and have you decided which channel we should watch?"

Sometimes Rena was too smart. She had conveniently selected the evening news to make her point in this case. Aven thought to himself, "Why doesn't she consider the diversity in commercials, in the numerous game shows, and in the family-life drama situations that offer information and entertainment to the Russian citizens throughout the day? Cooking, exercise, comics for the children, the fascinating impromptu news-shouting shows where the journalists have at each other in the most entertaining fashion...and the weekly opera on RPBS."

"Why, Aven, what *are* you thinking about? Have I been turning the dial too quickly for you?"

"No, Rena, I really wasn't thinking about anything. Just watching the news."

Rena's attack on the news was not made in jest. But her dial-spinning orgy, done without anger, prevented this issue from intruding on their relationship, much less on Aven's sense of confidence about the economic plan and his and his nation's destiny. He could not say the same about Rena's recent research, which had its origins in the night they had gone to the Big Game.

Aven became privy to Rena's explorations during a particularly cold spell in January, nearing the second anniversary of their new world. They had returned from dinner at Pero's. Rena suggested eating out in an effort to combat the somber cold and gray of the elements. They had tried without success to reach Gaylord and Sonny and then trudged the modest distance through the wind by themselves. Aven was happy to feel the relative warmth of the flat as they returned.

"I know the walking is good for us, but I'll be happy when the weather turns."

He rubbed his hands together and soon reestablished enough of the circulation to take off his gloves and other garments.

"Sit down, and I'll have *warm* tea for us as quickly as possible."

Rena did his bidding after planting a light kiss on his cheek. It was clear that her lips would require more time to thaw. The breathy sounds of the kettle whistle came quickly.

"This should help. But I am glad you thought of Pero's. His grandmother keeps coming up with winning ideas, and the Minskvasser went well with the bass. Those California wines are not bad—a nice fruity aftertaste, though not all that subtle. Pretty much what California's all about from what I understand."

Aven was becoming accustomed to these long silences on Rena's part.

"I know you enjoyed dinner. You ate all of the fish this time....Holy mackerel, was that the last time we were at Pero's—almost two years ago?"

"That *was* a long time ago, Aven. So much has changed. Even Pero's. The food was wonderful, but I miss the intimacy of the old place."

"It was different before they decided to expand, but think how many more people can enjoy his grandmother's recipes."

"I don't think Pero had any option. Do you remember Servo's comment as he brought the check?"

"No, what did he say?"

"That with all of the competition from the express food chains, Pero felt that he could no longer compete on the limited volume of six tables. He has done a wonderful job of maintaining the quality, but Servo felt that the strain was wearing on Pero."

"But in a sense, that's the beauty of competition. Pero is just responding to the desires of his customers."

"Most of those people eating tonight may have been *cash* customers, but I don't think many of them were *Pero's*. Not the way we used to be. He had time to talk with us, and there was a warmth and camaraderie in his manner. Tonight Pero seemed a harried old man, unable to say much beyond the perfunctory hello. I'm not even sure he recognized us."

Aven wondered to himself why it was that so many conversations with Rena quickly turned to how much better it was in the "good old days." Rena didn't use that term, but he knew that is what she was feeling. Rather than defend the market, he decided to change the subject and the mood.

"Not to change the subject, but you haven't said much about Hester lately. I trust she's well, and long since recovered from Mellors', ah, his ungracious departure?"

"Funny you should ask. She's been on my mind a lot lately. In a way she has recovered from that first-class heel, and I think she realizes her mistake. If Hester had it to do over, she wouldn't have let him stay around for ten *days*, much less ten years. But that's all history that can't be cleansed from the record or, I'm afraid, from her psyche."

"Don't you think you're being just a bit hard on Mellors? After all, they...."

"Not nearly hard enough. That jerk's no doubt running around Moscow from one tramp to another, happy as a lark."

"He does seem to be in good spirits, but...."

"What would you expect? He can forget their years together the minute he hits the next bed. It's not been quite so easy for Hester, however. She's still not gotten over it, and she continues to have periodic episodes of depression. I went to the clinic with her just last week. You know, Aven, Hester's doctor is located at the new MIST outpatient clinic."

"Oh yes, I understand it's quite a place."

"It's quite a place all right."

The change in her tone of voice was dramatic.

"Ever since that barbaric sporting event, I've wondered what MIST would be like once the students arrived. Hester and I didn't get to the main campus area, but the clinic was a phenomenon unto its own."

"Doesn't sound as if there is anything wrong...."

"That's because I haven't finished. Don't get me wrong, Aven, but from what I see happening, this new world of yours is not moving in a way that makes a lot of sense. From the looks of things, it's going in the wrong direction. The clinic is only the latest example. You know I've been doing work on women and the pressures that society places on us in regard to our sense of self, particularly our *physical* self."

"I sure don't see the connection between that and the direction of society. In fact, tonight you were the one who insisted on walking halfway across the Alaskan tundra because the exercise would do us good."

"That's not what the MIST clinic is about, Aven, and by the way, I'm not so sure we need a health spa on every corner either. But the MIST clinic has another mission."

"I never thought it was simply another health spa, it's a health *clinic*, isn't it?"

"More like a combination auto-wrecking-salvage and high-gloss painting yard all rolled into one."

Aven was unable to stifle either the yawn or the involuntary glance at his watch.

"...it is getting late, and I'm off again on the evils of your world."

"Rena, I have enough faith in the world we're creating to be able to listen to constructive criticism, even from a beautiful lady who hasn't made love to me in longer than I want to remember."

"Aven, I am sorry...."

There was a glimmer of a smile as she spoke these last words, but the serious tone returned as she continued.

"The MIST clinic is a fairly attractive building, quite welcoming in appearance and design, and the halls and waiting rooms on each of its eight floors offer a comforting, almost seductive environment, both of color and of sound. What goes on in the closed offices is another matter."

"You really aren't expecting to find illness an aesthetically pleasing event?"

"We are not talking about *illness*, Aven. It's more a *sickness*, and it's society that seems to be in need of treatment, not the poor creatures sitting in the melodious MIST waiting areas. It took us some time to find Hester's physician. She and a handful of general practitioners, internists, and gynecologists are hidden away in the basement level. Do you have any idea what goes on in the eight floors above the ground?"

"Not really, but I'll bet that problem will soon be corrected...unless I fall asleep first."

"Hold on. Let me get this off my chest. I've been in a fury from the moment I left the place. The top *four floors* are devoted to surgery."

"Rena, come on now, you do recall what MIST is all about?"

"Aven, the clinic is an *outpatient* facility, like your typical drive-through car wash, or bank, or Donald Molay's. Patients are in and out in a matter of minutes, or hours in the more sophisticated procedures, and the best and brightest Russian medical talent spends most of its effort working on eyes, cheeks, and hairlines, and removing or relocating wrinkles. You can select the shape of your nose, mouth, and chin in the first-floor showroom, between nine and ten in the morning, and have the whole job done before five the *same day*. The entire fifth floor is devoted to vacuum-surgery."

"I don't think I know what that is."

Aven could hear the weariness in his voice.

Rena's had lost none of its energy.

"They used to call it 'liposuction,' a disgusting process of sucking and scrapping what society has determined to be excess fat from all the little nooks and crannies that we want to expose to the world. They don't use that ugly term any longer. I guess it didn't convey the kind of image the doctors of surgery and advertising wanted to project. Too close to blood-sucking, which is what it amounts to. Now, it's called *Assuage d'Adipose!!* Tres chic, don't you think?"

Aven could feel the stress of his eyelids along with the gravity of Rena's commentary.

"Most of these poor creatures have been persuaded of their illness by the sick society we seem to be creating. They're almost all women. The men are too busy doing the selling, sucking, and slicing. Most of the victims are in their forties and fifties. Younger women have their special needs taken care of on the three floors below the butcher shops. These patients find their salvation through diet."

"It's a wonderful system, Aven. Too bad we had to wait for the Amerikans to lead the way. First, we persuade these impressionable kids to befoul their systems by selling them every variety of diet our research physicians can dream of, each diet promising ever greater popularity and romance. Then, when all of the powder, pills, and false panaceas fail, real sickness sets in. The *abnormal* diet specialists, who occupy the entire second floor, get their opportunity. Somehow these blood-sucking leeches don't object to the fattening of their own pocketbooks. I doubt if they're interested in much else."

Aven had never heard her speak at such length and with such indignation. But the weight of his eyelids refused to yield.

"Rena, I don't really know why, but I can't keep my eyes open for another minute. I've got to get to bed."

"I really didn't have much more to say, and it will keep until morning. Go on to bed. I'll join you in a while."

Aven was unsure when Rena had come to bed that cold night in January. Breakfast was waiting for him. Much as he enjoyed eggs and onions, Rena's commentary had done little to enhance his appetite. He learned of some eating disorders appetizingly referred to as anorexia/bulimia. Seemingly opposite in nature—the one of self-induced starvation and the other of "voluntary" forced feeding followed by self-induced vomiting—the disorders had their highest incidence among women, mostly in their teens, the majority of whom came from upper middle-income families.

"It's quite convenient, as they not only worry about their weight to the pathological point of self-destruction, but they, or their parents, have the funds to pay the doctors to keep them alive. The more success the *healers* have in saving the young, of course, the more business for the top four floors as these women age. I think it's what the surgeons and diet specialists call cooperative medicine."

His indigestion did not persist, nor did Rena's words linger in his mind. Work at MOP, along with the steady stream of good economic news, was more than an adequate antidote for any concern he might have felt regarding the foolish behavior of a few of the nation's women. He knew Rena exaggerated. It was the essence of the social critic. The fall-off in intimacy between them was bothersome, but the rest of his world provided considerable stimulation. And the recognition he received as director of MOP nurtured in him a warmth that was both erotic and exhilarating.

It was in early summer, past the second anniversary of the new economic order, when Aven became aware of the drive to MOP. The road had been widened on two occasions. It now contained eight full lanes, with six allotted to the natural flow of traffic. The limo was in one of the six lanes moving with the morning commute. The trip to work was just a brief interlude prior to the pleasures awaiting him at MOP.

Aven didn't bother to look up from his paper as he spoke to the driver.

"Are we here already? Seems as if you just picked me...."

"Sorry, sir, but there must be an accident ahead. No small wonder, the way these local maniacs drive."

Aven looked up from his paper. There was a car parked in each of the lanes on his left, and there were cars in front and behind these vehicles, extending as far as he could see.

"Unusual to have an accident on this road...six lanes, uninterrupted, and the weather conditions are perfect."

They remained motionless for a short time longer. As the driver pulled up to the MOP entrance, Aven looked at his watch. He had left the flat at six-fifty; it was seven-thirty-three.

"Good-bye."

"Good-bye, sir. Perhaps I should come a few minutes earlier tomorrow?"

"Perhaps. We can decide this evening."

Aven's path to the elevator was clogged with members of the MOP staff, each with an odd expression—a blend of bewilderment and levity. Aven gently forged through to see firsthand the source of these emotions. It was the elevator itself.

PING

The elevator doors remained open until any one of the assembled group moved to within a half meter or so. When this happened, the doors closed quickly, only to reopen as the trespasser retreated behind some invisible but very real line. Given the berth they apparently required, the elevator's doors re-opened. Not necessarily to the same tune.

PINK

The MOP workers were not about to be denied. Taking up the challenge in the spirit in which it was cast, they were rebuffed each time, and entrance to the elevator was disallowed as if by some mystical force. Aven watched as the workers persisted in their futile forays.

PANNNNK...

PING PING...

PANG PUNG PUNG PUNG...

Finally, as if frustrated by the slow-witted workers, the mysterious force indicated its desire to be left alone.

PINGPINGPINGPINGPINGPINGPINGPINGPINGPINGPINGPING-
PINGPINGPINGPINGPINGPINGPING...

Aven decided to walk, and he shouted above the din, "Would someone please call the maintenance section. It appears the elevator requires servicing."

Gaylord's desk was unoccupied, but the sound of voices directed Aven to his own office, where he found Gaylord and Sonny engaged in conversation.

"Good morning, gentlemen, or should I say afternoon. Getting to work this morning was a rather interesting experience, all in all."

"Hello, Aven."

"Mooornin, Aven. You talking 'bout the elevator? Probably just needs a little TLC."

"Yes, the elevator, but also the accident. And if you don't mind, what is TLC?"

"Sorry, Aven, I mean its monthly maintenance. Elevators are just like women. If you want to ride them, you're gonna have to service them regularly. What accident?"

"It's not really important, Gaylord. What's on the agenda today?"

Sonny responded.

"Aven, just keep doing what we've been doing of late. The economy is on a roll, and it will pretty much feed on itself so long as we keep the road ahead well oiled."

Gaylord appeared ready to utter one of his wry witticisms but thought better of it as the squeaky voice of Paula filled the room.

"Morning, gentlemen. Is something the matter with the elevator? It was shut down for repairs."

"Morning, Paula. Nothing serious, just due for its monthly maintenance."

"Oooowee, Gaylord. I think I know what you mean. But not to worry, things are going so well out there in the shops. The entire economy is taking off with retail sales leading the way...just what it's all about."

"That's good, Paula. Sonny was just talking about the economy. Looks like we're all on a roll."

"Right you are, Aven...."

The self-congratulatory conversation continued for some time, dominated by Paula, who was particularly excited about the opening of a new chain of clothing stores designed to carry the most daring of fashions for men as well as for women. It was sometime after lunch, during a break in the discussions about the economy, that Aven touched on Rena's discontent. He wasn't specific, nor did he suggest that the problem was of any real significance for Rena or for himself. Nevertheless, Paula leaped on the opportunity.

"Trust me, Aven. Nothing lifts a woman's spirits more than a good honest-to-God shopping spree, and whatever you might think, your Rena is no different than other women. Barbie's opens two weeks from Saturday. Put it on your calendar."

Nothing could be clearer to Aven than the futility of argument.

While Aven had agreed to Paula's edict, Rena had a far different attitude.

"Aven, you're kidding."

There were several variations on this theme, all played in moderately good humor, but Rena had little interest in a shopping trip and even less in spending time with Paula. She did, however, confront the matter of Aven's wishes. These were of concern to her, and as the Saturday in question neared, Rena yielded.

"OK, but please, let's meet Paula at the shop. The less time I have to spend with her...."

"Fine."

Saturday arrived. The limo came on time. Little was said over breakfast or on the drive to Barbie's. The shop was located in another of Moscow's redevelopment areas. Paula had explained how much classier a tone the new development lent to the neighborhood. The Big Top stood adjacent to a large retail mall that was home for some four hundred shops. Aven had been in on a number of MOP sessions where he, Paula, and his staff had explored the many subtle ways in which fantasy fabrication could be facilitated.

Paula's experience in Amerika, particularly at RSJ & S, proved to be invaluable in these efforts, efforts that had already borne fruit in the booming consumer expenditures. Rapid improvement in production had eliminated the problem of "monetary overhang" and the inflationary threat it posed when the Amerikans first arrived. Excessive spending was no longer of concern. In fact, to the delight of everyone at MOP, the Russian consumer had discovered the Amerikan VISA card. Gaylord suggested that the Russian version might be called "Poverty Passport," when they hit on the perfect name. Without application, every Russian citizen over the age of fifteen received the small plastic card that Paula had dubbed "HUSH." Even Gaylord could see the genius behind Paula's inadvertent suggestion. With access to such a card, the typical Russian citizen would have little to complain about.

"I think this is it, sir."

The driver's comment broke in on Aven's thoughts and the quiet between him and Rena. Both doors opened. As they got out of the limo, Aven could feel the grin spread across his face. Rena, too, had a look of wonderment.

"Rena, are you thinking what I'm thinking?"

"I think so, Aven."

"It's just like when I was a boy...only bigger."

What Aven was speaking of was the building that stood before them, with the gay, multicolored sign with old-fashioned lettering:

BARBIE'S BOUNTEOUS BIG TOP BOUTIQUE

But it was not the sign that so quickly transported them back to an earlier time. It was the building. No, it was the tent. The traveling circus was pretty much a thing of the past, but for Aven and Rena, who had watched the bears and ponies and men dressed in the funniest outfits entertain them in the small ring within the tent, the pleasures and the visual memory were easily recalled, as if that time of childhood innocence was missed too much. The tent that stood before them, made of a more durable material than the canvas of old, was of exactly the same shape that Aven now saw in his mind, only larger in area and much taller.

"My parents used to take me, too. It's a lot bigger, but I must say, Aven, I like it."

"Well, hello there."

They both recognized the voice.

"Isn't it just awesome? Oweeeeee, how I wish my great granddaddy could be here now. I had the place designed in his memory. Rena, you're going to love it. All just the way grandpa would have done it, I'm sure."

Aven was certain that Rena knew nothing of Phineas T. Barnum. But *he* knew, and he couldn't wait to get inside.

"Hi, Paula. We do love it. Reminds us of our childhood…what a wonderful idea."

"Hello, Paula. It was nice of you to suggest we meet like this. And I do love the feel of the circus you've created with the building. Perhaps we should take a look inside."

"Oh, I hope you do more than look, Rena. I know I will…oweeeee…as they say, shopping is the ultimate aphrodisiac."

"Really, I didn't know that. Did you, Aven?"

"No, actually I didn't, Rena. I thought it was power."

"Oh, I thought it was love."

"Come on folks, let's get busy, ah, I mean, let's see what's hot."

As they walked to the entrance, Paula explained that Barbie's was divided into three areas, rings, as they were called. The first, which they were nearing, was the Latest Loop, where the most modern chic products were put on display, usually with live models. The center ring, the largest, was for women. It was called the Ladies Circle. The third ring, for men, had been given the lusty moniker of Bull Ring.

"Oh, good, I think we're coming in at the start of a new product demo. Let's check it out."

Aven was reminded of those first days of the occupation when Paula, in her enthusiasm, would move across the combo room in a grand and sweeping manner. She was every bit as enthusiastic in introducing the products of free-market

capitalism as she had been the ideas—perhaps more. As they entered the Latest
Loop, they encountered a gaudily dressed young man with top hat and cane.
The band on his hat was white, and the crown had red and blue stripes running
in a vertical direction. He was wearing a sweater, with three bold stripes, the
same colors as his hat, and his pants and shoes were white. A candy-striped cane
spun in his hand as he barked his message:

> Hurra, hurra, hurra…step right up, ladies and gentlemen,
> hurra, hurra, hurra…the exotic, titillating, and mysterious
> Bobbsie Twins are about to give a live and in-the-flesh dem-
> onstration of Barbie's fresh and finest fantastic fashion
> find…the newest design in multifashion bra wear…you've
> never seen anything like it in your life…hurra, hurra, hurra,
> no charge, eeeeeevery thing aaaabsolutely freeeeee…hurra,
> hurra, hurra.

"Oweeee…let's hurry."

Aven and Rena followed Paula, who was clearly excited. Aven was both excited and somewhat overwhelmed. Rena was holding Aven's hand. Only a few
other people were in the Latest Loop area. Paula had explained that this would
be a good time to visit Barbie's, since the weekend was usually quiet. The biggest shopping day was Monday, and Barbie's, along with all of the other stores
that catered primarily to women, had major sales that day. Time spent with the
family on the weekend prevented many women from doing what they most
wanted to do—shop—and looking forward to the sales helped them overcome
the sorrow of Saturday and Sunday. In fact, these sales for women had become
institutionalized a few months earlier and, at Paula's suggestion, were called
"Blue Mondays." The demonstration area was on a platform only a few meters
in front of them. A group of fifteen or twenty other shoppers had gathered
around two scantily clad women.

"Aven, what an awful spectacle. And don't they remind you of Mila and
Jenna…you know, from the ministry…your old secretary, and Igor's."

Aven was having precisely the same thoughts. The two women did not
seem happy being where they were. He was also reminded of Mila and Jenna.

"I'm sure you're mistaken. Mila and Jenna were much too talented to be
working in this manner."

"Aven…do we really have to watch this tawdry display?"

"Rena, come on now, we only have to *look*, not buy…and if you want, you
can close your eyes."

He hoped that his humor would satisfy her. It didn't.

"Paula, if you don't mind, Aven and I would really like to move to the Ladies Circle."

When Aven first entered Barbie's, he had been instantly distracted by the barker and the incognito-bra demonstration. He didn't have a strong impression of the Latest Loop itself. The Ladies Circle would, on the other hand, create a lasting impression. From the instant they opened the wide swinging doors into the center ring, Aven's visual and auditory senses were confronted with a Herculean task, and it was to take some time before he understood where he was and what he was seeing and hearing. There was no doubt in his mind but that Rena was having the same experience. Paula, too, seemed very excited, but she had been in this state for some time.

The sound was overwhelming, but with overtones of familiarity. And before Aven could make sense of the music, the area's visual forces joined in the bombardment. Aven and the others stood transfixed in the midst of an overpowering swirl of color moving around and about them in every direction imaginable. They remained without voice for a time.

"My God, Rena, what is this?" shouted Aven.

"I haven't any idea."

"Oweeeeeeeee."

And then, as if by magic, both the sounds and colors took form. Aven was spellbound...and delighted. He realized where they were and what was happening. He spoke in a voice mixed with awe and admiration.

"Paula...Rena, this is fantastic. It's a carousel. The music, from the old calliope we used to love so much, and the colors whirling around are just like those handsome steeds we rode with such delight and fear, round and round and up and down...."

"Oweeeeeee, I hope my great granddaddy's listening."

Rena ignored Paula's squeal.

"You're right Aven...almost. When we used to watch the carousel and listen to the whistles and organ pipes and dream of riding those gallant horses that flew by us in a blaze of color, we were on the *outside*. Here it's like being at the center, where the man who collected the tickets used to stand, watching it spin all around us."

The brilliant reality of the Ladies Circle had set in. They were in the midst of a brightly lit circular area, well over a hundred meters in diameter. The colors that were whirling about them were actually the women's clothing on the shelves encasing the center ring of the Big Top. These were no ordinary shelves, however. The clothing—sweaters, blouses, skirts, scarves—was displayed along the rounded walls of the room, with each set of wall shelves approximately three meters in height. There were, as Aven counted, twenty such sets of wall shelves extending many meters up the walls. This gave the room a towerlike feel. What had created the whirling and blurred effect was the fact that each of the twenty shelves was moving at its own speed, in alternating counterclockwise and clockwise directions.

"With all of the clothes on the wall shelves, and the shelves themselves in constant motion, how does one get close enough to buy anything?"

"I was thinking the same thing, Rena....Paula, can you tell?"

"Oweeeeeeeeeeeeeeeeeee. Just look a little bit harder. There are so few shoppers here today, and it might not be obvious...see what I mean, and isn't this simply a killer kind of place. I mean, are we talking major league or...?"

"I think I see what Paula's talking about."

"I think I do too, Aven."

The scene before them, unique as it was, became intelligible. The few customers near the merchandise on the ground level ahead of them were standing on small platforms, each of which had a handrail on three of its sides. Each platform was large enough to hold several shoppers. The customers standing on the platforms on the ground level were, Aven and Rena realized at about the same time, *moving along with the shelves!* Having come to this discovery, it was only an instant before the two of them looked higher up on the walls. Sure enough, they saw several more platforms, each moving in pace with the particular level the customers had selected. While Paula wasn't entirely clear about the engineering, she seemed to think that the platforms were guided to the level the customer desired by magnetic control. Once on the level of choice, you just waited until the segment of the shelf you were interested in arrived before you and then engaged the magnetic control once again and moved along with the shelf, keeping you motionless with respect to the items of interest.

"This is really wonderful, Paula. The customer stands on the platform, and without taking a single step, the entire contents of the store is brought before her."

"And there's a dressing room every twenty meters on each of the levels. When a selection is made, the customer orders the item by voice electronics. What could be easier, or more fun...oweeeeeeeeee."

"It is a rather interesting concept, Paula, and I'm sure many Russian women can't wait until Monday. But wouldn't it be dangerous to have all of those women climbing the walls?"

Paula looked as if she didn't quite understood Rena. Aven did, and he made a quick calculation in his head.

"I don't see why there should be any problem, Rena. There's about a hundred and sixty *thousand* meters of shelf space here in Barbie's Big Top—plenty of room."

"And besides, with scads of shoppers, it just adds to the excitement...oweeeeee...let's say we take a look ourselves. We've been gabbing long enough."

Again in grand manner, Paula led Rena and Aven to the closest shelf. As they approached they saw one unoccupied platform and stepped onto it with some hesitation. Aven quickly took charge. He noticed that as their platform moved, another rose from below floor level ready for the next set of customers.

"What would you like to do, ladies? Stay on the first level or move up?"

"Oweeeeee, let's go everywhere."

"Let's *stay*."

"Perhaps we should see what's on this level, it's going to be time to leave soon."

"Oh that's no problem. Barbie's is open all the time, you know, a twenty-four-seven kind of place."

Aven decided to ignore Paula, especially since Rena had her fingernails pressing rather forcefully against the back of his hand.

"Come on, ladies, you're going to have to make up your minds, unreasonable a request as that might seem."

"The fingernails would soon draw blood," he thought.

"Well then, I'll pick...let's look at the sweaters."

"Oweeeeeeee."

Aven watched as the first-floor shelving passed before them. The shelf moved speedily, but he could recognize the various garments, and besides, an audio message was delivered to them from the speaker mounted on their personal platform announcing the sections as they approached from the right. They were on a counterclockwise level. Along came the camouflaged bras, ladies intimate nightwear, a very small section of flannel pajamas—Paula had noted that these were only for bluehairs—and several other sections, before they were alerted to the arrival of the sweater species—v-neck, scoop-neck, square-neck, plunging-neck, turtleneck, no-neck, pullovers, wraparounds, two-button, three-button, cardigan, solids, plaid, and combinations of these. Aven wondered how women had the time to decide which of the variations they wanted.

Paula offered an explanation.

"The more choices, the more people will buy, like the old Model-T Ford. That lovable but unsophisticated Henry just didn't have a clue about selling. All he ever cared about was whether or not his silly black car would work."

Rena chimed in at this point.

"I wonder how you can tell if these sweaters *work* or not."

Aven was sure she had drawn blood but refused to look at his hand or at Rena. Instead he engaged the magnet—or whatever it was that brought their platform in motion with the shelf—so that the sweaters remained motionless in front of them.

"Oweeeeeee, oweeeeeeeee, oweeeeeeee…Aven, how did you know?"

Aven was perplexed.

"What?"

Rena's fingernails dug deeper.

"Why, yes, love, how *did* you know?"

"Ladies, I don't know what either of you is talking about."

"Oh, Aven, you've stopped at just the right place."

Aven and Rena looked at the sweater in front of them. "Barbie's incredibly soft, silk and angora off-shoulder sweater, embroidered with faux pearl beading…it's a totally funky garment, really first-class Monday night attire…."

Aven wasn't sure how to respond. The white sweater that Paula was holding up to herself was attractive, if somewhat ostentatious. He did notice that it came in several other colors—peach, tea rose, carnation red, daffodil, aqua, spearmint, porcelain blue, and cornflower blue. But as Paula's joy mounted, Rena seemed less excited all the while, and Aven's hand was beginning to throb.

"Aven, I'm really very sorry, but I'm beginning to feel quite sick. Would you mind terribly if we left?"

"Oh, Rena, that's a pity. Perhaps you need to make a pit stop."

"Actually, Rena's been working nonstop these days, and Barbie's is a bit overwhelming for the first time…."

An expression of regret flickered over Paula's face but did not linger.

"No problem. Remember, I brought my own car. You two run along. If you don't mind, there are a few more things I wanna check out…oweeeeee. But you should walk through the Bull Ring on your way out. They say it's totally dyno…."

Perhaps they should have listened to Paula. Instead, at Rena's insistence, they headed for the nearest exit. It took them past a small section of the Ladies Circle devoted to women's cosmetics and beauty aids. There were very few people left in the store, but several customers were gathered around one of the counters. Neither Rena nor Aven could avoid stopping. On one of the countertops that had been draped in a white sheet, a middle-aged woman was lying on her side leaning on her elbow. Much of her body was covered with a slimy, claylike substance, pale green in color except for the buttocks area, which was covered in pink. Her head was wrapped in a towel, turban fashion. She was applying the last dollops of the slimy clay material, this time blue, to her face. As she did so, the woman behind the counter, dressed much like the barker in the Latest Loop, began speaking.

Laaaadies, do you notice that your skin needs help…that it's showing the stress of your demanding lifestyle and the inevitable effects of inattention? Are you going soft in all the wrong places? And gents, you might be seeing the veeeeery same thing but are reluctant to say anything to the little lady.…Weeeeeell then, come to the rescue with our Magic Spa Therapy Muds. These natural mud formulas, developed at the woooorld-renowned Frivola Spa in Italy, quickly renew the lady's skin and body firmness, revive its resiliency, and help her to recapture a more youthful texture. Each Frivola treatment cleanses, adds vim, and refreshes. Our model, the world-renowned Maid Fejee, is demonstrating Frivola's creamy blue clay emulsion facial, guaranteed to remove dulling surface skin cells and reveal, once again, the healthy gloooow that's itching to emerge. The green body mud can be spread aaaaaall over…it will bring back your lost elasticity.…And, if your man is toooooo embarrassed to say so, your mirror will tell you when to use our sensational pink contouring body mud. It firms, it tightens, and it is especially wonderful at removing the appearance of "orange peel" skin…so hurra, hurra, hurra…

They left before the barker had finished.

"Oh the cruel hand of fate," Aven thought to himself. "If we had gone out by way of the Bull Ring, Rena might well have found amusement in the things we sell to our Russian men. Instead, it's going to be a long drive home, and I probably won't hear the end of this for some time."

Aven was only partially right. It was a long drive home. He found himself thinking of what they had recently witnessed. Gaylord was right, there was a lot of old Phineas in Paula. And Aven thought he understood more profoundly than ever the genius that was Amerika. He was not justified in his concern regarding the longer term consequences of the shopping trip, however. After leaving the limo, Rena was never again to mention Barbie's Beauteous Big Top Boutique.

THE END OF
THE MIDDLE
■■■■■■■■■■■■■■■■■

April 1999–2000…FOURTH YEAR OF ECONOMIC EXPANSION
**** MILLIONS OF NEW JOBS CREATED **** INVESTMENT
OPPORTUNITIES AND FAMILY INCOMES RISING WITHOUT
REKINDLING INFLATION **** UNEMPLOYMENT DOWN
DRAMATICALLY **** SUCCESS OF NEW POLICIES NOW
READILY APPARENT **** STRAIN ON FINANCIAL INSTITUTIONS
NOTED **** RUSSIAN OPTIMISM OVER ECONOMIC GROWTH
NOW SHARED THROUGHOUT THE WORLD **** EXPANSION TO
CONTINUE **** GOVERNMENT WILL NOT IGNORE LESS
FORTUNATE: SAFETY NET CONTINUES TO BE PROVIDED ****
SUPPLEMENT TO FREE MARKET IN DEALING WITH AIR AND
WATER POLLUTION MAY BE NEEDED **** GOVERNMENT
DEFICIT LESS ALARMING **** EMERGENCY DEFICIT CON-
TROL REGULATIONS WORKING **** FURTHER DEREGULA-
TION IN TRANSPORTATION AND BANKING NEEDED ****
FINANCIAL INSTITUTIONS TO BE GIVEN GREATER FREEDOMS
**** PRIVATIZATION OF GOVERNMENT SERVICES UNDER WAY

April 2000–01…FREE MARKET POLICIES PAYOFF **** ECONOMIC
EXPANSION NOW IN FIFTH YEAR **** UNEMPLOYMENT CON-
TINUES TO FALL **** RAPID RISE IN BUSINESS INVESTMENT
**** TREMENDOUS GAINS IN EMPLOYMENT AND PRODUC-
TION WITHOUT INFLATION **** PAST PROBLEMS PLAGUING
ECONOMY AVOIDED **** NEW TAX REGULATIONS IN PLACE
**** GOVERNMENT DEFICIT REMAINS **** FOREIGN TRADE

DEFICIT REMAINS **** NEED FOR FURTHER REDUCTIONS IN
GOVERNMENT REGULATIONS: BENEFITS VISIBLE IN AIRLINE,
BANKING, RAIL, AND TRUCKING **** PRIVATIZATION CON-
TINUES: PUBLIC RAIL, OIL, AND POWER SOLD **** AGRI-
CULTURAL REFORM UNDER WAY: FREE-MARKET POLICIES
REQUIRED

renA renOOO

■ ■ ■ ■ ■ ■ ■ ■ ■ ■ ■ ■ ■ ■ ■ ■

*T*he Russian economy was in full bloom. By the turn of the century, it had become the envy of nations around the world. The few nations that had not fully freed their markets were themselves seeking immersion in the consecrated waters. They looked to Russia by way of example. Composition of the daily news banner, so crucial in the initial months of the revolution, had been delegated to the lower level staff at MOP.

The remaining economic concerns—and none were significant—were generated by the very success of the Russian economic machine. While unemployment was near record lows, a few unfortunate individuals remained in need of public assistance. The only consideration was in seeing to it that such assistance did not reduce work incentives among the more productive members of the society. This was easy enough, as the government safety net was kept at a realistically low level. The nation's concern with such matters as air and water quality and the occasional alarm expressed regarding traffic congestion were seen more as a manifestation of economic success than cause for alarm. Aven knew that too zealous an effort to mitigate these minor irritants could severely damage the entire Russian economy. Progress was slower in freeing up the nation's transport and financial systems, though here, too, there was no question that these last vestiges of the old regime would soon yield.

Aven luxuriated in his nation's economic success. He did encounter a few personal inconveniences, particularly the traffic, and one rather ugly, though isolated, event in the park. These were not significant. If there was an air of dissonance during this period, it remained in his relationship with Rena. And, more particularly, in how he came to see that relationship.

He was beginning to feel unmistakable signs of impatience with Rena. Not really with her, but with her failure to acknowledge the world around her. The world that he believed in so deeply and had had so much to do with.

"The entire world is singing praise to the Russian revolution. It wouldn't hurt her to say something complimentary every now and then. Women were born to nag, but Rena's had the benefit of a university education...and of living in the midst of the greatest economic revolution the world has known...perhaps I've been too forbearing. Perhaps I should take a more active role in her education...."

These thoughts began seeping into his consciousness.

Aven could not remember the last time the two of them had shared breakfast, nor when he had last eaten eggs and onions. And he had little interest or time in preparing them himself. He was feeling rushed in the mornings as the drive to MOP was taking longer and longer. Plans were under way to deal with the matter, but as of midsummer, early in the revolution's fifth year, Aven was allowing forty minutes for the commute. The comfort of the limo permitted Aven to work on the way to MOP, and thus the extended travel time presented no real burden. The six lanes of traffic into the heart of Moscow represented the blood flow surging through the veins of a very healthy patient. Indeed, the leisurely drive only added to the energy Aven brought to his work.

"Good-bye."

"Good-bye, sir."

"I wonder if it's working yet?"

PINGPINGPINGPINGPINGPINGPINGPINGPINGPINGPINGPING-
PINGPINGPINGPINGPINGPING...

"I wish the staff would stop teasing the elevator."

Aven walked to the second floor. The fact that the elevator had been acting up again did not cause him any difficulty.

"But it must be getting to some of the Labor and Industry staffers on the fourth and fifth floors," he thought.

"Gaylord, good morning."

"Mooooornin, Aven."

"Is there something we can do about that elevator?"

"Why, is it working?"

"Well, you might say so, the way our economy worked before we had the benefit of your Amerikan wisdom...and humor."

"Thank you, Aven. It may be time for a new elevator, or perhaps a redesign of MOP. We could eliminate all the difficulty with a single-story building."

"But then, how would the workers amuse themselves in the morning, and what would you have to joke about?"

"I'd find something."

In the more than four years of work with Gaylord, Aven had learned that if this stream of inane conversation was ever to end, the responsibility was his.

"Gaylord, did that banking matter get resolved last week? I'm beginning to think we need to exercise a bit more pressure."

"As a matter of fact, Aven, I asked the finance group to meet with you later this morning. And I think your intuition is correct."

In the week of the revolution's birth—Aven's rebirth—the Amerikan economists emphasized two points relevant to the Russian banking system. First, that a modern free-enterprise system of banking was absolutely essential to the long-term health of the economy, and second, that for all intents and purposes, the Russian economy had been without any banking system whatsoever. With all investment decisions centrally planned, Russia did not require a financial system to mediate such issues. In addition, consumers always paid with cash. There was no need to establish any system of consumer credit to stimulate consumption, since so little was available to purchase in the first place. The problem with the old system was not in creating *demand*; that was quite adequate. MOP's primary function, in fact, was the modulation of demand in keeping with the meager supply available to the consumer. Thus, most Russian banks performed the function of savings banks. Not much different, Aven was told, than the old blacksmith shop in the Amerikan Wild West, where the gold panner might deposit his modest amount of ore for safekeeping. The only Russian institution that functioned at all like a modern bank was the Bank for Economic Affairs, which approved all foreign loans and other credit transactions. With the revolution, all of this was to change.

The Amerikan economists had recommended fairly tight controls on the fledgling financial system. Such controls were not intended to remain in place for long, lest they stifle the initiative of the young banking executives who would be trained during the early phases of the revolution. However, once in place, these regulations proved difficult to remove. Sensing the need for firm action, Gaylord had asked the MOP financial staff to call together the heads of the nation's several major banking institutions in an effort to expedite the deregulation process. Three MOP staffers along with six of the nation's most influential bankers would be meeting with Aven shortly. Only a few details needed clarification.

"That's fine, then, Gaylord, as long as we protect the deposits, the bankers should have no fear of venturing beyond the regulations that were meant only to help them crawl as infants. They must be persuaded that they are well past that point now."

After the introductions, Aven wasted no time in focusing on the issue.

"Gentlemen, I'm not satisfied with the progress we've made in shedding ourselves of these many regulations, regulations whose usefulness has long since passed. Your institutions must join more quickly in our free-enterprise system. Continued reluctance to do so will soon hamper the nation's economic ascendancy. I don't think we need to spend much longer in discussion. The time for action is upon us, and has been for too long. Our staff has drawn up the necessary policies to bring your institutions fully into the twenty-first century."

As Aven handed the two-page memo to each of the bankers, he concluded, "They need no amplification."

The six bankers began to peruse the memo without enthusiasm. Gaylord had warned Aven that these men would not yield easily. They had become quite comfortable working within their cocoonlike environment, protected from the vigor of the marketplace by stringent government regulations. Little by way of creative initiative was asked of them in such an environment. Their institutions were held in place by layers of red tape.

One of the older men, overweight and obviously disturbed, began the counterattack.

"But Director _____, this memo would lift virtually all of the rules under which we operate. I'm sure you're aware of the difficulty we had in finding and training workers who could properly assess individual and business creditworthiness, men and women who could read and understand the most basic of accounting statements and who were familiar with the vast assortment of modern money management techniques. If we remove all regulations, including the strictures on lending, why, I shudder to think what would happen to the public confidence. And without that trust, our banking system cannot function...I'm sure you understand that."

The other bankers nodded and mumbled their agreement.

"Gentlemen, it's you who don't understand. We are not here to debate. This memo *is the new policy.* If the implications are not clear, I ask that you trust me and the efficacy of the free market. The latter will provide you and your colleagues with far more satisfactory guidance than the volumes of regulations that have been cluttering your desks, and minds. Now, are there any *further* questions?"

The fat banker, who had evidently been chosen as spokesman, persisted.

"Forgive me, Director _____, but with all due respect, we have far more exp—"

"Perhaps *too much* experience, in a protected environment."

"Please, please, I beg you, let me finish. Our citizens have become accustomed to government protection of the banking system. Without such protection, the trust we have built over these past four years could evaporate overnight."

"Suit yourselves, gentlemen. I'm sure that the MOP personnel section will be able to locate replacements if you so desire, and the public confidence will remain as strong as ever. Read the memo again. We have no intention of eliminating government insurance on any deposits. We know full well how important such protection is. By having it in place, we *assure the fact that it will never be needed.*"

The bankers were looking again at the MOP memo. Aven could see a change in their collective expressions. The large man spoke again, with far less belligerence.

"Do we understand correctly, Director _____, that each bank in the nation will now be free of all regulations and limitations placed on its lending activity?"

"That's correct. Where you choose to lend will be governed solely by profitability. The market will provide ample discipline…"

"…and the government will *continue to insure all deposits?*"

"That's absolutely correct. You all can read, I assume."

The bankers, one after the other, appeared to regain their confidence. They responded to Aven in unison.

"Director _____, we are with you one hundred percent. Your plan to install free-market principles into our nation's financial system will be a boon to us all."

A more relaxed conversation followed. As the bankers and the MOP financial staff departed, Aven turned to Gaylord.

"I think we should have our staff meet with the airline executives, next week if possible."

"I'll take care of it, Aven. But what about the boys who play with the trucks and trains? Shouldn't we free the lot of them all at once?"

"Why not? The sooner these overly comfortable executives face up to the exhilaration of competing in a free-market environment, free of regulation and subsidy, the better off we'll all be."

Aven paused and leaned back in his chair, letting his mind wander.

"Oh, Gaylord, just think of all we've accomplished in such a short time…and we've only scratched the surface. By the way, that was a good meeting. It took a while, but I do believe those overfed bankers got the idea."

"Not only got it, Aven, but took to it like sharks at a feeding frenzy. You really had them drooling at the end."

The movement to speed deregulation in the transport industries occurred not long after the bankers had gaily left MOP. The transport industry executives departed with somewhat less enthusiasm. Deregulation would indeed impose the rigors of competitive markets, but they were offered nothing comparable to the government-guaranteed deposit insurance that provided the bankers such peace of mind.

Having completed their work well before midafternoon, Aven asked Gaylord if he wanted to take advantage of the pleasant summer weather.

"That sounds like a great idea, Aven. Let's see if Sonny wants to join us."

Gaylord made the call from his own office, while Aven remained at his desk, idly turning to the books behind him. He had had little occasion to refer to them these past two years, but the ideas they contained continued to provide the Russian people with ever-increasing material abundance. As his glance fell onto the picture of Rena at the lake, he couldn't help but feel a slight pang of regret and vexation.

"It's a shame she insists on searching out the unfavorable news above all else. Not only a shame," he thought to himself, "but tiresome as well. She talks and writes as if the isolated problem is commonplace."

Sonny joined them as they left MOP in the late July afternoon.

"Why don't we head in toward Red Square? I understand there's a quite unusual show at the museum."

"Sounds good to me, Gay-babe."

"Listen, fellows, if you don't mind, I'd rather not take the time, and besides, I've seen the show. It's fabulous. I wouldn't mind seeing it again, but some other time."

"Aven, what's with you lately? Pretty soon you're going to be an expert on modern art *and* music. You've been listening to that weird stuff all the time. But fine, we can check out the show later. It's gonna be around till the end of the month. Where *would* you like to walk?"

"The park. I haven't been there in over a year, maybe longer. Before you arrived, I used to walk there every morning and evening, sometimes during lunch as well. Come on, we can do the full loop and still be back within the hour....Is there a problem of some sort? You look as if I've suggested we shoot ourselves in the foot."

"Naw, Aven, ah, sounds like a great idea."

"That's right, Aven, like Sonny-bo says, a *great* idea, especially with *three* of us."

"Well, then what are we waiting for?"

Sonny and Gaylord quickly caught up with Aven, and the three continued on side by side. It was only a few short steps before familiar sights and smells addressed Aven's senses.

"It really has been a long time," he thought to himself, "...and looks like a lot has happened."

The widening of the road did intrude on the park space. It had not impacted at all on the longer dimension of the park, some seven city blocks in all, but the feeling of openness had all but vanished. The walkway was now only a few feet from the eight lanes of road, nearly full to capacity despite the hour. Separating them from the stream of traffic was a narrow strip of grass, most of which was occupied by an endless row of benches. The benches were occupied mainly by isolated individuals who, best as Aven could determine, were mostly men. Many were lying on the bench, facing away from the walkway, toward the slow-moving cars a few feet away. Others sat with a fixed gaze upon their face. The park greenery, laced with a variety of flowers vaguely familiar to Aven, along with the warmth and brightness of the summer afternoon, provided a vivid contrast with the mood conveyed by these men.

They had been walking in silence for several minutes, almost as if in awe of the powerful contradictions so close at hand.

"Who are these people? Don't they have anything better to do than sleep or stare the day away?"

"Sonny-bo, why don't you explain to Aven. These are what your economist colleagues call the voluntary unemployed. You know, Aven, for the economy to function smoothly, there has to be a small amount of slack, including some unemployment. These are the folks who volunteered."

"That's not exactly what we mean by the term, Gay-babe, but close enough. And of course, these men and women are paid for their work, out of the safety net. Not too much, mind you."

"Right on, Sonny-bo. You can see for yourself, Aven, if the pay was too high, we'd soon run out of benches."

"It seems to me that even with space for more benches, there's something immoral about paying people for not working."

"I'm not so sure about that, Aven. I can think of a few people I'd like to pay for not working, might even be the ethical thing to do in some cases."

"Don't try to be a wiseacre, Gay-babe. I think we've established to most everyone's satisfaction, if you can earn a wage in the market, the question of ethics does not arise. These people around us are simply incapable of performing productive work."

"Aven, what he means to say is that these folks are too sick, physically or mentally, too high on drugs, too ignorant, too lacking in productive skills to make it in the labor market. And, of course, they come by these attributes *voluntarily*."

"Gaylord, you're not trying to pull my leg, are you?"

Not a great deal more was said on the subject. They were approaching the part of the park where the food concessions used to be located. For an instant, Aven thought of suggesting Luigi's pizza. The trees on the side of the path away from the road were abruptly replaced by a thick hedge well over three meters in height. This, too, was new to Aven.

"Isn't that the central park area, beyond the hedges, where McDonatelli's used to be located?"

"That's right, Aven. They're still there, and according to Paula, they feed over thirty-five thousand customers."

"Wow, in a *week*? That's really impressive."

"I think Gay-babe means a *day*, Aven...."

"Who would have thought? But come to think of it, when we first brought your Amerikan Beeg Meks over, almost twenty years ago, they were a smash hit as well."

"Yeah, Aven, and that was before we had perfected the freeze-dried pizza process. McDonatelli's pizzas are a hell of a lot tastier than what we used to pass off for food, fast or otherwise."

"Sounds delicious. Why don't we have a look?"

"That won't be easy. The entrance is on the far side of the hedge, quite a distance."

"That's peculiar, it means you can't really get there from the park."

"Well, Aven, I think the reason for the hedge is to keep out the traffic noise and fumes."

"Sonny-bo's right on again, Aven. Mix those auto fumes with a mushroom and onion pizza and we're talking a real gas attack. And snarfing a slice of pizza with the voluntary unemployed peeking in might also cause a bit of indigestion."

"Put that way, the hedge makes good sense."

Aven looked at his watch. They had been walking for almost a quarter of an hour.

"I guess we should turn back," he thought, and as he did, the warm light of the afternoon sun was pushed from the park.

Aven glanced upward. A large cloud, the only one in the sky, had made its way between the men and the source of warmth and light. While the drop in temperature was not apparent, the premature grayness was. The trio had come upon a break in the row of benches, in whose place was an unusual sight. Lying where the benches had been were six coffinlike objects that appeared to be made of a durable cardboard, obviously very light in weight. The boxes were between two and three meters in length, with a pentagonal shaped opening. The five-sided receptacles lay side by side, their open ends close to where Aven and his companions were standing and the closed ends only a few centimeters from the eight lanes of traffic, which had grown dense with the afternoon commute.

"Mobile homes."

"What?"

"Aven...sorry, I might have failed to mention them. Sonny-bo's trying a bit of economistic humor. They're portable sleeping shelters. We've had them in the States for years. They fold up and weigh about five kilograms."

"Gaylord, between Sonny's effort at humor and your failed clarity, I'm missing the point."

"Let me try, Gay-babe. We came upon this idea in the late eighties, Aven. The number of men and women without a place to sleep...."

"Yeah, Aven, we used to call them the homeless. 'Happy Campers' turned out to be more appropriate, and you gotta admit, Dan Quayle can really turn a phrase."

"That he can, Gay-babe. Our cities were having a difficult time locating sufficient housing, or at least a place to sleep, and the number of happy campers increased. Mind you, the number was never all that large, and a lot lower than our bleeding-heart liberals claimed. These campers also liked to move around."

"Like birds migrating south every summer...."

"You might say that. At any rate, these portable sleepers fold up, and the happy campers take them from place to place."

"And if you notice, they're built to be stacked in rows, beehive fashion. In some of our more popular and hospitable camping grounds like New York City and Santa Cruz, California, the hive often occupies several city blocks, extending to twenty or more levels."

"For a while, Aven, we exported them to your country, but you're beginning to develop enough of a demand to warrant your own production facility. One opened in Moscow last year."

"Be a major industry soon, right, Sonny-bo?"

Before the conversation could continue, Aven became aware of the presence of several individuals who had appeared as if from nowhere.

"Something we can help you fellas with?"

Six men were standing a few feet away. It was clear that the mobile homes belonged to them. Aven could recognize two as Asians, perhaps from Tibet. The others were Russian citizens, all fairly young, not over thirty to thirty-five years of age, and of varying height and weight. From the clothing covering their bodies and the looks on their faces, Aven realized they were among the voluntarily unemployed cadre of men they had been passing along the walk in the park. The person who had spoken was well built, though there was nothing attractive about the sound of his voice, which was seething with sarcasm.

Sonny and Gaylord responded simultaneously.

"Uh oh."

Gaylord added, "No, man, everything's cool. We were just leaving."

Sonny joined in, "That's right, awful good to see you fellas. Take care now."

"I don't think you fellas wanna leave just yet. Why, we've hardly had a chance to get acquainted."

One of the Asians added his voice to the fray.

"He's right ya know, ain't nothing like an exchange of gifts to improve relations."

"What my friend Stilts is talking about, *gentlemen...*" (the stench of sarcasm was even greater than the odor coming from the six men), "...is the fact that we could get to know each other a lot quicker...and you could be on your way. Wouldn't cost very much at all. Three of you, let's see, how 'bout a thousand rubles each?"

Aven's anger had been increasing from the moment these slovenly clad and foul-smelling men had arrived on the scene. Slowly at first, but with this last blatant attempt at extortion, Aven exploded.

"Just a goddamn minute. Who in the hell do you sons of pig-eating camels think you are?...Do you have any idea...?"

As the strangers moved closer, Aven felt Gaylord's arm on his, pushing him gently away from the six men. Gaylord picked up the conversation where Aven had left off, in a different style and manner.

"Hey, easy now. My friend here means no harm. A little hot-headed, that's all....And a thousand rubles, nooooo problem. Don't you agree, Sonny?"

"Right on, Gay-b-babe. Sounds like a deal to me."

Aven wasn't sure which was more stunning, the appearance of the six thugs or Gaylord and Sonny's cowardly capitulation. He was about to resume where Gaylord had interrupted him, but didn't. The force of Gaylord's arm and expression somehow kept him still.

The trace of a smile appeared on the Asian's face. A sneer remained on the other faces. The Asian spoke for the group.

"Sounds like a done deal—no muss, an' everybody leaves friends. You fellas feel free to come down here whenever you want. We're always happy to renew acquaintances, isn't that right, fellas?"

Stilts's five companions nodded as if to second the invitation.

Aven followed Sonny's lead. He took a thousand-ruble note from his wallet and handed it to the sneering Russian. The sneer seemed riveted to his face. The three departed, walking back along the path that had brought them to the six happy campers. Aven's fury detracted substantially from the pleasures of the walk. So, too, did the sight of the men and women sitting or lying on the benches along the way. For the first time since they had met well over four years ago, Aven's feelings toward Gaylord were anything but positive. They had walked on for some time. Aven finally dared to look back over his shoulder. The six extortion artists were nowhere in sight.

"Gaylord…."

"I know what you're thinking, Aven."

"I don't see how. How could you possibly allow…."

"Aven, please, hear me out."

"I think you should, Aven. Gaylord and I have had a lot of experience in these matters, like anyone else living in New York."

"Not just New York, Sonny-bo. Aven, what you saw happen back there used to be commonplace in my country."

"*Commonplace?* Six muggers walk up to you in broad daylight? A few feet from the traffic, in plain sight of hundreds of drivers?"

"I know it was upsetting, Aven, especially the first time. But listen for a minute, you've certainly lived enough to know that crime of one sort or the other will always be with us. Imperfections in character and inequality of income assure it. We are unlikely to eliminate the first, and the economy can't function without the latter."

Aven could feel the resentment ebb as Gaylord continued.

"Now, the best way to circumvent confrontation in these situations is to simply avoid putting yourself in a vulnerable position in the first place."

"You mean we shouldn't have walked in the park?"

"Either that, or have ample security where you choose to walk."

"He's right as usual, Aven, and in our country we do both. Stay out of the parks populated by the happy campers, and secure the others."

"More important though, Aven, and Sonny will agree, you might not be able to provide adequate security in every place all of the time. Sometimes you need to know what to do when confronted by happy campers."

"That's what bothers me, Gaylord, giving in without a fight. Those bums will think it's always that easy."

"I'm sure that they'd have preferred we refuse their modest demands. Then they would have gotten our money, and our skulls as well. No, Aven, we handled the situation to perfection. A straight business deal."

"Right on, Gay-babe. And if they're still craving some physical action at day's end, they always have each other. Really, Aven, there's only one sensible way to think. It's all *business*, and the bottom line is you want to *come out ahead*."

As if the confrontation in the park had never occurred, Aven's mood was transformed. The lessons of the past half hour, both physical and intellectual, had been powerful. And as with all knowledge, he felt stronger for its acquisition.

The three men parted a short while after returning to MOP. Aven shook Gaylord's hand warmly.

"Thanks, Gaylord. You were, as Sonny always says, right on about the park. The lessons were well worth the few rubles…in fact, I think I had a good time. See you in the morning."

In the time following the instructive event in the park, work at MOP continued apace. The easing of government regulation was well under way in the transport and banking sectors. In the former, more and more firms were competing for the Russian travel ruble. A host of institutions were springing up all over the financial landscape. In major city and small village alike, banks had become fiercely aggressive in their lending policies. Production, employment, and profits rose to record heights throughout the economy. The elevator continued to act up from time to time, but otherwise, the mood at MOP echoed the euphoric state. Aven's encounter with the happy campers had long since faded from his memory. It was this healthy attitude that contributed to the mild argument with Rena.

"Aven, we have to talk."

This was how Rena had greeted him on that late fall evening. These words were all the more jarring, since he hadn't seen her for several days. Rena had been off on another research project. She had taken to frequent and extended travel, and the more she was away on these morbid muckraking ventures, the less she wrote and the less success she had in publishing the few essays she managed to complete. Aven attributed her melancholy to the nature of her work. In much of what she had done, Rena was simply out of step with the vast majority of citizens.

"Am I permitted entrance into the flat, and a glass of wine?"

"Yes, of course, Aven. Come on in. You won't believe what's going on, and somehow we, you…I don't know, it just can't continue."

If he was to have wine, he'd have to get it himself. He did, and poured a glass for Rena. During the next two hours, he managed to consume several glasses of the calming liquid. Rena's glass remained where he had first placed it, its contents undisturbed.

"Aven, we've been visiting several of the major urban areas."

"We" referred to Hester and Ivan, both of whom were without regular employment. Rena had offered them work with her. Rena earned very little these days, and much of what she paid Hester and Ivan came from Aven's salary, but Aven had not objected. Aven's mind wandered, and he lost some of what Rena was saying. Her initial criticisms focused on the "obscenities of prosperity" as they impacted women, middle age and older—the clothing/cosmetics/surgery/ suction/high-medium-low impact aerobics/dance/yoga/jogging/walking/ meditation/Zen/hot tubs/saunas—moist and dry///////. Aven had listened to too much of this. Rena's complaints soon blended into one screaming condemnation of economic success. More recently, she had turned to the "barbarisms of poverty" as they impacted younger women and girls.

"…the rise in crime, and not just petty shoplifting, no, Aven, I'm talking about violent crime. More and more young women and girls, teenagers and younger, are taking part in robberies, assaults…murders….Aven, *are you listening to me?*"

Aven refilled his glass.

"Yes, Rena, I'm listening, but you don't have to shout. These are isolated instances after all."

"They're not isolated, and if I'm shouting, it's because no one seems to be listening."

"I am, you know that."

"Well then, do something! Young girls, if they're not running loose on the streets, are running in gangs, fourteen-, fifteen-year-olds, collecting their monthly dues to buy guns for themselves. Aven, do you know how many gangs there are in Moscow alone?"

"I really haven't been paying a great deal of attention, Rena."

"You, or anyone else."

"Rena, it's not as if I haven't been busy these past six years. And you talk as if so little has been accomplished. Perhaps…."

"Oh, a good bit has been accomplished, Aven. And some of us are better for it. But some of what we are accomplishing is making us *all* poorer. These young girls don't join because it's fun. They're *born into the gangs*, born of young women who have lost all hope, young women who have never met their fathers…young men themselves, long since dead, or in prison, or on the streets half crazed with what this society has done to them."

There was much Aven could have said at this point. Rena's irrational discourse had brought the incident in the park vividly to his mind. Rena continued.

"These miserable creatures have become our throwaways, cast off from families already broken, beaten and abused as children. Some of them are on the streets even before their teens, doing every horrible thing imaginable, if only to stay alive for another day. Aven, why? Tell me why we are ignoring them?"

"They could solve much of their own difficulty with a little restraint, particularly in sex, if they'd just have more sense and fewer babies. It's not as if these people are ignorant of birth control, one pill a year. And we do pay attention to them. A good deal of attention, if you ask me."

"Don't you understand, Aven? Having babies often seems like the *right* and *best* thing to do. They know too well that the only time they'll *ever* have a chance to have a child is in those few years when they are still healthy enough. Oh yes, we do pay attention to some of them as long as they have a half ruble to spend. Your men at MOP find ways to court them. I suppose you don't know anything about the new advertising campaign, a Paula brainstorm, I'm sure. It's called 'Be All You Can Be—Be a Callous Cookie.'"

"Rena...let's stop. It bothers me more than you know to see you so upset, and I hope you believe me, I've never heard of that ad campaign. I doubt if it was Paula's idea, and I don't like it at all. 'Callous Cookie' is hardly an image anyone would aspire to. I promise I'll look into it first thing in the morning."

"Look into what, Aven?"

"The ad, of course."

"That's all...?"

The tears were pouring from her eyes. Aven left his chair. He picked Rena up as gently as he could and carried her to the bedroom. She was far too exhausted, physically and emotionally, to do anything about eating, much less prepare for bed. Aven tucked her in, clothes and all, and kissed away some of her tears.

"I'll look into everything, Rena."

The next day, Aven discovered that an over-zealous member of the public relations section had installed the "Callous Cookie Campaign" in an effort to increase beer and cigarette sales among younger working women. Aven suggested that they drop the slogan and find more subtle ways of increasing sales. He also had every intention of inquiring about the other issues, but didn't. Rena's concerns were greatly exaggerated, and the continued rush of economic success diverted his attention.

The news of Sonny's departure came as a shock, but in truth, Sonny was no longer needed. The finale lunch for the upbeat Amerikan economist was given added zest by a special video presentation Paula had arranged for the senior staff. Traffic was lighter than normal that morning, and Aven arrived at work a few minutes early.

"Good-bye."

"Good-bye, sir."

PINGPINGPINGPINGPINGGGGGGGGGGGGGGGGGGGGGPING-
PINGPINGPINGPINGPIIIIIIIIIIIIIIINGPINGPING

Only two or three individuals were watching the elevator. These periodic seizures had lost their novelty for most of the MOP staff.

"Morning."

"Good morning, Gaylord. Is there something wrong."

"Not really, Aven. It's just that…"

"It's Sonny, isn't it? I know how you feel. I'm going to miss him, too. Where's he going?"

"Back to the States. Seems as if they've become rather desperate for his services. He asked if he could return at the end of the month, but no luck. You know, Aven, Sonny and I are much more than friends and colleagues. We've become soul brothers."

Aven had little taste for extended morbidity.

"Oh, I didn't know that. Hhmmm, sole brothers. Does that mean you wear the same size shoe? Or do you have similar taste in seafood?"

"Thanks, Aven. I know you're trying to help."

"Why, not at all. I'm quite serious."

"Well then, my serious but unlettered friend, perhaps you need a lesson in spelling."

"Spelling?" Aven had succeeded. The two rows of glistening white teeth had returned as Gaylord responded.

"It's soul, S-O-U-L, and there's nothing fishy about our relationship. We've developed an honest spiritual and emotional kinship, closer than any I've had before. But I am feeling better. As usual, a conversation with you always helps."

The remainder of the morning passed quickly. Aven and Gaylord had a brief conversation with some of the MOP staff. Aven had to intervene in a dispute regarding payments to the small indigent population residing in Moscow. He sided with those recommending a reduction in government outlays, and the matter was settled forthwith. The lunch for Sonny was pleasant. Good food and wine as usual. The senior members of MOP sat around the dining table well satisfied with all that they had been party to. Per Paula's request, the farewell comments were brief. Paula had a special "treat," as she put it, and wanted to proceed as expeditiously as possible. With Sonny's final words, Paula rose from her seat.

"Ooooweeeeeeeeeeeeeeeeeeeeeeeeeeeee….Gentlemen, you'll soon be every bit as jazzed as yours truly…oweeeeeeeeeeeeee."

Paula paused for an instant, as if to pull herself together. She walked towards the dining room kitchen and office, opened the door, and announced, "We're ready for the video presentation."

Aven was aware of the multimedia capabilities of the dining area. Over the past few years, he had witnessed several slick presentations dealing with new products or methods of production that were about to be introduced into the economy. He had enjoyed all of them, and was looking forward to whatever it was that had Paula so aroused.

"Before the video, a few words of explanation are in order. You're all familiar with the recreational development area north of the city."

"Paula, do you mean Sidney Land, the eleventh Wonder of the World?" It was the head of parks and recreation, Janos Vatts, who had spoken.

"Yes, precisely, and I'm sure you remember the origin of Sidney Land."

"Why, yes, Paula, an Amerikan concept brought to our country by good old Gorby as he was retiring. If memory serves, it started in California, then Florida. One in every state now. Good clean family entertainment, and ours is doing very nicely as well."

"Not quite, Janos. All but Nevada. Indeed, your Moscow Sidney Land is doing well, but not well enough. Attendance peaked at the park well over four years ago. An average of fifty thou a day. Not bad, gentlemen, but there's a gaping pocket in the entertainment market out there just waiting to be filled."

Gaylord leaned across the table to Sonny and whispered, none too softly, "I think she means a pocket to be picked."

"Hush, Gaylord. Now then, your Sidney Land is just too family oriented. Parents can take the kids once or twice a year at most, and then only for the few years until the little brats grow up. Oh, sure, new customers are born every day, but you gotta admit, even for the little duddly dipshits, there's always going to be a limit on how many times they can ride the Fantasamagora Falls before they're boaging their cotton candy all over the place."

"I think we see your point."

Aven broke in on his staffer's comment.

"Isn't it also true that the number of children per family is declining?"

"And many couples are opting to enjoy the pleasures of a two-family income instead of a two-child family."

Gaylord added his contribution.

"Right you are, gentlemen. I don't know why it's taken us this long to make the necessary adjustment, but what counts is that we have. Gentlemen of MOP, hold on to your hats. The video you're about to see is gonna blow you away. We call it the EPTOC CRUX. Doesn't stand for a thing, but it has a nice ring."

The room darkened as Paula's piercing voice gave the signal to begin.

The letters E-P-T-O-C C-R-U-X grew larger, and the music swelled to a dramatic crescendo, followed by the fanfare of an army of trumpets. The music faded, only to assume a more gentle, pastoral quality as the helicopter camera panned effortlessly over the city of Moscow on its way north. Sidney Land soon came into view, and the voice of the announcer repeated much of what Paula had been telling them. As the announcer spoke, the helicopter altered direction, heading easterly from Sidney Land.

...only a short twenty kilometers to the east...the charming crystal lake, under state control, had been underutilized for years...but no longer...thanks to the combined genius of Amerikans from Florida and Nevada, we are proud to present the world's finest, and most modern gaming center....

A small lake came into view, soon in its entirety. Something stirred inside Aven. A clouded sense of recognition.

"It's the lake, *our* lake."

The absence of trees and cabins had obscured his memory for an instant.

...each of the four major casinos has a hotel capacity of fifteen thousand guests, housed comfortably in the six thousand uniquely designed rooms. There is a gaming area on each of the twenty stories....

Four pavilions surrounded the small body of water, and each stood as tall as the length of the lake itself. They were quite oddly shaped, but a smile came to Aven's face as the camera moved slowly to each in turn.

"A club, diamond, heart, and spade...brilliant!" he thought.

The four giant and cleverly shaped casinos glimmered as the sun reflected from each of them. They were painted in bright metallic colors of red, silver, black, and blue, matching the glistening lake that they dwarfed.

...bus service direct from Moscow center will commence before the onset of Spring...

"In less than a month...."

Aven was beginning to share Paula's excitement.

"Oweeeeeeee," he said to himself.

...every five minutes. There will be no charge for transportation and only a nominal room fee. Plans are under way to increase the bus service by late July....A sky tram will also be running every minute, direct from Sidney Land, as soon as the expanded childcare facilities there are completed.

The inspirational scenes of the lake and its surrounding development faded. Aven found himself viewing the inside of a large gaming room—bright lights, music, green-clothed tables with smiling, glamorous, and well-dressed men and women obviously enjoying themselves. Beyond these tables, he saw row upon row of elderly men and women, mostly women, none as well dressed as those draped over the men around the tables, furiously interacting with the small machines before them.

> ...the largest gaming arenas in Amerika will be no match for the EPTOC CRUX....

The gaming room faded from the screen. The lake and its four monumental vaults reappeared, slowly receding in the distance, along with the bucolic sound of violins. The trumpet fanfare grew louder in pace with the expanding EPTOC CRUX. The viewers remained silent for some moments, as if stunned by the glamour of what they had all just witnessed.

"Paula, this is fantastic. Do we have any other literature? We need to get the word out to the public."

"Oh, Aven, I wouldn't worry about that. Your citizens will become addicted to the pleasures of EPTOC soon enough, but we do have copies of the brochures that will be going out in the Sunday edition of the news, a week before the opening. They're in my office."

Aven took one of the brochures home with him that evening. It was informative, containing the most impressive shots that he had seen on the video. He was hoping that Rena would be home. She was, but her dour greeting dissuaded him from broaching the subject immediately. He did so not long after dinner.

"Rena..."

"Aven, what is this?"

"A wonderful new concept in...."

In his excitement to show Rena EPTOC CRUX, he had omitted many of the details. He began from the beginning.

"Our lake?"

Her voice was hardly audible.

"Yes, Rena, and isn't it wonderful? So many more people. I can't wait to get back."

"Aven, that's not *our* lake."

It was clear that she didn't yet recognize the lake. He was about to show her the location of their favorite spot on the picture in the glossy pamphlet, but Rena had already left the room. She must have worked late that night, as Aven fell asleep in an otherwise unoccupied bed.

THE END?

■■■■■■■■■■■■■■■■

*A*pril 2001-02…ECONOMIC POLICIES TO CONTRIBUTE TO RIS-
ING STANDARDS OF LIVING IN THE FUTURE AS WELL
**** GOVERNMENT DEFICIT REDUCTION PLANNED ****
INFLATION ABSENT THROUGHOUT STRONG ECONOMIC
GROWTH **** EMPLOYMENT GROWTH DRAMATIC: ALL
REGIONS BENEFIT **** TURKMENS, TADZHIKS, AZERBAY-
DZHANIES SHARE IN PROSPERITY **** ESTONIANS AND
LATVIANS CONSIDER RETURN **** GROWTH IN JOBS NOT LIM-
ITED TO LOW-QUALITY, DEAD-END POSITIONS **** RUSSIAN
ECONOMIC RECORD FAR SURPASSES OTHER INDUSTRIAL
NATIONS **** DESPAIR OF EARLIER DAY HARD TO BELIEVE
**** GOVERNMENT INTRUSION INTO THE ECONOMY GREAT-
LY REDUCED, BUT OVERREGULATION STILL PRESENT IN
BANKING, TRUCKING, NATURAL GAS **** AUTO PRODUCERS
TO BE FREED OF MILEAGE STANDARDS AND OTHER IMPEDI-
MENTS TO EFFICIENCY **** BENEFITS OF PRIVATIZATION
APPRECIATED ACROSS THE CONTINENT **** CHALLENGES
REMAIN, INCLUDING GOVERNMENT AND TRADE
DEFICITS **** CALLS FOR PROTECTIONISM TO BE RESIS-
TED **** FIRST DEMOCRATIC ELECTIONS ONLY A YEAR OFF

April 2002-03…MALAISE, DEMORALIZATION, AND IMPOTENCE OF
EIGHT YEARS AGO VANISH **** RUSSIAN CITIZENS FEEL AS IF
THE WORLD WERE BORN ANEW **** TIDE OF HISTORY NOW
FLOWING IN RUSSIAN DIRECTION **** RESPECT RESTORED
TO RUSSIA **** NATION BRIMMING WITH SELF-CONFIDENCE:
A MODEL FOR THE WORLD **** PRODUCTS ONCE UN-

IMAGINED NOW COMMONPLACE **** FORMER LUXURIES NOW CONSIDERED THE NECESSITIES OF LIFE **** RUSSIAN CAPITALISM EMERGES TRIUMPHANT **** SAFETY NET FOR THE POOR TO PROMOTE INDIVIDUAL INITIATIVE **** REGULATION MAY BE REQUIRED IN PROTECTING AIR AND WATER **** ENVIRONMENTAL REGULATIONS TO BE BASED ON SOUND ECONOMIC PRINCIPLES **** UNPRECEDENTED ECONOMIC GROWTH IN EIGHTH YEAR: TESTIMONY TO WISDOM OF POLICIES **** ALL SEGMENTS OF THE NATION HAVE BENEFITED: ETHNIC GROUPS DO PARTICULARLY WELL **** INFLATION A THING OF THE PAST **** COMPETING POLITICAL PARTIES FORM: PLATFORMS TO BE UNVEILED EARLY NEXT YEAR **** NEW ECONOMIC AGENDA NOT FULLY ACCOMPLISHED **** GOVERNMENT DEFICIT REDUCTION DESIRABLE **** FOREIGN TRADE DEFICIT REDUCTION DESIRABLE **** CHALLENGE FOR THE FUTURE: CONTINUE PRIVATIZATION ALONG WITH REDUCTION IN GOVERNMENT REGULATION **** TREND OF PAST 100 YEARS REVERSED **** VITALITY AND CREATIVITY OF RUSSIAN PEOPLE, NOT GOVERNMENT, MAKE A GREAT NATION

GOODBYEFOREVER
■ ■ ■ ■ ■ ■ ■ ■ ■ ■ ■ ■ ■ ■ ■ ■

*T*he glorious expansion of historic proportion and duration showed no signs of abating. The increasing debt among consumers and at the national and international level was now seen as confirmation of the faith that lenders had in the economic vitality of the Russian people and nation. Most government regulations, necessary evils in the early years, were at the lowest levels consistent with rapid economic growth. So, too, was the nation's safety net. Two political parties were being established, and the first presidential election was less than a year off. Aven had little interest in these matters, and his time was spent accepting the accolades he so richly deserved. He was invited to countless banquets put on by the nation's professional and industry associations. Gaylord was his frequent companion at these happy events.

Rena's problem showed no sign of diminishing. If anything, her moodiness and hostility grew more extreme. Aven's indomitable optimism provided what cohesion remained between them. Thanks initially to Rena's prodding, but more recently to the leisurely pace at MOP, Aven had cultivated a taste for the arts, particularly in painting and music. He now understood their significance to Russian culture. No longer the plaything of the idle classes, art and artists offered to society an introspective and deep understanding of its essence.

It was during one of his many visits to the Russian Museum of Modern Art that Aven thought he had found a way to reach Rena. But his efforts proved futile. If anything, they exacerbated the problem. Rena's reaction to the Post-Minimalist show was not all that different from the revulsion she had expressed some years ago at Barbie's.

"Aven…really, don't you have anything better to do with your time than visit these pseudo-sophisticated construction sites that try to pass for art exhibits?"

He had suggested visiting the exhibition of street-artist work that was on display in one of the smaller galleries not far from their flat. Inspired by a young Amerikan graffiti artist who had died over a decade earlier, a number of Russia's youth had been moved to take their work from the sidewalks and vacant walls throughout the city into the fashionable galleries frequented by some of Moscow's most sophisticated and wealthy art clientele. This effort to rescue Rena from her long period of despondency was no more successful.

The museum visits ended, but Aven refused to capitulate to Rena's stubborn joylessness. It was a Monday in late March, a few days before the eighth anniversary of the revolution and a few weeks before the first serious democratic election in the nation's history. The drive to MOP had taken just under two hours, and Aven had accomplished most of the day's work in the limo. The elevator was missing. It would be some time before a replacement could be installed. As it turned out, when the Amerikans introduced the equipment eight years earlier, they had decided on a unique design for both the shaft and the cab. The machinery used in the elevator's construction and assembly had long since been dismantled. At the moment, there was no firm date on when a replacement would be available. Most of the MOP workers took the news with good humor.

"Aven, Gaylord, I will be leaving for Amerika on Friday."

This news was not altogether unexpected. Paula's services were being utilized more infrequently with each passing year. For a time, she herself seemed not to mind, spending most of her days shopping, when she wasn't having her hair fixed.

"I think it's time for me to return to RSJ & S, and besides, I hear they're gonna have some mongo going-out-of-business sales back home, all over the place, I think…oweeeeeeeeeeeee-eeeeeeee."

"Does that mean Gaylord…?"

"No, Aven. I'm going to pass on the sales. If you don't mind, I'd kinda like to stick it out with you."

Aven knew he was not going to miss Paula. Even though they had worked together on many vital projects, he'd never developed any real feelings for her. That Paula had been extremely useful in what he had achieved and what he had become, Aven had no doubt. There were no regrets on his part, and to the extent that he thought about their relationship, he was certain that it was quite symmetrical.

Gaylord was another matter. Aven was far more pleased with what Gaylord had to say that morning than he was distressed with Paula's declaration.

With so little to occupy him that afternoon, Aven's thoughts returned to the "rehabilitation of Rena," as he had come to call this last vexatious concern. The image of "that first night" would not leave his mind. He had forgotten the last time they had made love. But "…that night…after the concert…our own…the concert…OF COURSE!"

The commute seemed to take forever as he was anxious to get to his flat. Despite the delay, he was feeling happier than he had in a long while. Aven had never been more hopeful. Nor more confident.

"Next Friday."

Aven grinned to the point of straining his facial muscles. A look of bewilderment crossed Rena's face. So much had happened to them, and to Russia, since that night, that night when they were both students at Moscow University, that night of the concert. Aven had no intention of forcing Rena's memory. He continued smiling. The first signs of recognition appeared on her face.

"Oh, Aven, that was a long time ago, wasn't it?"

There were tears in her eyes as she slowly rose from her desk. They held each other tightly for a long time.

"Next Friday, what?"

"The concert, of course."

"That doesn't sound like such a good idea. You know how I feel about modern.…"

"I don't think you're being fair. When you introduced me to Mozart and Haydn, it was music that I couldn't understand at first, but at least my mind was open."

"Perhaps, but you never really did open your ears."

"I did. More than you gave me credit for. I doubt if I would have become interested in the work of our young composers had it not been for Bach and all of the others."

"Do you suppose Bach would consider that a compliment or an insult?"

The conversation continued on in this vein for some time. Aven entreating, Rena unyielding. Slowly, however, the tide began to shift.

"Well, you are right. I've never been to a modern music concert, ever."

"One evening won't hurt you, and this Friday's concert is important to me. It's important to Russia. Several new works have been commissioned, compositions written by the most talented of our young composers in honor of our new nation. Rena, the concert is important to *us!*"

Rena sat quietly. She finished the wine in her glass.

"I'll go…for us."

Shortly after Rena's assent, they went to bed. Their lovemaking that night was restrained, almost tentative, as if their bodies were being introduced for the first time. The concert became Aven's sole preoccupation. He could think of little else. During these few days he had honed his knowledge of contemporary Russian music, spending his MOP time reading everything he could about it.

Gaylord expressed concern over this fixation.

"Don't you think you've read enough already? Seems to me you oughta be able to enjoy a concert without having to pass a bar exam."

"If you would do a little reading yourself, Gaylord, you'd know that the most sophisticated work these days is written without bars."

"Yeah, Aven, I understand. That's what they mean by this stuff being so dry."

"Gaylord, if you don't mind...."

Aven returned to the flat in time to dress for the concert. He had no real difficulty persuading Rena that the special circumstances surrounding the concert required formal attire. He realized that the two of them made quite a handsome couple. Confirmation of this fact was repeated at Pero's and as they were escorted to their center front-row balcony seats.

The small concert hall had been refurbished especially for the evening's performance. Additional seating in the balcony area had been established for members of the international press. Several television cameras had been discreetly installed. The three hundred elegantly attired concertgoers—the elite of Moscow society fortunate enough to obtain tickets to the concert—were to be joined by a television audience numbering in the millions, within and well beyond the Russian borders.

The program itself was a splendid work of art, numbering well over fifty pages. The advertisements for Russia's most elegant commodities were done exquisitely, and the high-fashion clothing was modeled by the nation's most beautiful young people. Aven was slowly leafing through the pages, one by one. The center page contained the evening's program.

***** WORLD PREMIER CONCERT *****

PROGRAM

MOSCOW CONSERVATORY CHAMBER HALL
April 1, 2003

Andante Movement   F. J. HAYDN
(Prussian Quartet, Op. 50, No. 4)   1732–1809
      Conservatory String Quartet

Trio for Diverse Voices   F. J. YNDAH
  I Sneeze   1982–
  II Snore
  III Seduction
      Conservatory Vocal Quartet

Music Unprepared   J. F. HADNY
  Fast   1983–
  Slow
  ????
      Conservatory Chamber Pot Players

*** *INTERMISSION* ***

Ode to a Banana Slug   H. F. DAYHN
  Smooth   1965–
  Flexible
  Slooooow
  Indelicate
      University Chorus/Student Conductors

"Aven, what's Haydn doing on the program?"

"Just the second movement. A short piece of older music is often first on the program. People object, but I guess the idea is to introduce concertgoers to something different. Also, given the traffic and parking congestion, it's convenient to have a piece that not too many patrons care about anyway."

"Oh."

"Rena, you *are* going to enjoy the program. Yndah and Hadny are among the most brilliant of our young composers. Neither one of them yet twenty-one years of age, and both obviously destined for greatness. Yndah is a student of Sannis Nakexis, the world-renowned Greek composer, and Hadny spends his summers in Poland working with Krzysztof Rekipender. You've probably heard of him."

"Actually not."

"As a matter of fact, I'm not sure what he's written, either. But, Rena, surely you've heard of Hannah Dayhn. She's one of our leading women composers, somewhat older than Yndah and Hadny. A product of old Gorby's era. Made one of the first cross-cultural exchange visits to Amerika. California, in fact, at a small resort area, Santa Cruz or something. They say she worked with David Harsiron and Lou Opec."

"I don't think I've heard of her either."

The lights in the hall dimmed, and a ripple of polite applause greeted the four musicians, who bowed, took their seats, and began the caterwauling. The cellist was the last one to finish warming up. Aven had bet on the second violin. The musicians began the Haydn, despite the fact that people were still scrambling for their seats.

"My God, why don't they keep those inconsiderate dolts out of the hall."

"It's really not a problem, Rena. Remember, not too many people really want to hear the Haydn anyway."

"I see."

The oddly melodic Andante ended shortly after it had begun, and the four musicians left the stage to a smattering of applause. Aven actually enjoyed the piece. He took pride in his open response to all forms of music, and applauded without restraint. Rena was sitting motionless. The four music stands were quickly replaced by four singers. It was several minutes before the thunderous audience approval ebbed, and then only grudgingly. The vocalists, two men and two women, bowed in appreciation. They took their places on the stage, one man and one of the women standing arm in arm. The other two performers were situated quite a distance from each other and from the cuddling duo. The hall was still.

"I think you're going to enjoy this. Yndah is a master of the motivic fragmentation. It's a short piece, but rich in harmonic bifurcation. Shhhhh. Let's listen...."

For the next three minutes the only sound in the hall came from the four young performers on stage. Those listening sat immobile, as if transfixed by Yndah's creation.

Ah   Ah   Ah   Chooooooooooooooooooooooooooo
            ZZZZZZZZZ

                                                        Ah
Cho
     o
        o
          oZZZZZZZZZZZZZZZZZZZZZ
                                   John   Marsha

ZZZZZaaaaaa**aaaaaaaAAAAAA**
                    choo

                                        John   Marsha
                                        John   Marshaa
                                        John   Marsh**aaa**
                                        John   Mars**haaaa**
                                        John**Marshaaaaa**

Chooooo
        ZZZZ
        zzzz
        ZZZZ
        zzzz   aaaa   zzzz   **aaaa   zzzz   AAAA   ZZZZZZ**
AAAAAAAAAAAAA

JOHN!   MARSHA!
      john   marsha
         JOHN   MARSHA
         JOHN   MARSHA
            JOHNNNNNNNNNNNNNNNNNNNNNNNNNN
maaaaaaaaaaaaaaaaaaaaaaaaaaaaaaaaaaaaaaaaaaaaaaaaaaaaaaaaa**RSHA!!!**

ZaZaZaZaZaZaZaZaZaZaZaaaaaaaaaaaaaaaaaaaaaz
                                        z
      johnmarshajohn   z
                                    z
                                  z
                                z
AaAaAaAaAaAaAaaaaaaaaaaaaaaaaaaaaaaaaaaaaaaaaazzzzzzzzzzzzzzzzz
  ChooooooooJohn   AaaaaaaaMarsha

                                                        a
choo

The audience remained still for an extended period after the overtones of the fine soprano's voice had reverberated throughout the hall. The four singers bowed to indicate an end to the brilliant Yndah work. Applause began cascading from row to row, both in the orchestra and in the balcony. In his excitement, Aven was unaware of Rena for several minutes.

"Rena…"

She returned his glance.

"Aven…"

Most everyone else was still applauding. Aven put his arm around Rena and squeezed her gently.

"You'll like the instrumental piece, I'm sure."

Rena's body was unbending. There was an unusual tautness, in response not only to his arm but to his glance as well.

The ovation ran its course. The four singers had come back for six bows, the last three holding the hand of a smiling young man, obviously Yndah. After the bows and applause had ended, several young men and women, all dressed in dark work clothing began to move about on the stage. Four or five were struggling with a piano. Their difficulty was caused by the fact that each of the three piano legs was of differing length.

"That's what they call an ill-prepared piano."

Rena made no comment, and Aven was not sure she had heard him. A large anvil was the next item that gave the workers a fit, although they had a much easier time with the mounted sirens, chimes, and numerous cymbals that were placed, seemingly at random, on the stage. Four moderate-size amplified speakers were the last items to appear.

Several instruments were also located in the aisles behind where the couple was sitting, and two large drums were placed in the rear of the orchestra section of the hall. When the workers had completed their mission, they took a brief bow, to which the audience responded generously.

A stillness, rich with anticipation, again filled the theater. It was broken as the Chamber Pot Players began assembling. Aven counted thirty-one musicians in all, including those located in the balcony and orchestra section.

"Rena, Hadny says that the electronic instrumentation allows him to work as he wishes, in no way bound by interests, abilities, and temperaments of musicians. He has total *control*, and at the same time, the musicians on stage are permitted to pick and choose among a variety of options in the score. They have total *freedom*—an extraordinary example of the freedom-control polarity.…"

"Aven, can we leave…?"

The words came to him in muffled fashion. Aven was not sure what Rena had actually said, or meant. Before he could reply, however, the Pot Players had commenced. The piece began with a thunderous roar from the four speakers.

ZZZZZZZZZZZZZZZZZZZZZZZZZZuuuuuuuuuuuuuUUUUUUUU**KKKK**
ZZZZZZZZZZZZZZZZZZZZZZZZZZuuuuuuuuuuuuuUUUUUUUU**KKKK**
ZZZZZZZZZZZZZZZZZZZZZZZZZZZuuuuuuuuuuuuuUUUUUUUU**KKKK**

eeeeeeeeeeeee

skiiiiiizzzzzz

THOMP
THOMP
THOMP

la la la la la la la la la la la la la

BONGGGGG**GGGGGGGGGGGGGGGGGG**GGGGGGGg g g g g   g

FIZZZZZZZZZZZZZ
                            Z
                              Z
                                Z
                                  Z
                                    Z
                                ZOOOOOOOOOOOnnnnnngngngngngnnn

iiiiiii
    eeeeeeee
                    THOWOPPPPAAAAAAAa a a   a   a

"Rena," whispered Aven, "his use of the inverse retrogression is spine chilling."

Rena seemed frozen in her seat, as if deeply moved by the sounds that were coming at her from all directions.

ting

ZONGGGGGG

stummmmm

tic tic tic tic tic tic tic tic tic tic tic tic tic tic

wap

EEEEEEEEEEEEEEEE
E
E
E
e
e
e
e
e

e

e

s
p
l
a
tttttt⊤⊤⊤⊤⊤⊤⊤⊤⊤⊤⊤⊤⊤

Aven had never before been so moved. There was something about the Hadny that touched the core of his being. He was going to say something to Rena, who was rocking back and forth in her seat. He realized that she, too, was touched by the young Russian's genius.

fizuuuuuk
stemamamamamamam

BOP

tadaaaaaaaaaaaahhhhhhhhhhhhhhhhhhhhhhhhhh
tadaaaaaaaaaaaaaahhhhhhhhhhhhhhhhhhhh
tadaaaaaaaaaaaaahhhhhhhhhhhhhhhhh

ping g   g   g   g

Aven couldn't keep still. He needed to share his feelings with Rena. As he turned to do so, he saw that her movement had become more agitated, and he detected a faint utterance from her throat.

"Rena…I think you're disturbing the people around you."

She seemed not to hear him. Whatever sound she might have been making was soon engulfed in the roar of the electronic instruments so totally under Hadny's control.

ZZZZZZZZZZZZZZZZZZZZZZZZZZZZZZZZZZZZZZZZZZuuuuuuuuuuuuuuukkkk
ZZZZZZZZZZZZZZZZZZZZZZZZZZZZZZZZZZZZZZZZZZuuuuuuuuuuuuuuukkkk
ZZZZZZZZZZZZZZZZZZZZZZZZZZZZZZZZZZZZZZZZZZuuuuuuuuuuuuuuukkkk
ZZZZZZZZZZZZZZZZZZZZZZZZZZZZZZZZZZZZZZZZZZuuuuuuuuuuuuuuukkkk
ZZZZZZZZZZZZZZZZZZZZZZZZZZZZZZZZZZZZZZZZZZuuuuuuuuuuuuuuukkkk

BAMMMMMMMMM
        BONGGGGGGGGGGGG
                bip bip bip bip   bip   bip

    eeeee
                                        skizzz

THWOPPPPP

In the moving pauses that were so artfully created, Aven once again became aware of Rena. As he turned to quiet her, the sight before his eyes seemed
unreal. So, too, did her vocal activity. Rena was rocking violently back and
forth. Gasping and wailing cries poured from her mouth. Tears flooded from
her eyes. Aven could not tell whether his own emotions were those of alarm or
of anger. He put his arm on hers to quiet her, to no effect. Something had to be
done. Finally he spoke, not loudly, but with a firmness that was unmistakable.

"Rena, please control yourself. You're spoiling the performance...a world
premier. *Please*, I must *insist!*"

Nothing.

"Rena, *damn it*, we're sitting right in the middle...."

Aven did not finish. Rena's rocking had ceased, as had the wailing and the
tears. Aven watched and listened in utter astonishment at what soon followed.

ting

dowaaaapapapapapap pa   pa   pa   pa   pa

THWOP
        THWOP

                          THWOP

Rena rose from her seat. It was not long before the musicians, press, television representatives, and listeners alike turned their attention to the balcony,
front-row center. What they saw and heard was a performance never to be forgotten.

Rena was tearing her program into shreds, page by page. When she
finished with her program, she made a frenzied and successful effort to remove
Aven's. She repeated the rending of the program, casting page after page into
Aven's face. Each physical assault matched with intemperate verbal abuse.

"DAMN YOU, AVEN—DAMN YOUR FASHION DESIGNS—DAMN
YOUR SOPHISTICATED LIQUOR—"

She carried on this way through each page of the slick program.

"DAMN YOUR SEDUCTIVE PERFUMES—DAMN EVERYTHING

IN THIS PROGRAM—DAMN EVERYTHING AND EVERYONE IN THIS HALL—DAMN YOUR MUSIC—DAMN YOUR ECONOMY—DAMN YOUR COUNTRY—DAMN YOU—DAMN YOU—DAMN YOU—damn you—damn."

She turned and lurched toward the aisle. As she left the theater, silence returned to the hall, but not to Aven's crown. A minute, two, three passed, as the pounding in his head grew louder. He wasn't sure he could stand the pressure for much longer, until he realized it was not his head at all. Upon looking up, he discovered that not a person remained seated. Every man and woman was cheering, yelling, applauding.

BRAVA…BRAVA…BRAVISSIMA…ENCORE…ENCORE…BRAVA…

Aven's eyes regained a degree of clarity. The entire audience, in both the balcony and the orchestra section, was looking to him with smiles of approval and appreciation. He had no idea how long the ovation continued, but once he understood what had happened, he was able to nod and smile to the many admirers all around him. Aven enjoyed talking to the excited concertgoers during the intermission. The Ode to a Banana Slug was somewhat long and slow moving, but he was not sorry he stayed until the last Indelicate movement.

Aven did not return immediately to the flat. He had been cornered in the lobby by a number of the city's major business leaders. A reception was to be held for the composers Yndah, Hadny, and Dayhn at a nearby restaurant, and Aven had been easily persuaded to attend. It was an exuberant affair, and the noise and excitement of three world premiers lingered long after the performance. Aven was not entirely certain what the young Hadny had said to him about Rena. Something about her "impromptu coda providing a rich melodic counterfoil," but it was obvious from the composer's gestures that he was as impressed as the audience had been earlier.

It was well past midnight before he left. For a brief period of time in the early hours of the morning, traffic on the city streets moved at a fairly brisk pace. This morning was no exception, and he arrived at his flat in no time at all.

"Good night."

"Good night, sir."

Aven entered quietly. To his surprise he found their bed empty. He also found an envelope on the pillow at Rena's side of the bed. The mild feeling of concern receded as he thought to himself, "She's gone to spend the night with Hester. Perhaps she was more upset than I thought."

Aven was confident that Rena would be fine in the morning. Given the lateness of the hour along with the quantity of celebratory champagne he had consumed at the gala reception, he fell asleep as his head hit the pillow. He woke without benefit of the alarm. It was Saturday, and he had no reason to be at MOP. The news lead that morning was not surprising:

RUSSIAN COMPOSERS ELECTRIFY THE MUSIC WORLD
New Works Capture the Spirit of the Nation

The story itself said nothing about the Dayhn, nor was there mention of Rena. Aven realized that the writer for the morning edition had had to file her story well before the concert's completion. After pouring himself another cup of tea, Aven opened the note from Rena. There were several pages, a fact that struck him as odd. He had no difficulty recognizing Rena's gentle, feminine script. He was not, however, prepared for her words.

> Dearest Aven—
> I'm not sure I know where to begin, nor how to say what I feel. Writing this is the most painful task I have ever faced. I think I should apologize for my behavior earlier this evening, though I'm not sure why. I'm not even sure that anyone noticed me, my anger, my tears, my screams. Did you, Aven? You asked me to join you, and I agreed without enthusiasm. Indeed, my worst fears were realized. With the exception of the few short bars of the Haydn, thrown as crumbs from an opulent table to some undeserving beggars, the sounds we heard were not worthy of human attention. They were devoid of all feeling and emotion, incoherent, isolated, isolating, the work of men and women who can think and feel only through the perverted logic of the computer, or whatever the latest technological fix might be. Machines designed and sold to us as the means of easing the human burden and freeing the human spirit, but in fact, irrelevant to both. Worse than irrelevant—but I am wandering, Aven. Whatever my feelings, there can be no excuse for my conduct, and I want you to know that I regret it. Aven, the excess of emotion and anger that you witnessed this evening has been building for a long time, longer than I care to remember, and as painful as it is to admit to you and to myself, I'm afraid I meant what I said. All of it. Aven, I loved you completely and more deeply than I had ever imagined possible. I still love you, Aven, but not what you've become. It's impossible to differentiate how

much this crazy and inhumane society has made of you from what you have helped society become. Our love, once so deep, began to change almost from the moment you took the directorship at the ministry. I won't ever forget that Sunday morning, before this nightmare started. Do you remember? We made love most of the morning. In so many ways, Aven, we've never since been able to capture those feelings. We've talked so little these past years, but I know I've never felt warmth from you comparable to that morning. It was as if you had been drained of all feeling. I felt an emptiness the moment I returned from Hester's. Perhaps things would have worked out differently for both of us if I had spoken sooner, but in my own way, I *was* speaking to you. I know now that you couldn't hear much of what I was trying to say, but Aven, it wasn't for lack of my trying. What was I to say amidst the roar of the basketball crowd? You seemed to sense my feelings in that inane circus tent, and you did have the good sense not to take me to the environmental desecration that was once so much a part of our lives. True enough, for a time, I was able to speak to you about my concerns—with the exploitation of women, the fostering of such false and self-de-structive values—but even then I think you were playing at listening. You never expressed a word of regret about what had become of Mira and Jenna. Before this crazy new world of yours, they meant something to you, not just as good work-ers, but as people, people who had feelings for you and you for them. Our streets and parks are becoming uninhabitable, our men, women, and young children tossed aside with as much concern as the opening Andante this evening. This is what our society is becoming—an emptiness, overflowing with the physical and human debris. Aven, this is the society you've been so proud of. This is the society you have helped to create, you and your insane economic thinking. Do you have any idea what you've so effectively constructed? A world void of humanity—void of all there is that allows us to walk upright and to see ourselves as more than animal, of our abil-ity to work together collectively and as the social beings we were meant to be. And our special relationship with the earth—no other creature on earth has the ability to destroy the very nature that gives it life. Sheep that overgraze will find their numbers dwindle long before they have devastated the land that sustains them. The grass will return, and then the sheep. But we are more than sheep. We have a responsibility to understand that and not rely on your Darwinian process to save humanity. But, Aven, your new world makes of us animals. In your world we sell our labor and our land, our very individual and collective soul, to the highest bidder. The disposition of our humankind is left to the blind hand of self-interest. Aven, I didn't think I would ever be saying this, but I fear for our survival—yours, mine, all of Russia. Worse, I feel so helpless. You know that I never backed away from "lost causes." As long as we could hold on to our feelings for each other, there was no such thing. But the world you have so effectively fostered—the dog-eat-dog world so cruel, crass, competitive, fixated on tawdry commercialism—seems to have drained from us much of this ability....I love you, Aven. If you can believe me, I care for you more than I do for myself. Our nation was beset with difficulties, many very serious, when first we met, but oh how I long for those days. Our country did seem to be changing for the better, slowly, but moving in the right direction. You've moved so much higher now. We never did finish our discussion about Hayek, and I won't forgive myself for not talking to you about him.

Aven had some difficulty focusing on the remaining few words.

Aven, I'm leaving....I know we will never see each other again....Please, even if you feel otherwise, please don't try to find me. I'm afraid we left each other...many years ago.

—Rena

Aven sat quietly for some time. He surely hadn't expected such a letter from her. It occurred to him that she was more troubled than he might have imagined. Within a few minutes, he replaced the letter in its envelope and was on the phone.

"Hi, Gaylord....Fine, it was a wonderful concert....Listen, Rena's going to be staying with Hester this evening. Would you like to join me for dinner...? Great, I haven't seen it either. I'll pick you up at six."

Part III

NOTHINGTOFEAR

■■■■■■■■■■■■■■■■

Aven had no recollection of Saturday's movie. Nor was Sunday a day of note. The Monday morning news was waiting at the door.

BARNUM FINI FINDS FULL CAPITALISM FIRMLY FIXED
Free Elections Follow Forthwith

He admired the MOP staffer's work. It had taken longer than anticipated, but as the eighth year came to an end there could be no doubt as to what had been achieved. Laissez-faire capitalism, first pronounced by the gentle Scottish patriarch well over two hundred years earlier, had now been promulgated in its purest form. Aven allowed his mind to wander.

"Old Adam would have been pleased...."

He thought it an odd coincidence that both women had left him on the same day but knew that Rena's departure was only temporary.

The Amerikans had advised against prolonged election campaigns. The political staff at MOP was easily persuaded, and the historic election was set for early May. During the past year, two political parties had been established, platforms written, and candidates selected. The campaign was to open on the first of May. In addition to limiting the length of the campaign, opening the election on this day provided a fitting alternative to the May Day of old. Aven's interests had been elsewhere, and he happily delegated full responsibility for political matters to his subordinates.

The dishes and dust were left untouched as he walked from the flat. Rena's absence voided any real stimulus, and Aven's limo was arriving shortly after five. The morning commute now required just under three hours, an inconvenience that Aven had promised himself he would attend to soon.

"Good morning."

"Good morning, sir....may be a bit slow this morning. More traffic than usual on the road to MOP, and I understand there's a detour near the park area."

"Yes, it is taking too much time."

Aven turned to the work he planned to do during the drive. Three hours later, the limo crept into the MOP entry. Several hundred people were lined up at the front entry, standing two or three abreast, in a state of considerable agitation. These individuals appeared to embody a cross section of Moscow's population, men, women, mostly adult, of various ages. From their attire, it was obvious that they represented equally diverse occupations as well. Something told Aven he should avoid contact with them.

"Perhaps we should use the side approach."

"Very good, sir."

The side entrance was not accessible to pedestrian traffic, and Aven made his way into MOP undisturbed. The agitation had entered the building. Members of MOP he had known for years, unflappable men and women who had dealt with innumerable crises, were scampering about in a manner suggestive of enormous apprehension. Aven walked quickly to the rear stairway and entered the office moments later. Several staff members were gathered around Gaylord. Aven said nothing as he walked past the gesticulating group. He had the phone in his hand before he was fully seated.

"Gaylord, I think we should talk...immediately."

The door opened as he returned the phone to its cradle. Gaylord's teeth were as white as ever.

"Mooornin, Aven. I thought you'd never call."

"Good morning, yourself. I'd have called earlier, but a few thousand cars got in the way. And if you don't mind, could we get serious for just a moment?"

"Hey, Aven, I know the importance of being earnest. What's on your mind, any special problems I should know about?"

"I thought you might be able to tell me. What in the hell is going on around here? That mob outside, and the MOP staff, they're all acting like we hit ten on the Richter scale."

"Nowhere near a ten, Aven. And I'm not sure you'd even want to call it a *natural* disaster, more man-made I'd say. Nothing we can't handle with a good MOP."

Aven's patience was waning, and his mood must have caught Gaylord's attention. The gleaming teeth receded. His voice lowered, both in pitch and volume.

"Aven, I think we've got problems."

"More than one?"

"I assume you saw the gathering outside? From what we can learn, MOP staff members are having the same experience throughout Russia."

"Gaylord, why are they here? What do they want?"

"I'm not sure where to begin, so much seems to have hit the fan. But one thing's certain, Aven...."

"What's that?"

"That mob outside is serving no useful purpose, nor is our staff at the moment. We're gonna have to get everyone calmed down as quickly as possible and then face up to the real calamity. Trust me, Aven, it'll be clear to you soon enough. But first things first. The Russian people need immediate assurance that nothing's really amiss. Once they've regained a sense of confidence, the rest should be easy, but they need to know someone's in charge."

"Who?"

"You, Aven, and I've taken care of all the necessary details."

"Damn it, Gaylord...if you don't get to the point, I'm going to join the crowd."

"We've made arrangements for you to speak at ten-thirty. The speech will be broadcast on radio and TV across the nation."

Aven looked at his watch. It was nine-thirty. "That's wonderful, Gaylord. I haven't a clue of what this is all about, nor the first notion of what to say. And even if I did...but I suppose we have time to spare?"

"Not to spare, but enough. Here, take a look."

Aven took the folder from Gaylord.

"Gaylord, how can I give a speech on a subject I know nothing about?"

The extent of his assistant's composure prompted Aven to open the file, which contained a single yellowed page with a fuzzy pencilled reference at the top:

Inau al spe ch///F. L. P./Marc 4, 19 3

"What is this? Some kind of address, given nearly a century ago? What's this got to do with...?"

"In 1933, the only successful modern-day Democratic American president took office with his nation in chaos and many predicting revolution. In one brief moment, with the right words, he turned the entire game around. Not the economy—we had to wait for Hitler and Tojo to help with that—but the American spirit."

"I really am interested in history, but perhaps another time. Besides, this says 1903, and your president's initials were F-D-R, not...."

Aven stopped as he realized the source of his confusion.

"Right, this is FDR's first inaugural...."

"Gaylord, our elections are set for *next* month, and I don't think I'm running."

"FDR's speech *bought time*, exactly what we need. A couple of weeks. Then, with the start of the election campaign, *and* the opening of the baseball season...."

Aven understood instantly. Over the course of the next forty-five minutes, he and Gaylord worked over the speech, shortening it considerably. They finished with time to spare.

"Hey, Gaylord, I like it."

"I do too, Aven, and after lunch we can begin to deal with the easier problems."

A stage with a speaker's rostrum had been set up in front of the two large entry doors. The somber grayness of the reflecting glass provided an impressive backdrop, and as Aven walked onto the platform, he was greeted by prolonged and vocal applause. He needed no introduction. Gaylord had informed the gathering some hours earlier that they could expect to hear from the MOP director before noon. Aven was prepared to fulfill Gaylord's promise. The MOP staffers were assembled off to the left of where he stood. Numerous TV cameras were in evidence, in addition to a bevy of microphones. Aven began to speak, pausing again and again in deference to the applause of his audience:

> My fellow citizens, this is a day of national consecration. The first day that we as a nation are on our own. It is thus incumbent upon me to speak with a candor and decision which our present situation impels....This is the time to speak the truth, the whole truth, frankly and boldly. Nor need we shrink from honestly facing conditions in our country today. This great nation will endure as it has endured, will easily overcome the trifling snags, and will prosper....

Aven had reached the high point of the speech. He and Gaylord had seen the next lines as crucial. All he need do was speak with his normal buoyancy.

> So first of all let me assert my firm belief that the only thing we have to fear is fear itself—nameless, unreasoning, unjustified terror which paralyzes needed efforts to convert retreat into advance....

Gaylord was right. Aven could feel his own power blend with the magic of the words. He paused as he finished the sentence. The applause was deafening. The crowd began jumping up and down, and the expressions of apprehension that were prevalent earlier in the day vanished. The now deliriously happy throng soon began to applaud and chant in uniform cadence.

Ah-VEN Ah-VEN Ah-VEN…

Aven could feel his face redden as he modestly sought to quiet the crowd. Finally, with a number of lingering Ah-VENs, quiet returned. He continued:

> In a short time from now, a leadership of vigor will meet with your understanding and support so essential to victory in all we hope to accomplish. The minor snags we face are only material in nature. Compared with the perils which our fore-fathers conquered because they believed and were not afraid, we have much to be thankful for. Nature offers her bounty, and our own efforts have multiplied it. And so my fellow countrymen, we face the few days that lie before us in the warm courage of national unity, with the clear consciousness of seeking old and precious moral values, and with the clear satisfaction that comes from the performance of duty by old and young alike. We do not distrust the future of our newfound democracy. Until our leaders are firmly in place, I ask you to put your faith in me and in MOP. We look to the future with our heads high and our hearts filled with opti-mism.

It did not take long for the chant to return:

Ah-VEN Ah-VEN Ah-VEN Ah-VEN Ah-VEN Ah-VEN…

It was several minutes before Aven requested silence, and several minutes more before his appeal was granted. The edited speech had been completed, but Aven was able to provide a short encore.

> Thank you…thank you…thank you very much…thank you very much….And now, the best thing we can all do is to re-turn to our work. May first, May Day, will be upon us in no time. The start of our nation's inaugural free and democratic elections, and our seventh full season of major league base-ball. Thank you, and bless you all….

Ah-VEN Ah-VEN Ah-VEN ah-ven ah-ven

The sound of his name finally receded. The MOP staffers had also returned to their offices.

"Aven, you were brilliant. I've listened to recordings of FDR, and you were better."

"Thanks. I enjoyed it, and the audience certainly seemed to like what I said."

"They liked *you*, Aven. I have a feeling you could have told them that Armageddon was around the corner and they'd have cheered. And reminding them of the baseball season opener, Aven, baby, face it, you're a natural."

"Perhaps, but politics is not my game, never has been. I've been quite happy at MOP...and by the way, don't we have some work to do? Or did FDR's words do the trick?"

"*Your* words and FDR's. There are a few minor details that we oughta tend to. Let's try the staff room for lunch, and then we can talk."

Eating in the staff lunchroom was something he had wanted to do ever since he accidentally burst into the place that first week of the Amerikan occupation. Gaylord felt that their presence would reinforce the confidence his speech had provided to the MOPers. Their entrance created a stir among the workers. The staff members who already had their food were jammed tightly around the several counters. Aven and Gaylord hadn't been in the room more than a few moments when those in line as well as the staffers packed efficiently around the counters began to applaud and then to chant:

Ah-VEN Ah-VEN Ah-VEN...

This was the third time within the hour that Aven had been confronted with what at first was an awkward experience. He now found no cause for embarrassment and let the MOPers continue. They stopped of their own accord, replacing the uniform acclaim with individual variations:

"Way to go, Aven."

"Great speech, Aven."

"You made us all proud to be MOPers."

"We were terribly concerned this morning, but now...."

"I just knew you'd have the answers."

Aven accepted these individual compliments with ease.

"Thank you, all of you...."

Gaylord interrupted, both with his hand on Aven's arm and with his own voice.

"Indeed, Aven appreciates your confidence and support. And in the next week or two, we are going to need your most dedicated efforts. If we work together and follow Aven's lead, dealing with the few problems that have come along will be a piece of cake. When you get back to your desks after lunch, you'll find a revised and extended work schedule. But we should be back to normal well before May Day."

The impact of Gaylord's message was softened considerably by his concluding words, and the MOPers returned to their meals and conversation. Shortly, Aven found himself standing before the salad and yogurt compartments. He decided on a plain yogurt and plain Perrier. Gaylord selected the same. These were the only items available.

The dining area was less crowded as they left the serving line. Aven acknowledged the smiles of welcome from those around him and, once situated, spoke quietly to Gaylord.

"Gaylord, this is not much of a selection, is it? One flavor of yogurt, and no tea?"

"The food delivery was delayed this morning, but that's really the least of our problems. I'll tell you about it when we get back to the office."

With a wink and a flash of white, Gaylord returned to his frugal lunch. Aven did the same. Having extended good-byes and other words of encouragement to those around them, they left the lunch area and walked down to their office. Once inside, Gaylord was on the phone to the receptionist.

"Please hold all calls for the next two hours...and send out a reminder to the MOP staff. We'll be having the special meeting sometime before six this evening. Until then, everybody should just go about their work as if nothing's happened....Thanks. Good-bye."

"Gaylord, *what's happened?*"

"Happened? Well Aven, actually not all that much. I'm sorry there's no tea today. Would you like some Port instead?"

Gaylord brought the wine to the small conference table and poured for both of them. Aven said nothing.

"I'm not sure where to begin. A lot seems to have hit at once...."

"Why don't you just start, somewhere, anywhere, will be fine."

"Okay, Aven, but I don't want you to be upset. Some of this may come as a surprise to you...."

"No problem. I love surprises."

"Not these. Maybe we can start with the fact that there's no tea."

"Why not? Might as well deal with the tough issues first."

"Aven, I think we both need to be serious for a moment. The morning delivery truck was delayed. In fact, it hasn't yet arrived. The commute into the MOP area was much heavier."

"I know, many in this morning's crowd drove in."

"Not only that, but the accident in the park...."

"What accident?"

"A major accident. At least two hundred killed, and many hundreds more injured. Had to close the road for several blocks."

Aven listened to Gaylord with increasing astonishment. The number of happy campers had been growing rapidly. There was no accurate count, since the relevant MOP section was not particularly concerned with this aspect of the city's population. A few overly involved citizens argued that there were many thousands of campers in Moscow and in every major city in the land, but no one knew for sure. Whatever their numbers, many slept in the park area near MOP every night. The campers stacked their mobile homes one on top of the other. The park area, with many benches removed, provided space for over one hundred units along the ground. Within the past month or two, the number of stacked rows had grown to nearly thirty.

"Aven, there's been about three thousand campers in the park every night. Not a bad use of space. The problem developed when the diners at McDonatelli's objected to the view. We tried to resolve the issue amicably. The MOP staffer in charge suggested rearranging the tables at McDonatelli's. But even if they couldn't see the campers, the pizza crowd objected, and the campers not only looked down on the diners, but lately they've had a lot to say as well. One thing led to another, and last night, around three in the morning, a group of young pizza patrons took matters into their own hands. It wasn't all that difficult. They went running past the stacks of sleeping campers and pushed them over. The moment a few tumbled, the entire edifice toppled. The emergency rooms in every hospital, already overcrowded, have been working nonstop. I don't think we'll have the park cleared of debris, human and otherwise, for several more hours. The entire area is sealed off, and to avoid undue alarm in the city, we've required the ambulances to proceed at normal speed and without siren. But Aven, the accident is not the only problem, or the most serious. I don't think anyone in this morning's gathering even knew about the park."

Gaylord's tale had stimulated many emotions in Aven. Absent, however, was any sympathy. The story rekindled his feelings for the six homeless thugs he encountered on his last walk in the park. Whatever he might have felt for the dead and injured, he recognized that the event was a calamity for the city.

"You spoke of 'other' problems...."

"Yes, and I'm not sure where...."

"Don't bother just yet. Let's try to deal with one at a time."

"Fair enough, Aven. I think you're right. Any ideas?"

"Let me think."

They both sat quietly for some time. Paula's words kept mingling with his own thoughts.

"Gaylord, it seems to me that few if any of our citizens care much about the campers themselves. Most of them are without family or friends, all pretty much lost to society, and useless as well."

"That's basically the story, Aven."

"Then, all that really matters is how the incident *appears* to the average citizen. Surely we can find something of value to report....*Gaylord!*"

Gaylord came close to knocking over his wineglass, so abrupt was Aven's cry. "What?"

"I think I've got it."

Aven walked to his desk and brought back a notepad and pen. He wrote for a moment, crossed out the few words, and started again. This modest ritual was repeated several times.

"This will do. Tomorrow's lead."

Gaylord took the pad and read the single line. He looked up at a beaming Aven, reciprocating instantly. Gaylord's glance returned to the pad:

DRAMATIC FALL IN MOSCOW HOMELESS

"Aven, it's a winner. The kind of news that'll make everybody happy. And with your talent, the other problems are gonna be a breeze."

"As they say, there's no time like the present. What other little snags need mending?"

Gaylord didn't go into detail on the "snags" that had hit the nation in the past couple of days. There were too many. Nevertheless, his recitation took several minutes.

"The timing of these developments is incredible. How can so many things go haywire in a span of seventy-two hours? And why now? We've had eight great years with hardly a hitch, and then Paula leaves...almost as if she knew something."

"In many ways, Paula's a lot smarter than people think. Who knows? Maybe she did sense some problems, but, Aven, she's gone, and we're here."

"And left with more than a few tangles. But I think if we work on them for the next few days, we'll be all right. Come May Day, we'll have...."

"A whole new ballgame...."

"It's clear that we can't clean the mess all at once, and it's equally obvious that some of the problems are quite trivial. Go back over the list one more time, slowly, and I'll see if we can't set some priorities."

For the next half hour, Gaylord went over the litany of problems that had surfaced, and Aven organized the items into general categories. They worked over the list, and without much difficulty, a strategy emerged.

"I think we're in agreement. With everyone's cooperation we should be out of the woods in a week or so. We might even be able to relax for a few days before May Day, and then, as you said, a whole new ballgame."

"Actually, a doubleheader."

"A double what? What's that?"

"Oh, an old American idea. On Sunday afternoon they'd usually play two games for the price of one. Never happens anymore. Nobody wants to spend that much time at the ballpark, and it takes half the day to get there and park anyway."

"Amerikans used to see two games on *one ticket?*"

"Yeah, that was a problem, too."

The plan that Aven and Gaylord developed delineated two sets of problems, major and minor. It was agreed that Aven and the relevant MOP sections would deal with the former, with responsibility for the more numerous but trivial matters delegated directly to the appropriate MOPers. The latter included intractable learning difficulties and violence in the classroom, small-farm bankruptcy, domestic brutality, racial and ethnic hostility and conflict throughout the nation's cities, petty corruption amongst elected and appointed government officials, and moral turpitude within the church. While these minor irritants seemed to have visited Russia all at once, and with some intensity, Aven had every confidence in the ability of his MOPers. None of these problems would be eliminated, and some would be with the nation for a while. What was essential was persuading the public that solutions were indeed *possible. Believing* in a solution was, after all, half the battle, and the selling of this message would buy the necessary time until May Day arrived.

The remaining few items seemed worthy of Aven's special attention and skill, each being of sufficient complexity to require a full twenty-four-hour session. Gaylord set up meetings with the appropriate industry leaders, the first to begin at seven that evening. Not only did Aven want to get to work as quickly as possible, but the early evening starting and *ending* time would permit good news to reach the nation first thing each morning. Gaylord did most of the talking at the special MOP orientation meeting that he had set for six. Aven spoke briefly at the conclusion and was greeted with another warm and vocal ovation. Despite the extended work hours, the MOPers left the assembly hall beaming with confidence.

Aven and Gaylord climbed the single flight of stairs to the combo room on the fifth floor.

"Any idea when the new elevator parts will be installed?"

"I don't think they've found the old plans yet. We might have to widen the shaft to standard size after all, and, Aven, I sure hope those fat bankers can make it. Maybe I should order some oxygen along with the food and drinks."

They entered the combo room. The MOP section representatives were seated at the large conference table. It was several minutes past seven before all ten of the nation's leading bankers arrived. None were smiling, and most were drenched in perspiration. As they settled around the table, Gaylord opened the meeting.

"Good evening, ladies and gentlemen. As you're aware, the past few days have been a bit ticklish for many of our major banking and financial institutions. Nothing funny, mind you, but nothing that MOP can't deal with either. Director, Aven _____, whom many of you know personally..."

Gaylord nodded toward Aven, who smiled at the sad and damp faces around the table.

"...has decided that restoration of confidence, both in your institutions and amongst yourselves, is our nation's first priority. We expect to have a resolution in place within twenty-four hours. Ample food and drink will be available for all of you, and we will take a short break every four hours. Director _____ will take over for the rest of our meeting."

As Gaylord turned again to Aven, some members of the group, both MOPers and bankers began to chant.

Ah-VEN Ah-VEN...

Aven quickly silenced them. *"Please!"*

He looked directly at the bankers.

"The schedule that Mr. Creamer laid out may seem Spartan, but our nation has no other choice. Nor do you. I've asked the MOP finance section leader to outline the problem—problems, actually, since there are two distinct matters that will require our attention. After his presentation, we can open the floor to general discussion. I'm confident that a solution will emerge before too long."

The nature of the twin financial difficulties was set forth in considerable detail by the MOP section head. As he proceeded, using prepared charts and the blackboard to illustrate and clarify issues, the ten fat banking executives continued to perspire, their faces maintaining a reddish tone. The story, all too familiar to them, contained elements of ineptitude, shortsighted greed, and corruption. While a portion of the responsibility lay with Russian consumers and government officials, there was no mistaking where much of the culpability lay. The MOPer's monologue continued for several hours, with modest participation from others in the room. After a short break, the group returned to their seats. During the pause, Aven had had a brief conversation with the section head and Gaylord about how best to proceed.

All eyes turned toward Aven as he began to speak.

"This has not been a pretty story. Let me summarize. We stand at this moment with two major financial complications, both the result of, let us say, an overextravagance on the part of several elements within our nation. Despite, and perhaps because of, eight years of record economic progress, many consumers as well as public officials have, in their understandable enthusiasm, been *spending* and *borrowing* more than might have been prudent. And at the same time, in an effort to accommodate these desires and simultaneously maximize profits, you have been overly *zealous* in granting loans of *questionable* value."

Aven paused, and the bankers seemed to relax somewhat.

"Would you say that this is a fair characterization of what has been happening?"

It was not clear to whom this question was directed. Several of the bankers in the room were nodding as if in agreement. Most, however, were still perspiring.

"Well, very good, then let me—"

"Aven, forgive my interruption...."

It was the one female MOPer in the finance section who was speaking for the first time.

"Indeed, the massive increase in consumer spending and borrowing can be attributed to a benign ebullience on the part of our citizens. After the dark days before capitalism came to our country, it's not difficult to comprehend their behavior. But with all due respect, Aven, I think there is perhaps a bit more culpability on the part of our public officials and bankers than your comments might suggest. I don't say this simply to be critical of these individuals, or of your trenchant summary. But rather, in the hopes of facilitating a resolution this evening, ah, morning."

"No forgiveness is required. We are here to resolve these matters. By all means continue. A woman's touch is always welcome."

"Well, sir, ah, Aven, the massive government borrowing that we have been observing for the past eight years is not the result of overspending. In fact, in many areas we have had significant *reductions* in government spending. The debt has swelled to the extent it has primarily because we have *eliminated most taxes*."

"But I thought that the Gapper theory...?"

"What? That a dramatic cut in tax rates would *increase* government receipts? Oh, Aven, that was one of the greatest PR triumphs of all time; RSJ & S couldn't have done a better snow job."

"Gaylord...."

"I think Gaylord's correct, sir. The cut in taxes was really designed to force a reduction in the size of our government. And it did. The supply-side theory was pretty much a Trojan horse. Also, if I may make one additional point?"

"Go ahead, but I'm somewhat surprised to hear that the Gapper curve was a delusion."

"More a voodoo incantation, I believe."

"Gaylord, if you don't mind, can we get back to the issue at hand."

Aven motioned for the female MOPer to continue.

"Thank you. The issue of our bankers' behavior is slightly more delicate."

Aven noticed that the bankers, all of them, had taken handkerchiefs to their foreheads as the MOPer spoke.

"I'd say that 'overly zealous' is a most charitable characterization. Aven, many bankers knew that their loan policy was a disaster. Some went so far as to lend money to friends and relatives, never expecting to collect interest, much less the principle. Our guarantee of bank deposits, coupled with the elimination of all regulations on lending policy, removed all sense of responsibility. Bankers knew that whatever they did, the government would be there to bail them out, and the billions of rubles that will be required to do just that has exacerbated the debt problem. Now, not only is the banking system near collapse, but many foreigners have become reluctant to lend. Russian bond prices have plummeted on the world market, and interest rates are well above thirty percent. Our financial institutions are close to a panic."

Aven was clearly upset. The bankers were drenched. No one at the table spoke for several minutes. Finally, Aven did.

"Well, the problem seems more complex than my initial characterization, but by no means beyond solution. We clearly have some criminal conduct to address. This concerns only a few rotten apples and can be dealt with by the judicial system in no time at all. Of far greater concern are the very high interest rates, the loss of bank funds, the nation's credit standing, and the potential financial panic. We need to find a way to cast all of this in a more positive light. Remember, in a few days the nation's attention will be riveted on the campaign and, of course, baseball."

Aven's upbeat conclusion provided ample stimulus for the group, and the next several hours were devoted to constructive discussion. Gaylord had been discriminating in his invitations to the bankers. None present were directly involved in outright criminal activity, and they joined with only modest reservation in an aggressive and open dialogue. Aven said little during this period. It was sometime after the third or fourth break when he picked up his notepad and soon joined the conversation.

"Well, ladies and gentlemen, I think we've achieved consensus. It's well past six, and I'm sure you'll be happy to call it a day. Gaylord and I will be staying on to deal with some minor woes in the transportation sector, but it does seem to me we've got the financial matters under control. The criminal and incompetent bankers will be removed within the week, and the financial furlough should buy us the necessary time. Confidence will return, and it will be back to business as usual before we know it. You can all be very proud of what we have accomplished here."

"Aven, have you thought of how we're going to sell all of this to the public?"

It was the female MOPer who had redirected Aven's thoughts.

"As a matter of fact, I have. What Gaylord is speaking of is the manner in which we cast our decisions. The key is to put on the proper spin. Public *reaction* to any policy depends entirely on *perception*."

Aven walked over to the blackboard standing near the conference table.

"This is it. What do you think?"

The group required a few moments to read the board and a few moments longer to comprehend its meaning. Within minutes, uniformly broad grins spread across every face in the room, Gaylord's included.

"Good. I like it, too."

INVISIBLE HAND REDIRECTS BANKING RESOURCES
Financial Community HOLIDAY Celebrates
Record Interest Rates

The expansive smiles remained as the MOPers and bankers left the room, each offering Aven their warm congratulations and right hand. Gaylord turned to Aven as the impromptu celebration ended.

"One down and four to go. At this rate, we're gonna be out of here in less than a week. But seriously, Aven, are ya sure we can keep this pace, back-to-back meetings without a break for five days? Only mad dogs and Englishmen...."

"These are maddening times, Gaylord, and we don't have a choice. By the way, where did you come up with the idea for a bank holiday? It's magnificent."

"I'm not sure. I know it wasn't Reagan's. He liked to think of every day as a holiday."

Gaylord paused as he glanced at his watch.

"Aven, we've got exactly ten minutes before the transport officials and the MOP section make an appearance. Perhaps we should both try to get some rest."

"You go ahead, Gaylord. I don't work well if I've overslept."

Oversleeping was not one of the problems they confronted over the next several days. Nor could they be counted among the English, human or canine. But in a near superhuman effort, Aven and Gaylord worked for an additional ninety-six hours, listening to variations on the banking and financial crisis themes as they applied to the nation's transportation system, air and water quality, and medical and health services.

It was nearing seven o'clock Saturday morning. The MOP health section representatives and several executives from the Russian Assembly of Physicians Extraordinarius (RAPE) had left a few minutes earlier. In keeping with the free-market teachings of Doctors Friedman and Hayek, RAPE was a purely voluntary association, open to everyone interested in practicing medicine. Abolition of the restrictive certification process allowed any individual willing to undergo the market test the freedom to hang up a medical shingle. Many did, and the cost of services fell dramatically.

Along with this healthy increase in services and reduction in cost came a modest deterioration in the quality of repair. Those individuals who were ill-suited to the profession did not fare well, nor did their patients. But a prolonged cold or a misdiagnosed sprain was a small price to pay for the vastly expanded offerings. Among surgeons, however, where salaries were particularly high, the incidence of failure was equally high. Of late, a disquieting number of wounded patients had taken direct action against their deficient doctors. RAPE sought to protect their members against such unwarranted violence. Unfortunately, patient hostility had grown to the point where surgeons could no longer afford the costs of self-protection. In effect, the cost of malpractice insurance had become prohibitive.

"Well, Gaylord, I think we deserve a rest. You know, it's a funny thing. When you and Paula and the Amerikan economists arrived, it took less than a week to make the new world, about the same time we've spent this week."

"MOPing up. Took only a few hours longer this time. Weren't we on the road to Rita's 'bout now?"

"I think so, talking about pretty much the same thing, carving ribs."

Aven's eyes turned to the blackboard, where he had written out the Sunday morning lead:

SURGEON'S SALARIES RISE
AS PATIENT DEMANDS ESCALATE

"And the market solution remains every bit as good for our surgeons today as it did for Rita's rib chefs."

"In any case, Aven, tomorrow's story on opportunities in surgery should ease the crisis."

Gaylord joined Aven in savoring their work before speaking again.

"Aven, I don't know 'bout you, but all of a sudden I'm feeling drowsy, like maybe a nap might be nice. Nothing too long, mind you. Two, three days at the most."

"I *have* kept us going at a brisk pace, and a short nap sounds good to me, too. We certainly do have things under control."

"At least until May Day."

"Right, and then it's a whole new ballgame, a doubleheader to boot. I'll get the limo."

Traffic was light for a Saturday evening. As the limo left Gaylord behind, Aven began to realize the extent of his tiredness.

"Good night."

"Good night, sir."

Aven entered the flat, dimly aware of the pile of newspapers at the door. The bed was unmade and empty. Sleep was instantaneous — almost.

"I wonder when Rena...."

"Eight o'clock? It's dark? It can't be the...."

He had slept for over twenty-four hours.

"My God, it's Sunday evening...."

As he got out of bed, undressed, showered, dressed, and went for the morning news, other elements of reality came to him in discrete intervals. Rena had not yet returned. Nothing in the apartment had been disturbed since the previous Monday morning. Sunday's paper was at the door, placed neatly atop those from the previous four days. Aven brought them into the dining area and prepared some tea. The solitary apple in the basket on the kitchen counter was the only item of food that was both available and appealing. He cut it into several wedges, which he took, along with a cup of tea, to the table. The Sunday lead was familiar, and Aven turned to the news editions of earlier in the week. There were four in all.

"Where's Tuesday's?"

He sat for a moment pondering this small mystery, before recalling Monday's chaos. After his calming speech to the nation that afternoon, MOP had placed a twenty-four-hour hold on further news. With the first full day of meetings, the good news was rolling from the nation's presses once again. Aven read portions of Wednesday's lead story. There was no question about the media's effectiveness in handling the financial crisis. And the banking holiday itself remained in place without a murmur of public dissent. Consumers had been reassured, and daily spending continued apace, thanks to the ubiquitous HUSH card.

Aven had almost forgotten the terror-filled eyes of the transport officials.

Airline accidents had increased during each year of the revolution, and in the past week alone, thirty-six major incidents had occurred around the Moscow Aeroport. At the start of Wednesday's meeting, there had been several thousand confirmed deaths, and more were expected in the days ahead. Deregulation had, as forecast, stimulated a rapid increase in the number of airline firms. Competition was stiff, stimulating all manner of cost reductions in pilot training and maintenance supervision. Some firms that had taken these healthy measures a bit too far soon lost customers and ceased operations. An added problem, beyond equipment and pilot failure, was the fact that the dramatic reduction in airline profit taxes brought a commensurate reduction in public expenditures on air traffic control. Pilots flying into the Moscow airspace during busy parts of the day often had to land without aid of traffic control. With the heavy rains, this became a challenge, even for the most experienced airline captains. As he glanced at Thursday's banner, Aven recalled the good feelings that had eventually pervaded the meeting:

RECORD-SETTING PACE IN AIR TRAVEL
Moscow Departures Exceed Arrivals
by Ever-Increasing Margins

During the meeting on transportation, a few minutes had been devoted to a similar situation in train travel, particularly along the Moscow rail commute line. Fatalities had been growing as a result of the overused equipment and less than sober conductors. However, train passenger travel constituted a minuscule portion of the urban commute, and it was decided that little should be done about mayhem on the nation's railroads. This was in keeping with the long-standing policy to stimulate automobile travel and production. For several days prior to the emergency meeting, gridlock overtook the Russian commuter. Tens of thousands were caught each morning, unable to move, and many of these motorists simply abandoned their cars and proceeded on foot.

An added complication was the fact that the exhaust from these idling engines added to the smog-laden skies. In the past week alone, on those occasions when traffic began to move, well over two hundred motorists had been found slumped over their steering wheel, dead. Loss of life aside, these deaths further complicated the morning commute.

Air quality had not been the only topic of conversation during Friday's session. Industrial waste and chemical emissions into the nation's rivers and lakes were impacting on water quality in many areas. While the brackish water caused some mild illness among the very young and the elderly, many working-age adults found the odor and color aesthetically unattractive. Aven, along with most of the MOPers, agreed that in seeking solutions to these complex pollution problems, care must be taken so as not to hamper the nation's economic growth. It was clear to all that more study was needed. At Gaylord's suggestion, a public interest group—Reduce Air Pollution and Effluents—was formed to look into the matter.

Aven perused the headlines that ran across Friday and Saturday's editions:

HEALTH-CONSCIOUS RUSSIANS
ABANDON AUTOS IN DROVES

NEW CITIZEN COMMISSION TO STUDY ENVIRONMENT

The tea was cold, and two hours had passed since he had gotten out of bed. It was nearing midnight.

"There's no way I'm going to be able to sleep."

Aven took his cup and the pieces of apple core to the sink. He returned to the front room and dialed Gaylord's number.

"Hi...yeah, I guess we were both tired...no, not much. Listen, Gaylord, Rena's out for the evening, and I'm wide awake...well then, why don't we take in a late movie...great, I'll pick you up as soon as the limo can get here."

Despite the twenty-four hours of sleep, Aven found himself nodding off during much of the film. He joined Gaylord for a beer and was back in the flat sometime after three in the morning. As he had done the preceding night, he fell asleep straightaway, without bothering to remove his clothing, and without Rena.

MAY DAY MAYDAY

■■■■■■■■■■■■■■■■■

*T*he torrid pace had exhausted the MOP staff, but so effective was the previous week's activity that their presence Monday morning was not required. It was close to noon when Aven decided to get out of bed. He didn't spend much time in the shower. Returning to the bedroom he noticed the empty bed and Rena's letter on the dresser where he'd left it several days earlier. Aven took the letter from the envelope, more out of curiosity than anything else. He knew that Rena had left the concert under duress, and he assumed that the dramatic dissonance of the Hadny offended her traditional musical sensibilities. Nine days had passed.

"Surely she is overreacting...." Much of what she had written seemed remote, as if the author were a stranger. An occasional passage did evoke some feeling.

> I loved you...more deeply...not what you've become...we were so in love....I felt an emptiness...never...a word of regret....I love you, Aven...we will never see each other again...don't try to find me...

These words had about them a tone of finality that began to trouble him. During the past week, Rena's absence had not entered his thoughts. But with national tensions eased, he felt no guilt in dwelling on a purely personal matter. He went out for the morning news and was soon seated with the banner and cup of tea before him.

NATION WAITS IN SUSPENDED ANIMATION
May Day Countdown Begins—14 Days

"Indeed, not much of interest is likely to transpire until the first of May, and Rena will surely return to her senses and to me by then."

Aven's normal optimism permitted no other conclusion.

"But why would she write with such finality? Of course she'll be back. We've been together for close to twenty years. But that look in her eyes at the concert, and the sound of her voice...."

Aven sat for some minutes engaged in this mental tennis match. Finally, he put aside the paper along with the negative thoughts about Rena and spent some time putting the flat in order. The last cup was washed as the limo arrived. Aven took Rena's letter with him as he left the apartment.

"Good mor..., good afternoon."

"Good afternoon, sir. We're all very proud of you."

"Why, thank you, but I don't think...."

Aven didn't finish the thought. The limo made its way into the flow of mid-afternoon traffic. Aven arrived in much less time than the normal morning commute, which was fortunate, since it was near closing time. He glanced up at old Igor's portrait as he walked past the elevator shaft. He knew his mind was overly tired, but for the briefest moment it seemed that Igor's forced smile had relaxed considerably. In fact, Igor looked to have an enormous grin on his face. The few MOPers in evidence seemed relaxed and greeted Aven with enthusiasm and admiration. Gaylord, too, was effusive in his welcome.

"Oh thanks, Gaylord. You're not far off the mark. I have been treated like the conquering hero, why, I'm not sure, but...."

"Don't be modest, Aven. You conquered the toughest foes a nation can confront—demoralization, depression, malaise. It's the stuff that leads to revolution. Ask that old peanut farmer from Georgia."

"Fine, Gaylord...I'm not sure I know what you're talking about, but there's something else that's on my mind at the moment."

"The poor guy who got himself trampled in the Reagan landslide. Not really important, though. What could be on your mind at this triumphant hour?"

"Rena."

"Rena?"

"Yes, Rena. You do remember, don't you?"

"Well, in fact, I do, Aven. But you've said so little about her lately that I was beginning to wonder if you might not have forgotten."

"We have been busy, and...and Rena's been upset. I haven't seen her since the concert. She's gotta come soon."

"Whoa, Aven. Slow down. What's happened to the man who last week tossed off solutions to every problem imaginable? Sounds like you wanna talk to Ann Landers."

"Gaylord, I don't have any problems with Ann Landers, whoever she might be. It's Rena."

"Seriously, Aven, Ann Landers was a kind of Adam Smith for the lovelorn, but she's not around. You're gonna have to settle for me."

Aven spoke at some length. Gaylord listened in silence.

"That's pretty much it. I guess you could say the concert was only one of many things that annoyed her. With each event, her anger and depression intensified. And now she's gone. Hasn't been back since that Friday night, well over a week. I am beginning to miss her, but I'm more annoyed than anything else. What do you make of her behavior? An exaggerated female temper tantrum? How should I respond when she returns...?"

Gaylord's stillness continued. A bottle of port was opened.

"That's it? She just flew out of the conservatory in a Hadny-like rage, and you haven't seen or heard from her since? Somehow that doesn't sound like Rena."

"There is one other thing...."

"What's that?"

Aven handed the letter to Gaylord, who took his time reading it.

"Aven...."

"What do you think?"

"Aven, this is not your typical female temper tantrum. I think she means it."

"Means what?"

"Every word she wrote, including her love for you, and...."

"That she's not coming back? Ever? I can't believe that. Rena's far too intelligent. She wouldn't be so foolish. Her parents gave up many opportunities, lived more like paupers, just for their beliefs. It isn't possible that Rena would repeat their mistakes, is it?"

Aven emptied the bottle of port into his glass and with considerable deliberation emptied the glass.

"Gaylord...I think you're right."

"Aven, I'm really sorry."

"No, don't be. There's no point in allowing Rena's misguided behavior to cause you any pain. Nor me, for that matter."

"But..."

"Listen, she's a grown woman. If she wants to spend the rest of her life chasing idealistic illusions, so be it."

"But, you and Rena, you've been lovers for as long as I've known you. You can't just...."

"We *were* lovers for a long time. But from the first day of the revolution,

Rena began to harp on everything that was happening. To be honest, my feelings for her changed as well. The passion seems to have been drained from my system, almost as if it were planned so that I could dedicate myself to the revolution without distraction. Don't you see, Gaylord, Rena's leaving is easy to understand and the right thing for both of us. I doubt if she has any regrets. Nor do I. Gaylord, thanks, this conversation has been...."

Aven did not finish the thought. Both men sat quietly for an extended time.

"Aven, we've done a number on this port, and I'm getting hungry. Would you like to continue the conversation over dinner? Do you have any plans?"

"No plans at all. But I think we've pretty much exhausted the present topic."

The restaurant was not crowded, and they were shown to their seats quickly. It took some time, however, to decide on what to order. Pero's menu had grown along with the number of tables. The first several pages offered an array of appetizers, soups, and salads. Several pages followed cataloging a multitude of pasta, fish, poultry, and meat dishes. The last section provided an equally expansive choice of desserts. After studying the larger volume, the two men required some time to skim the smaller companion folio of aperitifs, fine wines, beers, and liqueurs. Once they had made their selection, the food was brought to their table within a matter of minutes. Aven's stuffed sole hadn't fully thawed, and Gaylord's mussels were discolored. Neither ate much, and the waiter's blatant apathy dissuaded them from comment when the check arrived.

"I'm sorry, Gaylord, the food used to be a lot better. Our waiter's a zombie, and Pero's not around to complain to."

"I think he had to sell the place to a consortium of express food automats. McFly's, if I'm not mistaken."

"Oh."

"Come on, let's get out'a here. We can get some tea somewhere else."

"Fine with me. How about that new place, McLatte's?"

"Isn't the old teahouse near the university still open?"

They spent the next two hours drinking tea and talking. Throughout the dinner, and for a time in the teahouse, the topic of Rena's parting did not enter into their conversation. Gaylord made an oblique foray but did not pursue the matter.

"Aven, ah, earlier, when we were talking about Rena. The two of you haven't made love in months?"

"Longer. I stopped counting, and even on those rare occasions, it wasn't like it had been before, when we were younger...."

"Before the revolution?"

"You might say."

"Well, then, I was just thinking. It's not really my thing, but maybe you'd like to, ah...."

"Gaylord, what are you trying to say?"

"Well, maybe you'd like to have a woman? I'd be happy to tag along."

"You mean stop in at one of McPleasure's outlets? That's thoughtful of you, Gaylord, but to tell you the truth, I haven't missed sex all that much. These past eight years...I don't know, the directorship at MOP, the revolution...."

"Yeah, all pretty orgasmic."

"In a way it has been. Maybe after May Day and the elections. But not tonight, Gaylord."

They left the teahouse shortly after Gaylord's aborted proposition. Aven slept soundly and woke in good spirits. The morning news felt much lighter than normal. In fact, beyond the robust and inviolable advertising sections, the front section consisted of a single page, half of which was taken up with the day's banner:

MAY DAY COUNTDOWN CONTINUES: 13 DAYS

There wasn't a lot more to say until the election and baseball season openers. With the nation's crises in suspended animation, the next several days were likely to be short on stimulation. At the same time, they promised a serenity that was not unwelcome to Aven. A phase of his life was coming to a close. He would remain as director, but MOP itself would be moving from the nation's center stage. Russia would soon have her first democratically chosen president and legislative assembly. Very little of substance transpired at MOP, with the exception of the political section. There activity continued apace, but without Aven's involvement or interest. Aven was pleased with how quickly the modest hurt of Rena's departure had ebbed. In fact, he began to see bachelorhood as an opportunity. He made a mental note to himself about getting together with Mellors after May Day.

When Aven entered MOP on Monday, toward the end of April, he could sense a change in the air. The Moscow Giants were opening the season at home next week in quest of their fourth consecutive title. In last year's Global Series against the Hanoi Dodgers, the Giants had been extended to their fullest before squeezing home the winning run in the tenth inning of the deciding game. Hopes ran high for the boys in orange and black, and in this regard, the MOPers were no different from the average fan.

"Hi, Aven."

"What do you think of the new kid at short?"

"He's crazy to keep Lefty in the bullpen this season."

"That's gotta be an all-time bonehead trade."

"Think we can do it again?"

"Aven, got any extra seats for the opener?"

"We should have it wrapped up by August."

"Are you crazy, no way's that gonna happen."

"Nowadays, these guys are just in it for the rubles."

In the halls, at lunch, in the gym, MOP rang with anticipation. Occasional references were made to the election campaign. On Wednesday when opening-day fever normally peaked, the building was strangely subdued. As Aven entered his office, he quickly understood the source of the MOPers' letdown. It was relayed to him by an unsmiling Gaylord.

"Three or four days at a minimum? Across the nation?"

"I'm afraid so, Aven."

"Well, a lot of people are going to be very disappointed, but at least there's the election campaign kickoff."

"That could make matters worse."

"I don't understand what you're talking about, Gaylord. The opening political forum will be televised nationally. Without baseball, voters can pay closer attention to the debates, at least until the weather clears. Why should that make matters worse?"

"Have you ever seen an American political campaign?"

"No, I haven't. But I understand that our political MOPers used the Amerikan system as a model, or at least as the starting point. Not unlike the planning of our economy."

"Well, Aven, I think the best thing we can do right now is pray for sunshine."

"Or, better yet, look at the sunny side of things. Seems to me, Gaylord, since the game has been postponed, we can go to the debates instead. Where are they opening?"

"In the Music Conservatory Theater."

"Great, call and tell them we'll be wanting two seats. I wouldn't miss it."

"I'll call, Aven."

With the heavy rains, Aven decided to delay his departure. It was Friday, nearing the eve of a long-awaited May Day campaign. As usual, nothing of much significance was on the schedule. The limo arrived at the flat shortly after eight, and Aven reached his office well before lunch.

"Thank you."

"You're welcome, sir."

Aven was careful to avoid the puddles that had accumulated on the pavement but could not keep the heavy rain from his head. The dampness followed him into the building.

"Well, good morning. And look what the cat brought in."

"Morning, Gaylord. Looks can be deceptive, you know. I feel fine, but I am sorry about all the rain. It's really unusual for this time of the year."

"It's an unusual time of the year, Aven, what with no opening game."

"But the election debates, they begin tomorrow. You haven't forgotten, have you?"

"Is there a way to? No, you're right, Aven. They should provide some distraction, but it's not as if I haven't seen my share of election campaigns. After a while, they sort of...."

"This is my first, and the first for all of Russia. Maybe after two hundred and fifty years they'll lose their luster for us, too. I'll let you know. Today, however, it'll take a lot more than the monsoon outside to dampen my spirits. Which reminds me, I'd like to have the political MOPers fill me in on what they've been up to these past months."

"I'll give them a call. How 'bout lunch?"

"Perfect."

Aven was greeted warmly as he entered the dining hall. The MOPers seated around the long dining table took up the Ah-ven chant, which had reverberated through the MOP halls since his now famous "nothing to fear" address. Aven had become accustomed to the ritual almost from the start, and he smiled in appreciation. The verbal salute ended as the waiter approached. Another ritual, of longer standing, was the collective groan in response to the fixed menu. Turkey dumplings appealed to Aven, but he joined in the friendly jeer nevertheless. Disparate conversations broke out as the waiter departed.

"Gentlemen, excuse me. I'd like to use some of our lunchtime for business, ah, light business...."

The casual talk around the table ebbed as he continued.

"Most of you know that I've stayed out of politics throughout the revolution, and as a result, I guess I have some catching up to do. Leigh, you've been leading the political section."

Vassily Advasser was one of the few members of MOP who had made a successful transition from the KGB. In his youth, he had attained a well-earned reputation as a ruthless adviser in all political matters. With the Amerikan occupation, most of the elderly secret police staff were given an early and generous retirement. Finding suitable alternatives for the few younger members of the KGB had provided MOP with some awkward moments. Vassily, however, had a winning personality, allowing him to transfer his KGB skills to the political section at MOP with ease. In a manner similar to Aven, he had risen quickly, and with his recent promotion had become the youngest person to head any of the MOP sections.

"Aven, I'd be happy to fill you in. It's all quite simple. We owe much to our comrades across the sea. The Amerikans had been refining their own political process for decades, and only recently have they felt satisfied with their election campaigns. We expect our system to be as efficient and practical...."

"Leigh, I think Aven would like to hear about some of the details. Can you tell us who the candidates are? How were they selected? And what about the parties? I suppose there are two? What are they called, and what are the issues, if any?"

"Gaylord's right, Leigh. That's exactly the kind of information that will be useful in following the campaign."

"I think we can answer all of those questions."

"Before dessert?"

"Easily, Gaylord. There are, indeed, two formal parties, with space on the ballot for a write-in candidate. The Amerikans learned long ago that the ability to select beyond the official candidates is a wonderful device, permitting a diversity of options that are meaningful to the handful of idiosyncratic voters and meaningless in the election outcome."

"Leigh, it looks as if our MOPers have learned well. What are the two parties?"

"Naming the parties proved to be one of the more complex tasks, but we finally settled on Democratic Movement and National Unity, Demo and Nu for short. What do you think?"

"Well, I don't know what the other choices were, but...."

"Leigh, I can see the inspiration for the Demos, but National Unity. Wasn't there a third party...?"

"Right, in the 1980 campaign, the start of Amerika's own revolution...."

"But why didn't you use Reagan's party? Something like Government of the People?"

"Actually, Gaylord, that was our first choice, but the Amerikans vetoed the idea. They were afraid if we used the name, it might change their luck. Can't say that I blame them, but Nu has a nice ring to it, and both names evoke good feelings—democracy—unity."

"Do they stand for anything else?"

"Of course. The party platforms define the core issues. I have several copies."

Vassily reached under his chair and brought up a stack of legal-size pages, which were passed around the table.

PARTY PLATFORM

ABORTION We remain opposed to the economically (and morally) indefensible crime of abortion and all other crimes which impinge on individual FREEDOM and LIBERTY.

ALCOHOL Alcohol is the chief cause of poverty, broken homes, domestic violence, juvenile delinquency, vice, crime, political corruption, wasted manpower, and highway accidents. We therefore support continued restriction on its use, within the context of individual FREEDOM and LIBERTY.

ARTS Our nation has always been distinguished by its rich and full artistic cultures. We seek to foster the arts without controlling their content, providing such artistic endeavor conforms to local community standards of DECENCY and PUBLIC MORALITY, within the context of individual FREEDOM and LIBERTY.

CHURCH AND STATE We believe in the freedom of the individual to worship in accordance with his beliefs and shall foster a climate where such diversity of religious views may flourish, within the context of individual FREEDOM and LIBERTY.

CRIME Our primary concern shall be the safety of property (and lives) of law-abiding citizens, not the rights of criminals. We promise speedy and appropriate justice in all cases of criminal activity, and where appropriate, the DEATH PENALTY must be employed WITHOUT DELAY.

EDUCATION A sound economic policy must incorporate a commitment to quality EDUCATION at the LOCAL LEVEL.

EMPLOYMENT A sound economic policy must incorporate a commitment to full employment.

ENVIRONMENT A sound economic policy must incorporate a commitment to a clean environment.

FAMILY VALUES The family is a sacred institution and basic unit on which our society is built. We oppose any action which might weaken or limit traditional PARENTAL AUTHORITY and cohesion of the TRADITIONAL FAMILY UNIT.

HEALTH A sound economic policy must incorporate a commitment to a healthy workforce. In this regard, all matters of OCCUPATIONAL health and SAFETY are properly LEFT TO THE judgment of the EMPLOYER.

INFLATION A sound economic policy must incorporate a commitment to LOW inflation, LOW interest rates, and LOW WAGES.

TAXATION A sound economic policy must incorporate a commitment to LOW and NONPROGRESSIVE TAXES.

UNIONS A sound economic policy must incorporate a commitment to the freedom of workers and employers AGAINST the COERCIVE powers of LABOR UNIONS.

WELFARE We are sensitive to the needs of our nation's blind and physically disabled citizens, and fully support all PRIVATE CHARITY to enable these poor citizens to live in dignity and economic security.

WORLD GOVERNMENT We are opposed to all efforts that deny the SANCTITY of our nation's SOVEREIGNTY.

"Each of these points, ah, what are they called?"

"Planks."

"Thanks, Gay."

"No, planks, with a 'P,'"

"Gaylord! Leigh, these planks seem fairly innocuous. Is this all there is to the platform? And which party...?"

"Both parties. The Demos and the Nus use the same platform. It's less confusing to the voter. The brevity comes out of the Amerikan experience. Party platforms had gotten out of hand, providing an opportunity for every crackpot to have his say and to argue over for weeks on end. Became a completely debilitating exercise. The vagueness allows real freedom for the candidates."

"Uh oh...."

"What's the problem, Gaylord?"

"Nothing, Aven. I was just..., oh, look, here come the candidates now."

Aven, who thought he had been following the discussion, was suddenly perplexed. As Gaylord spoke, the waiter arrived with the main dish, and the MOPers began chuckling and eating.

"I seem to have missed the joke, but I would like to know something about the candidates."

"I think Gaylord was referring to the waiter."

"No, Leigh, the turkey dumplings."

"We interviewed hundreds of applicants, mostly men. Again, we patterned our search after the Amerikans."

"We? At MOP? I thought I,...I mean the party...?"

"That's the way it used to be, Aven, but along with arcane platforms, political parties went out of fashion in Amerika some time ago. The Amerikans we spoke with thought MOP was in the best position to make the selection, at least this time."

"The same group picking *both* candidates?"

"Aven, the Amerikans assured us that if we used their optimal candidate profile, we'd wind up with two winners."

"Or losers."

"True enough, Gaylord, both can't be winners."

"Do these two winners or losers have names? Faces?"

"Yes, Aven, names, faces, *and* histories. Here, take a look. One of these two men will soon be our first democratically and freely elected president."

Vassily handed two folders to Aven and gave a similar set to Gaylord.

"These are the candidate dossiers. I just brought the two copies. Both men, Yurri Karterev and Yanos Boris Andrezun meet the suggested profile to perfection."

As Vassily spoke, Aven opened the first dossier. It contained a glossy photograph and a single-page biographical statement. It didn't take long to digest the contents, and upon doing so, Aven passed them along to another MOPer at the table. Gaylord did the same.

"Leigh, you sure you haven't made some kind of mistake? Yurri and Yanos, they look like...."

"Aven, I guarantee they are *not related*. These men fit the physical profile we've been working with—forty-two and handsome. The kind of alluring appearance that goes well on television *and* in person."

"Your bio sheets say they've earned law degrees and have had extensive experience with local government, Yanos as parks and recreation leader and Yurri as an adviser to the home militia. That's all? Leigh, this is the best you've been able to come up with after months...?"

"Aven, it's not what Yurri and Yanos have done that counts. It's what we can do with them. The Amerikans have become masters at *creating* attractive leaders from scratch. I assure you, we have not deviated from their advice."

"Perhaps. And these law degrees? The bio sheets indicate they both have, ah, M.O.D.s...?"

"Mail order degrees, of course. Very popular in America."

"Perhaps, Gaylord. But both men were reluctant to say much about their law school experience, and we saw no reason to press them. Their wives, however, are well educated and ambitious women.

"Uh oh...."

"What's the problem now, Gaylord?"

"Oh, ah, nothing at all, Leigh. I just noticed my dumplings are gone."

"As a matter of fact, they were better than usual. But, Gaylord, with May Day only a few hours away, these turkey dumplings will soon be a distant memory."

A number of the MOPers who had sat quietly throughout Leigh's informal orientation murmured in agreement with this forecast. Aven pushed aside his own reservations and joined in the upbeat mood.

"Gaylord, Leigh's right. And if the Amerikans can do it, we can do it even better."

With Aven's optimism again setting the tone, the lunch gathering soon broke up in a jovial mood. The rain showed no sign of abating, prompting Gaylord's recommendation for an early start to the holiday. Aven agreed, and the MOP staff was given the afternoon off. This was not the only weather-induced alteration. The indefinite postponement of the baseball season had prompted a change in the election debate schedule as well. The opening salvo, originally set for late the next evening so as not to conflict with the national pastime, had been moved to late afternoon. Only Gaylord had been less than enthusiastic about the adjustment.

As they left for home, Aven returned to the subject.

"Gaylord, I don't understand your objection to the change. At prime time, many more citizens will be able to watch, and with the rain and nothing else to do...."

It was clear that Gaylord preferred not to join in the conversation.

"Which reminds me, I assume you were able to get us tickets for tomorrow?"

"No trouble at all. They had plenty of seats."

"They did? I guess it's because of the rescheduling."

"That must be it, Aven. We'll see soon enough. How 'bout some food now?"

"I think I'll pass. Thanks, anyway. I'm still full from the dumplings. I don't feel like doing much. Probably just read for a while and get to bed early. But Monday should be exciting. After all, it's May Day."

"It's gonna be May, *MayDay*, all right."

Aven felt a trace of regret as he entered the flat. With so much new on the horizon, so much to anticipate, he missed being able to share his thoughts with Rena. Momentary anger replaced the regret, only to be shunted aside itself.

"Yurri and Yanos will have a few problems themselves. Nothing MOP won't be able to help them overcome."

Aven picked his way through an uninteresting dinner and television fare. His one phone call went unanswered. It was to Mellors. Aven called several times over the weekend to no avail.

The rains continued. The morning news, snugly wrapped in its plastic sleeve, was leaning against the door.

GIANT PITCHERS WELCOME RAIN DELAY

Moscow's pitching staff had been severely banged up during spring training. The story also provided extensive information on the alternate scheduling options, depending on when the weather cleared. Under any circumstances, the league commissioner promised that the Giants would open at home. Aven found the other headline of the day farther down on the page.

MAY DAY INTERCOURSE
OPENS POLITICAL SEASON

The format for the Karterev-Andrezun debate was described briefly. The story also provided information similar to what was on the bio sheets as well as a synopsis of the issues likely to be raised during the first head-to-head bout of the inaugural campaign. In contrast to the baseball coverage, the political reporting was quite skimpy. Absent also was any real sense of excitement or anticipation. Aven's mind drifted as he lingered over the news and some tepid tea. His call to Mellors again went unanswered, and the rest of the morning passed in an equally unproductive manner. Eventually the limo arrived.

"Damn. Where did I put it? Perhaps Rena...."

"Good afternoon."

"Good afternoon, sir. Awful weather."

"I'll say. Especially without an umbrella."

Aven tiptoed into the conservatory lobby, which was virtually empty. Vassily had offered a behind-the-scenes look at the battle site. Gaylord agreed to join them despite having seen more than his share of televised tussles at home. Aven was shaking the moisture from his coat as Vassily appeared, followed closely by Gaylord.

"Leigh, Gaylord, hello. I don't suppose either of you brought an extra umbrella?"

"Sorry, I just have the one."

"Me neither, but you can share mine during the debate."

"Thanks, Gaylord...."

"Ah, Gaylord, ever the comedian. Come on, let's go into the theater. The pregame activity ought to be in full swing."

Vassily opened the door to the rear of the orchestra section. In contrast to the quiet lobby, the stage area was alive with activity. For an instant, the mad and jumbled events of the historic concert raced through Aven's head, and he lost sense of where he was. The sound of Vassily's voice clarified the scene.

"...and the preparations have been under way for several days. Most of the people you see are the senior advisers who will provide on-the-spot advice throughout the debate. The others—the tech staff and sound engineers—are making their final check. Yurri and Yanos are backstage with the makeup crew and their trainers."

Aven had not expected such a crowd. There had to be over fifty individuals onstage, some moving about in an urgent fashion, others clustered in groups and speaking in hushed voices. Aven's idea of a head-to-head debate had evoked a much different image.

"A far cry from the Rhetoric Club debates we used to hold at MU," he thought, but it immediately occurred to him that there was more at stake today.

"Leigh, I see what you mean by pregame activity. Looks pretty chaotic...."

"Wait till the debate."

"Gaylord, don't be silly. The show, ah, debate itself will go off without a hitch precisely because of these advance preparations. They only *seem* frenetic to you, Aven. Every person on stage, as well as those working in the wings, is a highly trained professional. And from the shine on their shoes up to each minuscule bit of data in their heads, Yurri and Yanos have been prepped as near to perfection as is humanly possible. Once the debate begins, the advisers will provide instant polling results to the candidates, not only on how they are scoring but also on the issues foremost in the viewers' minds."

"During the debate? I thought it was 'one on one.' How...?"

They had moved down the aisle and were now only a few meters from the stage. Aven could see the answer to his question as Vassily explained.

"Head-to-head on camera and for the theater audience as well. In a few minutes, they'll be screening off the advisers, who will remain in direct contact with the two candidates through the teleprompters. Yurri and Yanos will also be wired for sound, so their advisers can speak to them when appropriate."

Aven lost his concentration as an image from his childhood intruded. A wagon pulled into town and in an instant transformed itself into a magical stage.

"We've got Yurri and Yanos wired like puppets."

As his mind refocused on the scene at hand, the feelings of ennui from the morning returned.

The pair of speaker stands, each with its see-through teleprompter, had been set in the front portion of the stage. Both stands were draped in red bunting, contrasting nicely with the several golden carnation wreaths placed nearby.

"Leigh, one of the rostrums is quite a bit higher off the floor. Is that...?"

"Yes, perhaps I didn't mention this the other day. The candidate specifications called for very much the same physical attributes, except for their height. At first the MOP staff didn't understand. The height difference makes it easier for the voters. The Amerikans also said something about the greatest political debates of all time...."

"Lincoln-Douglas?"

"That's it, Gaylord. How did you know?"

"Not that difficult, Leigh. Some time ago, actually, in the mid-nineteenth century, we had the first—some say the only—political debates in America. Two men, both excellent speakers, who had a lot to say. A deadly combination. Most believe that Lincoln lost the debates but won the war. I used to think so, but I'm not sure anymore. The debates were a winner, the standard of comparison ever since. Seven times the two of them got together, talked and argued for hours. They were just doing battle for a senate seat from Illinois, but what they had to say concerned the nation—never been anything like it since."

"Until now!"

Leigh spoke in an assured manner.

"Gentlemen, Yurri and Yanos—Yanos, by the way, is the shorter one—will be doing seven head-to-head debates as well. One each day this week, and the seventh is set for election eve. We've limited this campaign to seven days, and of course, Lincoln and Douglas didn't have access to computer-based cueing and meteoric mood monitoring. Otherwise, everything's the same, if not better."

"I think you missed just one small point, Leigh."

"What's that? Oh yes, there was no TV then, either."

"That wasn't what I had in mind. I never met the man, but we did have to learn a fair amount about Abe Lincoln. I'd say I know Abe pretty well, and I'll tell you something, Leigh, ol' Yurri Karterev ain't no Abe Lincoln. As for Yanos Andrezun and Stephen Douglas, I don't know, they are close to the same height."

"Gaylord, I think you underestimate the ability of our trainers, as you'll see shortly. People are starting to enter, and we should probably take our seats. Who has the tickets?"

"I do. The seats are in the balcony. Your regular seats, Aven."

"In the first row?"

"Of course, the special seats reserved for the MOP director and his la...."

"Maybe we could sit here in the orchestra. It doesn't look all that crowded. Would you mind checking? I'd just as soon not go up to the balcony."

"No problem. I'm sure Leigh doesn't mind."

"Of course not."

"We can sit right here. When I called for seats, they said the orchestra was unlikely to fill up."

The start of the debate was approaching. Aven found himself seated in the fourth row of the orchestra section. He and Rena had agreed that these seats were too close to the stage, at least for acoustic purposes. He didn't think the same applied to the debate, and it would be interesting to be able to see the candidates close up. Vassily continued to discuss various aspects of the debate and the upcoming campaign.

"You'll see, a week will be ample time for the voters."

"Maybe too much."

"Oh, I don't think so, Gaylord. And besides the seven debates, Yurri and Yanos will be visiting all of the major cities, shaking hands, eating herring, and getting to know the Russian people. There's really no better way for the people to meet the candidates than in the flesh."

"Uh oh."

"What's wrong now, Gaylord?"

"Why, ah...I think the debate is about to begin."

"That's weird."

"What's weird?"

"The hall is half empty."

"Must be the weather."

"I'm sure that's it, Gaylord."

"And don't forget, it is being televised."

"Uh oh."

At that moment the hall darkened and two bright amber lights focused on the speaker stands. Yurri and Yanos walked onstage, acknowledged the smattering of applause, and took their places. Yanos required some assistance in mounting his elevated podium. Music filled the theater. Aven didn't think it was classical, and he was positive that it wasn't modern Russian, either. He turned to Gaylord.

"What's that?"

"It's clearly one of the campaign songs, for Yurri or for Yanos, right, Leigh?"

"As a matter of fact, it's the theme for *both* of them."

"Both?"

"It's an old Beatles tune—'I Wanna Be Your Man.'"

"Shhh, they're about to begin. Remember, there's no moderator, just Yurri and Yanos, one on one, and I think the Nus won the toss. Yanos goes first."

> Welcome! How good it is to be with you this May Day. My fellow Russians, it is hard for me to express what is in my heart—and mind—at this historic moment. That I have been selected as the candidate of National Unity is a very great honor. Our time is short, and your responsibility enormous. Let me begin with the essence of Nu.

Their seats provided an intimate view of the candidates. Aven noticed that Yurri and Yanos did look very much alike, and very much like the photographs he had seen. The photos, however, had not done justice to the spectacular head of hair atop each. Yanos's voice was well modulated, rich, and fatherly. The only visual distraction was his greenish-blue eyes, which seemed to dart about nervously.

> I stand foursquare behind the Nu platform, every plank, every slat, splinter, and nail. And I know you will want a president who believes in FREEDOM and LIBERTY for all deserving citizens. A president who will help maintain our great TRADITIONS. A president who believes in the SANCTITY of PRIVATE PROPERTY and who will keep government off of the back of workers and owners alike. There are many issues facing our great nation, and I am confident that tonight and throughout the seven debates—debates that my party has suggested—you will have ample opportunity to know precisely where I stand. When you do, on the eighth of May, you will vote the straight Nu ticket. Thank you very much.

As Yanos took a step back from his podium, a rustling could be heard among the small gathering. Gaylord coughed. Aven was experiencing an ill-defined feeling of discomfort as Yurri began to deliver his opening remarks.

> Welcome! Indeed, how fitting that we can be with you on May Day. My fellow Russians, it is also hard for me to express what is in my heart and mind at this historic moment. In view of the shortness of time and the urgency of our situation, allow me to get to the essence. Like my esteemed colleague, I too stand foursquare behind, and on, every last plank in my great party's platform—FREEDOM and LIBERTY for ALL CITIZENS, ah, for all DESERVING citizens. Finally, let me conclude with the following observation: A casual reading of the Demo and Nu platforms will reveal a degree of similarity. But don't be fooled; there are profound differences between the cracks. And I am confident that the debates, which, by the way, history will reveal were first proposed by the Demos and not by the Nus, as my worthy opponent would have you believe, will shine light into every Nu chink, every Nu chasm, and every Nu crevice.

Yurri directed a militant glare toward Yanos, indicating the conclusion of his opening comments. His voice was not unlike Yanos's, though his eyes seemed more firmly rooted in their sockets. The rustling in the hall resumed. Gaylord coughed again, and Aven continued to feel out of sorts. Vassily seemed comfortable.

"This is going to get interesting right away. Both candidates have been drilled in the importance of the attack mode. Yanos was a bit slow off the mark, but Yurri seems to be going for the jugular right from the git-go."

"Leigh, is this a debate or a dog fight?"

"It's a *political* debate, Aven, with very high stakes."

> My esteemed opponent, inadvertently, I am sure, has rather plainly demonstrated his inability to distinguish truth from fantasy. Any thoughtful reading of history will show that the Demos haven't come up with an original idea in over a century. To make matters worse, the opposition candidate has been *opposed* to any debates whatsoever.

> Is the representative from Nu calling me a liar?

Indeed. And a liar of the lowest form. But we are not here to make personal judgments. Such judgments are properly reserved for the voter...and I have the utmost faith in the wisdom of the Russian citizen. Perhaps my worthy opponent would like to explain precisely how he intends to deal with the nagging homeless problem.

I will ignore the personal insult. My esteemed opponent is indeed correct. The election will be decided by the Russian people. You ask about the homeless? Of course I assume you mean our nation's "happy campers." The most recent data show the number of campers to be at an all-time low, and more to the point, our polls show public concern to be at a similar level. The few "happy campers" that remain are the direct product of alcohol abuse. And I must say, if my opponent, as well as other prominent members of his party, would control their own public inebriation....

Is the Demo candidate calling me a drunkard?

Indeed I am, though I agree with my able opponent, we are not here to cast aspersions at each other but rather to flush out the core differences in our approaches to the nation's concerns. Perhaps the candidate from Nu would like to enlighten us on how he plans to deal with the nation's transportation difficulties.

My worthy foe may wallow in the gutter if he wishes, but I have no intention of responding to his slanderous personal attacks. On the matter of transportation, the latest polls show an overwhelming preference for the automobile....

The wave of restlessness grew as it spread through the orchestra section. Aven noticed that several people were leaving their seats. He himself found these early moments of the debate disappointing, bordering on the banal.

"What do you think so far? They've both mastered the subtle technique of thrust and parry, attack your opponent's character and put yourself on the high road. This is really exciting, isn't it?"

"Leigh, both candidates seem to be experts at climbing in and out of the gutter."

"Gaylord, I doubt that that's the way our Amerikan advisers would characterize the process."

My personal use of prescription drugs has nothing to do....

...the problems can be traced directly to outside *financiers*...it is worth noting that the Demo party chairman, Miss Goldie Cohenberg....

It is not my place to charge my worthy opponent with anti-Semitism...our polls indicate that teenage pregnancy encouraged....

The voters are not interested in whether or not I've ever been arraigned on child molestation...what is at issue....

...energy shortage, and our latest polls indicate...shock therapy.

To suggest that my wife suffers from severe bouts of depression is beyond the bounds of normal decency....

Of course our party welcomes the establishment of an independent prosecutor. It's the Nus, ah, I mean the Demos....

The feeling of unease was becoming more pronounced, bordering on nausea. Aven's mind turned as well. Less than a month had passed since he had sat in the music hall listening to the inspiring work of Russia's young musical talent.

"What a contrast. Our young musicians have so much to say, and Yurri and Yanos...."

He looked at his watch.

"Hang on, Aven. Only ten more minutes."

"I know, Gaylord, but there are *six more* debates...."

"They're nearing the end. A few rough edges, but otherwise a super show, don't you think?"

Aven paid little attention to Vassily, and even less to Yurri's and Yanos's concluding remarks. Both candidates appeared to be well satisfied with their efforts. As the hall brightened and the few remaining viewers departed, frenzy returned to the stage. The many advisers had come from behind the curtain.

They all seemed to be talking at once, indiscriminately to both Yurri and Yanos.

Despite his mood, Aven smiled to himself.

"Rena would have much to write about."

He could feel his grin ebb as he spoke to Vassily.

"It's hard for me to imagine what the voter might have learned from this spectacle we've just witnessed. Leigh, I know I'm ultimately responsible for everything that takes place at MOP. Perhaps I should have assumed a more active role in the work of the political section, but...."

"Aven, come on, don't be down on yourself. You've done a brilliant job getting the economic pot boiling and in keeping the lid on. You can't hold yourself responsible for every detail, and besides, this was just the first debate. A pretty dismal showing, I agree. What about it, Leigh? Why don't we meet with your political staff in the morning? We'll have the viewer response by then and a better idea of where we stand."

"As you wish, Gaylord, but I must say, even with the rocky moments, this evening's debate went pretty much as planned."

The confident overtones were absent from Vassily's voice.

"Well then, Leigh, we're going to have to do something about the plan. Gaylord's right, we'll know more in the morning. I just hope it isn't too late already...."

The rain had eased, and the prospect of Giants baseball softened Aven's mood somewhat. Aven had no desire for food, and he spent the next several hours with a pot of tea and the novel that he had been flirting with over the past several weeks. Images of Rena blended with the fictional characters, almost as if she, too, were a creation of the author. But with or without her, the story penetrated very little into his consciousness. The debate fiasco dominated his thoughts throughout the evening and beyond. He could not recall a night of such fitful sleep, and visions of two bloodied pitbulls locked at each other's throat spoiled what little sleep he did manage. He woke to heavy rain and the morning news.

NOMINEES NURTURE MERCILESS MAY DAY MESSAGE

WHEN IT RAINS
IT POURS
■■■■■■■■■■■■■■■■■

*L*ittle of his appetite had returned. The news report of the May Day debacle didn't help, nor did the steady downpour. Aven knew the rains would end and he would soon experience the vicarious pleasures and pains that were part of being a Giants fan. But would such diversion mask the pain of a Yurri presidency? The thought of a runt like Yanos was even more disheartening. It was in this mood that he arrived at MOP in time for the political powwow with Vassily. After a few words with Gaylord in his own office, the two walked up to the combo conference room.

"Any news on the elevator front?"

"As a matter of fact, I think they're about ready to make a decision. Shouldn't be more than a few weeks."

"It's been months. I suppose getting it down to weeks represents some progress. What's holding them up now?"

"Not sure. I think it's something about the music."

"Music! Gaylord, you can't be serious?"

"I am. Seems that electronic music causes the equipment to jam at awkward moments. Hardly an insurmountable problem though."

"Surely not like Yurri and Yanos."

"I know what you mean, Aven. That wasn't a very encouraging start to the election, but we may be underestimating the MOPers. Leigh has been in some pretty tough situations during his days with the KGB. We oughta give him a chance."

"If you ask me, it'll be a small miracle if he gets us out of this mess, with all of six days to work with."

"And Yurri and Yanos as well."

"Right. Make that a *large* miracle."

Vassily and his staff were seated around the conference table. Only Vassily appeared to be in good spirits.

"Good morning, Aven, Gaylord. I trust you both slept well. Nothing like a good night's sleep to get the day off right."

"Good morning."

Aven made it clear that the greeting was for all of the political section.

"As a matter of fact, Leigh, I've had better nights, which, if I'm not mistaken, has something to do with why we are here this morning."

"Well, yes, of course. I didn't mean to suggest that we are without problems, but...."

"And perhaps you'd like to start with the extent of the problem. I assume your staff has the ratings for last night's farce...?"

"Aven, I don't think that's fair. Yurri and Yanos are...."

"Leigh, I think Aven's being quite forbearing. You know as well as I that Yurri and Yanos were duller than yesterday's dumplings. Why don't we forget the excuses and see if we can't do something about the remaining debates. Do we have the ratings for yesterday's...?"

If the political staff needed additional reasons for depression, Gaylord and Aven had provided them. After a prolonged and embarrassed silence, one of the MOPers began speaking.

"There is some good news. Sparkling ratings were recorded at the start. Data for the major urban areas show that well over sixty percent of the households were tuned to the debate. In fact, that represents *one hundred percent* of all of the TV sets in use at the time."

"I'm not sure if that's good or bad news. What channels were carrying the debates?"

"Ah, all of them, Aven."

"Who's idea was that? Leigh, didn't you think to allow for some choice, just in case the debates bombed?"

"Actually not. The Amerikans have had so much experience. In a sense there is good news from the later ratings. Go ahead, Kneelzun."

The MOPer continued.

"Yes, well, the ratings did change over the course of the debates, declining at each sampling. After the first hour only fifteen percent of the viewing audience remained."

"Oh, that is top-notch news, and did you have a reading for the bitter end? We should probably check those homes to see if there's anyone alive."

"In fact, Gaylord, the ratings dropped to zero not long after five PM."

"Well, that's *truly* stellar news indeed. The two candidates are so rotten they not only stink up the Music Conservatory but in little more than an hour are able to drive every Russian citizen from his Rube-tube. And just how do you all propose to continue this pathetic political parody? At the rate it's going, Yurri and Yanos will end up in a dead heat, *without a goddamn vote apiece.*"

"Don't forget, they're both family men, Aven."

"Somehow, Gaylord, that doesn't make me feel a whole lot better."

Aven's visible anger and depression were aspects of his personality that none of the MOPers had seen before. These combined with the disappointing start to the campaign began to cast a pall over the meeting. No one said a word. The MOPers were too intimidated, and Aven was obviously too furious.

Gaylord, as always, seemed to manage a degree of detachment from the proceedings.

"Gentlemen, I assume that this long silence has produced a wealth of ideas. Surely, Leigh, with your past experience?"

"Well, Gaylord, no disrespect intended, but I think you underestimate Yurri and Yanos. In fact, we all have.…"

"*Leigh.…*"

"No, Aven, please hear me out. I think the problem last night was that both men were too *tightly* controlled. We were feeding them information and lines from the moment the debate began."

"And what are you suggesting?"

Aven made little effort to modulate his feelings.

"It's simple. We've gotta let Yurri be Yurri and Yanos be Yanos. These two men are decent, ordinary Russian citizens with a lust for political office. And it's not as if they haven't had a wealth of experience."

"That's right, parks and recreation and the home militia. Pretty much all anyone could ask for in the way of expertise."

"They do have loved ones to lean on as well. Yurri's wife is quite intelligent, and Yanos has always listened to his father and, more recently, his wife, too. There's no question about her credentials. And, Aven, don't forget both men have law degrees."

"Leigh's got a point there, a duo of dubious diplomas."

"We like to think of them more as creative credentials, useful with a malleable electorate. We can argue qualifications ad nauseam, but under any circumstance, we all agree that last night's program didn't work as well as we might have wished."

"It was a catastrophe!"

"All right, Aven, have it your way. The fact remains, we must find a way to alter the format, and with next to no time in which to work.…"

"I'm delighted to know that there is something we can agree on. And just how do you suggest we proceed?"

"As I said, we have to loosen the reins, unleash Yurri and Yanos. From the start of the training period, I've had this uncomfortable feeling that the handlers were being overly cautious. If we let the candidates speak what's in their hearts and minds...."

"Uh oh."

"Gaylord, why the doubts? In your own country, isn't that when the great leaders are at their best?"

"That's what they say, Leigh, but...."

"Sorry to interrupt gentlemen. I'd like us to get back to the present moment if you don't mind. Gaylord, I don't see all that many options at this point. And Leigh's suggestion has merit in its simplicity. Just cut the wires and it's hard to imagine Yurri and Yanos doing worse on their own. Unless anyone else has a better idea?"

No response was forthcoming.

"Okay, it's Leigh's alternative approach. We can take stock in the morning."

"Thanks, Aven. I appreciate your confidence. We'll get the word out immediately. Yurri and Yanos will be campaigning throughout the city for much of the day, pressing a lot of flesh. They'll meet up again this evening for the second debate in Kiev. Trust me, I've got a good feeling about what we're doing."

"I hope you're right. I must say, I hardly share your optimism, but my opinion's not at issue. What matters is how the citizens react to Yurri and Yanos, free of their keepers, and we'll know soon enough. Gaylord, I think we've done as much as we can this morning. We should let Leigh and his staff alone so they can get to their work. Gentlemen, I trust the situation will have changed by the time we meet again."

"Aven, I can guarantee it. My staff and I look forward to the renewed campaign and to seeing you in the morning."

The scene was similar to that at the onset of the meeting. As Aven and Gaylord departed, Leigh was the only member of the political section with a smile on his face.

"Gaylord, I don't understand that man. How can he be smiling?"

"Hard to explain. Maybe it has to do with his KGB training. Weren't those fellows taught to smile while they worked?"

"Whatever the explanation, he damn well better deliver, or I'll give his jaw real cause to sag."

They continued down the stairs without speaking. The feelings of disquiet and anger were new to Aven, and nothing that had occurred in the combo room provided him solace. His record as director had been unblemished, until

May Day. And now, for the first time in his experience, crucial events seemed beyond his control. The political process would grind on, and he could do little to intervene. He hadn't eaten since lunch yesterday, but he declined Gaylord's suggestion to go to lunch.

"Not yet thanks, Gaylord. Those turkey dumplings are still doing a number on my stomach."

Gaylord brought some tea to the office. Aven continued to express feelings of distress, and Gaylord listened sympathetically.

"Aven, I know it's a long shot, but Leigh might be onto something. Don't forget, the weather's gotta break in a day or two also."

"Not to take anything away from the powers of your Amerikan baseball, but you don't really believe that that will be enough to ease the financial situation or the traffic, and it's hard to imagine Yurri or Yanos doing much....We've come so far, and now...."

"Aven, I think you're taking all of this too much to heart, as if it's all you have to think about."

"What else is there?"

"Maybe what you need is a good woman?"

"Gaylord, do me a favor. Talking about Rena won't help. She's a part of my past, and I want to keep it that way. I'd be happier not having to think about her."

"I didn't mean Rena necessarily, though I'm sorry if I uncovered old wounds."

"*She* may have the wounds. I just don't want to think about her."

"I'm sorry."

"Apologies aren't necessary, Gaylord, and I promise you, if, by some act of God, we survive this week, the ladies of Moscow will once again have much to be thankful for."

Aven got up and walked to the window. There was nothing in the continued downpour to suggest outside intervention.

"On another subject, do you know anything about Mellors? I've been trying to get in touch with him. I meant to ask you last week. He's not listed in the MOP directory. Do you have any...?"

"Mellors, oh yeah, the handsome dude who used to work in the family support section. He got one of the first McPleasure's franchises a prime location in Red Square."

"Red Square?"

"Where else, Aven? I'm sure you and Rena never managed to get down there at night. Probably just as well."

"Gaylord, what *are* you talking about?"

"McPleasure's has been one of the most rapidly growing chains. They serve as a magnet for a multitude of subsidiary products, adult books, toys, photography, overnight travel tours to Thailand, Korea, Greece. I understand some enterprising young couple has even been experimenting with a bestiary. They were talking at lunch a while back; Mellors must have made a small fortune. Seems he had access to an entire stable of young fillies, the most alluring of Moscow's young women, and, ah, men. Business boomed, and the overflow created a financial bonanza for everyone else. Rumor has it that even Lenin's been having wet dreams. As I understand it, Mellors was asked to join the national franchise organization. He probably spends a lot of time on the road, which explains...."

"Just like politics, I guess I should have paid more attention to the nation's sexual progression. They're both as fascinating as they are foul. If we didn't have Yurri and Yanos to worry about, I'd suggest we look into the matter ourselves."

"Don't worry, Aven. It'll keep, and there's no doubt, those two yahoos present a yawning problem."

Later, during lunch, Gaylord persuaded Aven that he should spend some time with the various MOP sections that had been helping to keep the lid on.

"With the May Day letdown, spirits have sagged. A visit from you would do a lot."

Aven succeeded in suppressing his own discontent, and their travels through the halls of MOP in the afternoon did alter the mood. So much so that his appetite returned. He joined Gaylord for dinner at Donald Molay's. The meal would have been quite acceptable save for the fact that the enchilada verde was cold. As advertised, they did have their food within ninety seconds of placing the order and were able to arrive at Aven's flat in ample time for the second debate.

"You don't happen to have any Acid Quench?"

Gaylord explained that it was the enchilada and had nothing to do with the forthcoming debate. Aven had never before required such medication. They settled for herbal tea, which Aven located after some exploration. Gaylord was the first to notice the time.

"Well, Aven, hold onto your hat. The unleashing of Yurri and Yanos oughta be something."

Gaylord turned up the volume.

"Gaylord, the tea's fine, but next time I'll have Acid Quench."

As Aven spoke, the musical fanfare filled the small room and the television screen brightened.

KARTEREV vs ANDREZUN (ROUND 2)
May 2, 2003
KIEV

A Public Service Broadcast
STATION OWNERSHIP NOT RESPONSIBLE
FOR THE VIEWS EXPRESSED

The music faded, and a view of the debate scene, similar to the conservatory stage with its two spotlit lecterns, emerged. Aven stared at the screen in disbelief as Yurri and Yanos came into focus.

"What in the hell…?"

"I haven't any idea. Looks more like the start of the fifteenth round. I can't believe this is what Leigh had in mind."

Gone were the well-groomed and slickly coiffured contestants of the previous afternoon. Yurri had a wound above his left eye, and the blood hadn't fully dried around the bandage. His tie was askew and his shirt badly stained. The steadiness of his gaze was absent as his eyes darted around in their sockets much like Yanos's had earlier. Yanos' left eye was swollen shut. Yanos had no tie, and his shirt was deeply stained. Neither man was smiling. The announcer's mellow voice indicated that in this evening's second debate the Demo candidate would be speaking first. Yurri grasped the sides of his podium, as if to steady himself.

> Good evening, fellow citizens. It's a a a pppleasure for me to be with you again. After a day in the streets, I know fffirsthand how deep the emotions are in this campaign, and that is why I intend to speak to you fffrom my heart. I trust my eststeemed opponent will have the courage to do the same. Thank you.

"Oh, God."

"Aven, I don't think he can help."

Yurri stepped back. The smirk on his face appeared to be causing him some pain. Yanos stepped forward, cast an angry glance at his opponent, held tightly to the side of his lectern, and began speaking in a lusterless voice.

> Good evening, comrades. I, too, spent the day amongst the energetic Russian citizen. There is mmmuch that I want to say this evening, but I cannot overlook what has just bbbbeen said. For my worthy foe to question my courage borders on

blasphemy. It is well known that he and his Demo candidates have shunned every opportunity to cccconfront the issues we face today. He, in fact, is the master of ccccowardly cccconduct, an artist at gutless guile. Thank you....

Gutless cccconduct and cccccowardly guile, indeed. The candidate from Nu has a facile tongue. But he is too clever by three quarters. Since last we mmmmet, I have asked my staff to investigate this man who asks for your trust. Can we trust him? I thththink not. Take, for example, his maternal grandfather, and in particular this man's mmmmmilitary record during the great war....

It grieves me to see my honorable adveveversary slither in the slime...worse yet is his avoidance of the ppppppressing issues we face—traffic, air quality, crime...and I'll be happy to match my grandaddy's military record with his any day. Everyone knows that the Demo candidate bought his way into the home militia and that his entire thhthhthree months of duty was spspspspent....

Neither Aven nor Gaylord was to learn how Yurri occupied himself while on duty with the home militia. Aven had almost broken the remote control in darkening the screen.

"It didn't work. Now what? I think the only satisfaction is going to come in firing that asshole, Leigh, along with his entire section. Gaylord, what are we going to do now?"

"I'm n-n-n-n-not sure, Aven. But canning Leigh may not be such a good idea. Might be convenient to have him stay in charge. Somebody's gotta be responsible, and at this point...."

"I understand, but the thought of having that grinning ape around MOP one day longer...."

"Aven, there's not a hell of a lot we can do tonight except pray. We do have a meeting set for the morning. Let's hold off any decision until then."

"We certainly don't have much choice, and right now I'm too upset and tired to make *any* decisions. If you don't mind, I think I'd like to be alone for a while."

"I don't mind."

Gaylord paused before closing the door.

"Aven, you're not going to believe this, but something tells me we are gonna get through this week in good shape. I'll take the limo. See you in the morning, and don't forget to pray."

Aven did not pray. He wouldn't have known whom to pray to or what to ask. He didn't sleep much, either. The rain and the news awaited.

MOSCOW CITIZENS RUB ELBOWS WITH CANDIDATES
Lasting Impressions Made on Karterev and Andrezun

He cast the paper aside. Neither the tea nor the toast was any more appetizing. In a perverse way he felt anxious to get to MOP.

"That son of a lame goat better not be smiling. I suppose Gaylord's got a point about deflecting the responsibility, but...and the campaign has all of four days to run, *including today*. Rena picked a great time to walk out....Where's the god-damn limo?"

"Good morning, sir...."

Aven closed the limo door. There was a noticeable diminution in traffic.

"The poor slobs are surely not home watching reruns of the debates. How could anyone be interested? Whatever, at least it cuts down on the commute."

His thoughts turned to the financial reports that had been assembled since his brilliant colloquy on fear. HUSH card charges had reached an all-time high as the public continued to react to the bank holiday with equanimity. Despite the shortened travel time, Aven was able to read the several other crisis communiqués that were awaiting him in the limo. Nothing had really been accomplished in the several areas where he and his MOPers had worked so effectively to keep the lid on, but such failings paled in comparison with the present political fiasco. Aven had not, however, expected the degree of public nonchalance that was apparent, almost as if a catatonic spell had been cast over much of the populace.

"Good morning, sir..."

"Morning, Av..."

"Good mor..."

It must have been evident in his step and expression. He was not in the mood for even the most perfunctory greeting, and he walked to his office without a word.

"Moooooooornin, Av..."

"What time's the meeting."

"They're waiting for us now. But, come on, Aven, you're gonna scare Leigh and his group half to death."

"Gaylord, the election's on Sunday, in *four bloody days!*"

"That's gonna be a lot of blood...."

"Maybe, but not many days...."

"I still think everything'll work out...."

"Sure it will, with divine intervention...."

"You took my advice and prayed...."

"Gaylord!"

"Okay, Aven, let's see what Leigh and his little band of angels have come up with."

They walked to the combo room in silence, entering to find a band of fallen angels. The political MOPers seemed incapable of taking their eyes off the conference table. Aven thought he could detect a mumbled greeting as he and Gaylord joined the group. Leigh managed to turn his eyes to Aven, but the effort was painfully obvious.

"Well now, come on, gentlemen, it's not as if the Giants lost the opener."

"Gaylord, if you took a vote, it wouldn't surprise me in the least if Leigh and his staff opted to pass on the humor this morning. I'm sure they'd much rather get right to business."

Aven turned toward Leigh and continued after an anger-laden pause.

"Terribly sorry, Leigh, but for some inexplicable reason, Gaylord and I didn't watch all that much of last night's debate. We had the tiniest peek at the two bumbling braindead boneheads, babbling and bloodied...."

As he spoke, Aven could feel his face redden as Leigh's whitened.

"Leigh, in exactly four days we're going to have an election in this nation. You know? An election, where people *vote*? The project *you* and this sorry group here have been working on for months!"

"Ah, excuse me, Aven. Leigh, what happened? Maybe if you go over some of what occurred yesterday, we'll have a better feel for the situation. Yurri and Yanos looked like...."

"Turkey shit!"

"Aven, let him answer."

Some time passed before Vassily responded. When he finally did, his voice was hushed and tentative. Absent, without a trace, was the self-confidence he had exhibited throughout round one of the campaign. The reasons for this vivid turnabout were not hard to fathom. No one could have anticipated the reception given to Yanos and Yurri as they brought their campaigns to the streets of Moscow.

"I had planned to accompany Yurri during the first part of the day. It was a walking tour through the newer housing projects beyond Red Square, culminating in an informal meeting in Gorby Park. A chance for the citizens to get to know Yurri face to face. Despite the rain, Yurri and his staff were in high spirits at the start. None of us could have guessed...."

The story of Yurri's morning was as savage as it was simple. Notice of the walking tour had been widely circulated. There were, however, very few spectators in evidence as the party emerged from their vehicles.

"We had anticipated some problems because of the weather, but...."

The party had walked for several blocks before encountering a single individual. The few people that they did meet initially were surprisingly indifferent to the presence of the Demo candidate.

"The early morning optimism was fading, and then, as we turned off the main street, we noticed a small gathering. Our spirits rose until...."

They had come upon a small group of men who were anything but passive.

"For no apparent reason, these men, no more than ten or so, began hurling angry words at Yurri, who, to his credit, did not respond in kind. Instead, he acknowledged the vitriolic abuse with a smile and a wave of his hand. At that moment, I felt that he was destined to political greatness. Alas, I didn't know what lay ahead."

As Vassily's monologue continued, Aven found himself listening with increasing interest and even greater incredulity. Yurri's party had continued past the first group of angry men, only to have the experience repeated time and time again throughout the tour. Small groups of working-age men had greeted Yurri with unremitting hostility. If there was any alteration in the pattern, it was the fact that the animosity directed at their party did, at times, extend beyond mere verbal assault.

"I can't even tell you what they were saying. All too quickly the hateful words came at us, punctuated by eggs, tomatoes, and an occasional rock or bottle. Yurri continued to press on, waving and smiling, as if he were oblivious to the rage around him."

The Demo entourage had finally arrived at the park, all, with the exception of Yurri, visibly shaken. Many of the men they passed along the way had joined in a pugnacious procession to Gorby Park. Nevertheless, the gathering at the park was not large. Their level of ferocity was well out of proportion to their numbers.

"Yurri made several attempts to quiet the mob, clasping his hands above his head as if to acknowledge the jeers, smiling, and asking for quiet. Of course, it didn't work. The scorn continued to pour down, intermingled with the rain and refuse. There may have been the sound of gunfire as well. I began to fear for our safety. Curiously, Yurri seemed oblivious to all of this, almost as if he enjoyed the verbal and physical assault, a natural politician. It was some time before we could persuade him to leave. A few of the derelicts followed us back to the parking area, and we were not completely free of their abuse for some time. We canceled the afternoon excursion. Yurri had been scheduled to visit the university, but we all needed time to recover and do the best we could to have the candidate cleaned up for the flight to Kiev. Of course, Yurri wasn't at his best for the debate. Nor was Yanos."

Leigh looked towards his despondent section members as he continued.

"When I returned to MOP, I learned that Yanos, who had been scheduled to visit MIST and MU, had much the same experience. The students were no more civilized than the men on the streets. And we've gotten isolated reports of radical political activity among some disaffected intellectuals. Secret meetings and rallies. It wasn't a day I want to see again, ever."

Vassily's glance turned down to the conference table, and the room remained still for several minutes. Aven was trying to comprehend what he had heard. Gaylord's voice broke the silence.

"In other words, we have two candidates who can't be let out of their cages. Just what have you and your staff decided to do about the rest of the campaign?"

"We haven't been able to think...."

"We're all quite aware of that. Gaylord's asking about the last four days of the campaign."

"I'm sorry, Aven."

"Goddamn it, Leigh. I know you can't think, and I know you're *quite* sorry. Those factors will indeed be relevant when we review your personnel file. Right now I want to know about the campaign, at least what's left of it."

"Aven, yesterday's events have upset our staff, and they're not thinking as well as they might...."

Several of the downcast MOPers looked up from the table for the first time, as if in gratitude for Gaylord's understanding.

"There's no question about letting Yurri and Yanos back on the streets, but we can certainly keep the campaign on TV....And how did last night's debate go? What were the ratings?"

The MOPers who had shown a momentary spark of appreciation looked from one to the other. It was painfully evident that no one wanted to speak. Aven's reservoir of patience had long since run dry.

"A sorry lot that can't think. Can't any of you speak either?"

"Director _____, they, they were, ah, low." Kneelzun's voice was barely audible.

"How low?"

"Sir, we, we started with five percent of the sets tuned in, but that number fell off quickly."

"That's pretty much the way we saw it, wasn't it, Aven?"

Aven did not respond immediately. His mind began to wander.

"Gaylord, at this point, there's not much I feel I can contribute. It all seems so absurd and futile."

"Politics is a funny pastime, Aven. But for the next few days, or until the rain ends, it's the only game in town. If you want, I'll stay with Leigh and his staff and see if we can't put Humpty-Dumpty together again. If it weren't so nasty outside I'd suggest you take a walk."

"That's the first intelligent idea of the morning. And I appreciate your trying to help, for all the good it'll do. I'll check back in this afternoon."

"Around two would be good. Be sure to take your umbrella. And, Aven, something'll turn up. I feel it in my gut."

Aven knew that Gaylord meant well, but there was no way he could share in his optimism. He left the combo room without reply and was soon out of the building. The melancholy patter of the rain seemed fitting. He walked without energy or direction. The few individuals he passed were hidden from view, as were the drivers ensconced somewhere behind their shimmering windshields. So much of the area had been altered, but he still recognized the park. He was heading down the path towards McDonatelli's, passing the same forlorn individuals of an earlier walk.

"Must be nice to be in their shoes, without responsibility, ambition, hope...without Yurri and Yanos."

As he approached the park area where the mugging had taken place, Aven became aware of a small gathering of men and women. No more than fifty in number, they were standing in a semicircle. He left the path and walked toward the group. Mostly college age, they stood arm in arm, sharing the few umbrellas in their possession. Aven remained at the outer edge, unnoticed. All eyes were focused on two individuals who were talking intently to each other in the center of the group. The two hugged, warmly kissed, and unclasped their arms to the applause of the rain-drenched contingent. The man acknowledged the greeting, and the woman stepped to the side.

Aven had experienced the sensation once before, on the morning Mzzz. Paula T. Barnum first walked into the Boris Stemtide auditorium. The sight of Rena served as a momentary release. Gone were his anger, self-pity, and frustration. In their place, nothing, an emptiness through which he toppled. The male voice that broke his descent was located at the margin of his memory.

> Brothers and sisters, a specter is haunting our land. The specter of decency, integrity, and compassion for our fellow citizens. The three established powers of our nation have entered into an unholy alliance to exorcise this specter: Nu...Demo...MOP. They would have us believe their materialist cant.

Aven's mind was torn between Rena and the speaker.

"Who is he? What right has he...?"

Recognition came.

"That's the *same* son of a slimy snake...."

These thoughts were interrupted by enthusiastic cheers, which themselves ebbed as the speaker continued.

> True enough, as they will so proudly tell you, the modern corporation has allowed our beloved Russia to enter and now to lead in the well-established world market. So, too, however, have the corporate executives conquered for themselves exclusive political sway over MOP, and our pseudo-political apparatus as well. Rest assured, comrades, it matters little who is foisted upon us. Yurri from Demo, or the Nu Yanos, the work of MOP will continue.

For an extended time Aven could not take his eyes from the speaker, the young, aggressive member of the legal section whom he had dismissed in that first wondrous week. The events of eight years ago came into focus.

"I didn't like him from the moment he opened his mouth, and it's obvious that he has learned very little since then—nor has he shaved. Trying to look and sound like Marx. How pitiful! *Worse!* To inflict his heresy on our gullible students, and how they appear to idolize...."

> You need only look around you to see what they have wrought, these captains of industry. These men and women whom we are taught to emulate. They have pitilessly torn asunder the fragile ties that bind each of us to this earth and left nothing of the human bond other than naked self-interest. The callous exchange of rubles. The corporate leaders and their lackeys have shredded the sentimental fabric that binds the family—husband, wife, child—who now exist only through work, and their work is their only existence. In place of simpler desires, a never-ending stream of new wants has been created, requiring for their satisfaction the products of distant lands and climes, thus destroying within each of us the noble feelings of independence and self-sufficiency. And in the process, our leaders have created for us an urban nightmare. They've obliterated all rural life. These are the *genuine* fruits of our economic miracle, a loveless and meaningless ex-

istence amidst an environment unfit to inhabit. Fruits that are not easily digested, fruits that MOP has so well and for so long hidden. *Too* long, but *not* well enough....

The bearded rabble-rouser had his admirers transfixed. Aven, too, was experiencing a singular sensation, both mesmerizing and distasteful. In turning his gaze from the counterfeit revolutionary, the hypnotic aura lessened as the visceral revulsion intensified. Rena, too, had her eyes riveted on the speaker, with a look of adoration that twisted Aven's stomach, seemingly beyond repair. Aven wanted to bend over to ease the pain. He tried to scream at the speaker, *"You bloody fool...,"* and at Rena, *"You're worse than he is...."* He wanted to yell at the students, *"Go back to the classroom where you belong...."* He remained erect and mute.

> ...and so we ask you to join with us in this struggle. A struggle that will not be won with the first shot, nor without frequent disappointment. But prevail we will, and in place of this grotesque society, we shall have a true association, in which the free development of *each one of us* is the condition for the free development of *all*. Let the men from Nu and Demo and their puppeteers tremble at our revolution. We have nothing to lose but our deformity, and a world to win.

The applause reached its crescendo in an instant. At first clapping in rhythmical disjointedness, the students were soon clapping in unison. A smile of appreciation broke through the man's scruffy beard, and Rena's eyes, aglow with passion, remained fixed on the guru. Aven's pain continued. He was fighting within himself, deeply conflicted over what, if anything, he should say.

"She's got to be told...."

As he was deciding, a chant rose up, synchronized with the measured applause.

I-VAN I-VAN I-VAN I-VAN I-VAN...

"Ivan....Hest...."

Aven stood at the outer edge of the buoyant rally for several minutes longer. He turned and began walking back to MOP, oblivious of the rain that beat down around him in ever-increasing intensity.

JESUS SAVES

■■■■■■■■■■■■■■■

*E*motional and psychological difficulties in others had rarely drawn his sympathy. Such problems were beyond his comprehension. And why not? These problems had never visited him—until May Day. Aven was well beyond the park area. Despite the distance and the downpour, the students' jackhammer chant continued its assault on his senses. As he plodded along, other names—Rena, Mellors, Yurri, Hester, Paula, Yanos—cooperated with Ivan's in the pounding. For a time he lost track of where he was. The buildings, the signs, the street he was on, became as one with the grotesque melange that had captured his psyche.

"Gaylord...."

The rains had turned to a delicate drizzle, and the grinding in his head slackened. He looked at his watch.

"After three...when did I?...afternoon meeting...."

He stopped for a moment to orient himself.

"Pero's...."

MOP was several kilometers behind him. Aven turned and resumed his doleful stride. A general feeling of malaise had taken hold, anesthetizing much of the pain. Aven walked back to MOP without purpose or hope. For some reason, he found Igor's smiling portrait particularly offensive.

"Aven, where on earth have you been? It's well past four."

Gaylord's greeting did nothing to alter Aven's mood. Gaylord was not alone. Four individuals had risen from their seats around the table. Each was smiling more broadly than the next. The entire scene was violently askew. Aven found speech impossible.

"Well, you're back, and that's all that really matters. Here, I'll take your coat."

Aven offered no resistance. Gaylord hung up Aven's rain-soaked coat and solicitously escorted Aven to the smiling guests. Three men and a woman. The men were wearing dark blue suits, white shirts, and somber-toned ties. With well-groomed gray hair, they appeared to be in their seventies. The woman, short, stocky, and somewhat younger, was wearing a handsome red dress. Her hair, a coiffure of short shimmering silver strands, provided a dramatic enclosure for her eyes, which were barely visible, engulfed beneath layers of exotic coloring. Her face was laminated with a deep tan paste, while a finer metallic red substance coated her lips. Aven felt a trace of laughter, the first in some time. He shook his head abruptly, as if to free himself of the unearthly sight. Gaylord's voice finished the job.

"Let me introduce you to the answer to our prayers. I think we're out of the woods."

Aven had no idea what these words meant.

"Aven, I want you to meet the Reverend Jeri Phalvel and Paddy Roberzun...and the Bakkoffs, Yumme and Tamara." The three men, whose broad grins seemed permanent, shook Aven's hand, as did Tamara, whose smile turned demure.

"We didn't get very far with the political section. Leigh and I agreed to keep Yurri and Yanos off the streets, limit the campaign to the thirty-second attack spots, and hope for the best. I took a call for you around noon. It was from the Reverend Phalvel. I think you should hear what he has to say. He and his colleagues are members of the Russian Orthodox Church, actually from the political section located in Zagorsk. They've been here since two this afternoon. I think it best if we start from the beginning. Reverend Phalvel, if you don't mind...."

"Not at all, Gaylord, and if *you* don't mind, would you be so kind as to bring more tea?"

He spoke in a rich and paternal manner, much as a man of the cloth might. Aven had taken a seat at the table in close proximity to the others. His mind and heart were elsewhere.

"Aven, as we've been explaining to Gaylord, there are two *fundamental* challenges facing our great nation. The first concerns our economy...."

"Praise the Lord."

The Reverend Bakkoff's timorous voice did give the hint of musical training.

"Amen, Yumme."

Bakkoff's wife spoke as if to boost her husband's ego.

"Thank you, Yumme. As I was saying, there has been much analysis of the issues, but all of it without God. With all due respect, Aven, the spiritual and moral aspects of the matter have been left undiscussed. This is the single greatest problem facing our economy today. Our huge spiraling debt, the national gridlock, the urban pollution, and the tragic growth of our happy campers, these will be solved only on a spiritual basis."

"Praise the Lord."

"Amen, Yumme."

"Oh, indeed, we've come a long way with the establishment of free markets in Russia, farther than any might have dreamed, but in our lust for wealth we have forgotten Him. In a fallen world, free markets won't set our people free. Indeed, we have created a system of enterprise that facilitates the marketing of sinful things, a system that, if not checked, will soon destroy our families and our churches."

The mere absurdity of the Reverend Phalvel's smiling diatribe began to help Aven refocus his thoughts.

"This man's a lunatic. And what does that say about poor Gaylord?"

The depression lingered, but he was taking some perverted interest in the clergyman's argument. He tasted the tea. Its warmth also competed with his languor.

"Reverend, forgive me, but I was under the impression that your, ah, our churches have been guaranteed protection for some time now, isn't that right?"

"Legally, yes. For about thirty years, in fact. Article fifty-two of our constitution guarantees the freedom to profess any religion and to celebrate any and all religious rites."

"That's what I thought. Then I don't understand why...."

"The problem, Aven, is that the wonderful progress we began to see after 1977 — with our youth, the middle classes, and the intellectuals returning to the Church in greater and greater numbers — has all but vanished. The Russian revolution is in danger of foundering, unless we heed His Word."

"Praise the Lord."

"Amen, Yumme."

"I really don't understand what God's word has to do with our economy."

"Ahhhhhhh."

The Reverend Phalvel continued after the collective gasp.

"Aven, *everything*. Was it not He who sanctified private property? Did He not write in the book of Exodus, 'Thou shall not steal,' and in Acts, 'While you still owned the land, wasn't it yours to keep, and after you had sold it wasn't the money yours to do with as you liked'? Was it not Matthew who asked, 'Have I no right to do what I like with my own?' It is plain for all who wish to see, He has, in His divine wisdom, chosen to consecrate the essence of our free enterprise system. But we have become lazy and careless and far too tolerant of the evil that lurks within."

"Reverend Phalvel, Gaylord, I'm sorry. It's been a long day, in fact, a long week, with little end in sight. Would you mind if we...."

"Aven, hear him out."

"Thank you, Gaylord. Aven, I'll try to be brief. I'm sure you agree that our economic system thrives on individual initiative. Indeed, individual enterprise is its motivating force."

"Reverend Phalvel, if I'm not mistaken, that was one of *Adam Smith's* great discoveries."

"With respect, Aven, the Reverend Smith was only *preaching* the Gospel, *His* Word."

Aven glanced at Gaylord, who responded with a reassuring smile and nod of his head.

"And yet, in a misguided effort to appease the weaker elements in society, we have come perilously close to *destroying* the best elements of human ambition, encouraging the *worst*."

"Praise the Lord."

"Amen, Yumme."

"You remain skeptical. Let me give two examples. On the one hand, our welfare system is an abomination. It fosters dependency, discourages work, and flies in the face of His Word. In Exodus we are told that in our legal system we *must not* show partiality to the poor."

"Reverend Phalvel, you can't be serious. Surely, with the present level of our Safety Net...."

"The state has *no business* providing *anything to the poor!*"

These words came thundering from the clergyman in a manner that at first startled Aven, who quickly recovered.

"I don't know about your God, Reverend Phalvel, but there are some members of our society in need of assistance."

"Aven, He is your God as well. And He has always recognized the need for assistance, *private* assistance. We call it charity. Too many of our citizens have forgotten Paul's message: 'Thin sowing means thin reaping; the more you sow, the more you reap.' And Aven, listen closely, for Paul continues, 'Each one should give what he has decided in his own mind, not grudgingly or because he is made to, for God *loves* a cheerful giver.' Think about it Aven. The state has no business doing the Church's work, and to compound our sin, not only are we indulging the indigent, but of greater transgression, we coddle the criminals amongst us."

"Surely you can't quarrel with our efforts to control crime. Why, as I understand it, the prisons are overflowing."

"Precisely, and that overflow is like a sewer rupture, contaminating society."

"We've been building prisons."

"You will never have enough prisons, so long as you choose to permit, even encourage, the most vile of the criminal element."

"Reverend Phalvel...."

"And that's exactly what we've done. When was the last execution, and how long was that grisly murderer allowed to plead his case? *Years!*"

"These are complex...."

"We've *chosen* to make them complex. His Word could not be simpler. 'He who sheds man's blood, shall have his blood shed by man.' Nor will He tolerate our conduct for long. Yumme, may I have the book?"

"Praise the Lord."

"Amen."

The Reverend Phalvel took the book from Yumme.

"Aven, we've been put on this earth to serve Him for as long as *He* decides. If we fail Him, we forfeit the privilege of inhabiting His planet. Listen to Paul's words to Timothy:

> You may be quite sure that in the...*last*...*days*...there are going to be some difficult times. People will be self-centered and grasping; boastful, arrogant and rude; disobedient to their parents, ungrateful, irreligious; heartless and unappeasable; they will be slanderers, profligates, savages and enemies of everything that is good...preferring their own pleasures to God.

The Reverend Phalvel's voice took on a forlorn quality, and his smile receded as he read. When he finished, he calmly closed the book. An eerie hush came over the small gathering. Aven noticed that the Reverend Bakkoff began to shiver, while his wife held tightly to his hands. He also was struck with the timing of the message of Armageddon so soon after his own private world seemed to have collapsed. For a brief moment, Aven was prepared to engage in serious conversation.

"Reverend Phalvel, I'm beginning to see your..."

"*His*, my son...."

"...sorry, *His* point. But it's a message without hope. What does *He* propose we do if the end is near?"

The broad grin returned to the Reverend Phalvel's face.

"Aven, my son, we need only to follow Him, for therein lies our salvation."

He opened the book, reading briefly from its pages:

> ...if my people who bear my name humble themselves and

pray and seek my presence and turn from their wicked ways, I
myself will hear from heaven and forgive them.

There is no need to worry; but if there is anything you need,
pray for it, asking God for it with prayer and thanksgiving.

The Reverend Phalvel's state of ecstasy was obvious. Mrs. Bakkoff released
her husband's hands. Mr. Bakkoff stopped quivering.

"Praaaaaaaise the Lord."

"Amen, Yumme."

"That's *it*! All we have to do is *pray*? And the debt will vanish, the roads
and air will clear, and Yurri and Yanos will grow up? Perhaps we should pray for
the eradication of all poverty, illiteracy, disease...not just here, but everywhere
on Earth and Mars and....Gaylord, you've asked me to hear them out. I have.
Patiently. *For over an hour!* Its been a *fascinating* diversion, but..."

Aven stopped mid-sentence. It was as if he had not said a word. In fact, he
might as well have been uttering the most profound praise and thanksgiving.
The adoration bestowed on him by the four visitors said as much.

"Aven, the last few weeks have been trying, and you *have* been patient. Our
visitors appreciate it."

"Gaylord, I don't know if it's you or me, but one of us is losing touch. You
too? You think all we need to do is *pray*?"

"If you recall, Aven, the Reverend Phalvel spoke of *two* fundamental problems. We do need to pray and trust in the Lord."

"And tithe ten percent!"

"Well, Aaaven, that'll take care'a itself, if ya'll elect the propa fella on Sunday."

Aven looked to his left with a start. These were the first words from the Reverend Paddy Roberzun. They left his tongue in a soft and lilting manner, with a
dialect peculiar to the southernmost provinces of Russia. Aven regained his balance.

"If it's all the same to you, Reverend, given a choice between Yurri and
Yanos, I'd prefer to pray."

"That's the point, Aven."

"Gaylord, you're talking in circles."

"Aaaven, ah think what the genelmen means is that ya'll can do a powerful
lot betta than Yanos or Yurri, a whole heap betta."

"You're suggesting we not only pray to the Lord but also vote for Him, or
one of His representatives perhaps?"

"That's close, Aven, but I think the Reverend Roberzun's thinking of someone more down to earth."

"There *are* only two candidates."

"But, Aaaven, the Lord, in His wisdom, saw to it that ya'll could have mor'en two."

"He's right, Aven. Remember, we've allowed for *write-in* candidates."

There appeared to be no letup in the madness. Aven listened in disbelief. Despite his better judgment, he found himself a reluctant participant.

"And I suppose you have some shining white knight in mind, who at the eleventh hour will save us from Yurri and Yanos?"

As if to compound the lunacy, Tamara Bakkoff reached across the table and tenderly put her left hand on Aven's arm. The hand was adorned with several colossal rings. Her voice was more gentle.

"Wah, Aaaaven, that whaat knaat's you."

Her eyes fluttered as she finished, distracting him briefly from the impact of her words. He looked at the others around the table. Their expressions were identical, what Aven imagined of the proud father upon first sight of his newborn son. He realized they were waiting for his first words as well. Aven played the role of wailing monster to perfection.

"*Enough!* Gaylord, get these people out of here. *Now!* I'm tired. I'm hungry. If it isn't Marx, it's Jesus, and *I don't intend to work for either!*"

Again his words seemed to have little impact. Gaylord whispered something to the Reverend Phalvel, who nodded in agreement. Almost immediately, the four visitors departed.

"Aven, you need to pull yourself together. The Reverend Roberzun will be back in a while. In the meantime, I'll call up for some food. What would you like?"

"Gaylord, why are you doing this to me? I don't want to put up with that smooth-talking hustler for another minute. Let's get out of here. We can get some food at Pero's or somewhere. I just need to get away from all of this craziness."

Gaylord's persistence, while out of character, continued. They remained in the office eating MingDonald's To Go, which was delivered to MOP in surprisingly good condition. For a while, Gaylord allowed Aven to set the tone of the conversation. As Aven was applying the last bit of plum sauce to his mushu pork pancake, Gaylord returned to the craziness.

"Aven, we don't have a lot of time to waste. There's no question in my mind we can get you elected. You can do the job, and at this phase of the campaign, there's not a single viable alternative."

Aven was struggling to keep the contents within the folded crepe. Gaylord's remarks didn't help.

"You know, I've never gotten the hang of these."

"Getting you elected will be easier, I promise."

It was clear Gaylord had no intention of changing the subject. Aven acquiesced. He asked a series of rhetorical questions designed to dissuade Gaylord from this maddest of all proposals. Gaylord replied to each, calmly and thoughtfully. Aven could not have identified the precise moment when the transformation occurred. Gaylord's answers, which at first seemed merely logical, soon became persuasive. The election code did allow for write-in candidates. Neither Yurri nor Yanos was capable of dealing with the complex issues the new leader would confront, and Aven couldn't argue with the fact that he himself was better prepared than anyone else to do so. His lack of experience in political matters allowed him to run as a citizen politician. Lack of party identification would only enhance this image. The absence of a slate of candidates for the National Assembly proved to be an insignificant matter. The election code allowed for the president to fill any vacancies on the Assembly, *if he chose to do so*, for whatever reason such vacancies might arise. Even the fact that the election campaign was nearing the halfway point did not present a significant obstacle.

Rain remained in the forecast through the balance of the week, and without the distraction of baseball, four days seemed ample time in which to establish a viable candidacy. Two questions remained unresolved, the medium through which he would speak to the voters and what he would say. Aven had raised these issues, seeing both as serious obstacles. Gaylord didn't have an immediate answer but assured him that both matters were trivial and would be resolved when the Reverend Roberzun returned.

"You have me nearly convinced. It's not a crazy idea, if...."

"Relax, Aven, the Reverend Roberzun assured me he'd be able to handle the details. He should be here before long."

"Okay, I'll relax. And, Gaylord, I do appreciate what you've done. You've given me a renewed sense of confidence that for a while seemed gone forever."

"It was never gone, Aven."

"Perhaps not. Can we change the subject for a minute?"

"Shoot."

"I'm willing to use their help, but you have to know, I find the four of them a pretty sleazy lot. My atheistic bias may be showing, I realize...."

"I know what you mean, especially Roberzun, but they can help. After all, they claim to have some pretty powerful friends."

"So they say. But why *are* they bothering? I doubt they care all that much about air pollution and bank holidays. The Church has been around a long time, and it's not going to go away."

"No, it isn't. And from everything I've read, you Russians sure as hell are a religious people. Even under the most repressive circumstances, Stalin and his followers were destined to fail. They did manage to decimate the Church physically, but for some reason, faith is a tough light to snuff out. I think it's essentially a matter of influence. The elders were starting to regain some not so long ago. And Phalvel is right about the last few years. The Church and its symbols have been huckstered in the marketplace along with everything else. Hard to be taken seriously with Jesus' face plastered on every T-shirt, shopping bag, and tea mug in sight. You know, Aven, perhaps better than I, that there was a time under the tsars when the Phalvels and Roberzuns of the world carried a lot of weight in your society. They and the wealthy classes had it pretty much their own way. My best guess is that that's what they're hoping to regain."

"If so, they're about to nominate the wrong man."

"Yeah, but they don't know that, and there's no point in spoiling their fun, is there?"

"None that I can think of."

Aven hadn't felt as much at ease in days. The thought, however remote, of moving up from his position at MOP took on a fascination that was seductive and comforting.

"President...."

He liked the sound and the idea.

"The first thing...."

Aven luxuriated in images so at odds with those of earlier in the day. He was finishing the last sip of cold tea when the Reverend Roberzun returned.

"How ya'll doo'en? Gaylord, Aaaven, I trust ya'll had a good dinner an ah readah to do the Lord's work?"

Aven bit his tongue. Gaylord came to the rescue.

"Reverend Roberzun, we're as ready as we'll ever be. I've been able to convince Aven that he's the man for the job. Now all we need to do is win over a few million voters. Earlier you suggested that the Church could help. What did you have in mind?"

"Wah, television, a'course. With onla foa days left...."

Aven was content to have Gaylord carry on much of the conversation with the pastor, whose refined drawl was beginning to grate on his nerves.

"Four days, with rain, should be adequate, if—and that seems to me to be the kicker—if we had access to TV. It's my understanding that the Demo and Nu parties have bought up all of the prime-time commercial spots."

"Not quate aul. Those elitist po-liticos din see fit to buy enna time on RCBN. They musta felt noboda was wachin."

"RCBN?"

"Aven, that's the Russian religious channel. When Leigh said the debates were on *all* channels, he probably wasn't paying any attention to RCBN. Hardly anyone does these days."

"An it's a gol-darn shame. A numba of ah young telepriests have had to plead paavatee righten front of the camera, and lately, the more desperate been resorten to hunga strahks."

"That's too bad, Reverend Roberzun. But with a new format, I think RCBN will work out just fine."

"Even if no one watches?"

"Aven, no one's *been* watching. All we have to do is put you on opposite Yurri and Yanos."

"If they *know*."

"They'll know."

Gaylord glanced at his watch.

"We have hours before MOP sets the morning headline."

"Gaylord, you *are* a genius. We'll get an audience, all right, and I suppose you've figured out what I'll be saying?"

"Not that much of a genius."

Gaylord turned from Aven to the Reverend Roberzun.

"Reverend Roberzun?"

"Wah yes, genelmen, ya'll take a look at this."

He removed two sheets of paper from a large manila envelope.

"Wha doan ya'll read this, then ah'll be happa t'explain."

Aven glanced at the page and then read it in its entirety.

"What do you think, Gaylord?"

"Not bad. Needs some work on the grammar, and a few of the references are out of date. How do you feel about it?"

"It's got possibilities. I'd feel better if we could tone down some of the religious cra…, ah, jargon, but otherwise, I agree, not bad. Reverend Roberzun, we like it. Where'd it come from?"

"We lahke t'call it 'The Speech.' Bout twenna fahve years ago ah gave some thought to running fa po-litical office m'self. Thought the Lord was callen, but it jess wassen the raht tahm."

"Well, with a little work, this time it's gonna make Aven a winner. And I know it's late, but if we're gonna be on God's network in the morning, we better get to it."

They spent the next hour working over the Reverend Roberzun's opus. Aven thrust himself into the enterprise with optimism and confidence. Gaylord was able to suggest some minor alterations. The Reverend Roberzun smiled but said little. They also wrote the banner for the morning news. It was nearing midnight when their fruitful labor ended.

"Aven, we'll do the recording in the morning. The first showing is set for

noon tomorrow, with repeats at four, seven, and midnight. Four shots a day until Sunday. What do you think?"

"Whatever you say, remember, you're the po-litical genius. I'm just a little
ol' citizen doing his best. Are we going to be doing anything besides The
Speech? I'd like to get out and, how do they say it…?"

"Ah think ya'll mean press the flesh."

"Aven, can we talk about the remaining details in the morning? This has
been one hell of a long day for all of us. We've got The Speech, and RCBN.
The rest can keep. Whadda'ya say?"

"Amen."

"Fair enough. It has been a long day."

The traffic and drizzle had eased. Aven was in his flat soon after leaving
MOP. It had been a day of wild emotional swings, reaching its nadir in the
park. Aven's feelings of despondency had vanished, obliterated from his consciousness. He had never felt more in control, more assured about the future—
Russia's and his. Sleep came quickly and was deep and undisturbed. He woke
in the same mood. If anything, the immediacy of the campaign emboldened his
spirit. As the morning news proclaimed, he would soon be offering himself in
the cause of national salvation.

RELIGIOUS LEADERS TURN TO MAD AVE
MOP Director Speaks on Channel 666

In an obvious well-meaning gesture, the MOPers had used his nickname.
He would have preferred a degree of formality but was not otherwise troubled.
There could be no doubt about the outcome. His talents and qualifications
were unique in their own right. And, of course, there was the competition.

"Good morning, sir."

"Good morning."

Aven walked past the cavity where the elevator was soon to be located. The
halls of MOP had assumed a distinctly upbeat flavor as supportive greetings followed him to the office.

"Moooornin, Aven. Sounds like your own private voting section out there."

"I'll say. I hope it's not because they want me out of MOP."

"I doubt it. Anyway, you won't be *out* of MOP, just *over* it. Providing, that
is, we do the tape before noon. The audiovisual people will be here at ten.
Shouldn't take all that much time. The Speech itself takes less than four minutes."

"Maybe I should run over it."

Aven rehearsed The Speech several times. They made some modest changes in the text itself, but most of the time was spent in facial expression and vocal inflection. As with any political message, there were a limited number of key ideas. They concentrated their efforts on highlighting each of these. The Speech was to be taped in Aven's office. There was a brief moment of panic when it appeared that the MOP library had misplaced its only copy of the Bible. After the makeup crew did its work, the filming went smoothly and quickly. So polished was Aven's performance that they decided to go with the first take.

"Hey, Mad Ave, ya'should'a been'a actta."

Aven assured the cameraman that politics took far too much time to allow for such frivolous pursuits. The last of the equipment was removed shortly after eleven. Gaylord took a bottle of champagne from the ice cabinet.

"I think we've earned this."

The conversation meandered. Despite Aven's very real euphoria, he could feel a trace of anxiety. Normal stage fright, they both decided. The taping had been completed, but Aven had not yet spoken heart to heart to the Russian people. Until he had, and until the reviews were in, doubts, however superficial, would remain. As the moment of Aven's political debut arrived they moved into the outer office and turned on the television. It took a moment to figure out how to tune in the three-digit channel. Aven's tanned and handsome face finally appeared. The music faded. The Speech took three and a half minutes, during which time neither man spoke.

> My fellow citizens, I am going to talk of controversial things. I make no apology for this. For the past several days throughout the political campaign, it seems impossible to legitimately debate the issues without being subjected to name calling and the application of labels. How long can we afford the luxury of this family fight when we are at war with the most dangerous enemy ever known to man? We've come to a moment in our history when party labels are unimportant. The RIGHT philosophy, God Over Politics, is. Only through these beliefs, G____ O____ P____, will we be able to rediscover, reassert, and reapply Russia's SPIRITUAL HERITAGE to our national affairs.
>
> It saddens me to see discontent in the land today. The men who would be our leaders, who in an earlier time did those things that strengthened FAMILY and TRADITIONAL VALUES, now seem to have lost faith in us. And many of us seem

to have lost confidence in ourselves. For days now, we have been told there are no simple answers to the complex problems that are beyond our comprehension. Well, the *TRUTH* is there are *SIMPLE* answers—they just are *NOT EASY* ones.

It's time we asked ourselves if we still desire the freedoms intended for us by our *MAKER*. Today we face a harsh but simple choice: either we follow *HIS WORD*, accepting the responsibility for our own destiny, or we abandon the revolution and allow others to plan our lives for us. Have we the courage to choose *HIM*?

Have we the *COURAGE* and the will to face up to the immorality and discrimination of all progressive taxes and return to His Word?

Have we the *COURAGE* to spend time studying the issues, making ourselves aware, and then conveying that information to family and friends?

Have we the *COURAGE* to allow our children to *PRAY* when they are moved to do so, *in* the *SCHOOLS* as well as in their churches and homes?

Have we the *COURAGE* to insist that our leaders do their utmost to promote *FAMILY VALUES*, not ignore or weaken them?

Have we the *COURAGE* to face the deprivation in our midst? We are a humane and a generous people, and we should accept without reservation our obligation, *VOLUNTARILY*, to help the unfortunates who, through no fault of their own, must depend on their fellow man. But we must not perpetuate poverty by substituting a permanent *GOVERNMENT DOLE* for a paycheck. There is no humanity or charity in destroying *SELF-RELIANCE*, *DIGNITY*, and *SELF-RESPECT*, the very substance of moral fiber.

These are the *SIMPLE TRUTHS* that we face together. Now

many of you may be thinking, I'm *NOT A POLITICIAN* by profession. To that charge I happily plead guilty. I am a *CITIZEN, CALLED* to stand up for my own values and beliefs. My candidacy is based on my record and, for that matter, my entire life. Let me be completely candid: no man has a patent on virtue, but I believe I offer something more than words....I believe I can do the job that has to be done.

My fellow citizens, you and I have a *RENDEZVOUS WITH DESTINY*. Together, we can preserve for our children this, the last best hope of man on earth, or we can sentence them to take the first steps into a thousand years of darkness. If we fail, at least let our children and our children's children say of us we justified our brief moment here. We did all that could be done. But take heart. We need not contemplate failure. Have *FAITH*, and *VOTE G__O__P__*. Then with *HIS HELP* we shall indeed be as a city upon a hill with the eyes of all people upon us. Thank you, and God bless you.

Gaylord used the remote to darken the set. Some time passed before Aven dared speak.

"Was that *me*?"

"It was you, Aven, and you were brilliant...first time on television, as if you were conceived with a teleprompter in your brain. Let's face it, you're the quintessential communicator. It wouldn't surprise me if Yurri and Yanos threw in the towel before Sunday."

"I doubt if they'd have enough sense...and I suppose we ought to wait for the polling data before closing up shop at MOP. In the meantime, we can talk about the rest of the campaign, the 'details' we put off last night."

"Hard to imagine needing much beyond The Speech. What do you have in mind?"

"Well, I'd like to have a shot at 'pressing the flesh' myself. You saw how they responded last month when we did the 'nothing to fear' number. To be honest, I found the crowd reaction exhilarating. Getting out among the voters would probably raise their spirits as well."

"I grant you, Yurri and Yanos have been wretched. The baseball postponements did come at a hell of a time, but I'm not so sure...."

"Not so sure about what?"

"Taking your campaign into the streets."

"What are you talking about? I thought we agreed that I was a natural...?"

"You are, Aven, but right now it wouldn't be all that wise."

"I still don't know what you're talking about."

"I'm not entirely certain myself. The fact of the matter is, there have been a number of incidents of violence. You saw what Yurri and Yanos looked like at the second debate. Apparently things have gotten worse. We've had reports of isolated shootings, roving mobs, not just in Moscow, all pretty ugly stuff. Sounds like there's a lot of anger in the streets right now. Leigh persuaded me that we ought to keep the campaign on television."

"You and Leigh may be overreacting. You know, yesterday morning, when I left the meeting with our saviors, I took a walk in the park."

"And, as I recall, you didn't look too happy about it when you returned."

"I wasn't, but that's not the point. There was this rally. You may or not remember that young wiseass lawyer that we fired some years ago."

"Ivan, I remember...."

"How did you know his name?"

"He's been somewhat of a rabble-rouser lately. We've gotten reports from the MOP security section. All pretty harmless stuff. It didn't seem worth bothering you with. Ivan's an unreconstituted Marxist."

"I'm not sure how harmless he is, he and his fawning followers, but under any circumstances, he was doing his feeble impersonation of Marx, all to the delight of a mob of cheering young people. Beyond the intellectual violence, the whole scene couldn't have been more peaceful."

"No, that's right. The real mob anger has been directed at Yurri and Yanos and their party headquarters."

"Gaylord, doesn't that tell you something?"

"About what?"

"About the Ivans in our midst."

"Sure, they're harmless, if not irrelevant. Why should *anyone* hassle them?"

"Maybe *they're* the ones promoting the violence."

"Unlikely."

"You know, Gaylord, we had a disagreement about Ivan once before. If elected I have no intention of allowing Ivan or any of his ilk the license to pollute the minds of our youth."

"Aven, you needn't be angry. There's no *doubt* who will be elected, and once we deal with the few problems now on hold, it'll be nice to have the Ivans around, for comic relief, if nothing else. In a way, they're like a court jester; they can criticize the king in a way that few find offensive and most can ignore."

"There's nothing funny about him, or his followers, or what they stand for. But you're right, it's silly for me to be upset. And the problem will take care of itself, all in good time. I'm *sure* of that."

"Aven, every society seems to have an Ivan or two and their adoring group-ies. I don't expect they'll ever go away."

"If you don't mind, let's drop the subject."

The extent of disagreement between them was rare. Aven found himself at odds with Gaylord on both counts. He reluctantly agreed to limit his campaign to The Speech. He had dealt with Ivan once before and would do so again *after* the election. Of more immediate concern was the voter response. They didn't have to wait long for the polling results. An excited Kneelzun burst into the of-fice a short time after noon. They stared at the survey data, questioned the en-thusiastic MOPer, and looked once again at the viewer analysis. During the thirty-minute period covered by the survey, all of the TV sets in operation had been tuned to Channel 666. Not a single Russian citizen had seen the Nu and Demo attack messages broadcast in competition with The Speech. Their ela-tion was tempered by the fact that only a modest number of sets had been in op-eration. They knew, however, that The Speech would be repeated several times over the course of the campaign. As it turned out, Kneelzun's data for the re-maining three broadcasts of that first day, including the seven o'clock encoun-ter, changed little. The few sets in operation were tuned to Aven, who fell asleep early in the morning knowing victory would be his. Only the size of the man-date remained in doubt. This issue was to be resolved the following day in what can only be considered a remarkable turn of events.

Aven and Gaylord had finished lunch and were reviewing the all too famil-iar survey results with Kneelzun when the Church contingent burst into the of-fice. The broad grins of yesterday were modest in contrast to the expressions that now dominated their bodies. Yumme Bakkoff was quivering uncontrollably but seemed no less ecstatic than the others.

"Praise the…"

"Son…"

"Mah whaat naat…"

"Ya'll won't…"

"Praise…"

"Ya'll…"

"My son…"

Aven looked questioningly to Gaylord, whose expression made it clear he knew nothing of what had prompted the visit, much less the peculiar verbal bal-let. Nor was it evident whether or when the gibbering would cease. Aven did what he could to calm the four, greeting each in turn. Gaylord joined in the en-terprise. Kneelzun was of little help, remaining paralyzed in astonishment. A semblance of sanity was finally achieved.

"Gentlemen, gentlemen, and Mrs. Bakkoff, if you don't mind, I'm sure

Aven would love to hear what you have to say, but not in quadraphonic sound. Reverend Phalvel, what prompts all the excitement?"

"Well, Gaylord…"

"Praise the Lord…"

"Ya'll…"

Finally, as if realizing the nature of their behavior, the ambrosial ambassadors quieted themselves. The Reverend Phalvel was soon able to respond.

"Our apologies, Aven, and Gaylord, and…?"

"Oh, sorry. This is Doctor Kneelzun. He does the survey work at MOP."

"Well, we're pleased to meet you."

After the round of introductions, the Reverend Phalvel continued.

"There is an explanation for our exhilaration. We've just received the most divine news, as if He had planned it."

"Praise…"

"That's enough, Yumme. Ah, Tamara, please try to keep him quiet if you don't mind. As I was saying, He has answered our prayers, all of ours. Aven, He's picked *you!*"

"Forgive me, sir, picked me for what?"

"Jeri, if ya'll don'mahnd, let me try t'xplain. Aaaven, those two po-litical clowns have thrown in the towel. Thass raat, Yurri and Yanos gonna give their concession speeches t'naaht.

"*Before* the election?"

"Aven, my son. There will be no election."

The grinning apostles stood with their attention riveted on Aven, apparently anticipating some response. He had none. None, at least, that he could articulate. Finally, Gaylord, who had appeared deep in thought, asked a series of questions that helped to disentangle the situation. Vassily Advasser was called to join them for a time. The MOP political section leader was able to confirm most of the story that Gaylord had drawn from the Reverend Phalvel and his colleagues. Aven began to comprehend the significance of all that had developed. Yurri and Yanos had indeed decided to withdraw. Both men recorded concession statements in the middle of the night and quietly disappeared. Rumors were rampant as to their whereabouts, but the best guess was that they'd fled the country along with their National Assembly candidates. Nor could anyone be located at the Moscow offices of the Nu and Demo parties. A visit to the premises suggested that the party workers had left in a hurry. The fallout from this political implosion was to be monumental.

"Gaylord, if you don't mind, could we go over the election code once again? Do I understand we win by default?"

"Wa, Aaaven, ya'll should have more faith. We laak t'think of it as destiny."

"Either way, that's right, Aven. *We win!* The way Leigh explained it, the election code was designed by the Americans, taking advantage of the depth of their experience, particularly during the last two decades. The code incorporates the most sophisticated political innovations. These simplify the election process and require minimal voter knowledge or participation. At the same time, recognizing the complexity of the times, a great deal of authority is granted to the chief executive. As long as the people choose wisely, they are assured of an effective leader. More, in fact. The two-party system remains intact, while avoiding unnecessary campaign expenditures. Even though elections are scheduled at six-year intervals, they needn't be held unless the opposition party offers a viable candidate. A constitutional amendment prohibited the Americans from keeping Ronald Reagan in office beyond his eight glorious years. The new Russian code precludes such a tragedy. An effective leader who is without significant opposition can stay in office indefinitely. If we pick wisely, the people not only get the most effective leadership but also will have continuity. And now, with no other announced opposition, we are permitted to call off the election. I'd like to think of it as destiny, too."

"Praise the Lord."

"Amen, Yumme."

"Aven, my son. Our church elders couldn't be more pleased. I think you know how proud we all are."

"Thass raat, Aaaven. Seems t'me ya'll ken be thinking 'bout waat y'gonna say come Sunde."

"But, Gaylord, Reverend Phalvel, no one's said a word about the National Assembly. Shouldn't we have some ideas? Some names? What kind of government...?"

"Remember, the president can fill any and all vacancies...."

"*If you choose to!* Aven, my son, in the early stages of your reign, it might be wise to forgo the assembly. All you'll really need is a group of *trusted* advisers. I can feel it deep in my heart, son, with *His* help, you're going to be a great president."

There was nothing subtle about Phalvel. Aven understood exactly what was happening. He said nothing but knew that the Reverend Phalvel and his cronies were in for a rude awakening. The meeting soon broke up amidst several rounds of congratulations. Aven and Gaylord stayed in the office long enough to watch the taped concession statements. Yurri and Yanos were obviously beaten men. Neither looked into the camera, and both mumbled something about wishing the nation well. It was not a pleasant scene. Aven was sorry he had watched. Soon after these lamentable performances, Gaylord was called to the phone. MOP was receiving word of intensified violence and random shootings. Apparently, the street thugs were furious over the withdrawal of such attractive targets. With his ascension to power so close at hand, Aven agreed to remain within the safe confines of MOP until nightfall.

"Everything will be back to normal in no time. I did get some good news along with the reports of rage. The weather forecast promises clearing by Saturday evening. It probably makes sense to have the inauguration in the morning. With you installed as president and the Giants opening in the afternoon, we oughta be back to business as usual."

"I hope so, Gaylord. I'll be glad to get to the ballpark myself. But I'm not sure. You know, I think one of the problems is that we've been without strong leadership for too long. As a matter of fact, if you listened to what Phalvel was saying, he might just as well have been talking about another time. Sounded like we were anointing a new tsar, not electing a president. It was almost as if he'd forgotten everything that's happened in the twentieth century."

"I was thinking the same thing. Actually, for some folks, that century would be best forgotten."

They decided on MingDonald's To Go again, doubling their previous order of mushu pancakes, and talked late into the evening. Work on the inaugural speech and other arrangements began in earnest the next morning. The Reverend Roberzun sent some material that he thought might be useful. Aven did find it stimulating. He labored over the address with monasticlike devotion while Gaylord looked after the inaugural day activities. Hardly a word was exchanged over the next two days as they went about their respective tasks, both of which were completed by midday Saturday.

"Chinese *again?*"

"What would you like?"

The pizza arrived late and was thus free. It was cold as well, but given the price, they ate with gusto.

"Speaking of free, I was thinking about the MOPers in our political section. There's not going to be much of a need for them, is there?"

"I hadn't thought about it, Aven, but I suppose so."

"Not that I'll shed any tears over Leigh's departure. He never was among my favorites."

"But he was good, at least until he tried to manage Yurri and Yanos. No one could have done much with those two. He used to work with the KGB, right?"

"He did."

"Well, I wouldn't worry about him. He'll find a place."

"Maybe we should keep him on after all, to look after the rabble-rousers."

Aven could sense Gaylord's slight displeasure.

"Let's forget Leigh for now. Tell me about the arrangements for tomorrow. I trust you've made plans worthy of the youngest *tsar* in over a century."

Taking his lead from Phalvel's delusions, Aven had become fond of the more ethnically appropriate reference. However, he used the term mostly in jest.

"And I do want to go over the speech with you."

Aven was surprised and frustrated to learn of the security arrangements. He had hoped to be able to speak directly to his subjects in Red Square. Instead, the address was to be given from MOP's second-floor balcony overlooking the open space in front of the building. More bothersome was the fact that a protective shield would surround him.

"Even though you won't be able to see the crowd, they will see you. We thought that was the best way to arrange things, especially with the outfit you'll be wearing. Appearing in the open is too dangerous. With so many sophisticated weapons on the market, the MOP security section was adamant. Besides, our entry area will be able to handle quite a good sized crowd. I'm sure most citizens will be watching on TV anyway, if they're not already on the way to the ballpark."

The extended confinement within MOP added to Aven's desire to mingle with his constituents. He did what he could to impress upon a diffident Gaylord the extent of his impatience. The remainder of the evening was spent in rehearsing Aven's maiden peroration.

"What do you think?"

"I'm not sure."

"Come on, Gaylord, what kind of answer is that?"

"Something about the style, almost an archaic feel to it. You don't think it might be a bit too pious and forbidding?"

"You mean the fire and brimstone? Perhaps we should tone it down just a bit. After all, if I'm going to become a tsar, I might as well start speaking like one."

They worked well into the evening. It was one of their less cooperative endeavors, as Aven found himself resisting many of Gaylord's emendations. He accepted a few without enthusiasm, more to mollify Gaylord than anything else. When they concluded their labor, it was evident that neither was fully satisfied. Aven forced aside a trace of resentment. He poured a small quantity of wine into two glasses as a peace offering. Gaylord readily accepted.

"Cheers, Aven. To the new and proper president—and tsar."

"I'll drink to that."

They departed, tired but with their friendship intact. Despite his weary state, Aven had little desire for sleep. He made tea. The ninety-four channels offered nothing of interest, and he soon found himself standing before Rena's desk. She had removed most of her papers and books. A notepad was all that remained. It was not difficult to identify her delicate script, so often in opposition to the message itself. He opened the center drawer without thinking. It was empty save for two tattered volumes. He recognized the larger one. It was Adam Smith's naive monograph that Rena had read from that Sunday morning so very long ago. Aven smiled to himself, knowing that tomorrow morning he would be the one delivering the Word. The smaller of the two books was unfamiliar. Its binding was barely holding together. The identification it carried had long since faded but was not beyond comprehension. He smiled as he read the title, *The Road to Serfdom*, Hayek's brilliant philosophical treatise that Rena had partially understood. The *Theory of Moral Sentiments* was left in the drawer.

Aven took his tea and Hayek into the front room. He choose the Hadny Concerto for Disparate Drums and Mandolin, adjusted the volume to compensate for the wide-ranging dynamics, and opened the frail volume. The title page, with its ironic dedication to the "Socialists of All Parties" indicated it was a first edition, printed over a half century earlier. He vaguely remembered an extended foreword that Hayek had included some years after the initial publication date. It was missing. He glanced at the brief preface, which was followed by the table of contents and the familiar chapters on individualism, planning, the rule of law, security, and freedom. There it was! *Chapter 10!* Aven was not sure whether he had read correctly. The drums of Hadny were in the midst of a violent staccato orgy as background to the mournful sobs of the solo mandolin. As the music ebbed, reaching an elegant and prolonged silence, Aven reread the chapter title:

WHY THE WORST GET TO THE TOP

He did not read the chapter. The lateness of the hour overtook him. Under any circumstance, it was obvious that Hayek could not be referring to a society that so well met his divine purpose. Aven listened to the last several minutes of Hadny's silence. It was deeply moving. He slept well that night.

EPILOGUE

■ ■ ■ ■ ■ ■ ■ ■ ■ ■ ■ ■ ■ ■ ■ ■ ■

Well, this is not exactly what I expected to be doing when we first met."

The entrance to the balcony was a few feet away. Aven paused before taking his final steps.

"I don't think any of us knew just where we were headed then, Aven."

Gaylord turned into a small room off the corridor. He sat down in front of the television monitor and watched as Aven stepped onto the balcony. The panel in front of him contained several dials. He turned the one on the far left midway through its gradient. The center gauge was soon adjusted in similar fashion. It was several minutes before Gaylord turned both gradually back to their original positions.

Aven's reaction to the applause was restrained. He knew this was only the beginning of an adoration that would shower upon him. As the applause grew in intensity, the crowd below began their metered chant:

Ah-ven   Ah-ven   Ah-ven...

Both forms of adulation continued to wash over him for several minutes. Aven removed the note cards from beneath the folds of his purple velvet robe and smiled broadly at the crowd that he knew was watching. He paused in deference to the lingering applause. Until this moment, he hadn't fully realized the sense of fulfillment his election would bring. With the silence, he began speaking. The sound of his voice reflected his mood.

> Fellow citizens, it is with the deepest sense of *humility* and *awe* that I accept your summons. In this summons, from the peoples of all Russia, I read the *will* of the *Almighty*. And into my head and heart I take the Lord's Word, *acting on His behalf*, a *Sovereign President* of Russia shall I become. It is thus, before God, I swear this weighty oath: To *execute* throughout

Russia *His will*, to *destroy* throughout Russia the forces that would rob us of His divine guidance, to *burn out* the corruption in our midst, and to *cut out* dependency wherever it is found. Not self nor others sparing, for the Sake of the Great Russian Realm....

Gaylord was following Aven's every word and movement. He turned the leftmost dial abruptly. Aven paused, and as he anticipated, the applause was instantaneous. It persisted for a time and ebbed in response to his appreciative gestures. He began again, for a time, in firm but hushed tones.

We have strayed too far. But for the mirage of temporary glory and self-love and the all-too fleeting delights of this world, we have trampled down all spiritual piety together with the Christian faith and law. For the mania of short-lived fame we have scorned imperishable glory. We have raged against each other and have risen against God. *But no more!*

There was a visible breach in the sound. Aven paused, as if to punctuate the severity of his command. Gaylord, too, was motionless for a moment. The clapping and chanting reached a crescendo quickly. Gaylord turned both gauges to the left, as Aven, who had been calling for quiet, continued.

Comrades, today we find, in our great and bountiful land, disorder, discord, and disarray. But we will not, nor can we, look to others. We shall, ourselves, reestablish order, reintroduce harmony, and *return to Him*....

It is His wish that we return to our great enterprise and to the glory that He would have for us. More than once in our history, magnificent leaders have been called on to restore the kingdom in its times of trouble. In doing so, they have frustrated the thoughts and ill deeds of the wicked and have acted with both gentleness and ferocity. Mercy and gentleness for the good; for the evil, ferocity and torment. As our leaders have done before, so too shall I respond henceforth. I do not consider myself to be immortal, for death is the debt that all of us must pay for the sin of Adam, but for so long as He deems me worthy of His Work, *I cannot do otherwise*....

Ah-ven!   Ah-ven!   Ah-ven!   Ah-ven!....

By this point in his address, the chanting and applause had been calibrated to coincide with metric precision. The noise reverberated happily within the confines of the security screen from which he spoke, enhancing the feelings of pride that had overtaken him. As the quiet returned, so too did a tinge of humility.

> At this awesome moment in our nation's history, I ask that you join me in a moment of silent prayer....
>
> Godly people of Russia, given into my care by God! I invoke your *faith in Him* and *your love for me*: Be forgiving! Past evil cannot be undone. *I can* only *save you* from future oppression and extortion. Forget what has happened and will not happen again! Put enmity and hatred from you! Let us all join in Christian love! *Henceforth, I will be your judge and your defender.*

It was clear by his movement he had finished. Gaylord turned each dial through its maximum arc, slowly and sequentially. As Aven acknowledged the building applause, soon amplified by the roar of his name, a new chant enriched the cacophony.

LONG LIFE   LONG LIFE   LONG LIFE   LONG LIFE.

"Words fit for a tsar," he thought.

Ah-ven!   Ah-ven!   Ah-ven!   LONG LIFE AH-VEN   LONG LIFE AH-VEN   LONG LIFE AH-VEN....

Aven's arms were tiring, but he kept them raised in recognition of his subjects' blessing. The ovation seemed to take on a life of its own. It would ebb only momentarily. But end it did, with obvious reluctance. Aven finally left the balcony. The confidence and stimulation he had felt when comprehending Paula's lunchtime announcement of the "new" MOP director was eclipsed many times over. Gaylord was waiting as he walked into the MOP corridor.

"Aven, my apologies. The speech was wonderful. It was obvious from the crowd response, they loved you. And if the Giants weren't opening this afternoon, who knows, they might still be out there."

"Thanks, Gaylord. I'm sorry we squabbled last night, but I'm glad to see you finally agree. Nothing like putting the fear of God into the simple folk. They love it, and they love me. As a matter of fact, this overly protective foolishness has got to stop. What kind of leader can I be stuck away in MOP? Come on, let's get outside. I'm sure there's still a good size gathering hoping to see me in the flesh."

"I don't think that'd be a good idea."

"Why not? This is getting silly, you know?"

"It may *seem* silly, Aven, but security thinks otherwise."

"The hell with security then. If need be we can replace the lot of them."

Gaylord was unwilling to yield. Nor was Aven. The controversy quickly intensified. Their voices rose. Aven could feel the anger overtaking him. He finally held his breath and tongue for an instant.

"Gaylord, this *is* foolish. Why are we arguing? You heard the crowd. There's no danger in going among them. What *are* we arguing about? Is there…is there something else?"

For the longest time, the two men looked at each other. Neither spoke. Aven was waiting for an answer. None was forthcoming. Poor Gaylord simply couldn't find the words to tell him. There was not a *soul* left in Russia.